## AS HE LOWERED THE DRUM,
## THE METAL STRUCK A MATCH HEAD.

Instantly the pier was aglow with brilliant white light. Then came the sound—the deep, violent crack and boom that have measured Ireland's history like the regular ticking of a clock for centuries—and the white light burst into a billowing fireball, growing, destroying utterly whatever it engulfed.

The small man didn't have time to run, or scream, or even remove his arms from their embrace of death. The fire swallowed him and spat him into the sea. And then he was gone.

**THE HAND OF LAZARUS**

## THE FINEST IN SUSPENSE!

**THE URSA ULTIMATUM**                                      (2130, $3.95)
by Terry Baxter

In the dead of night, twelve nuclear warheads are smuggled north across the Mexican border to be detonated simultaneously in major cities throughout the U.S. And only a small-town desert lawman stands between a face-less Russian superspy and World War Three!

**THE LAST ASSASSIN**                                        (1989, $3.95)
by Daniel Easterman

From New York City to the Middle East, the devastating flames of revolution and terrorism sweep across a world gone mad . . . as the most terrifying conspiracy in the history of mankind is born!

**FLOWERS FROM BERLIN**                                      (2060, $4.50)
by Noel Hynd

With the Earth on the brink of World War Two, the Third Reich's deadliest professional killer is dispatched on the most heinous assignment of his murderous career: the assassination of Franklin Delano Roosevelt!

**THE BIG NEEDLE**                                           (1921, $2.95)
by Ken Follett

All across Europe, innocent people are being terrorized, homes are destroyed, and dead bodies have become an unnervingly common sight. And the horrors will continue until the most powerful organization on Earth finds Chadwell Carstairs—and kills him!

**DOMINATOR**                                                (2118, $3.95)
by James Follett

Two extraordinary men, each driven by dangerously ambiguous loyalties, play out the ultimate nuclear endgame miles above the helpless planet—aboard a hijacked space shuttle called DOMINATOR!

*Available wherever paperbacks are sold, or order direct from the Publisher. Send cover price plus 50¢ per copy for mailing and handling to Zebra Books, Dept. 100 , 475 Park Avenue South, New York, N.Y. 10016. Residents of New York, New Jersey and Pennsylvania must include sales tax. DO NOT SEND CASH.*

# WARREN MURPHY
### AND
## MOLLY COCHRAN

# THE HAND OF LAZARUS

**PINNACLE BOOKS**
**WINDSOR PUBLISHING CORP.**

*For Megan and Mark . . . Always there when we need them.*

PINNACLE BOOKS

are published by

Windsor Publishing Corp.
475 Park Avenue South
New York, NY 10016

First printing: April, 1988

Printed in the United States of America

# PROLOGUE

## THE LEGEND

On a small hill overlooking Moon Lake in Ardath is Bounfort Castle, home of the Shrine of Eternal Peace and one of the most sacred sites in the history of Christianity in Ireland.

Legend has it that one day in the year 988, while the castle's Irish defenders were under siege by a large army of Norsemen, the vision of a woman appeared on the castle's balcony. She spoke and was understood by all, although they were men of differing tongues.

And she said, "Let there be no violence here. Let this forever be a place of peace."

Then the figure of Mary, Mother of God, rose in the air, and lingered for long minutes before vanishing. The Norsemen retreated, and Our Lady's command has been heeded since that day. Bounfort Castle has never again been attacked by enemies, not even when Cromwell's thugs were ravaging the entire countryside.

Through the years, the castle fell into decline, but a small section has been restored and is now maintained by the government of the Republic of Ireland. Medieval banquets with entertainment are given there nightly for visitors, and religious functions are held occasionally at the Shrine of Eternal Peace.

> —From the Official History
> of the Village of Ardath,
> County Kerry, 1961.

# *BOOK ONE*

# CHAPTER ONE

A dot of light, bobbing with the waves, illuminated the weedy yellow furze on the hillside above the lake. There were no houses there, no cars. A well-worn dirt road had once wound through the reeds as far as the pier, but when the fish had mysteriously abandoned the lake, the road had grown grassy with disuse. Now only a single narrow groove outlined the footpath taken by children to play on the pier.

The light moved in a waving horizontal line from left to right, over the scrub brush and the lush red rhododendrons of the hills, then stopped when it struck the rotting pier. The bright circle traveled down the pier onto the green-gray scum floating on the water. Then, with a click, the light was gone.

A man, the one holding the flashlight, nodded. The two others with him pulled in their oars. The boat, now safely out of the strong current that ran down the center of the lake from the river's entrance to its exit, drifted silently forward toward the pier.

The men were dressed identically, in black sweaters and American-style jeans. Their heads were covered, their faces smeared with bootblack. As they approached, the man with the flashlight, the leader, threw out a length of rope and tied it expertly around one of the pier's supporting posts.

He was first out of the boat, a swift, surefooted figure that moved in the starless night like a creature who was comfortable only in darkness.

He rigged up a pulley. The men in the boat attached lengths of rope around two ten-gallon metal drums still in the boat. In the darkness, the drums floated and weaved above the water like huge, slow-moving birds.

First one, then the other raised his drum silently onto the pier. They heard a scratching, the faint sound of splintering wood.

"What's that?"

The leader spat in response.

One of the men hoisted a drum, grasped it in a bear hug, and walked heavily from the concrete pier. In seconds he had disappeared into the rhododendrons along the hill. Beyond where he had gone, in the distance, was the black silhouette of Bounfort Castle.

The second man, short and thin, wrestled to lift the drum, his knees buckling.

"It's wet," he grunted. "I think it's leaking."

"Then watch it," the leader hissed.

"Think I want to drop the bloody fucking thing? There's something underfoot."

"Shut up."

His feet skidding, the short man shuffled awkwardly toward the pier's base. "Damn it, me feet's slipping on something, I tell you."

Disgustedly, the leader snapped on the flashlight. The lines in his face flattened with shock. "Stop," he commanded.

"What?" the short man said, craning over his shoulder to see the illuminated spot.

And for a split second, before the leader tossed the flashlight away and dived into the water, the man saw.

Matches. The pier was strewn with them. "Pigshit," he growled. The drum was too heavy. He had to put it down. It hit the pier with a thump.

The metal struck a match head.

Instantly, the pier was aglow with brilliant white light. Then came the sound—the deep, violent crack and boom that have measured Ireland's history like the regular ticking of a clock for centuries—and the white light burst into a billowing fireball, growing, destroying utterly whatever it engulfed.

The small man didn't have time to run, or scream, or even remove his arms from their embrace of death. The fire swallowed him and spat him into the sea. And then he was gone.


The explosion marked the climax of one of the most eventful days the village of Ardath had experienced since the Earl of Bounfort jumped to his death from a parapet of the castle in 1583.

The day had started with Mad Hattie, the village's most certifiable lunatic, who that morning had been even madder than usual, chasing some children through the woods with rocks, and pelting young Billy O'Glynn soundly enough to send him to the hospital with a broken arm.

"She's got the strength of a devil," Mrs. O'Glynn shrilled as Morty O'Sullivan, natty as always in his pressed policeman's uniform, escorted the aromatic Mad

Hattie to the Garda station. But since Hattie claimed to possess the ability to curse a man and all his family into an early grave, not even the mean-tempered Mrs. O'Glynn and her bullying son were willing to test Hattie's supernatural associations, so the charges against the old crone were dropped.

Then came Molly Logan's soup. A chowder it was, thick and fishy, two potfuls, the Friday night staple at Grady's Pub, which was packed to bursting.

There were nine ladies from the village Irish dancing class whirling and beating frenzied tattoos with their feet while their poor husbands sweated like horses following them around the floor. Old Lanigan, too, was present, as he was most evenings. Lanigan started his drinking promptly at 8:00 A.M. six days a week, and generally kept up a heroic pace until he collapsed at around ten in the evening. No one ever minded much, though, since the old man didn't weigh more than a hundred pounds and was easy to cart home. Doctor O'Connor was there with his grandfather. The elder O'Connor weighed considerably more than Old Lanigan, but held it better, so long as no one was fighting. In his youth, Doctor O'Connor's grandfather was the bare-knuckle champion of County Kerry, and still, at the age of eighty-eight, could not resist the impulse to occasionally swell someone's nose with his famous left jab.

Mrs. O'Glynn was wailing about the condition of little Billy's arm while she assuaged her maternal wounds with several pints of Harp.

And on that night of Molly Logan's soup, a couple of wild-looking German cyclists were present, skintight elastic shorts and all, as well as an aggressively healthy American couple, a pair of stout English ladies, and the town's constable, Morty O'Sullivan.

Morty was the first to feel the soup. Rising suddenly from the table, his face green and expressionless, the policeman knocked his bowl to the floor with trembling hands and then lunged, staggering, into the concertina player who'd been hired for the evening. There was a wild shriek as he spewed the solid portions of his dinner square onto Mrs. O'Glynn's lap, then a lot of commotion as Doctor O'Connor's grandfather dragged him outside.

The concertina player, taking one look at Mrs. O'Glynn, was next, followed shortly by the stout English ladies and the American couple. One of the Germans made a valiant attempt at restoring order but he, too, fell victim. So did Mrs. Logan, the cook; most of the dancing ladies and their husbands; and finally the proprietor, Jim Grady himself. In the end, Old Lanigan and Doctor O'Connor's grandfather were left in charge with strict instructions to close up the pub immediately.

And they would have followed those instructions, surely, had not Brian O'Flaherty arrived and complained that he'd only a pint in him and a terrible thirst from an evening's hard work.

Brian was dressed, as he was most nights, in his poet's shirt and harlequin pants that were meant to resemble the garb of a thirteenth-century troubadour, which is what he imitated during the nightly shows at Bounfort Castle.

His presence at the pub was always welcome. Brian sang like McCormack himself, it was said by the older members of the village, and he could dance like the wind and drink like a fire. All qualities that made him welcome wherever he went in Ardath.

With him was Kathleen Pierce, also decked out in antique clothes. She was not one by nature to frequent the pubs, but she seemed to follow Brian like a shadow, although the wiser ones would say more out of boredom recently than affection.

Convent reared, Kathleen Pierce possessed the kind of wan beauty that always seemed on the brink of turning one way or the other, either to waxy forgettableness or to a raging, fiery bloom. But her features never did either, remaining suspended in a bland sort of embryonic state. She was blonde, and wore her long hair pulled back like the schoolgirl she'd been until a few years before. Her blue eyes were slightly elongated, like the porcelain figurines of Chinese ladies sold in the souvenir shops, and her nose was straight and short.

Altogether, it was rather a lovely face, despite the ridiculously tall conical hat she wore as part of her medieval persona. There was only one thing wrong with the face, as Brian had told her before. Her lips were thin and perpetually taut, as if on the verge of rictus. If one looked closely, one almost expected her to pull them back in a snarl and reveal two rows of fanged teeth.

But Kathleen never snarled, never smiled, and rarely spoke. She made no difference one way or the other to the pub and its doings, but as Brian's girl and a lifelong Ardath resident, Kathleen was always included.

So Brian was complaining about his thirst and Old Lanigan felt compelled to pour a drop for the lad. And one for his lady. And one for Doctor O'Connor's grandfather, who'd worked up a mighty sweat from hauling all the sick away. And then one for himself, for all his trouble. And a round for the house, to celebrate their deliverance from the killer soup.

By an hour before the four-thirty summer sunrise,

14

things were well underway. Old Lanigan had passed out behind the bar. The Germans were singing revolutionary songs with guttural verses while Brian O'Flaherty, his poet's shirt stained brown with stout, countered them with Gaelic fighting marches at full throat. Kathleen Pierce had fallen demurely asleep in a corner. The others spread themselves out on the bar or stumbled around the tables in varying but extreme states of besottedness.

And then, like a herald of the Last Judgment, the sky was illuminated with a dreadful, brilliant light. The windows blew in with a blast of shattered glass. A roar swelled in the distance.

Some screamed. A dozen or more fell to their knees in prayer and sudden repentance before scurrying outside. In the village, the dark houses flooded with light as people crept out in their nightclothes.

"A bomb," one of the Germans said thickly. "This is Ireland. These things happen."

Brian O'Flaherty smashed his fist on the table. "This is *southern* Ireland," he said. "They don't happen here."

The German shrugged.

"Bloody fool," Brian said, rising to join the frantic exodus.

Five hundred yards from the explosion, where the lake current speeded up as it poured back into the river, a man in black curled himself into a tight ball in the mud beneath a grassy overhang. He hugged his knees to stem the cramps in his sides. He pulled off his sopping hat and, with pained eyes, lifted his face toward the breaking dawn.

One of his men was dead. The other knew how to get

15

to the place with the explosives and leave unseen, but the dead man was a problem. If the body—or what was left of it—washed out to sea, there would be no complications. But when operations like these went wrong, he knew, there were always complications.

All because of some matches. Matches! The finger of fate had poked at him before. It was inevitable in his line of work. But not like this. Some stray matches on a pier might have blown the plan wide open.

He shifted his seat. The cramps were easing. Maybe not wide open. The accident could be covered. Tricky, but it could be covered.

*Unless it wasn't an accident.*

Suddenly the man in black felt a shiver of cold. If someone had known about the plan . . . placed the matches there deliberately . . .

He shook his head and pulled himself to a stooping crouch. He would have to find out. Somewhere in this gossipy little town, someone knew about the matches. He would have to find that person, and if it was someone who knew more than he should, destroy him.

The sun's rays were turning from cobalt to red. He checked his watch. Four-fifteen. The days began so early here, he thought. It would make his work more difficult.

But not impossible. He had already performed the impossible by emerging unmarked from the explosion. He had swum underwater until he thought his lungs would burst. The distance had been enough to put him out of danger. He had been well trained. The plan would go through.

Feeling his way along the muddy lakeshore, he loped, crablike, for some distance and then scrambled over a polished stone and ran into the woods behind Bounfort Castle.

The place where he had touched the stone was smooth, with only the faint muddy outline of a hand that would wash away with the first wave. Inside the outline of the fingers were only blank spaces, devoid of whorls or ridges.

The man left no fingerprints. He never did.


At the pier, the townspeople of Ardath stared at the wreckage in stunned silence. The concrete pier had extended twenty feet out into the water. Now it was only half that long, ending in a jagged rip of stone. Pieces of the concrete were visible where they had been blown up onto the shore.

"Kids," Mrs. O'Glynn said at last, with the finality of an invalid roused from her sickbed to pronounce judgment. "It's them no-good Houlihan boys what's always getting my poor Billy into trouble—"

"Oh, shut up, woman," Doctor O'Connor's grandfather said. "Anyone can see it's but a play for the insurance."

The other old-timers of the village nodded in agreement.

"Was it Mr. Bonning, then, who owned it?"

"It and everything else," Kathleen Pierce said quietly.

"Ah, you poor darling," Mrs. O'Glynn cooed in sympathy. "She's dead right, you know. Who knows anything about this Bonning except that he come dancing in here cocky as you please, and proceeds to buy up everything in sight, turning Kathleen's poor mother into the street like a beggar woman. And him not even a Catholic."

17

The last remark caused a murmur of assent. "Aye. Ask Widow Pierce what kind of a man Bonning is," someone shouted.

"The Widow Pierce is not about to be a party to your accusations," a woman said, pushing her way through the crowd. "And Mr. Bonning has been in this village for ten years. Because he's not a busybody doesn't make him a stranger."

"Moira," Mrs. O'Glynn exclaimed as the townspeople made way. The men automatically doffed their hats in deference, as much to Moira Pierce's still-magnificent beauty as to her status as former first lady of Ardath.

She clasped Kathleen by the shoulders. "I've been sick with worry over you, girl," she snapped. "Get home with you. I'll talk to you later."

Her daughter turned and walked sullenly away.

Brian O'Flaherty made a conciliatory gesture, but Moira slapped him away roundly. "Drunkard! You'll not keep Kathleen out all night again, or I'll beat you myself."

She turned to the crowd. "As for Mr. Bonning, I thank the Lord he came when he did to buy that monstrosity of a house, and I'll thank you not to involve him in your imagined scandals!" She stalked away, her red hair flowing behind her.

Brian smiled with appreciation. "Ah, widow or not, there's no other like her still."

"Better to stay with the daughter," Mrs. O'Glynn said, smiling slyly. "My guess is that the Widow Pierce is out to make another rich marriage for herself."

Everyone laughed except for Father Ambrose, puffing to reach the outskirts of the crowd. "What's happened?" he pleaded, hands fluttering.

Doctor O'Connor's grandfather shrugged. "Looks like it blew up."

"Good heavens," the priest said, crossing himself as he surveyed the wreckage. The crowd around him did likewise. "Was anyone hurt?"

"Not that we know."

"Ah, he's a clever one, that one," Mrs. O'Glynn said.

"Who?"

"Mr. Bonning."

"I beg your pardon?"

"Ah, Father, the woman's talking out her ass again, forgive me." Doctor O'Connor's grandfather dutifully crossed himself, but his expression never changed. "More than likely, it was a bunch of youngsters with bangers. And I'll wager Billy O'Glynn headed the lot."

"Why, you wicked old fossil," Mrs. O'Glynn shrieked. "It was you said the thing was done for the insurance."

"Sure and you pounced on my words like a cat sniffing fish."

"Now, it won't do any good for us to speculate who did it," Father Ambrose said, stepping between them. "We need the police. Where is Morty?"

"Took sick, Father," Doctor O'Connor's grandfather said. "Something he ate."

"I ate it, too," Mrs. O'Glynn said proudly. "It was probably all part of Bonning's scheme, to kill us all. Oh, Father, it's sick as a dog I am."

"Then go home to your bed, where no one but your poor husband has to hear you," Doctor O'Connor's grandfather roared.

"Stop, stop," Father Ambrose shouted. His small frame seemed to tremble all over.

Mrs. O'Glynn and Doctor O'Connor's grandfather harrumphed at each other, then went their separate ways, dispersing the crowd with them. When Father Ambrose turned around, he was alone except for the stinking presence of Mad Hattie, cackling like a roosting hen.

"It's nothing, Hattie," he said, placing his arm gently around the old woman's shoulders. "Go on home now."

Hattie's cackles rose to a hoot. "But I know," she said, wagging a bony finger in front of her face.

"Know what?"

"I know it's just the beginning."

Father Ambrose led her away slowly. "Well, let's hope not." He patted her gnarled hand, as if to reassure himself.

The two figures shuffled down the village road as morning broke full over Moon Lake.

"Only the beginning." Hattie's laughter meshed with the sounds of birds and disappeared.

# CHAPTER TWO

Ten minutes late for the start of his shift, Detective Sergeant Michael Cormac walked into Cork police headquarters with a cardboard cup of coffee in his hand. The restaurant coffee was terrible, but the bitter, vaguely plasticine liquid they brewed at headquarters was worse.

Cormac sat at his desk, slugged down the final shot of thick and ancient goo like the vile medicine it was, then crumpled the paper cup with a grunt.

He sailed it past another detective filling out some reports. "Super's looking to see you, Mike," the other detective said, not bothering to look up.

"Screw him."

"Cormac," Superintendent Merrion rumbled from his door.

"As I was saying, a summons from my superior always warrants my first priority," Cormac mumbled. The other detective grinned.

Merrion's beady eyes were piercing. A sheet of smoke poured out of his office and engulfed him. "Get in here."

The superintendent was back behind his desk when

21

Cormac came in. There was a cigarette in his mouth, and the ends of three others smoldered in the ashtray. Methodically, Cormac ground out the three live butts.

"Never mind that," Merrion said.

"Damn fire hazard. I always fear for my life when I come in here."

"Leave my desk alone. The subject is you, not me." He narrowed his eyes and blew out a puff of smoke without moving his hands. "Where were you born?"

"What?"

"You heard me."

Cormac's eyes scanned one corner of the ceiling, then the other, then came to rest on Merrion's. "Italy, Frank. I meant to tell you. I'm really the brains behind the Cosa Nostra."

"Me sides is splitting from mirth," Merrion said sourly. "It says here you come from a dink town called Ardath." He flicked an ash onto an open folder.

"So if you know already, why bother asking me?"

"Just to see if you'd lie. Men from County Kerry are supposed to be compulsive liars." He looked up briefly. "So I guess you're from Ardath, after all."

"I see," Cormac said. "Is my being a Kerryman going to get me thrown out of the Gardai, then?"

"Not my luck," Merrion said, puffing like a chimney. "Whoremongering didn't get you thrown off, did it? Looks like we're stuck with you."

"Now, that's a low one," Cormac said, reddening. "I put up with six weeks of questioning about my personal life before I was accepted back into the Gardai," he said. "There's nothing about whoremongering in that file."

22

"Don't get your back up. It's just been one of those days," Merrion said.

"So what about where I was born? What does it matter?"

"Because that's where you're going."

Cormac felt his stomach knot. "Why?"

"You've got to look into something. Explosion on an abandoned pier. No casualties. Routine check."

"There's a Garda post in Ardath," Cormac said stubbornly.

"Only one man, and he was sick or something when it happened. Food poisoning, I was told."

Cormac sighed. "Ardath's not even in this jurisdiction. The Killarney district handles Ardath."

"Right," Merrion said. "But we got the word. This one's ours."

"What word?"

Merrion ignored the question. "So you're going. You know the town and the people. Find out what caused the pier to blow."

"Out of our jurisdiction?"

"Your jurisdiction is where I say it is. Me and that bleeding computer in Dublin. You should be proud, Cormac. It picked you out from thousands. Just because you had the good luck to be born in Ardath."

"No use in suggesting you send someone else, is there?" Cormac asked.

"No. Get a move on." The hint of a smile came to the super's face as he ground out a cigarette. "Look on the bright side. In Ardath, no one will be around to notice that you show up for work late every day."

"Terrific," Cormac muttered as he shambled

23

through the pall of smoke toward the door. "I'll go today, I'll be back tomorrow."

"Cormac."

"Super?"

"Pack a bag. A big bag. I don't want you to leave until you know exactly who caused the explosion and why."

"Sure," Cormac said, and slammed the door behind him.

From the station, he walked down the length of Barrack Street, past the rows of small, dirty houses and food shops, past the basement grilles stuffed to overflowing with trash, past the steaming, stinking breweries and the thick gray water of the river into Cork's Old City.

On the corner, almost directly across from the Crown and Beamish brewery, was the bar where he rented two upstairs rooms.

It was a perfect life for a middle-aged bachelor. He had a bed to sleep on, four sturdy walls to contain him, a never-ending supply of Guinness downstairs, and female companionship when he wanted it. No frilly lace curtains, no relatives to visit on Sundays.

The one adornment in the apartment was a bronze medal he had received when he was twenty-one years old, for saving Morty O'Sullivan from drowning. Cormac had been a cop then, too, but the medal wasn't from the Gardai.

His father and Morty's, lifelong friends until the day they were both killed in a bus accident, had the medal made in honor of Cormac's heroism. The medal was inscribed with only one word: VALOUR.

It was Cormac's only souvenir from the village of his

childhood, and he always kept the medal with him. Its ribbon had been torn off long before; several wallets had borne its imprint.

After he left Ardath and later Ireland, the medal had become the only physical remembrance Cormac had of his family.

They had all gone. Following Cormac, they left Ardath one by one, first his oldest sister, by marriage, to Edinburgh, then his father, in death. One of his brothers had become wealthy in Canada; two others and a sister, plus his mother, had gone to join him. His mother died there. Another sister died of pneumonia, and his youngest brother, according to the infrequent reports from the settled Canadian Cormacs, was prospecting for diamonds in South Africa.

Michael was the only one of his family left in Ireland now. Odd, he had thought more than once. He had been the first to leave, and now he was the last to remain.

His journey away from Ardath had begun in the factories of Belfast, then continued across the Atlantic to Louisiana, in America.

There were twelve lost years in America, years he didn't want to remember. When they were over, and he had nowhere else to go, he came back.

But not to Ardath. From the moment he left, Cormac had vowed never to see the village again. He took a room in Cork, labored at small jobs for a year, then reapplied to the Gardai. Through a technicality, his leave of absence was still in effect, and he got back on the force.

He was a joke for a while, at thirty-seven the oldest rookie in existence, but his work on a couple of homi-

25

cide cases singled him out of the mass of new recruits applying for training at detective headquarters. He was promoted to sergeant, and he was prepared to die a sergeant when his liver gave out.

And now he was ordered back to Ardath.

From the back of the cluttered closet he took a battered plaid cloth suitcase and opened it. It stank of the places he'd been, of the sea and the ports and the factories. There was a spatter of blood on it from a fist-fight in Baylor City, Louisiana, on the night he left. And inside, covered with the grime of more than twenty years, was a woman's photograph.

The sight of it shocked him. He had managed, somehow, to forget Moira's face for a while. He lifted the small square out of the bag and blew some of the dust off it.

Moira, with her laughing green eyes and a toss of thick red curls. Moira, more wild and young than Cormac could ever remember being himself, with her strong legs wrapped around him and honey on her breath and her bosom, white as a pigeon's, cradling his head.

He let the photograph drop back into the bag. He hoped he would not see Moira again.

Cormac tossed some clothes into the bag and zipped it. On his way out, he tore the medal from the wall and stuffed it into his inside jacket pocket.


Cormac had forgotten how hair-raising the road was that cut its way through the hills from Killarney south to the Ring of Kerry and the village of Ardath.

In the last gasp of the mountains, high on a hillside,

was a small luncheonette and tourist's gift shop with goatskin rugs hanging over the front railing, where Cormac stopped for coffee. He took the cup outside and stood by a retaining wall, looking down into the valley below.

It had been a soft morning, the land covered with a light rainy mist, but now the sun had come out, bright and mellow. Spread out before him he could see Ardath, and beyond it, Moon Lake and the river that fed it.

Even now, even after so many years and so much hurt, even after promising himself never to return, he felt his throat choke closed for a moment as he looked at the small town where he had spent his youth and the best of his dreams.

If he didn't belong here, he thought, here in this timeless place where nothing changed from generation to generation, where the water still ran cold and sweet and the green mountains rose up wild as the wind that shaped them, he didn't belong anywhere.

And that, he thought sadly, was the long and the short of it. He didn't belong anywhere.

Rising on the edge of the lake was Bounfort Castle. Even at this distance of a mile away, he could see the front wall of the old structure and the small balcony where the Virgin Mary was said to have appeared.

Smaller, to the right of the castle, was St. Benedict's Church. It was hidden now by trees in the full bloom of summer, but the Celtic cross atop the church—a traditional four-pointed cross with a circle designed around the intersection of the cross's two bars—jutted above the trees.

Before all that, nearer to him, lay the town. It was

just an intersection of two main streets, but clean, tidy, packed with shops and guest houses and homes over stores.

He tried to turn away, but couldn't. The beauty of the place held him, as it always had, with a cruel longing. To the left of the castle was another structure, the sprawling mansion that had been the Pierce mansion even when he was a boy. It was Moira Pierce's home, the place she had left his side to go to.

He drained his coffee cup, then started on the final mile to Ardath.


He drove directly to the Garda station at the end of Killian Street in town, not stopping to acknowledge any of the familiar faces he saw on the street. Inside the station, the feeling was worse. This was the place where his childhood dream of becoming a policeman had come true. But it hadn't been enough.

Morty O'Sullivan looked up from behind the desk and let out a whoop. He was a big young man with curly black hair and a handsome, regular-featured face. Even at thirty, he had laugh wrinkles in the corners of his eyes. An incipient potbelly was starting to encroach over his belt.

Cormac had not seen the young man in almost twenty years, but now he noticed for the first time that Morty just didn't look very bright. His face was happy and reasonably handsome, but it just didn't appear to be a very intelligent face. And why should it, Cormac thought. If he were bright, what would he be doing working as a cop in this godforsaken village? Sometimes it was best to be dumb.

"You're the big shot they've sent in from Cork, then?" the young man said as he stepped from behind the desk. He made a move to embrace Cormac, then hesitated. Cormac took him in his arms.

"The very same. Doing your job for you, as usual."

"It's a mystery, that pier business," Morty said gravely. "You should have seen the light from it. I was in bed, passed out cold, and it woke me like a blast from hell, it did."

"Find anything afterward?"

"We got orders not to touch a thing. I've roped it off and warned everybody to stay away."

"All right, then. Want to take a look with me?"

Morty's face lit up like a child's. "That I do. Oh, Michael, it's good to see you."

"Stow it," Cormac said grumpily, and Morty smiled.

They automatically got into Cormac's Ford. Cormac glanced sidelong at the handsome young officer. "Last I saw, you were the ugliest, skinniest kid in town," he said. Morty looked up at him adoringly. It settled well and familiarly on Cormac. "Leastwise, you're not so skinny anymore. Married?" He put the car key into the ignition.

"Thinking about it."

"Anyone I know?"

"In a way." The young policeman's expression changed. His cheeks flushed. "Moira Pierce's daughter, Kathleen. I don't expect you know her personally . . ." He stopped, looking guilty.

Cormac released the ignition key. It clicked in its slot. For a moment, it was the only sound in the car.

"Moira had children, then," Cormac said, barely audible.

"Just the one. Truth to tell, it'll be a while before the knot is tied. I don't think she thinks much of me."

"Better find yourself a fortune first," Cormac said bitterly.

Morty understood. "So you're a famous detective, then?"

"Just a detective."

"We all read about you. There was a story in the *Cork Examiner* after that kidnapping case that was in the news. It was even on the telly, only they didn't mention your name. But we knew it was you who solved it."

"A lot of people solved it, Morty."

"We kind of hoped you'd come back for a visit then. Once I knew where you were, I wrote to detective headquarters in Cork, but I guess you didn't get the letter."

"I got it," Cormac said. He started the car. They drove to the lake in silence.


At the blown-out site that was once the pier, Cormac opened his trunk and took out a big, hard plastic case. From it he took several clear plastic bags.

"Think it's something important?" Morty asked eagerly. "No one in town's spoken of anything else in the last two days."

Cormac shrugged. "I doubt if it'll mean much."

Dutifully he walked to the shore, picked up some broken pieces of concrete, and put them in one of the bags. Grunting as he bent over, he picked up a splintered piece of charred wood floating in the scum at the water's edge. As he placed it in another bag, he noticed a glint of metal sticking out of the mud. It was a long, thin sliver of aluminum, twisted into an irregular spiral. The ends were blunted, obviously melted.

"What do you take that for?" Morty asked.

"Dunno." He covered his hands in plastic and turned the piece over in them. "My guess would be a piece of a beer keg."

"Maybe it was kids after all, then. Kids drinking beer, maybe playing with firecrackers—"

"It's a piece of metal, not an eyewitness," Cormac said wearily. He rose, stashed the bags in his car, and went walking along the bank. "No sign of any boat?" he asked Morty.

The young man shook his head. "Not a stick."

It was useless, Cormac thought. More than two days had gone by since the incident occurred, and even the most ordinary police work had not been performed. If there had been a boat, all trace of it was gone now, caught up in the strong current that swept through the tidal lake. All because someone in Dublin chose not to have the matter investigated by local authorities.

Another political foul-up, he thought acidly. He was back in Ardath, with memories it had taken twenty years to forget, because of some politician in Dublin with his finger up his nose.

"Bastards," he muttered. He wanted a drink.

"Mike!" Morty was standing on the grass near the pier, waving his arms.

Cormac sighed. The kid wanted to help, but he was getting to be as much of an annoyance as his superiors.

31

Cormac ambled back, his legs feeling leaden. Even his body was bored. "What," he said flatly.

"I found this stuff on the reeds over there." The young man ran his thumb over the fingers of one hand. "Gritty, kind of. Stinks. Doesn't seem natural."

Cormac took Morty's hand, touched it, sniffed it. His boredom was gone. "Show me where."

Morty led him to an outcropping of brown reeds in a dank pool some ten yards inland from the shore. In the sunlight, they seemed furry, covered with soft brown down.

They tramped through the ooze toward the reeds. "I'll be damned," Cormac said.

"What is it?"

Cormac snipped off a few of the reeds and placed them in another bag. He touched his finger to one and tasted it. It had a bitter metallic flavor. Up close, the reeds were green, but speckled with fragments of dried wood pulp. "Looks like gelignite."

"What the hell is that?" Morty asked.

"A kind of explosive."

Morty was astonished. "For making bombs? Who'd want to blow up this old pier? It hasn't been used in years."

Cormac sighed. "There are a lot of bombs in Ireland, Morty."

"Aaah, they do that in the North. The only thing you blow up in Kerry is your wife's belly every nine months," Morty said.

"Let's hope so."

Morty looked at him, and Cormac's expression sent a chill of fear through the young policeman. "Well, that's a waste of a good bomb around here, then,'' Morty said lightly.

Cormac looked around. Morty was right. There was nothing in the area except a lake, a woods, the remains of a castle of undistinguished reputation, and a village where nothing ever happened. And yet, if his guess was right, someone had brought in at least one barrel full of gelignite—enough to blow a car or a house or a person to smithereens.

"I'll expect you to be quiet about this," Cormac said.

"Whatever you say, Michael."

"You don't want people getting alarmed or trampling all over each other and getting in the way of our work. Not until we know something."

"I understand."

"Good," Cormac said. "I'm going to walk around awhile. Why don't you take my car back to town?"

"I can walk."

"You sure?"

"It's part of my job, walking around town. . . . '' Morty laughed. "But then you'd know that, wouldn't you?"

"It's been a long time since I had that job," Cormac said. He thumped on the car impatiently. "I'll catch up with you later."

Morty nodded. "Maybe we can get a pint."

"Let's do that." Cormac turned away, and then said, "Morty, you don't have to tell anybody I'm in town."

"I won't, but I'm sure the town already knows it. It's hard to keep secrets in Ardath."

"Okay. Then let's just say I'm back on holiday. All right?"

Morty nodded and drove away.

After the young policeman left, Cormac spent an hour walking along the bank of the lake, almost up to the shore behind Bounfort Castle. But he found nothing to connect the explosion to anything else. There was no boat, not even a scrap of wreckage. Whoever had brought the gel-ignite in had simply vanished without a trace.

Back in Ardath, he wrapped the samples of metal and reed carefully into a package in the village post office and addressed it with a note to Superintendent Merrion. He gave it to a bus driver who would be starting his afternoon run to Cork in another hour. Then he called Cork Garda headquarters and left instructions to pick up the package at the bus station.

On Main Street, he stopped in a small confectionery store. An old woman was behind the counter. She looked up warily as he came in.

"Cigarettes, please," he said.

"Would you be smoking the same brand, then, Michael?" the woman asked. "John Carrolls?"

Cormac smiled. "You never forget, Mrs. Laughlin," he said as he paid for them.

"Don't be a stranger now," she said.

He stopped at the door. "Would you know anyone who's renting a room? I'm taking a few days holiday back here."

"You might try Doctor O'Connor's grandfather," she said. "You know where he is?"

"I do," he said.

He drove to a small house at the foot of Main Street and rang the doorbell. An old man answered.

34

"Why, Michael Cormac," he said as if Cormac had been gone from the village for a week instead of twenty years. "Where have you been keeping yourself these days?"

"I've been busy, Mr. O'Connor. I hear you have a room for rent?"

"That I do. Come up the stairs and take a look." He led Cormac to a small, tidy hallway on the second floor. "Have you had a good life, then?" he asked as he opened the door to a small but immaculate room with flowered wallpaper and a lace bedspread.

"Good enough," Cormac answered.

"Here's a new telephone for you if you want it. You'll have to pay for the calls, though, and part of the gas and electric. Heard you went north."

"For a while."

"They're animals, lad."

"I know."

"Not many of us remember the Black-and-Tans anymore. A rotten lot they were, too."

Cormac grunted.

"But if you ask me, the others are just as bad up there. The Irish."

"Maybe."

"I never thought I'd live to see the day when the IRA meant anything but good in the world, but I have. They've twisted it all around. The young people today, they don't understand right from wrong. They get to shouting them slogans—"

"I'll pay for the room now, Mr. O'Connor."

The old man sighed. "Right you are, Michael."

* * *

Cormac closed the door behind him and then sat on the bed, his thoughts running cold through his intestines.

He was no stranger to violence. As a child, his father had told him stories about the Black-and-Tans, the British mercenaries who ran roughshod over Ireland in the teens and twenties, beating and killing the rebellious citizenry at will. Cormac had seen for himself the brutality of civil war in Belfast, the first step in his travels. In that sad, hard city, he had seen the aftermath of bombing in the Catholic ghetto where he lived. He had seen the Shankill ablaze with fires from torches lit in the name of God and England. He had watched the long funeral corteges pass down his street, the sounds of widows' wailing hanging heavy in the still air, still stinking of cordite and burned flesh. He had seen children, their faces hideously burn-scarred, training for revenge with toy guns in dead earnest.

And he had understood. In service to a foreign nation that had abused Ireland and the Irish for four hundred years, the Protestant lepers of the North had killed and maimed and starved and humiliated his people until he could no longer bear Ireland's sadness.

He hadn't remained in the North for a year before moving on. He couldn't.

But the sadness had never touched southern Ireland in his lifetime. There was peace in Ardath, in fact in all of Kerry—so much peace that the people of the county had developed a reputation as complacent country bumpkins.

English tourists were abundant and welcome.

Watching British television was a normal evening's entertainment. The Irish in Ardath wore English clothes, ate English food, drank English liquor. The English and their Protestant descendants were not hated or feared here.

Not yet.

But then, if what Cormac had found at the lake was an explosive, what was the explosive for?

The lab results were positive. The brown substance on the reeds and on the strip of aluminum was gelignite.

Superintendent Merrion gave this report to Cormac the next day on the telephone and asked, "Why? Why?"

Cormac could almost hear the smoke hissing from his superior's mouth. "I don't know. I'm working on it," he said.

"You need more help?" Merrion asked.

"I don't think so. Not yet, anyway."

"When do you think you might have something?"

Cormac sighed, away from the telephone's mouthpiece. "I don't know," he said levelly. "There aren't any leads. If there ever were any, they were all cold by the time I got here. So I don't know when, or if, I'll ever have anything. Sorry."

"Don't 'sorry' me," Merrion snapped. "You get something, and fast." His voice crackled with authority. "And don't do too much talking around town, either."

"Hold on. Let me get this straight. I'm supposed to find out about the explosives, but I'm not supposed to talk to anybody about it? Is that what you're telling me?"

"Approximately."

"Wonderful. And how am I to divine all this information you want?"

"Use a goddamned crystal ball," Merrion roared. "Just find out what you can and don't tell anybody else anything, got it?"

"Impossible," Cormac mumbled.

"It's your job," Merrion reminded him. "To make things easier, whatever you need is yours. That's official. Just clean this thing up. That's official, too."

Cormac bit his lip. "All right, Frank. I think you'd better let me in on this. What the hell is really going on here? And don't give me that crap about the pier in this village."

The superintendent was silent. When he finally spoke, the anger was gone from his voice. "I'll be damned if I know," he said. "The only thing I'm sure of is that Dublin's gone wild over this, and if someone's butt is going into the thresher, it's not going to be mine."

"Well, at least that sounded honest," Cormac said. "Thanks a lot. You're all heart."

He heard the receiver slam down on the other end.

"Bastard," he growled before putting the phone back on its cradle.

He lit a cigarette and looked up at the ceiling. What was it all about? Who was pushing so hard to find a solution to a second-rate explosion in a second-rate town?

# CHAPTER THREE

Cormac hadn't been to mass in twenty years. His first Sunday in Ardath, he attended three times.

He passed the time between masses gobbling down coffee and pastries in the small reception hall next to the church, hoping that one of the villagers would inadvertently give him a lead on the shipment of explosives to Ardath.

Instead he got a continuous stream of welcomes back to Ardath from the townspeople who remembered him. They wished him well for his vacation in town. Many wanted to know where he had been for "the past few years."

As he was walking back into the church for his third consecutive mass, Old Lanigan said to him, "Seems you're a lot more religious than you used to be."

At the first mass, he had noticed a new priest celebrating and later was told that old Father Gervaise had died. Father Ambrose, who had been the old priest's assistant, had taken over the parish duties.

Morty O'Sullivan showed up for the nine-thirty services in a freshly pressed uniform, his carriage proud and his manner majestic. Hopeful mothers pressed their smiling daughters toward him and the men nodded as he passed down the pews after the service. He came to stand with Cormac near the coffee urn after the service. Mrs. O'Glynn lumbered up to him like a runaway cow.

Without preamble, she said, "I tell you, it's God's own curse upon us. There's no use looking for a criminal. It's the Lord's hand what's bringing us down." She stuffed a cookie into her mouth. "By the way, who do you think blew up the pier on Moon's Lake?"

"I'm not permitted to discuss the case at this point in time," Morty said, stiffening visibly with his own importance. Cormac suppressed a laugh.

"Aaah, then it's nothing you know. And how could you, poor lad? It's best we keep out of the Lord's work."

"I wouldn't call that explosion the Lord's work," Morty said. He looked around the church hall. "At least not here. The Lord may be listening."

"We've been cursed, son," she went on, crumbs falling over her ample bosom. "First Father Gervaise dies like he did, and then our town gets bombed. Not to mention half the town near to dying with Molly Logan's chowder."

Morty tried to cover a laugh with a cough. He glanced at Cormac and rolled his eyes. "Let's be fair, Mrs. O'Glynn. The other night wasn't the first time Molly turned deadly with her soup." He whispered to Cormac, "Mrs. Logan only took up cooking after she quit drinking. She's not got too much experience with the stove. As to Father Gervaise, well, he was old and his heart just stopped. We were lucky Father Ambrose was here at the time."

Mrs. O'Glynn snorted. "It's a curse, I tell you. For harboring one of the devil's own here in Ardath."

Cormac cocked his head toward her like a spaniel scenting prey. "Beg pardon?"

"I'm talking about Hattie O'Shea."

The spaniel head drooped in disappointment. He was well aware of Mad Hattie. "I don't think so," he said.

"And what would you know, Michael Cormac? Twenty years gone without so much as a letter to your poor ma until she had to leave her home and all she loved, so she did."

Cormac felt the pastries drying in his throat. He hated Ardath, he decided. Violently, desperately, emphatically hated it and every place like it.

"Excuse me," Morty said, walking quickly toward the church entrance, arriving just in time to intercept a pretty girl on her way out.

"It's Kathleen Pierce," Mrs. O'Glynn whispered conspiratorially as Morty followed the girl outside. "Morty's struck proper with her, he is, but she'll not be having any."

Cormac looked past the old woman, trying for a glimpse of Moira's daughter, but she could no longer be seen through the open door.

The bell rang for the next mass to begin. Mrs. O'Glynn stuffed an extra cookie in her mouth, as if she needed it to get through the next hour.

"That one's as stuck-up as her ma and not half as pretty, if you ask me. And wild. Staying out to all hours with that singer fellow. Oughtn't even to be coming to mass, so she oughtn't. Disgraceful. But then, with Moira for a mother, what could a body expect?"

Cormac reached into his pocket and closed his big

fist around the bronze medal he'd won for saving Morty. "Good day, Mrs. O'Glynn," he said and walked back into the sanctuary.

"Enjoy your holiday, Michael," she said.

"I was hoping to see you," Morty said, taking off his hat. The wind blew his hair into wispy black peaks.

"You're wasting your time, Mortimer," Kathleen said without slowing down.

"Maybe, maybe not. I'm a patient man."

She sighed. "Then wait. But you'll be waiting for nothing. I can find my own way home, thank you."

"Oh, no. I'll not have you walking by Moon Lake by yourself. It's not safe."

"I walk by there every day."

"Not this day. It's my duty as an officer."

Kathleen stormed ahead, with Morty following behind like a hound. "You don't have to hate me," Morty said, becoming breathless from the quick pace as they approached the woods near the lake. "I've done nothing wrong, and you know it."

She stopped abruptly, then turned to him. "No, you haven't, Morty," she said gently. "It was my fault, all of it, but it's done now."

"I thought you liked me."

"I did. I do," she said, her eyes lowered. "But things are different now, that's all."

Morty's face turned the color of ripe tomatoes. "Yes. Different with that Brian O'Flaherty," he said as if it were an obscenity. "A blowhard and a playboy, so he is."

Eyes flashing, Kathleen turned and ran ahead.

"Now stop, Kathleen. Listen to me just for a minute. You know it's true. He's nothing but big talk and lies. He'll do you no good, girl."

But Kathleen was long gone, running toward her mother's house beyond the lake.

Morty slapped his cap against a tree and doggedly followed.

Billy O'Glynn stood stock-still near the marsh around the west end of Moon Lake. He poised his father's rifle over the plaster cast on his arm and steadied the weapon. Then he stomped hard on the ground and sent up a whoop to wake the dead.

Out of the tall grass sprang an orange cat, gliding on the air. Billy followed it expertly with the barrel of the gun.

Cats were almost as good as rabbits for target shooting, except that you couldn't bring the carcasses home. He had dropped Old Lanigan's cat at fifty yards last fall. The bullet had gone clean through the animal's head, so fast that it didn't even have time to make a noise. To this day, Old Lanigan still roamed around the woods at night, calling for the mangy thing, clapping and making sounds with his mouth.

Taunting the old man was even more fun than killing the cat. Sometimes Billy would wait in the woods around twilight and mew in response to the old fool's calling. A few times, he had even brought his friends, and afterward they would roll on the ground with laughter remembering how Old Lanigan ran around the trees calling and clapping with all the hope in his heart.

43

He took aim and began to squeeze the trigger—softly, smoothly, slowly—then suddenly found himself on the ground with his father's rifle beside him and a piercing pain in his head while the orange cat bounded away.

It took him a few seconds to realize that he was feeling pain in places besides his head. His back was being pelted with rocks and clumps of earth. He spun around awkwardly on all fours just in time to see Mad Hattie slinging a double fistful of wet mud directly at his face.

"Get out of here, bitch!" he screamed, wiping off the cold slime.

"I know what you done," Hattie said portentously, her glazed eyes glowing with lunacy. "I seen you. I know."

Billy scrambled for the gun. "Crazy old hag. Don't come no closer."

"I was watching. Nobody seen me, but I was watching, don't you worry."

"Get away, I said." The old woman moved closer. Billy backed off a step, then another. "I'll kill you, I swear."

Mad Hattie stopped, blinking vacantly at the barrel of the rifle pointed at her.

"Get out." He waited. When there was no response, he screamed it. "Get out!"

Mad Hattie began to mumble, so softly at first that she was barely audible, the strange words flowing out of her mouth like running water.

"Muc, muc, seo dhuit do leici." She bent over and threw more clods of mud at the boy. Her eyes brightened as she spoke the ancient Gaelic words. Her voice grew strident. "Pig, pig, here are your mumps."

Billy felt a chill. The fingers sticking out of the plaster cast trembled. He wiped at the mud on his face.

"Mumps and bumps, lumps and clumps," Hattie cackled.

"Stop it," Billy whispered, crouching and walking backward slowly as if trying to disappear.

"Then the pig dies."

Billy pulled the trigger. At the same moment, he screamed as the rubber sole of his sneaker caught a patch of mud on the lake's embankment and he tumbled over a cascade of shiny, polished rocks to the water below.

Mad Hattie fell silent. She looked around, saw she was alone, and forgot immediately about the cat, the curse, and Billy O'Glynn. A thin veil fell over the old woman's eyes once again, and she wandered off. In the distance, she could hear a child screaming. It seemed like a perfectly natural sound.


Billy floundered in the water for a while, shouting obscenities and lamenting the loss of his father's rifle, before he saw the shore receding away from him. He had been swept into the strong rip of current that ran through Moon Lake.

Suddenly startled into action, he started to swim for all he was worth, but his efforts made little difference in the course he took. The water was carrying him toward the river, which rushed into the Atlantic.

As he watched the bushes and furze on shore grow small and blurred, he understood. He was cursed. Mad Hattie had pronounced sentence on him, and it was

45

being carried out with the swiftness of the supernatural.

He cried out feebly, but he knew, from all the stories and warnings he had heard since he was born, that it was no use. The cold waves lapped over his face. He tried to tread water, but the heavy cast on his arm kept pulling him over. He swallowed the salt water, spat and gagged, swallowed more. He felt his eyes grow heavy. Then he lost consciousness without ever seeing the two figures running from the woods to the embankment.

"Kathleen, are you all right? I heard a shot."

"Someone's in there," she screamed. "I saw somebody!"

"Get Doctor O'Connor," Morty said, tearing off his shoes. "He's in church." He dived into the lake without hesitation.

Morty swam out to the current, intersecting the spot where Billy O'Glynn's face bobbed on the surface. The boy was limp, making it difficult for Morty to swim with him. He put one arm around Billy's chest and stroked with the other, but the flow was too swift. He could already see the opening to the river snaking out in the distance ahead.

Sloshing wildly, he turned the boy around and slapped his face. "Billy! Billy, can you hear me?"

He hit him again. The child's tender skin was red and already beginning to bruise, but Morty struck him again. At last, the boy sputtered into consciousness, flailing his arms and scratching Morty's face and chest with his fingernails until they bled.

46

"Hold on to me, boy. That's it, take hold of my belt so I can have both arms free. Don't let go, now, you hear?"

"Yes," the boy said, coughing.

Morty turned at a ninety-degree angle and tried to put every muscle in his body into swimming across the current. Ahead of him he saw Bounfort Castle.

He pulled, feeling his belly knot and his nose sting, and at last the current slowed. He was past the worst of it. A small cave, cut under the rocky shoreline, was visible now. He stroked strongly toward it.

"In here, boy," he panted, heaving Billy into the rock-filled inlet. Together, they lay in the shallow water, too exhausted and terrified to speak. It was dark under the overhang of rock.

His heart pounding, Morty felt a swell of pride rise inside him. He had saved the boy from Moon Lake, just as Michael Cormac had once saved Morty himself.

*Valour,* he thought, basking in the mosquito-filled dankness of the cave as if it were sunshine.

Billy was the first to recover. "It stinks here," he said.

Morty laughed. "It's a piece of work you are, Billy O'Glynn." He sat up, sniffing. "But you're right. Something foul's afoot, I'd say from the wind around here."

The boy brightened. "By the flies." He pointed to a swarm of insects buzzing around a tangle of juniper and rhododendron bushes outside the cave. "Can I see?"

"If you can take what you find," Morty said.

The boy hesitated. "What do you think it is?"

47

"Wouldn't know. Dead deer, maybe. Nothing small, from the smell of it."

Billy stood up, and Morty marveled at the resilience of children. His own legs felt like warm jelly. The boy shooed the flies away, then separated the bushes.

He gasped before he screamed. As Morty scrambled over to hold him, he saw the boy's face contorted in utter, unspeakable terror.

"What? What is it?"

But Billy O'Glynn could no longer speak. His arms stuck out rigid in front of him, like a mechanical doll's. Throwing him aside, Morty dived into the bushes. The sight made him retch.

Lying in the flotsam of the cove, its legs broken and twisted, was the body of a man. There was no head. Its chest was unclothed and burned to blackness. One arm was severed at the wrist, the other at the shoulder. The flesh, where it was not burned, was wattled blue-white and covered with sores from the lake animals that had fed on it.

"Jesus Redeemer," Morty whispered, making the sign of the cross.

He heard a sound. Looking up, he spotted the doctor at the entrance to the cave. Behind him stood Kathleen Pierce, staring, immobile.

# CHAPTER FOUR

The Pierce mansion loomed in front of Cormac late that Sunday afternoon like an enemy fortress. He felt like a fool, a lone warrior who was both overage and overweight, confronting it. He took off his soft woolen hat and ran his hand nervously through his think gray hair as he looked through the open gates at the sprawling three-story building.

It would always be the Pierce mansion for him, even though the brass plaque bearing the Pierce name had been removed and replaced by a more cheerful one of painted porcelain with "Bonning" written upon it in runic script. And the house would always be Moira's for him as well, the castle where Cinderella married the prince and lived happily ever after.

He was prepared. Both Doctor O'Connor's grandfather and Morty O'Sullivan had filled him in on Moira's misfortune, but even the satisfaction of some sort of divine revenge failed to lessen the hurt he had lived with for half his life.

Moira McLaughlin had been the most beautiful girl in three counties. Looking back, it would have been foolish for a creature of such extravagant comeliness to marry the local constable, but no man thinks himself ordinary at the age of twenty.

When Moira agreed to marry Cormac, they had decided to buy a small farm on the outskirts of Ardath. Moira was going to call the place Tara, after the legendary seat of Ireland's ancient kings, and turn it into a bed-and-breakfast place for tourists. With the income from the place and Cormac's Garda salary, they figured to have enough for a car, a television, and a few extras. And as Moira once said, "Who knows? Maybe we'll discover oil."

But they never bought Tara. Lyle Pierce saw to that. More accurately, their plans were changed by Moira's sensible Irish eye for opportunity. When Pierce, at fifty, inherited the estate from his English aunt, he was between mistresses, and Moira, the local beauty, took his fancy long enough for him to marry her away from Cormac.

According to Morty and Doctor O'Connor's grandfather, the marriage quickly turned sour, with Pierce spending much of his time and most of his money at Deauville, where he commuted between the racetrack and the home of his French mistress. When he died, of a heart attack in what the papers described as the home of a "friend" in the south of France, Moira was left with the house, a small child, and monumental debts.

Moira struggled for more than a year with the legion of creditors before she finally found a buyer for the Pierce mansion. Mr. Bonning, the buyer, was a man about whom little was known in Ardath. He was an elderly widower who never socialized, belonged to no local organizations, and rarely left the house on the town side of Moon Lake.

Bonning had permitted Moira, who was destitute, to live in one of the out-cottages on the grounds. She had single-handedly reared her lone daughter Kathleen, sending her to a local school, and had never married again.

It was hard for Cormac to approach the place knowing that he might see her in passing. But a lead was a lead, and from what he could gather from the townspeople, the mysterious Mr. Bonning was the top suspect in their minds after Mad Hattie.

Of course, the townspeople were talking through their hats, he reminded himself. Bonning had lived among them for years. It was one of the peculiarities of life in a small town. Cormac had been back just several days after a twenty-year absence, yet they still regarded Cormac as one of their own, and Bonning as an outsider.

The estate owner was no suspect in either the explosion at the pier or the death of the man whose body Morty O'Sullivan had found on the lakeshore at noon. Still, both events had happened on property Bonning owned, and he might be able to provide some kind of a lead.

The body had already been wrapped in a heavy plastic bag and shipped off to the police morgue in Cork. Not even the dead creature's own mother would recognize him, Cormac thought, and he had a strong suspicion that he had found whoever it was that had been trying to move explosives down at the pier a few nights ago.

He had found him. But who was he? Who had that

person been back before a sudden blast had ripped away his hands and head?

Perhaps Bonning would know.

Cormac felt himself sweating as he walked through the open ironwork gate toward the house. It was a confection in blue and white, with its five chimneys and sloping eaves. No wonder Moira had chosen to live here, Cormac thought. Even though her reign had been short, she must have, for a time, felt like a queen. He stood on the porch, drew back his fist, and slugged the door with such ferocity that he let out an involuntary yelp of pain.

There was no answer, not to his knocking, or his ringing, or his shouts to open up. He spat into the flower bed and took a step backward, hands on hips, to see if he saw any movement inside the house.

To his right, just visible behind the shrubbery, was the figure of a woman throwing seed out of a bowl. She looked like a painting from another century, the loose ends of her hair floating on the wind, her skirt billowing behind her while birds gathered at her feet.

For a moment Cormac stood and watched her, allowing his eyes to rest on the back of a faceless woman whose movements were at the same time exciting and serene. Then she turned, and Cormac froze, feeling sweat on his upper lip and the sensation that a steel hand had just closed over his intestines.

It was Moira. The basket fell from her hands, and she stood still for a moment, the wind washing her hair over her eyes. She walked toward him, slowly at first, then more quickly.

He ran a hand over his hair, conscious of its grayness. "I'm looking for this Bonning," he said, trying to sound natural. He jerked his thumb toward the plaque on the wall, then felt foolish. He should at least have said hello to her.

Moira stared at him for a moment, searching his face, then looked down at her hands. "Mr. Bonning's away," she said.

"Doesn't he have servants?"

"Only me." She flushed. "I look after the house and mind things while he's away. He's let me stay on the grounds since the property was sold."

Cormac cleared his throat. "I heard. Where'd he go?"

"Nicaragua, I think."

"What?"

"Mr. Bonning's a bontanist. Just a hobby, but from what I understand, he's very well respected. He's gone to find some sort of plant."

"Oh, I see. Uh—"

"He'll be back in a few days."

Cormac grunted. "Well, I suppose I'll be back then." He stared hard at Moira's shoulder to avoid looking at her face. "I'm—ah—just passing through. I stopped to spend a couple of days, and wanted to pay my respects. My father used to mention a man named Bonning. I wondered if . . ."

Moira's face broke into a smile. "Oh, Michael, everyone knows why you're here. It's not every Sunday we find a headless body in Moon Lake."

They faced each other in silence. The sight of her almost took his breath away. She was as beautiful as he'd remembered. The hair still glistened red as burnished copper, and the eyes were as green as the sea. She had kept her figure, voluptuous and lean at the

53

same time, and her full mouth seemed ready, as it had those long years ago, to break into laughter. Finally Moira touched his arm gently. "It's been so long since I've seen you," she whispered. "Will you come have tea with me?"

"No, I can't," Cormac fumbled. He looked past her, his jaw clenched tight. "I don't want to."

She released him, embarrassed. "I'm sorry," she said quietly. A single furrow formed between her eyes. "I hoped you might have forgiven me by now."

He stared at her, longing to both kiss her and hit her. "I haven't," he said, turning away.

Not daring to look back, he walked toward the lake. He planned to look in on the cave where Morty found the body before walking back along the shoreline to the village.

By the time he reached the lake, the shock of seeing Moira had made his legs as weak as a puppy's. He stopped and sat down on the embankment to clear his head. Here the shore was lovely and grass-covered, as beautiful as everything else around the Pierce mansion. The water lapped up gracefully to the side, and its surface was clear as glass.

Barely more than a hundred yards away loomed Bounfort Castle, its gray stones black in silhouette against the slowly lowering sun. The Shrine of Eternal Peace, he thought bitterly. Not even that, he knew, would bring peace to his soul. Once Moira could have done that, a thousand years ago when he was young, but no longer.

He started to his feet. He would have to get moving. The middle of an investigation was not the place to pine for a woman.

Somehow, rejecting Moira—an act he had looked forward to for twenty years—had left him feeling empty and lost. As if she would have had him again, anyway, he thought. Moira looked half her age; Cormac looked twice his. He started to leave, then saw Moira walking in the distance toward the lake.

She didn't appear to notice him. She moved slowly, with her head down, then sat, as he had sat, along the water's edge. He watched her dip her hand into the water abstractedly.

*Is she acting for my benefit?* he wondered, then dismissed the thought. He was one of the forgotten things of her past, stored in her memory with her chip-faced porcelain dolls and red petticoats.

As he stood, transfixed on her, she suddenly wrenched backward with a piercing scream. Before he could respond, she was on her feet, shrieking; then she began running, falling over her feet, toward the house.

"Moira!" he called.

She turned toward him with wild eyes, her hands clasped over her mouth.

He ran to intercept her. "What is it? What's the matter?"

She clasped him around his shoulders. Her chest was heaving. "The lake," she said, choking.

Bewildered, Cormac hurried toward the spot where Moira had been sitting. His eyes passed over the thing more than once before he noticed the fingernails. Then it sprang into focus, like one of those drawings where the background becomes the image: a man's hand, severed at the wrist.

\* \* \*

55

In Grady's Pub, he found someone with a car who was willing to make the trip to Cork for ten pounds.

"Plus fuel," the man had said.

"That's all right," Cormac agreed.

"What do you want me to do?"

"Deliver this to Garda headquarters in Cork. To Superintendent Merrion. He'll know what to do with it." From behind his back he held out the severed hand, wrapped carefully in several layers of clear plastic.

"Jumping Jaysus," the man said. "I'll not be carrying no sliced-off hand for no measly ten quid."

"Plus petrol," Cormac reminded him.

"Why don't you be buying a morgue wagon, you and Morty, if you're going to be shipping parts of people out of this town every bloody day?" the man said.

"Yes or no," Cormac prodded impatiently.

"All right, then," the man grumbled. "But be putting that thing inside a sack so I don't have to look at it. It's bad enough I'll feel the thing crawling around inside the car, waiting for it to grab me throat."

Grady produced a paper bag and Cormac stuck the hand inside. He gave it to the man, who recoiled as if Cormac were giving him a live electrical wire.

"You put it in the boot of the car. This Merrion fellow of yours can take it out. I won't be touching it, so I won't."

"If you do, it'll come after you some night when the moon is full and you least expecting it," Cormac said, unable to resist taunting the Irishman's superstitions.

"You're not a funny man, Michael Cormac. You weren't funny as a wee one and you're not funny now.

56

Five pounds advance." He held out his hand. Cormac stuffed a bill into it.

After the man left, Cormac drank a pint more than he had planned to, but he didn't want to go back to his room. Moira would be there, in his thoughts. It was late when he finally lurched upstairs. He was grateful that he was too drunk to dream.

At eight o'clock the next morning, the telephone woke him. It was Merrion.

"That hand has fingerprints on it," he said.

"Well?" Cormac said thickly.

"You'd better come in, Mike."

# CHAPTER FIVE

Superintendent Merrion led Cormac through the smoky pall of his office and gestured with one of several burning cigarettes for him to sit down. The super's face, usually rangy and wolflike, instead looked drawn and sober. He sat smoking in silence for a while, then tossed the smoldering butt into the ashtray, where it ignited a strip of cellophane. He lit a fresh cigarette from the blaze. "The body belongs to Winston Barnett. His prints are on file in Dublin. You ever hear of him?"

Cormac shook his head no. Merrion slid a photograph across the desk. It was a mug shot of a man in his thirties, sooty looking, with the fanatical eyes of a zealot.

"Not much to look at," Merrion said.

"There's a lot less of him to look at now," Cormac said. "So who is Winston Barnett?"

"An anti-Catholic troublemaker from Belfast. He was with the Ulster vigilantes. . . . What do they call them?"

"The UDA. Ulster Defense Association," Cormac said.

"Right. He was with them and some other Protestant rabble-rousers. Got nailed a couple of years ago for possession of explosives. That's why his fingerprints were on file. The lab told me they had the devil's own time pulling the prints because that hand you sent in was so damned decomposed."

"I'll try to get fresher exhibits the next time," Cormac said.

"The big question is still what's a man like Barnett doing in the South. In Ardath, of all places. Aren't there enough Catholics for him to kill in the six counties of the North?" Merrion took a deep drag from his cigarette, then ground it out viciously. "God damn it, I wish I knew what was going on. Dublin's on my back every day about this homicide." He glared at Cormac as if the whole affair wcrc somehow his fault.

"I don't see a homicide, Frank."

"Well, what do you see?" the super snapped.

"Nothing, yet. There aren't enough facts. Maybe Barnett was trying to smuggle explosives in and blew himself up. That's an accident. Maybe it's ritual suicide. We just can't tell."

"I sent you there to find things out, not just to tell me what you don't know," Merrion said sourly.

"Any time you want to relieve me, I'm ready to come back."

"Don't get your back up, Cormac. The reserves are arriving. They're sending you a partner."

"What for? And who's 'they'?"

"They is Dublin, and I guess they're sending him so that we can get this thing finished up, that's what for," Merrion said.

"Who's the partner?"

"His name is Wells. Daniel Taylor Wells."

"He's from Dublin? I don't know him," Cormac said.

Merrion shook his head. "Not Dublin. London." He spat a piece of tobacco onto his desk blotter. "A Brit." He didn't look at Cormac as the Irishman sat speechless, his mouth fallen slightly open. "Supposed to be a big shot in terrorist cases."

"You can't be serious," Cormac said finally. "An Englishman coming to investigate a case involving a pro-English terrorist? In Ireland?" He stared at Merrion for a few moments, then burst out laughing.

"That's Dublin for you," Merrion said, shaking his head. "But it's not funny. Nothing is funny about this case."

"I'm not laughing because it's funny. I'm laughing because it's so frigging tragic. After five centuries of getting stabbed in the back by the bastards, we're still trusting the Brits to solve our problems for us."

Merrion threw a pencil onto his desk. "Be that as it may, those are the orders, and there's not much point in getting into a lather over it."

The two men sat quietly for a few moments. Each lit a cigarette. Then Cormac sighed, shrugged, and said, "All right. I don't make the rules. What do you know about this Wells?"

"I'll tell you everything we've got on him," Merrion said, opening a folder. He read, "Daniel Taylor Wells, forty-two, born in Brighton, England, educated at Sandhurst. Captain in the Seventeenth Fusilliers. Served in Vietnam. Retired nineteen seventy-eight, joined Metropolitan Police . . ." He closed the folder. "That's Scotland Yard."

"What's his rank?"

"That we don't know."

"What's that supposed to mean, you don't know?" Cormac said crankily.

Merrion glowered at him. "It means he probably outranks you, Sergeant." He waved his arms vaguely. "I know it isn't much. But I had to move heaven and earth just to get this paltry information on him. Damn Brits are as tight-lipped about their personnel as the Israelis."

"Scotland Yard," Cormac muttered.

"So I'm told. Probably C-eleven."

"What's C-eleven?"

Merrion sounded smug when he answered. "A special anti-terrorist branch inside the Yard."

Cormac shook his head. "I don't think so," he said.

"No?" the superintendent looked up questioningly.

"Somehow the idea of Scotland Yard sending a man to Ireland to help us out just doesn't ring true. I smell the hand of the SAS behind this," Cormac said.

Merrion dragged thoughtfully on his cigarette as Cormac mentioned the name of the special British Army unit that had been sent into Ireland to battle the Irish Republican Army. They were the Special Air Service. They were the elite of the British military, a combination of KGB and Israeli commando. They were ferocious, bloodthirsty and remorseless, as far as Cormac was concerned.

Merrion lit another cigarette, ignoring the ones already burning in his ashtray. "What makes you think he's SAS?"

"Just a hunch," Cormac said, remembering the stories of the English Black-and-Tans who had come to his country to restore order and instead instituted a reign of terror.

"Oh, you're great, Cormac," said Merrion. "You won't speculate on whether the bombing at the pier in Ardath was murder or accident or suicide because you don't have enough facts, but you can tell the occupation of a man you've never met because you get a hunch. Wonderful police work."

"Forget I said it."

"I already have. Anyway, you work with Wells. Whether he's C-eleven or your personal boogeyman from the SAS, he probably knows more about this shit than you do."

"Who doesn't?" Cormac said bitterly. "Well, when he solves everything, we can all get together and sing 'God Save the Queen.' "

"Better hope that he does. If this case isn't solved soon, you'll be singing 'God Save Cormac's Balls.' "

"Do you have a picture of this Wells? How do I recognize him?"

"A picture?" Merrion laughed. "I had to call in two years of favors just to get this much. There is no picture. He'll recognize you and make the contact. You just stay visible."

"All right. What are we doing about the press?"

"Nothing. As far as those vultures are concerned, we never found a body, we never found a hand floating in the lake. Dublin's put a lid on it."

Cormac blew out a stream of smoke. "Everybody knows about the body," he said. "There were dozens of people around when it was found. So when the hand turned up, I let them know about it, too. I figured it'd be a lot less mysterious that way, and maybe there'd be less talk."

"Maybe," Merrion said, but looked doubtful. "I'll have to leave that to you. Just try to keep it out of the papers."

"I think we're safe there," Cormac said. "There isn't any paper in Ardath." He stood up. "One more thing."

"What," Merrion growled.

"Can I get a transfer to the French foreign legion?"

"Clean this thing up, or we'll be looking for two vacancies," the super said. "Now, get out of here and get back to work."

In the squadroom, Cormac stopped to talk to Sergeant Willie Palmer, his sometime partner.

"If your face was any longer, you'd be stepping on your chin," Palmer said.

"I don't know," Cormac said, picking up Palmer's coffee container and putting it in front of himself. "Frank's all over me on this one."

"I don't know either," Palmer said. "You know how the super is. But he's worse now. He's getting real heat from upstairs in Dublin. I heard him mumbling something the other day about the prime minister's office sticking its nose where it doesn't belong."

"That, too," Cormac said. He sipped the coffee, then put the container back in front of Palmer. He forced himself to swallow. "Why is Dublin so gallopy about this one? An old pier blew up when some explosives went off. Now we got the body of some Protestant thug who was probably sitting on the barrel when it blew. Doesn't that sound like 'case closed' to you?"

"Except what was he doing there in the first place?

63

Was he taking the explosives out, or bringing them in? If he was bringing them in, what for? Still questions, Mike.''

"I think you should be working on this case instead of me, Willie,'' Cormac said disgustedly. "If you want, I can put a good word in for you.''

"No thanks,'' Palmer said. "When they start looking for sacrificial lambs, I don't want them to reach for me. You'll do just fine.''

"Thanks, partner.''

"Anytime.'' Palmer glanced at his watch and smiled slyly. "Shouldn't you be getting back? Who knows how many butchered bodies might be turning up and you not there to welcome them ashore?''

"You've got the heart of a Protestant bishop,'' Cormac said.

"And the well-saved ass of a sixty-year-old virgin. Go on with you, Michael. I don't want to be seen talking to you.''


Cormac drove back to Ardath and parked himself in Grady's Pub. If he had to work with a Brit, he decided, he certainly wasn't going to do it sober.

As in many other Irish villages, it seemed that every other storefront along the two busiest streets, West and Killian Streets, was a pub. But they were all geared for the summer tourist trade. Inside the barrooms were little tables where inedible sandwiches of dry ham on stale bread were served along with instant coffee, and tourists sat eating stoically, waiting for Barry Fitzgerald to walk in and lead the regulars in a chorus of "Wild Colonial Boy."

Cormac had learned a lot of things in his twelve years in the United States. One was that the native Irish knew nothing about making sandwiches fit for human consumption. The other was that he hated Barry Fitzgerald and every movie he'd ever appeared in.

He thought of going around to all the tourist pubs to make it easier for Wells to find him, but decided to hell with it. If Wells wanted to find him, let him track Cormac down. It should be easy for the great British detective.

Inside Grady's, he was greeted by the town's old-timers and Grady's regular customers in the effusive way he had come to expect, as if he had been out of town for the blink of an eye. No one ever asked him where he had been, as if life apart from Ardath did not exist. Instead, they regaled him with talk of the village.

Mad Hattie was in the news again. Apparently she had scared two American tourists in Ardath out of their wits by springing at them from behind the bakery and shouting something about ghosts pulling themselves out of their graves. But the main topic in Grady's was still Morty's discovery of the headless body in Moon Lake. Young Billy O'Glynn had been confined to his bed since the incident.

As to the severed hand with the incriminating fingerprints, the townspeople of Ardath were less impressed. Who cared about a fish-nibbled hand when you had the rest of the body to gossip about?

Old Lanigan was there, already beginning to nod off, as was Doctor O'Connor's grandfather. Molly Logan, who had gone back to drinking after her last culinary debacle, was holding her own with the best of them.

Since it was after working hours, much of the rest of Ardath was also at the pub, packed four deep at the bar. As the hours passed and the empty pint glasses of Guinness accumulated in front of him, Cormac began to eye the strangers in the place with a hostile wariness. Actually, there were no good prospects. Most of the faces were typically Irish or Norman, and most of them were regulars he'd seen before. There was only one bona fide Englishman in the place, but he was all wrong. Just to be sure, though, Cormac scrutinized him with his policeman's eye.

The man was tall, and rail thin. He wore an impeccable and expensive tweed sports coat, white gabardine trousers, and shoes polished to a high gleam. His hair was blond, his features ordinary but well tended, and his voice pitched to a grating whine. He seemed totally absorbed in a detailed conversation about bird watching with the two stout English ladies who'd moved into Ardath for the summer. Satisfied, Cormac dismissed him and kept his eye on the door.

A cyclist, complete with helmet and skintight stretch shorts, strolled in. Cormac snickered. "It's got to be him," he said aloud. Daniel Taylor Wells, master of disguise.

"Beg pardon?" Old Lanigan yelled, craning close to Cormac.

"Get lost," Cormac said gruffly, shying away from the alcoholic fumes emitted by the old man.

"Well, ain't himself the fine one," Lanigan sniffed to no one in particular. "The big detective, don't you know. And it took our own Morty O'Sullivan to be finding the headless killer."

"Who says he was a killer?" Cormac shouted.

"Who the hell's been killed?" He sloshed his drink on the bar. "Anyway, I'm on holiday."

" 'Twas Mrs. O'Glynn said he was a killer." Old Lanigan lifted his chin proudly. "And a true policeman's work is never done. Ask young Morty."

"Aaah, leave me alone." Cormac noticed a young blond-haired man at the far end of the bar staring at him. When Grady the publican came to refill his glass, Cormac asked who the man was.

Grady looked over his shoulder, then leaned closer to Cormac and said softly, "That's Brian O'Flaherty. He's been in town a couple of years now. Sings up at the castle for tourists." He paused just a single beat. "Sings with Kathleen Pierce. They're seeing each other off and on."

Cormac nodded. Old Lanigan leaned over and said, "What are you two whispering about, eh? What are you talking?"

"Give Old Lanigan a drink, too," Cormac told the barkeep. "Maybe that'll shut him up." As he waved his hand to include Lanigan in the drink, he knocked over the old man's tankard of ale, sending a jet of brown liquid pouring over the two stout English ladies and the foppish man. The three had been deep in a conversation about butterflies.

"It's all right," one of the women said graciously.

The man stood up. "Ought to be a little more careful, my friend." He lit a cigarette with a dull silver-colored lighter.

"I said I was sorry," Cormac said.

"It doesn't matter what you said, old bean. What matters is—"

"Don't 'old bean' me, you bloody Brit faggot."

67

There were a few chortles from people along the bar. The English ladies stood up, aghast, and drifted back toward the tables near the walls. The Englishman blinked twice, rapidly, the litttle red handkerchief in his tailored sports jacket quivering. He rubbed his manicured hands together.

"I say, you're in a nasty temper, what?"

"Jesus," Cormac sighed. "Leave me be."

"I expect you owe the ladies an apology," the Briton said archly, laying a limp hand on Cormac's shoulder. "As well as a visit to the cleaner's. Fair's fair."

Slowly, Cormac brushed the hand off him as if it were a fungus.

The Englishman smiled broadly. "My word, that's a switch. An Irishman getting soiled by the hands of a Queen's subject, eh, what?" He laughed in all innocence, his teeth showing like a horse's.

No one else thought the remark remotely funny.

Cormac's eyes narrowed into slits. "What's that?"

"Well, there's no need to take things so seriously. Surely you've heard Irish jokes before."

"Irish jokes?" Cormac said. "Sure, I'll bet I know more Irish jokes than you do. Here's one you've never heard before." Cormac thrust his right hand toward the Englishman's face and coldcocked him into a dead faint.

Cheers rose from the bar. Someone rang the bell above the bottles, signaling a free round for the house. Cormac looked at his hand. The Englishman was just coming to on the floor, but the blow had felt like it had barely grazed the target.

*Must have a glass jaw,* Cormac thought as he picked

the fool up by his costly lapels and propelled him out the door to the encouragement of the clientele.

Outside, he propped the man against the wall. The man's eyes darted left, then right. "I'm Wells," he said softly.

"I know," said Cormac.

"You prick."

"That'll teach you to tell Irish jokes,"

"I'm at the Park Hotel. Come over at nine." The blond man dusted himself off, then slowly walked away down the street.

Cormac went back inside to a deafening cheer from the bar. The young man at the far end of the bar, something O'Flaherty, raised a glass toward him in salute. Cormac nodded and moved to a spot in the corner of the bar, feeling satisfied with himself.


He showed up at the Park Hotel—the grandest and only regulation hotel in town—at five minutes to nine, checking to see he wasn't followed. He took the elevator up to the fourth floor, then followed the directions to the room. The door opened before he could knock.

"Come on in," Wells said. He closed the door behind Cormac. "So you knew it was me, did you?"

Cormac nodded. Even in his shirtsleeves, Cormac noticed, the Englishman looked like a dandy, in contrast to Cormac's own rumpled slovenliness.

Wells raised his eyebrows. "And you hit me anyway?"

"Couldn't resist," Cormac said, grinning maliciously.

"That's one I owe you," Wells said with good humor. Without his jacket, he looked more powerfully built than he had earlier. "Make yourself a drink." He waved toward a bar in the corner of the hotel suite's large living room. "If you can manage another one."

Just out of perversity, Cormac went to the bar and poured a large Scotch into a wide-topped glass. He dropped in a few ice cubes as he mumbled, "That'll be the day, when a Brit can tell me what and how to drink." He took a healthy slug of his drink and turned back. Wells was sitting in a chair, his feet up on the coffee table, reading a newspaper. "Don't you want to know how I made you?" Cormac asked.

"The cigarette lighter, of course," Wells said.

Deflated, Cormac pretended to ignore him. "That dull silver kind all you Brit militarists carry. You should get rid of it before the Russians have you for lunch."

"I already did." Wells lit a cigarette with a hotel match. "At any rate, it worked. I don't think anyone will suspect us of being bosom buddies."

Cormac waited for a few minutes while Wells read. When at last it seemed that the Englishman had forgotten all about his presence, Cormac boomed, "Well? What the hell am I doing here?"

Wells said from behind the newspaper, "I wanted to get to know you."

"Fine way of going about it," Cormac said.

"Oh, not so bad, really; I know you're impatient, excitable, trusting, lonely, stubborn, and that you resent working with me. Doubtless because of my nationality." He snapped the paper down toward his lap. There was a big grin on his face. "Am I right?"

70

"Holy Mary, spare me," Cormac said under his breath.

The grin vanished. "I want to know how you're going to respond."

"To what?"

The grin reappeared in a flash. "To anything." The Briton sat in silence, smiling, until Cormac felt his armpits getting damp and his toes beginning to cramp in his shoes.

"So? Do I measure up?" he said at last, his chin raised in defiance. "There are other men in the Gardai. I don't have to be here."

"You'll do," Wells said, still looking at the newspaper. "I just wanted us to spend some time around each other so I'll be able to operate with you and keep my own skin intact. A reasonable precaution, I'd say."

"Sounds pretty dramatic, considering the facts."

"Does it? Exactly what facts are we considering, Sergeant Cormac?"

"I'll tell you if you stop reading that bloody newspaper," Cormac snapped.

Wells set the paper on the table, neatly. Everything about him was neat. Cormac hated it. "Policemen should always read the newspapers. Interesting things to be found in the press," Wells said. "You were reciting some facts to me?"

Cormac sighed, then fiddled with his bronze medal as he went through his narrative: the blowing up of the pier, the trace of gelignite found in the reeds, the headless body, the severed hand, the identification. "Sounds like someone blew himself up to me."

Wells nodded pleasantly. His mustache was so well trimmed, Cormac noted, that it looked as if it had been groomed by a surgical team. "I'll let pass for a moment that the explosive wasn't gelignite, but something related to it. There's something else wrong with your facts, Sergeant. By the way, what is that coin you're playing with?"

Cormac pushed the medal back into his pocket. "Just a good luck charm," he said, feeling stupid. "What's wrong with my facts?"

"The hand, Sergeant Cormac."

"What about it?"

"It doesn't belong to the body."

# CHAPTER SIX

Cormac didn't like him. He didn't like his excessive neatness, his British precision, his habit of writing everything down. He didn't even like his damn striped cotton shirt, which never seemed to wrinkle. But he had to admit that Wells seemed to have his wits about him; he was able to follow the thread of a story from beginning to end without getting lost in side roads.

The two men talked well into the night. Cormac told the Briton everything he knew of the facts and where the different townspeople were during the incidents.

"Moira Pierce," Wells said aloud, writing the name on a list that included Billy O'Glynn, Morty O'Sullivan and the absent Mr. Bonning, new owner of the Pierce estate.

"If you want my opinion, that's not much of a list of suspects," Cormac groused. "Hell, Morty's in the Gardai. Billy O'Glynn's twelve years old."

"They aren't suspects. They're just people who know something. Perhaps they don't even know they know it. But they do." He picked up his pencil again. "We might as well put down the old woman, too. What did you say her name was?"

"You mean Mad Hattie? She wouldn't know anything. Doesn't even know her own name most of the time."

"Which is?"

"O'Shea," Cormac sighed. "Henrietta O'Shea, the seer of Ardath."

"Has she been here since before you left the village?"

Cormac nodded. "Aye, and she was crazy as a bedbug then, too. Old Lanigan and Doc O'Connor's grandfather pulled her out of her well two or three times that I can remember. Said she heard voices down there."

"Mad Hattie it is," Wells said, grinning, adding her name to his list.

"And Moira? What's she got to do with this?"

"She found the hand," Wells said crisply.

"A second before I did. She was scared out of her wits. There's no need to bring her into this."

"She might have been frightened," Wells said calmly.

"What's that supposed to mean?"

The Englishman made a dismissive gesture. "She might not."

"Why, you bloody, smarmy . . ."

"Oh, stop." Wells sat back in his chair and fluttered his eyelids in exasperation. "Now, if you're going to act like a crazy Irishman, you're going to hinder my investigation."

"Your investigation? This is my country, remember? Or doesn't that matter to you royalist machine gunners?"

"Just a moment, Cormac," Wells said, his eyes meeting the Irishman's levelly. "I think you ought to understand something from the beginning. I have no concern whatever about the troubles between your country and mine. If we've any hope of working together, this nation-alistic pap has got to go.''

Cormac clenched his jaw. "I just don't want a lot of innocent people bothered," he said.

"How about the guilty ones?" Wells snapped. "Do you worry about them, too?"

"God damn it, don't talk to me about guilt when we don't even know if a crime's been committed."

"I'd say that smuggling explosives is a crime," Wells said. "Even under a very gentle interpretation of the law. And when somebody gets killed doing it, I think we probably could find more than one crime involved if we looked."

"I suppose you plan to bust people's heads until you find out what's going on," Cormac shouted. "It's just what I'd expect from you bloody SAS bastards."

Wells smiled. "I'm with Scotland Yard," he said quietly.

"Sure. You can tell that to anybody you want, but don't go trying it with me. You've got the stench of Irish death on you, mister. You've got the look in your eyes of somebody who likes to kill. The worst terrorists in the North are you SAS murderers."

"Not the worst," Wells said evenly. "That prize goes to your charming compatriots in the IRA."

"We're not talking about the IRA, damn it."

"Aren't we?" Wells strode to the bed, picked up a briefcase, and took a photograph from it. "Look," he said, handing it to Cormac.

It was a picture of the severed hand, taken from the angle of the stump. "That was an execution, Michael."

He walked to the other side of the room while Cormac studied the picture. "Oh, it was handled with artistry, a

75

snag here and there, and probably smeared with sardine oil so that the fish would be sure to get at it quickly, but if you look at the fibers, they're cut as cleanly as a surgeon's work.''

Cormac ran his finger along the glossy surface, feeling nauseated.

"Your beloved Irish patriots up north specialize in this sort of thing, you know. Strap a man to a chair and then hack off his hands with a meat cleaver. They've even added improvements. Chain saws are quite popular these days, not to mention the electric drills used to puncture kneecaps. There's an entire hospital in Belfast devoted to the work of these Irish idealists.''

Wells paused to light a cigarette. "But the doctors can't keep up with the imaginations of these people. The kneecapping technique has been replaced in some areas by something much more interesting. A victim is made to stand on a sidewalk with his arms outstretched in front of him, as a concrete slab is dropped into his hands from the top of a building. Clever, don't you agree?''

Cormac tossed the photograph on the table. "What about your stinking Ulster Defense Association?'' he said bitterly. "I suppose they're different because they're Protestant.''

"No, they're not.'' Wells spoke quietly, but he stood perfectly still, his eyes fixed on Cormac with an intensity that seemed to emanate from every cell in his body. "Don't you see, Cormac? Religion isn't the issue here. We're not involved in some kind of holy war between Protestant and Catholic. And underneath all the rhetoric, the problem isn't between north and south, either, or even between Ireland and England.''

He sat down across from Cormac, so close that the

Irishman could feel the tension in Wells's muscles. "What we're dealing with is a vast, organized network of trained killers programmed to destroy what we know as civilization, piece by piece, person by person, at random. Who runs the IRA?" He lifted his hands. "Even the killers themselves don't know anymore. It's the thrill of the kill that feeds them now, a blood fever. And the Ulster vigilantes arc as sick and twisted as the IRA. Life means nothing to these people, any of them, regardless of their so-called ideologies. The credo of the terrorist is death. And in this, they're all the same."

Cormac toyed with the medallion in his pocket. An Irishman didn't side with an Englishman against the Irish, no matter what the circumstances. That was common knowledge. But what had happened to Ireland in the past twenty years had never happened before in the history of the world. His fingers fidgeted nervously. Cormac knew he was an intelligent man. But it was still hard to give up so old and comfortable a thing as his Irish hatred of the English. It had come down to him worn and sweet, passed to him through countless generations. How could he give up a distrust of an enemy so ancient that it had been old to his first forebears?

"You're the law," Wells said. "And so am I. As it is, there are too few of us to rid the world of all the murderers who are killing our families and crippling our countries. But we can stop a few of them. That's all I want to do. Whoever they are, whatever label they give themselves, if they're here, I'm going to get them. Are you with me?"

Cormac tightened his fist around his medal. "I'm with you," he said hoarsely. He felt the metal disk biting into his flesh. "But I don't have to like you," he added stubbornly.

Wells smiled. "Fair enough."

"But first, one answer, okay?"

"Depends on the question," Wells said.

"Why would a Brit be sent into southern Ireland on a matter like this?"

"I came at the request of your government," Wells said. "They probably have their reasons."

"If you knew those reasons, would you tell me what they were?"

"No," Wells said affably.

Cormac exhaled noisily. "I'll have another drink," he said, shambling over to the bar. He downed half his glass of Scotch in one swallow. "Anyway, I'll give the devil his due," he said. "It was a good guess that the hand was too small to belong to Winston Barnett's body."

"It wasn't a guess," Wells said. "I had other reasons."

"Such as?"

"I knew Barnett. The fingerprints were correct. The hand was his, but the body wasn't."

"How'd you know?"

"I checked at the morgue. Barnett had a broken right thighbone once. The corpse had no fracture lines."

"None of the other geniuses there figured that out?"

"They couldn't." Wells smiled. "They didn't break his leg." He walked over to Cormac and poured himself a drink. "I think I'm going to look at that castle of yours tomorrow."

"May the spirit of it settle in your black English heart," Cormac said, lifting his glass.

"What spirit?"

"It's called the Shrine of Eternal Peace, remember?"

"Ah, yes. To the Shrine of Eternal Peace."

They touched glasses. As Cormac drank, he felt a small shiver of fear. He hoped that the old chapel would keep its name.

Cormac woke, then lay in bed smoking. He thought about the previous evening and reaffirmed his judgment; He didn't like Wells. There was something a little too brittle, too precious about the Englishman for Cormac ever to think that he could warm up to him. But he had to admit that he looked forward to working with him. Perhaps Wells would be able to get this investigation off the penny. Once it was marked "closed," Cormac could get out of Ardath and back to the safety of Cork.

Meeting Moira over the weekend had been hard on him. There had not been a day in the past twenty years when he had not felt her in one part of his memory or another, but he had expected that the worst of the wound was healed. And yet when he saw her, and spoke to her, it was all there again, all the pain and confusion and hurt that had driven him from Ardath two decades before.

He was glad that she had not tried to call or contact him, because he didn't know how he would act if he had to see her again.

Or her daughter. To have to look at another man's child, the evidence of someone else's hands having been on Moira, would be more pain than he could stand. And he'd felt enough pain. After twenty years, it still hurt.

And nothing seemed to make it stop. Not the work, not the booze, not even the women. Hell, he'd even married one to get over Moira.

He gave a snort and shifted in his bed. No wonder Merrion had put him on this stupid case with an English faggot for a partner. The super probably figured it was all that Cormac's judgment warranted.

A whoremonger, Merrion had called him. Well, most men who married whores were, he supposed. Still, that was in America, he reasoned stubbornly. When you lived in a lawless place, you sometimes did idiot things for idiot reasons.

But just about everything he'd done since Moira married had been an idiot thing.

Maybe the pain would never stop.

He finally dressed and walked down West Street into the heart of town. He had a late breakfast at the Park Hotel, then dialed Wells's room. There was no answer.

Later, he walked out in the summer sunshine that brightly dappled the clean streets of the small town. He stood on Killian Street, the continuation of the road from Killarney. Far to the left he could see a sliver of Moon Lake, and the cross atop St. Benedict's Church.

He followed the road down the small hill. It ended at a crossroad. To the south, to the left, was Bounfort Castle and, beyond that, the Pierce estate. To the right was St. Benedict's. Killian Street itself turned into a grass-mottled dirt road that drifted down toward the lakeside, eventually ending in a footpath. At the end of the footpath was the bombed-out concrete pier.

Cormac went to the church, which was empty, then rang the bell of the rectory next door. In his youth, there were always nuns and priests buzzing around churches, but this one seemed completely empty. Then he heard the sound of singing from the back of the house.

He walked down a pathway of broken cement between the house and the church to a large garage in the back. Through the high windows he could see overhead lights.

The singing was coming from inside, tuneless, wordless singing that sounded as if someone was humming but was so abstracted that he'd forgotten to keep his mouth closed.

Behind the garage was the parish graveyard, bigger now than Cormac remembered from his childhood. The graves were neatly kept, and many had flower bouquets on them. Since Ardath was not a wealthy town and few had the resources to buy big monuments, most of the graves were marked only with simple headstones. The money would be better spent on food, Cormac thought. Or liquor.

He pushed open the side door to the garage. The singing was coming from a man who was bent over a long block of wood that was hoisted up on two sawhorses in the center of the garage floor. A sickly sweet smell curled into Cormac's nostrils as the door opened.

He called out, "Father Ambrose?"

The man tuned around. He held a long, curved woodworker's knife in his hand. He was a slight man with thinning hair and a sallow complexion. Cormac smiled when he saw the man was wearing a Roman collar under a red plaid shirt. His legs were covered by a pair of old paint-stained blue jeans.

"Yes? Oh. It's Sergeant Cormac, isn't it?"

"That's right. Michael, it is."

Father Ambrose laid down the long knife and wiped his hands on a cloth. "Forgive me for not shaking hands. You'd be weeks getting the stain off them," he said. He held up his blackamoor hands. "The curse of the woodworker."

Cormac stepped inside. "Leave the door open, if you

please," the priest said. "I keep forgetting. After a while, the smell of paint and varnish starts to make me heady."

"What are you working on, Father?" Cormac asked.

"It's going to be a hand-carved Celtic cross for the church grounds," Father Ambrose said. Cormac could hear the swell of simple pride in his voice. "You know, Father Gervaise, God rest his soul, built the church and, well, I guess it's vanity, but I wanted to leave something here that bears my mark for when I leave." He hesitated a moment, then sputtered, "Oh, what a rude lug I am. There's coffee over there in the pot. Are you game to try it?"

"It can't be worse that what I'm used to," Cormac said.

The priest poured two mugs of coffee from an antique electric pot on a workbench in the corner of the garage. Cormac sat on an unopened keg of roofing nails and looked at the wood that Father Ambrose had been working on. The section was ten feet long, and stashed in a corner, near the coal bin, was the crossbar. Both solid pieces of wood had been painstakingly covered with ancient Celtic religious symbols. The four arc-shaped wooden pieces that would form the characteristic Celtic circle around the junction of the cross's two members were on a shelf along the far wall. They had already been varnished and gave off bright glints of reflection from the overhead light.

"So how fares your investigation?" the priest asked as he handed Cormac one of the cups. The liquid was opaque black, thick and steaming.

"Investigation? I thought I'd made it clear to everyone that I was here on holiday."

"You tried to make it clear," Father Ambrose said.

He added with a chuckle, "You'd be the first vacationer ever to attend mass three times on one Sunday."

"Done in again by my religious fervor," Cormac said.

"You wouldn't be the first. That's how saints become saints," Father Ambrose said. He smiled. He was a little man, and he had mottled, stained teeth that looked strangely too large for the size of his head.

"You've found me out, Father. I'm looking into the body that was found on the shore of Moon Lake."

"I see. Have you got any identification yet?"

Cormac hesitated a moment. "Only tentatively. Somebody from outside of Ardath. You wouldn't know him."

"Maybe I would. I've been in many parishes. What was the name?"

"Winston Barnett. You ever hear of him?"

"Sorry, Michael," the priest said. "I can't say I have. What did he look like?"

"I really don't know, Father. Did you notice anything the night of the explosion?"

"No. I was asleep. The explosion woke me, but it took me a long time to . . . how do the young people say it . . . get it together and get down to the pier. So I didn't see anything that anybody else hadn't seen."

"In the days before the explosion," Cormac asked, "did you notice anything unusual at the pier? Any activity? Any strangers?"

Father Ambrose leaned back against a bench. "No. The only person I ever saw there was that vile O'Glynn boy."

"What's he do there?"

"Generally hunts cats or some other poor creatures.

Do you think the body—that person was killed when the pier exploded?''

"Seems logical," Cormac said. "So you didn't see anything at the pier that would make you think something out of the ordinary was going on?"

"No. I'm sorry. I didn't."

"And no suspicious strangers in town?"

Father Ambrose sipped his coffee and shook his head. "The only suspicious character I've seen around is you," he said, smiling. "They tell me you're from Cork."

"That's where I live now," Cormac said.

"Tell me, why is Cork so interested in an explosion here in Ardath? I thought that was Killarney's work."

"You're up on your police procedures, Father," Cormac said. "Honestly, I can't answer your question. Maybe, well, maybe with the troubles up north, they're a little spooky when it comes to any kind of explosion."

"That could be," the priest said agreeably. He drained his coffee with a sudden quick gesture and put the cup back on the workbench.

"You said you've been at a number of parishes?" Cormac asked conversationally.

"Aye. But none as pleasant as Ardath. I was born in Derry. It's much nicer here."

"I lived up north for a while myself," Cormac said. "Belfast. I guess Ulster would be pretty discouraging for a man of the cloth."

The priest nodded grimly. "Violence makes me ill. Especially when it's all for no purpose." A flash of pain showed in his eyes for a moment.

"It's our historical legacy. Or else God's curse," Cormac said. "I wonder if we Irish are doomed always to be fighting."

"What's saddest about the six counties of Ulster is that there's no solution," Father Ambrose said. "Most of the people there are Protestants. They feel British, so the British won't leave. And as long as the British are there, the IRA is going to be shooting at them."

"I never thought there was a problem that didn't have a political solution," Cormac said. "But I can't find one here."

Father Ambrose shook his head. "Maybe someday, when Irishmen are allowed to decide Ireland's destiny. Maybe then something can be done in peace." He walked back to the cross and picked up the knife again.

"It'll be a beautiful cross, Father," said Cormac.

"If it isn't, it won't be for lack of trying."

He seemed distracted. Cormac thought that perhaps just speaking of violence had upset the small man. He rose and said, "Well, I'll be on my way, Father. Thank you for your time. I was sorry to hear about Father Gervaise."

"He was a good man," the priest said. "But it was his time. He was very old."

"Everyone in town I've talked to says you are a fine successor to him."

Ambrose turned and smiled. "Thank you, Michael. I appreciate that."

At the door Cormac said, "It would be helpful if you'd not say anything to anyone about our talk."

"Of course. I understand."

"You know how gossip is in a town like this. I'd like people to keep thinking I was on holiday."

"I'll do all I can," Father Ambrose said.

* * *

Back in his room, Cormac called Wells, but the Englishman was still not in his room. He turned on the television and watched the test pattern for a while while listening to "Carmen" for the fifth time since he had been back in town. It was one of the things he missed about America, the round-the-clock television that was often an only companion on long quiet nights. Not so in Ireland. The broadcasting hours were short, and the rest of the time was taken up by test patterns and music he detested. Apparently the executives of Irish television felt a duty to enculturate their viewers before giving them "Dynasty" and reruns of "The Incredible Hulk."

He sat at the small table in the room and wrote a report for Superintendent Merrion back in Cork, outlining his meeting with Wells and the status of the investigation so far. He wrote seven pages, although he knew only two words would tell the truth: "No progress."

He had no cause to disbelieve Wells. If the Brit had said that the hand didn't belong to the body, that was that. But then whose body was it? And if the body didn't belong to Winston Barnett, who did it belong to? Wells had agreed that the body appeared to be that of one who was mutilated in an explosion.

But then where had Winston Barnett's hand come from? Had he been injured in the same explosion? What had he done then for medical treatment? Had he been driven away and taken to a hospital somewhere else?

He put in his report to Superintendent Merrion a request that hospital records be checked for the day of the explosion to see if anyone had been treated for an amputated hand.

He had just finished the report when the telephone

rang. It was Wells, saying he'd spent most of the day at Bounfort Castle.

"There's not a lot going on there," Cormac said.

"As much as anywhere else in Ardath. And at night they put on a show or something. I'm going back to see it. Want to come along?"

"Me?" Cormac thought for a moment about Moira's daughter. Someone had told him that she sang at the castle.

For an instant he was seized with fear. But that's irrational, he told himself. It was a small town. He would have to see the girl sometime. And it would be easier this way, from a distance, the first time.

"All right," he said finally.

"That seemed like quite a decision. Are you sure it won't hurt your social standing here, being seen with me?" Wells asked.

"I'll just tell people I'm trying to convert the poor Protestant heathen. They'll understand."

"I'll meet you at half seven at the castle," Wells said.


Bounfort Castle was rather ordinary, as far as Irish castles went, but the mere fact of its existence made it an attraction. So thoroughly had Cromwell and his troops destroyed everything of greater permanence than mud and straw in the seventeenth century that almost none of the thousands of castles in Ireland remained standing undamaged. It was a mystery how Ardath's tiny fortress had withstood England's barrage of destruction, and legends grew from it.

"That's the keep," Cormac said gruffly as Wells walked around the grounds admiringly.

"I know something about castles," Wells said, almost distractedly.

"Sorry," Cormac grumbled. "Forgot. Empire, cheerio-pip-pip and all that."

Wells ignored the sarcasm. "The keep's not surprising. The tower almost always survives. What I'm really astonished about is the west wall, the one with the balcony. It still looks sturdy."

"That's because your forefathers didn't get to it," Cormac said.

They stood on the grassy slope looking up at the balcony where the vision of Mary was said to have appeared.

It had once been the wall of only one wing of the castle, but now most of the structure had crumbled, and only the wing and the original castle tower remained. Inside the wing, the nightly entertainments for tourists were performed, and on the grounds where they now stood were held the frequent religious services commemorating the vision of Mary.

Cormac looked around. They were in a natural bowl in the earth, and the castle's balcony hung over them like a rock outcropping. Anyone on it would be as visible as if he were standing on a well-designed stage.

"If this place was never attacked, why is it a ruin?" Wells asked him suddenly.

"Time. Time wins all the wars," Cormac said. "But the legend says that the Miracle of Our Lady keeps it safe."

"It was a miracle that Cromwell passed it by, if you ask me."

"There's a story about that. It says that the English troops were ready to attack just north of here, but a terrible storm came up and they lost their way."

"That sounds quaint," Wells said.

"You don't have to believe it. But Cromwell and your British thugs leveled damn near every other castle in Ireland. Why not this one?"

"Maybe the vision of Mary recurred and Cromwell fled," Wells suggested.

The corners of Cormac's lips curled down. "Christ Himself, nailed to the cross and begging for mercy, couldn't turn you bloody English away." He walked back toward the front entrance to the castle remains.

# CHAPTER SEVEN

Dinner in the castle's small banquet hall was a pleasant affair designed expressly for tourists. Feeling vaguely uncomfortable amid the pairs of American and British visitors, Cormac edged in at the far end of one of the long wooden benches. Wells, who had entered alone a few minutes earlier, was sitting on the other end of the table. It faced the small raised stage where Brian O'Flaherty and Kathleen Pierce led the audience through several centuries of Irish music and poetry, beginning with a history of the castle. While the visitors ate, Brian's melodious voice resonated through the stone banquet room.

"It was during the latter part of the tenth century that the Danes and the Norsemen were expanding their control in Ireland," he began, as Kathleen's harp sang behind him.

"An army of these invaders marched on the quiet County Kerry countryside and laid siege to Bounfort Castle, then occupied by the peaceful Christian King Malachi.

"Seeing that the Irish inside the castle were greatly outnumbered, Malachi sent word to the Norse commander that he would surrender if the safety of his women and children were guaranteed. The Norse refused.

"Reluctantly, Malachi the Peaceful made preparations for battle. His plan was to engage the enemy on the sloping hillside in front of the castle while the women and children sneaked out from the rear of the building and escaped in boats that were anchored inside a small cave on the lakefront.

"Malachi and his small band of twenty-five men stepped forward in the bright sunlight of an early summer morning that day in nine eighty-six. Within minutes they were surrounded by almost a thousand ferocious Norsemen.

"With dignity, Malachi prepared himself to meet death, knowing that he had managed to save the women and children of the castle. But even as the Norse chieftain gave the order to strike, his tongue was stilled. He gaped at the castle, blinking in disbelief. His battle-ax dropped to his side. His men's eyes followed his, as did Malachi's, and when they saw the astonishing sight on Bounfort's battlements, the soldiers no longer thought of war or plunder or victory, but felt only the awe of men who have walked within the Mysteries.

"For this was the Miracle of Ardath."

The diners looked up. Even Cormac, hardened by a lifetime of listening to Irish barroom orators, was moved by the sheer beauty of Brian O'Flaherty's voice.

"There on the balcony of the castle, looking down over all of them, stood a woman in white, an ethereal, otherworldly figure whose words, when she spoke, could be heard and understood by all the soldiers below, although they were men of differing tongues.

"And she said, 'Let there be no violence here. Let this forever be a place of peace.'

"And such was the power of the vision that the bloodthirsty Norsemen fell to their knees alongside Malachi and worshiped this apparition that Malachi told them was Mary, the mother of his Christian God.

"The image remained for several minutes as the soldiers prayed before her. Then, as the men watched, the figure slowly rose off the balcony, hovered in the air for long moments near the turrets of the castle, and then slowly vanished without a trace."

The audience applauded. Brian raised his hands. "And so, ladies and gents, the Lady's command has been heeded since that day, and peace has reigned at Bounfort Castle for nigh a thousand years. So eat and drink and open your hearts to one another, for you'll find no discord here."

He smiled, but it seemed somehow hard and mechanical, the insincere goodwill of the professional entertainer. Kathleen said something to him, too quiet for anyone else to hear, then began a long run on her harp.

Cormac studied Moira's daughter with perverse fascination. She seemed ill at ease in the medieval costume she wore. Her voice was pleasant, but it seemed to quiver a little as she spoke her lines of poetry in counterpoint to the young blond-haired Brian. Even so, her touch on the harp was sure and light, and the music swelled to fill the room.

She was Moira's daughter, all right, Cormac thought. A beauty like her mother. But where Moira's eyes had always been warm and friendly, Kathleen's were wary and suspicious. They seemed never to smile.

Perhaps a legacy from her father, the drunken Lyle Pierce, Cormac thought.

It didn't surprise him that Kathleen was taken with Brian O'Flaherty. The young man charmed all the women in the audience with his poems and songs and dances, despite the undignified necessity of jumping off the stage after the diners finished each course to clear off the dishes and serve new ones.

As the evening wound down and the tourists were sated with Irish-named American food and a quantity of honeyed wine, Brian turned off the lights and lit one candle. On the wall, the shadows of the diners seemed to turn into the spirits of medieval barons at the end of a feast. The stone walls enfolded them into a time, centuries ago, when kings draped in animal skins, circlets of gold round their heads, walked with their wolfhounds to the barbaric music of reed pipes.

Brian began: "And now, my friends, our day is done. And though the battle's not yet won . . . ."

Kathleen's eyes darted toward him. Then, looking nervous, she played a long arpeggio to fill in the silence of Brian's forgotten lines.

"And though the battle's not yet won," he repeated abstractedly.

The audience began to fidget. Kathleen played another chord on the harp, but Brian silenced her with a gesture.

"No, the battle's not yet won, my friends." He stepped to the edge of the stage. "Nor will it ever be won so long as the devils of the North continue to divide our ancient and lovely land with their lies and deceits and the criminal oppression of the Irish people. These mongrels—Irish by nationality, but as English

93

as Oliver Cromwell in their black hearts—are the descendants of English convicts and spies, the worst that bloodthirsty England had to offer, sent to Ireland to take over our country."

Several of the British couples looked up in shocked dismay. One elderly pair got stiffly to their feet and left.

"It wasn't enough that they killed our kings and destroyed our castles. It wasn't enough to loot our monasteries, where the sacred scrolls, written by Irish scholars at a time when the English painted their faces blue and lived off raw meat, were kept.

"They burned our churches and outlawed our religion. They destroyed our books so that a nation, famous through all the world for its literature and poetry and a written history that chronicled events since the dawn of language, would be reduced to a land of peasants who could not read, and so would be deprived of the wisdom of their ancestors.

"The English took away our land, by force, murdering us with their guns and cannons and armies. Those Irish who lived were sent to the rock-filled, desolate wasteland of the west, where there was no water that was not salt and nothing could grow on the land. You may see our stone fences and find them quaint. Those stones were moved, one by one, by hungry men and women desperate for a patch of earth to grow a few mealy potatoes. And when the potato crop failed, we starved.

"Between eighteen forty-six and eighteen forty-nine, a million of us starved to death, our bellies filled with dirt and rocks and grass. But not everyone starved. There was food in Ireland, fat cows and sheep and milk. But they were for the English, raised by the English here in Ireland whose farms were kept by Irishmen, now held back by rifles from swallowing a morsel of the food they raised for their filthy British masters. As the cattle carts rolled by, the Irish watched, their mouths green with grass, their limbs too weak from hunger to move.

"Added to that million was another million more who fled Ireland in the death ships, crowded and stinking with disease. No one knows how many died on those ships. The survivors settled in Canada and America and everywhere else around the world, and Ireland was left with two-thirds of her population gone and her skies empty. The birds, you see, had all been eaten. The air, once filled with song, was silent. There was no more music in Ireland."

Brian paused and looked carefully over the faces of the tourists. "And yet we fought," he said, his voice a hoarse whisper. "We fought them with our cunning and our guile and our willingness to die to gain an inch of ground. We fought them knowing that we were outnumbered and underfed. We fought them without books, without guns, without laws. We fought them knowing we had nothing more to lose, and nothing more to gain except our freedom from the bloody yoke of British oppression that had strangled us. We fought them until they left our beloved southland, and we instituted a free government where we might work and worship in peace.

"But the British remain. They have held on to their stolen lands in the north. They call that part of our island by another name, Northern Ireland, as if the place of their infestation were another country.

"But it is not another country. There is one Ireland, a Gaelic Ireland, a free Ireland, and we will fight until the vermin of the North return to their lairs and leave us in peace. We will fight until the mockery of British rule is stopped. We will fight, and we will die, so that Ireland—*our* Ireland, our country, our home—will live forever."

He began to sing: "Seo dhibh, acháirde duan Ógláigh . . ." The Gaelic words of the Irish national anthem.

The audience rose.

> "In Erin's cause, come woe or weal
> 'Mid cannons' roar and rifles' peal
> We'll sing a soldier's song!"

When he finished, the room was dead silent. Kathleen threw on the lights. A few American visitors began to applaud. Cormac noticed that the English-looking faces were mostly averted from the stage, except for Wells's. He stood straight, his arms crossed in front of his chest, studying the fierce young man with the blazing eyes. Cormac walked to him.

When Brian turned away and left abruptly, Wells said, "Quite an impassioned young man."

"He's nothing but a saloon Irishman," Cormac said with disgust. The policeman's face was red with shame and anger. He had seen the likes of Brian O'Flaherty in a hundred pubs and bars on both sides of the Atlantic. The fervent nationalists, sopping with patriotism so long as their bellies were full and their lips wet with drink. "Let's get out of here," he said gruffly.

But Wells was still watching the empty stage, remembering the fire in the young man's eyes.

Cormac was still huffily silent as he left the castle. It took Wells a few minutes to catch up with him. When finally Cormac stopped, Wells put his arm on the Irishman's shoulder and laughed.

"All right, you don't have to overdo the false indignation."

"What are you talking about? Bleeding Brits all talk in circles."

"I meant, part of you loved that nationalistic claptrap back there."

"That's how much you know." Cormac continued across the grass at full speed.

The sky was growing dark. An Irish summer day seems endless, and when it does turn dark, the effect is ineffably final.

"I suppose I do love it," he said quietly. "The country, I mean." He looked over at Wells briefly. "It's not the same as an Englishman loving England, or an American loving America." He tightened his lips, trying to find the words. He had not wanted to be stirred by Brian's speech. He knew it had been no more than the venomous hatred and bigotry that had split his nation apart, couched in the beautiful words that were the gift of the Irish.

"You see, Ireland's like a mangy dog with sores all over its body and no teeth," he said at last. "You have to love it the way a mother loves her idiot child."

Wells looked around. Behind him, the castle loomed in majestic silhouette against the wine-colored sky and wild, flower-filled mountains. "Ah, but what a lovely child it is," he said quietly.

Cormac looked up at Wells, and for a moment, their eyes met in understanding. They walked together in silence.

"Who was that rabble-rouser, anyway?" Wells asked him.

"His name's Brian O'Flaherty. He was in the pub the night you arrived."

"You know him?"

"No. He's a latecomer to town, only here a few years. He wanted to buy me a drink when I hit you, so he can't be all bad," Cormac said.

"And the girl?"

"She's his sweetheart," Cormac said, attempting for a moment to hide the truth. But the truth was what they were both in Ardath to find. Dissembling wouldn't help, he knew. "Her name's Kathleen Pierce," he mumbled. "Moira Pierce's daughter."

"That's Moira who found the hand?"

"Yes, you suspicious British bastard," Cormac said hotly.

"Why are you being so testy over a simple question?"

"Because you're an anti-Irish paranoid," Cormac said.

"Anti-Irish? My father named me for an Irishman," Wells countered.

"Surprised your mother held still for that."

Wells smiled and thrust his hands in his pockets. "I was never her favorite. With my name, she thought I'd never amount to anything. But fortunately, the

98

family was large enough so that she let me alone about it most of the time. I'm one of eight."

"I am, too," Cormac said, remembering the poverty of his own childhood. "But I probably was raised differently from you."

"No doubt," Wells said factually, without any pride.

"Tell me how sad you are about growing up with nannies and lace collars. The poor little rich boy."

Wells laughed. "Not at all, Cormac. I had an extremely happy childhood."

"Too bad. I was hoping there'd be something about you that was human. Besides your name."

"My father wanted to give that name to his first-born, but mother wouldn't have it, of course. He sneaked it by her with me later."

"What were you named for, an Irish traitor who moved to London and became a millionaire?"

"No, my namesake was a machinist, I believe. Father met the man during the Boer War in South Africa. Bloemfontein. The Boers had started out well in the war, but the tide was turning. The British were bringing in troops from Canada, New Zealand, Australia. . . . As it was, the Boers didn't even own uniforms, but they still fought on valiantly. It was exactly the type of situation the Irish love."

"Maybe," Cormac said. "The Irish were there, you know. It was always my opinion that they joined the Boers just because it was chance to blow up some Brits on soil that wasn't Irish, for a change."

"Cynical, but probably true. At any rate, the battle at Bloemfontein was a dirty one, mostly hand-to-hand. It was the first time the British had been confronted with guerrillas."

"Guerrillas with guns, you mean. They'd met enough Irish who hated them, but they were only peasants with pitchforks," Cormac said indignantly.

"Who's telling this story?" Wells snapped. "Where was I?"

"Your darlin' daddy."

"Ahh, yes. Father was a coward, I'm afraid." He laughed. "He'd lost his weapons, and was being beaten to a pulp by a bunch of roughnecks. He didn't even know what nationality they were, since the Boers and the Irish dressed as they pleased. When he felt he was in an impossible situation, he fled to an entrenchment."

"To sit out the rest of the war," Cormac said. "Sterling."

"To survive, you suicidal Irish lunatic. Unfortunately, it was a Boer trench. And inside it was an enemy soldier. An Irishman."

Wells lit a cigarette and looked up at the sky, as if remembering. "Father was only twenty-two himself at the time, but he remembered the soldier as a mere boy. He must not have been more than seventeen. He was crouched in the entrenchment without weapons, his cheeks sunken and his eyes ringed with sleeplessness. Father said that when he spotted him, the boy backed away from him. It was a case of battle fatigue, most likely. My father said that the two of them were too tired and frightened to do anything except stare at one another. Finally he asked the boy his name, just to ease the tension of the moment. The boy said his name was Daniel Taylor. My father introduced himself, and while the battle raged on around them, they talked about their homes and their lives."

"Great soldiers, the pair of them."

Wells shrugged. "I once asked my father if he'd felt ashamed about being afraid."

"What'd he say?"

"He said only a fool regrets what's already done. The wise man learns and moves on. But then, I only knew Father as a very old man. He'd had enough time to think things over."

"And the Irish lad? Did your da kill him?"

Wells shook his head. "No. Before long, they heard the sound of footsteps coming toward them. 'Are they mine or yours?' my father asked. Taylor looked out over the entrenchment and said they were Boers. They'd lost the battle and were beating a retreat. The boy could have drawn fire to my father then, but he didn't. Instead, he climbed out and dashed toward the regiment. It must have confused them. His own men shot Daniel Taylor. My father saw him die."

Cormac stopped. Above, the moon was full in the starry sky. "That's too bad," he said softly. He was about to go on, when a wild shriek cut through the silence like a siren.

The two men turned around to face the castle, the source of the noise. "There," Wells said, pointing. "The keep."

He ran toward it. Cormac puffed behind him. Along the crenellated top of the castle's tower appeared a figure. It was an old woman, her skirts blowing, her arms flailing black against the yellow round of the moon.

"They walked out of their graves, they did! And they walk among us now," she shrilled.

"Bloody Christ, it's Mad Hattie," Cormac said. The two of them loped toward the entryway of the castle.

"Stop! Cormac!" someone shouted behind them. It was Morty O'Sullivan, running for all he was worth up the castle grounds. "Let me handle this. She doesn't know you. She might jump," he said breathlessly. "Been chasing the old bedbug for nigh on an hour. She's been breaking windows in the stores in town, yelling this gibberish. What a whore's job this is," he panted, pushing past them into the castle.

Cormac and Wells stood on the grounds, watching the bizarre spectacle above them. "And they wonder why I left this place," Cormac said.

"I rather enjoy seeing all you Irish in your native habitat," said Wells.

"You would." He turned to the Englishman, his eyes narrowed. "Speaking of which, I'd like to know what you're doing here. Don't you think it's about time I was let in on the secret?"

"Beg pardon?"

"I know you're this big-time antiterrorist expert. But for what's gone on here, I don't see why you've been called in."

Wells counted off the points on his fingers. "The explosion, for one thing. The body. The hand. The fingerprints of Winston Barnett, a convicted felon. The question of what happened to him. Isn't that enough?"

"No," Cormac said flatly. "All that points to is that some explosives, and maybe a killer, might be in the area. Or might not be. But so what? What's anybody going to blow up, the town library? And who's to kill? There isn't anything in Ardath of any value to terrorists or anyone else."

"Very astute," Wells said admiringly.

Cormac put his hands on his hips. "So? What's a big SAS man with your credentials doing here?"

"Scotland Yard."

"Come off it," Cormac said crankily.

Wells looked up, watching the figure of Hattie O'Shea dancing like a marionette against the backdrop of the moon. "The Pope is coming," he said without looking at Cormac.

The Irishman blinked, not knowing whether to believe him or not. He glanced up at Hattie, then at Wells. "The Pope's coming *here?*"

"I'm afraid so."

"What the bloody blazes for?"

"The thousandth anniversary of this castle," Wells said. "Next week."

"Oh, God."

"Dublin expects him to make a speech ripping the terrorists in the IRA," Wells said.

Cormac's heart sank. Slowly he looked up again to the tower. He could hear Morty's voice cooing to Mad Hattie, still teetering on the parapet, and for an insane moment, he saw in her a dark and twisted parody of the ancient vision of Holy Mary.

"The bleedin' Pope," Cormac said dully. "Assassination."

"That's why they sent me," Wells said.

Cormac gave him a sidelong look. "Leave it to Dublin."

"To do what?"

"To send a frigging English Protestant to protect the chief Catholic of the world."

Wells smiled. "Hattie's safe," he said, gesturing toward the castle entrance, where Morty was coming out, his arm around the old woman. "Buy you a drink."

Cormac took his bronze medal from his pocket and idly rubbed it with his thumb. "An Irish drink."

"Does it have to be a Catholic drink, too?" Wells asked.

Cormac felt shamed. He put the medal back in his pocket. "Smarmy Brit," he said, and the two men walked to the road together, the moonlight on their backs.

# BOOK TWO

# CHAPTER EIGHT

Brian O'Flaherty was still full of patriotic fervor as he walked with Kathleen along Killian Street toward Grady's Pub.

"They've got to be made to understand," he said loudly, still using his stage voice. "These tourists come to Ireland with their credit cards and their fine things and think they're going to see the lot of us shouting begorrah and talking about leprechauns. Someone's got to teach them that our struggle is the struggle between good and evil, right and wrong. . . ."

"You're getting tiresome, Brian," Kathleen interrupted, closing her eyes in distaste.

"And you're as bad as the rest of them."

"Don't dismiss me," she said hotly, "as if I were some village housewife telling you to cut your hair. You made a perfect fool of yourself tonight, ranting like some lunatic to people who don't care. Ireland, precious Ireland."

"It *is* precious."

"Nobody cares, Brian. Not about your sophomoric ideals or about this wasted second-rate country either."

"That's no way to talk, Kathleen."

"No way to talk is the right way to talk," the young woman said. The soft wind was blowing her hair in tangles across her face. "Ireland has a big enough share of talkers. It needs some doers for a change."

"So that's it. A doer, is it? A doer, I suppose, like your precious Seamus Dougherty."

"Aye, like him," she said. "Like me. Like anybody who doesn't just talk about Ireland to anyone who'll buy him a drink."

"Like you?" Brian erupted in a long peal of laughter. "What have you ever done for Ireland? You and your cozy little Catholic education and your cozy little job and cozy little mother? What do you care that Catholics are being slaughtered in the North?"

"You're right, Brian. I don't really care. I don't care about Ireland and I surely don't care about Catholics."

He started to speak but she spoke right through him. "I'll tell you something else. I know that all those precious Republicans you like so much and who are always spouting one Ireland, one Ireland, they're all nothing but a pack of Communists. And I don't care about that either."

"And Seamus Dougherty? He's a Communist too, I suppose?" the young man said.

"The worst of all," she said.

"But when he whistles, you jump."

"It doesn't have anything to do with Ireland, Brian," she said.

Brian worked his jaw, his forehead creased with hurt. "I just don't understand you, Kathleen," he said. "I thought we had something special."

"No," she said softly. "Not anymore."

"Is it because of Seamus?"

"Suppose it is?"

Brian kicked a pebble across the street. "He'll get you nowhere," he said bitterly. "Seamus may be a big man now, but not forever."

"And you will be?" she asked.

"I will," the young man said soberly.

"Write me when it happens." Kathleen hastened her step. "I'll not be going to Grady's tonight."

"Fine," Brian shouted at her back. "There's always company at Grady's."

"That's right," she said, turning to face him. "You mustn't miss a night of drinking with the boys." She stared at him for a moment, then turned a corner. Brian watched her walk off, back in the direction of the castle and the Pierce estate. Her long gown dragged on the road behind her and made her look like some brokenhearted princess from centuries before.

She slowed down. When she turned and saw that Brian was not watching her any longer, she walked off to the side of the road and threw up into the bushes. Then she tucked her long skirts around her and hurried toward her home.

Things hadn't always been so bad between them. When Kathleen had first met Brian O'Flaherty, he had seemed like a knight in shining armor come to rescue her from the endless tedium of her life.

If she had been born poor, she often thought, the sudden death of her father would not have been so shattering. As it was, the loss of that distant, often absent man changed her entire existence. It snatched away, in one instant, everything she had ever known.

Kathleen was ten years old when her mother received the telegram saying that Lyle Pierce was dead. She remembered the moment still, sitting in the large drawing room in her new lace dress while her mother and Toby, the butler, brought in pretty ribboned packages to place beneath the fifteen-foot-tall Christmas tree while "Hark, the Herald Angels Sing" played on the phonograph.

Moira had at first hidden the presents, telling Kathleen that Santa Claus would bring them, but the child had groaned that her mother still expected her to believe in fairy tales. Kathleen had just returned from her first semester at the famous Answell Boarding School in Dublin and had already been thoroughly disabused of the myths her mother and her tutors had filled her head with. Lana Pride, a strapping, bad-tempered girl in the first form, had even told her that babies were made by naked people gyrating on one another. While Kathleen didn't know what it meant to gyrate, it was a disgusting thought nonetheless.

At school, to believe in Santa and tooth fairies was an invitation to ridicule. Since her parents were spending the holidays in Barbados, Lana Pride didn't even go home for Christmas, thus achieving the height of sophistication among her fellow first-formers. She even claimed not to believe in Jesus Christ, although most of the other children agreed among themselves that Lana's apostasy was only for show, since she gladly accepted the Christmas presents her parents sent her.

Kathleen Pierce was a beautiful child, slender and delicate, with white-blond hair curling over her shoul-

110

ders. Her father insisted that she be dressed to perfection every day and in fact had selected the school in Dublin primarily because no uniforms were required and Kathleen would be able to show her spectacular wardrobe off to the world. Moira had objected to the expense of the clothes and the astronomical dry-cleaning bills they received every two weeks, but Kathleen's mother had easily been put in her place. She had come from nothing, as Pierce often reminded her, and did not possess the taste or refinement to live as a lady of substance.

But Kathleen would be different, he vowed. From the beginning, she would appreciate the lifestyle that wealth brings. She would know how to move and eat and speak with the ease and grace of a princess. She would grow up understanding how to handle servants. She would be a jewel in life, existing for adornment and adoration.

Kathleen was ashamed of her mother. Moira laughed too loudly, often went walking around the grounds of the estate without shoes and was an utter failure as a hostess. Even though Lyle Pierce, with his ball-bearing plant in Killarney, was the richest man in Ardath, Moira entertained only at her husband's express and forceful insistence. She said she didn't like parties where everyone talked boring nonsense and tried to impress each other with their expensive and uncomfortable clothes.

Pierce responded by calling Moira a yokel, a word that so impressed Kathleen with its hilarity that she used it in reference to Moira whenever her father was within earshot. He would always laugh when she did that and hold her on his lap and call her his beautiful

111

princess, while Moira would slip upstairs into her bedroom and look through her old picture album.

Kathleen had sneaked up to Moira's room once to look at the pictures for herself. She had been hoping to find something really secret—pictures of people kissing or perhaps even gyrating—but the photo album held nothing of even remote interest, just a lot of smudgy black-and-white pictures of ordinary people, most of them rather fat and not particularly clean. There were even a few brown ones of an old farmer couple. On the back of the photograph was a line in her mother's florid handwriting: Mother and Dad, 1937.

Mother and Dad! Kathleen scrutinized the picture. The woman had two teeth missing. She looked like she was young, but she wore her hair pulled back under a ragged old scarf. She was dressed in some kind of print housedress, with *socks,* and over it she wore a printed sweater. The man was skinny and hatchet-faced. He was short and about a foot narrower than the woman beside him. He looked as if he'd slept in whatever he was wearing. Mother and Dad . . .

*Then these trolls are my own grandparents,* Kathleen realized with alarm. The thought filled her with loathing. If anyone at school ever found out what kind of people she came from, she'd be a laughingstock. Lana Pride's grandmother, she was sure, would never go around with some rag on her head or be so lazy that she wouldn't even go to a dentist when the teeth were falling out of her head.

"What are you doing?" Moira asked softly from the doorway.

Kathleen slammed the album shut. "I was just looking," she said.

Moira sat beside the girl. She was smiling. "I'll tell you about them if you're interested," she said, laying the book across her lap.

"I'm not," Kathleen snapped.

"You see, here are your grandparents. . . ."

"I don't want to see them," the girl shouted, slamming the album closed on her mother's hand. "They're a bunch of ugly old stupid farmers and I hope they die!"

Moira slapped her across the face, so hard that the girl fell off the bed, howling wildly. "They *are* dead," Moira whispered hoarsely.

"I hate you," Kathleen screamed. "You're a damn yokel, just like them, and I hate you." She stumbled out of the room and ran to her father.

That night Kathleen could hear the sounds of an argument between her parents. It ended with a loud slam of the front door. Moira went ahead with her preparations for Christmas, as if nothing had happened, but Kathleen knew her father wouldn't be with them for the rest of the holiday. *She* had driven him out, the peasant who'd never belonged in the house in the first place.

And then had come the telegram. Lyle Pierce was dead somewhere in the south of France, and Kathleen was going to be as alone as Lana Pride on Christmas, and it had all been her mother's fault.

# CHAPTER NINE

"I've withdrawn you from Answell," Moira announced on the day before Kathleen was due to return. "Toby will go up to Dublin to pick up your things. Then we'll have to let him go, too."

Kathleen was dumbfounded. "What are you talking about? You can't take me out of *school*. Everybody's got to go to school."

"You'll have to go elsewhere," Moira said, looking at her hands. "We haven't got the money to keep you in Dublin. It seems your father accumulated some debts . . . in France . . . and they're for us to pay."

"Well, where am I supposed to go?"

Moira tried smiling. "I've talked to Father Gervaise. He may be able to get you into St. Anne's Convent School in Killarney. You'll be able to live there. I don't know how long we'll be able to keep this house."

"You must be crazy."

Moira stared at her daughter. "That's no way to talk."

"I'm not going to some convent school," Kathleen said flatly. "And I'm not going to live with you in some shack. What are you going to do, take in ironing?''

''I may,'' Moira said.

The following week, Kathleen was enrolled in St. Anne's Convent School. Kathleen cried when Moira handed her the blue uniform she would be wearing.

''It may not be forever,'' Moira said.

''I hope it is. I hope they keep me forever. I never want to see you again.''

''Maybe someday you'll change your mind,'' Moira said.


Life at St. Anne's was a test of endurance. It was an ugly place, its soot-darkened walls bare except for cardboard prints of religious paintings, its students a lackluster group of whey-faced girls with dirty hair. Kathleen made no friends among them.

Night after night, after having been forced to say her prayers in the chapel, she would lie awake in her bed and imagine what her friends in Dublin were doing. She didn't dare write to them; besides, word had probably already reached Lana and the others that Kathleen's father had lost all his money before he died. They no longer had any interest in her. She lived alone, like an exile, in the small cell in the old convent building where the out-of-town children were housed, waiting for the nightmare to end.

Since she didn't participate in any of the social activities or night talks with the other girls, Kathleen took to her studies with a vengeance. She learned to play the harp. She became the top student in the school, and the nuns liked her. Several times, Sister Frances

115

took her aside to praise her for her good work and to encourage her to be more friendly with the other girls. Kathleen responded politely, her face impassive, while she pictured Sister Frances naked, her head shaved, gyrating on top of a man.

Without exception, she despised the nuns at St. Anne's. She thought of them as crows, flapping and squawking and pretending to be holy, while beneath their powder and prayers, she could detect the peasant scents of unwashed armpits and the moist, corrupt clefts of their sex.

Once, when she had to deliver a message from one of the nuns to the principal, she heard sounds coming from one of the adjacent offices. The office belonged to Sister Theresa Marie, who was in charge of student activities, and the door was ajar.

"Shit," the nun said in the empty room. "Shit, shit, shit."

Kathleen didn't think she had heard correctly, but the possibility was too good to pass up. Moving close to the door, she lined her eye up with the slim opening.

Sister Theresa Marie was inside, sitting at her desk, with her hands folded in front of her. She didn't seem to be doing anything, just sitting, watching her knuckles turn white and saying "shit" a thousand times in a row. It struck Kathleen as a hilarious perversion of *Pilgrim's Progress* and the endless prayer that was supposed to be every Christian's goal.

"Shit. Shit shit shit shit shit. Shit. Shit. . . ."

Kathleen turned away, filled with loathing. She never told the other nuns or any of the students about the episode.

Later, in the school store, Kathleen bought a diary

with a key. Its cover was coated with plastic and smelled like new dolls.

"I want to love God," she wrote on the first page. "But how can I in this place?"

Then she locked the diary and hid the key.

# CHAPTER TEN

June 12

I am moving back with my mother for summer vacation. Some Brit named Bonning is going to buy Daddy's house and now we have to live in the gardener's shack. I remember that place. It is dark there and it smells. *She* doesn't even mind. She's used to living like a pig. Daddy said she never had anything before he married her. God must hate me to do this thing to me.

Moira, in fact, had not minded moving from the Pierce mansion to the small house near the estate's large front gates. The gloom of the mansion, built in the early 1800s by an unpopular English nobleman, was gone from the long-unused gardener's cottage. Moira hung bright curtains, painted the walls, and found herself in better spirits than she had been in in years.

It caused her some guilt to think that she might actually be relieved about her husband's death, but since she had no doubt that she *was* the peasant her daughter always accused her of being, she accepted her lack of sorrow without so much as a confession to Father Gervaise.

Besides, there was sorrow enough. Her failure to win her daughter's affection weighed on her like iron shackles. Through the years, she had watched Kathleen change from a lovely child into a cold, pretentious stranger whom Moira, had not Kathleen been of her own blood, would have dismissed from her thoughts as the spoiled offspring of spoiling parents. But she couldn't dismiss Kathleen. Whatever the girl might think of her mother, she would just have to learn to accept her.

She fixed a room for the girl, with a new bed painted white and a comforter she'd made herself. She decorated it with dried flowers pressed into picture frames and baskets of tall thistle and pussy willow from the lake. Over the doorway to the room she hung a banner that read, "Welcome home, Kathleen." It was a lovely room, suitable even for someone of Kathleen's exalted tastes.

When she brought Kathleen home from the convent school, the girl took a look at her room, tore off the banner absentmindedly, and closed herself inside with a slam of the door.

Moira opened it. "Kathleen . . ."

"This *is* my room, isn't it? Or do we sleep two to a bed like you did when you were growing up?"

Moira bit her lip. There would be no scene. Not today. "This is your room," she said quietly. "I only thought that we could talk."

Kathleen rolled her eyes and put her feet up on the bed. "What do you want to talk about?"

"You. How you've been getting along at school. The

sisters say you're a fine student. The best in your class."

"There's nothing to do there except study," Kathleen said. "And pray."

"Don't say it that way, darling. Prayer's a good thing. It can help if you're troubled."

"The same way shamrocks and rabbits' feet help."

"What?" Moira's forehead creased.

"It's all superstition, Mother," Kathleen said.

"God is not a superstition!"

Kathleen exhaled noisily. "Fine. What else do you want to talk about?"

"You do not have all the answers."

"And you do, I suppose," the girl said, looking slowly around the room. Suddenly Moira felt the smallness of it, the ordinariness.

"I want you to go to confession."

"I go every week. It's required."

"And you've told the priest that you don't believe in God?" Moira asked.

Kathleen felt something twist inside her. She hadn't meant for things to go that far.

"Well?" her mother said.

"What difference would it make?"


"Bless me Father, for I have sinned."

There was a long silence in the darkness of the confessional inside St. Benedict's Church. Finally, the old priest spoke. "Yes, my child? In what way have you sinned?"

"My mother doesn't think I believe in God."

"Do you?"

"I don't think it matters whether I do or not."

"Doesn't it matter what becomes of your immortal soul?"

Kathleen thought before answering. "I don't know," she said.

It was a long time before the priest spoke again. He told her to say a hundred Our Fathers and a hundred Hail Marys and to pray for enlightenment.

July 5

How can I pray when I don't know who to pray to? What kind of god is it who would kill my father and leave me with my mother? If I don't pray, will this god kill me too and turn me over to the devil? Or do I already belong in Hell?

Kathleen hated being home from school. As bad as life at St. Anne's was, she could at least pretend there that somewhere else, in another existence apart from the lunatic regimen of the church, she still lived in the Pierce mansion with its polished oak stairways and brass lamps, with her canopied bed and the rows of little ruffled dresses that her mother had long ago given to the so-called poor of the village. As if Mr. Bonning's cleaning woman, who lived in a shack on his property, had the right to call anyone else poor.

But when she was at home, and she walked past Moon Lake to the magnificent gates of the mansion and saw her own home looking small and dingy next to the house where she had once lived, all her pretenses were shattered and she was filled with anger and with pity. For her mother, who shamed herself in the domestic service of a stranger, and for herself. At summer's end, she almost looked forward to going back to Killarney and St. Anne's.

Late one afternoon, in her thirteenth year, she saw Sister Theresa Marie leaning on the convent gates as Kathleen was returning to her room after confession. The fence was in the rear of the convent grounds, and Sister Theresa Marie seemed to be draped on the spiked iron posts, as if impaled on them.

Kathleen stopped, for a moment wondering if the nun were again issuing a stream of sibilant obscenities, but Sister Theresa Marie was not speaking. She was sobbing quietly, absorbed in the activity with all her heart, like a child who had just discovered hiccups.

"Is . . . is something wrong, Sister?"

The nun gave no indication that she had heard the girl but spoke, softly, haltingly, between her outpourings of tears.

"If a man walk in the night, he stumbleth because there is no light in him," she whispered.

Kathleen moved closer toward the gate to hear the woman's stifled words, spoken into the folds of her black habit. For an instant, holding on to the black fence that separated her from the nun, Kathleen felt as if she were still in the confessional booth, but this time *she* was listening to the sinner.

"For we are stained by our guilt and punished by our wickedness," Sister Theresa Marie said. And then she looked up into the girl's face, seeing it for the first time and emitting a small gasp of recognition.

"It's all right, Sister . . ." Kathleen began, but the nun ran away, her eyes wide and rolling like a cow's when the spike is thrust into its skull at the slaughterhouse. Kathleen was left standing on the other side of the fence, her arms sticking through the slats, clutching helplessly at the air.

The following week, Sister Theresa Marie hanged herself in her cell. It was kept very quiet but word spread in whispers. Her head was uncovered, it was said. She was wearing her sleeping shift. The instrument of her death was the rope belt from her habit.

October 10

Was it because she said "shit"? Would God make a person kill herself for such a small sin? Or doesn't He care if one of us dies because there are so many of us? Does He do it for a reason? Or just because He feels like it? Did He kill Sister Theresa Marie for a joke maybe? Is that why He killed my father?

There was only one more entry in Kathleen's diary. It read, "God is the biggest killer of them all."

After she wrote the words, she locked the book away for the last time. When she went home on her next holiday, she threw the diary into Moon Lake.


Kathleen did not go back to St. Anne's Convent School. Instead her mother enrolled her in the church school in Ardath. Kathleen had decided that God, if there was one, had put her on earth to be His whipping boy, so she tolerated ancient old Father Gervaise and what she regarded as the equally decrepit nuns who ran the small school at St. Benedict's Parish.

She was graduated at fifteen, but just before her graduation, Moira excitedly told her, "You've got a chance to go to college. There's a scholarship to Edwards College in Dublin. It's a fine school.''

"That's grand," Kathleen said in her most bored voice, then rolled away on the bed, turning her back to her mother.

"You have to take a test to qualify. But with your grades, I'm sure you'll do just fine.''

Kathleen rolled over again and looked back at her mother. The woman's eyes were wide, expectant.

"This means a lot to you, Mother?" Kathleen said.

"It does.''

"I'll take the test then," Kathleen said.

The test was administered at the local school two weeks later. Three days after that, the mail brought Kathleen's test mark. She had scored zero. Every question had been answered wrong.

Moira was crushed. "You failed it deliberately, didn't you?"

"Of course I did," Kathleen said.

Moira raised her tear-streaked face. She still held the letter of rejection in her hand. "But why?"

"Why not?" Kathleen said feverishly. "It doesn't matter whether I go to college or not. There's no chance for me. I'll always be a peasant now, thanks to you. Since Daddy died, you've sunk back to your own level and you've dragged me down with you.''

"Don't you dare speak to me like that.''

"Go ahead and hit me, Mother," Kathleen said coolly. "It's your natural instinct. And maybe I'll hit you back. That's what's expected of people in our station, isn't it?"

Moira crumpled the letter into a ball and threw it into a corner of the room.

"Don't be upset," Kathleen said. "After all, I'm only living out the life you planned for me."

Moira began to speak but the girl's eyes stopped her. There was such a fury in them that Moira felt, suddenly, inexplicably, afraid.

She left the room then, and they never discussed the subject of college again.


And so the years went by for Kathleen, uneventful, leaden years tinged with the faint fried odor of poverty. She found herself a small job, but even though she was forced to live at home, she separated herself from her mother as she had separated herself from the girls at school and from the nuns who sinned secretly behind their black veils of holiness. One day, she realized she had separated herself from everything around her except her books.

And what treasures they were. From the joyful mysticism of St. Thomas Aquinas to the dark atheistic stirrings of Herbert Marcuse, Kathleen adopted the world of ideas and words as her own.

Until she met Brian O'Flaherty.

It had happened three years ago at a dance, and it was as a dancer that she best liked to remember him— light, fresh as a wind, laughing and bright and curly-haired and wonderfully wicked with his music and his easy cursing and his women who clung to him as if he were honeyed.

It was spring, and Bobby McFann and his fiddlers from County Clare had come to Ardath for the Country House dance held in the small social hall of St. Benedict's Church. The Country House dance was a tradition of long standing, having begun in the houses of farmers in the days when company was scarce and rural dwellers made their own entertainment.

In the old days, every neighbor within riding distance came to one house or another equipped with all the musical instruments they knew how to play and all the whiskey they could safely carry. Everyone played something, or sang, or was a good storyteller, or cooked or was a champion drinker.

They would gather in the house, cleared of furniture for the occasion, early in the afternoon, and the dance would go on until dawn the next day. Mothers dressed their eligible daughters in the finest gowns they could make, because the Country House dances were among the few occasions when young men and women could meet one another. For this reason, the normally stern Catholic mothers would delicately turn their backs when their offspring left the premises to dally in private.

As a result, the summer brought a flurry of weddings and the winter a crop of avowedly premature babies. It was a system that had worked well for hundreds of years, but St. Benedict's new social hall had put an end to most of it.

Now the dances began at eight o'clock and continued until eleven under the watchful eye of Father Gervaise. The old priest had even banned alcohol from the hall, but that was asking too much. As a concession, the women placed tables of food and drink outside, where those unable to resist temptation could imbibe in the open air.

Moira was in charge of providing hams for the food table, having obtained three of them as a gift from Mr.

Bonning. She still regarded participation in the Country House dances as a kind of community obligation, even though she had long ago given up any hope that Kathleen might take part in them. Her daughter had always said that she wasn't interested in the dances. Nothing, it seemed to Moira, interested Kathleen except her books. Piled in rows around the walls of her room like fortifications, they were ends in themselves for her, not paths to be followed to reach something bigger. For Kathleen, there was nothing to strive for, nothing to accomplish during her time on earth. It filled her mother with sadness.

Moira knew Kathleen was not happy that she was living in Ardath, where she had no future, but she could not imagine what *would* make Kathleen happy. When the girl had first started to go out with young Morty O'Sullivan, Moira had hoped that the romance would change Kathleen. But there had been no romance, apparently. Morty had meant no more to Kathleen than anything else. The girl took nothing, wanted nothing, gave nothing. She had become a cipher. Her natural beauty had already, at nineteen, begun to be washed out by the dullness of her spirit. There was no laughter in her, no fire, no feeling. Sometimes Moira thought of her as information without thought. The girl had almost ceased to live.

At night, alone, Moira would hide in the fragile, dog-eared pages of her photo album, poring over the frozen pictures of her past—her parents, strong and lusty, her father with a spine like steel wire, her mother large and soft and comforting—and remembering the sounds of love that came from them in the flea-infested cottage where she grew up. And then she would look at another, a secret face, handsome and craggy and proud above a policeman's uniform.

*Michael, oh, Michael, would it have been different for Kathleen if you'd stayed?*

But she would always close the book, knowing that nothing would have been different. Nothing would ever be different.

As Moira prepared to leave their house on the night of the dance, Kathleen came into the kitchen from her bedroom.

"Where are you going?" she asked.

"To the Country House dance."

Kathleen hesitated. "Perhaps I'll go, too," she said.

"If you wish," Moira said blandly. She was delighted but afraid to show her excitement, lest one chance word send Kathleen off on some angry tirade and cause her to change her mind.

At the dance, Kathleen kept to herself, near the walls, vaguely offended by the sweat and noise of the dance. Moira glanced at her occasionally and realized that her daughter had not a single friend in the village, not one person who would walk up to her to chat.

And then came Brian O'Flaherty. He was new to the village, having arrived in Ardath only two weeks before, and he walked in, carrying a jug over his shoulder, no less, and the girls giggled and the women clucked in disapproval and the men slapped him on the back and Bobby McFann began to fiddle a frenzy. It was as if the curly-haired young blond man had exploded himself into the room, scattering light with his very breath.

Kathleen felt a swift rush of air whoosh into her lungs. Never had she seen such a man before. He moved like an animal, glistening with sweat, his muscles bulging beneath his plain shirt, his lips full of sin and promise.

He didn't notice her. Kathleen hadn't expected him to. She watched, a mouse in the corner, as Brian sang and laughed and picked up the ladies by their waists and swung them above his head.

"Hello, Kathleen. I've brought you some punch."

She fluttered her eyelids, confused at the alien voice that broke into the concerted bubble of her attention. It was Morty, dressed in his new policeman's uniform, his hair so slicked back with brilliantine that it resembled patent leather. The sight of him so surprised Kathleen that she laughed out loud.

Morty flushed and looked down at his spanking new brass-buttoned jacket to see if he'd spilled something on it.

"No, you look fine, Mortimer," Kathleen said. "I just wasn't expecting to see you."

"It must be the uniform," Morty said shyly. "Wager you're not used to seeing it on me. Just issued, so it was . . ."

But Kathleen's eyes had traveled back to the dance floor.

"Anyway, I'm happy to see you're in such good spirits," Morty said.

Kathleen didn't answer. She had already forgotten him.

Brian O'Flaherty was dancing alone in the center of the floor, his feet kicking high in the old step dances that were so difficult that none but the most athletic would attempt them. The others stood in a circle around him, clapping in time to the fiddlers' music.

Someone passed Brian's jug around, and the men took a swigs from it in turn, toasting Brian's health.

"To the devil in ye," Old Lanigan shouted, and the clapping got louder. When it was done, Brian jumped high into the air and came down with a thunderous stomp on his heels, booming the old Irish prayer, "May God save you all from the ferocious O'Flahertys," and the place went up in one enormous cheer.

"It's a lovely night for a walk," Morty was saying from somewhere far away, but Kathleen didn't move, didn't blink. Something inside her quivered, ready to explode, something delicious and fleeting that she dared not disturb.

And then Brian, the golden god, looked at her, and in that instant the wall of shadow and darkness that had surrounded her like a shroud for all the years of her life tore apart in one blinding, screaming, shaking beam and she felt something like stars pour out of her.

"Kathleen," Morty said, alarmed. Kathleen's hands were wrung together as if in prayer, and her eyes were fixed straight ahead. Morty followed her gaze, and on the other end of it he saw Brian, moving toward her as if the two of them were connected by rays coming out of their eyes. Morty leaned back against the wall then and drank his cup of punch as Brian put his hand against Kathleen's waist and danced her onto the floor.

They danced together without a word. None was needed. Kathleen burned where Brian touched her, and she felt power in her own presence. She loved the smell of him, felt drunk on the moisture from his body. And she wanted him. More than she had wanted God, she wanted this man now. And she suddenly realized why she had come to the dance. She wanted a man.

He understood. They slipped out of the parish hall and, their steps lit by moonlight, walked toward Moon Lake with their hands entwined.

Moira watched them. Part of her twisted with worry because she suspected that Kathleen wasn't the first girl who'd walked with Brian to Moon Lake and would not likely be the last, if the stories she had heard about him were true. But she bit her lip and forced herself silent. She'd never seen anything like happiness cross the girl's face before. There was so much time for regret later, she knew. A stolen moment of joy was sometimes all the happiness there was.

"Your Kathleen's gone with that O'Flaherty creature, don't you know," Mrs. O'Glynn said smugly, folding a piece of ham and sticking it into her mouth.

"And what of it, you fat busybody?"

Leaving Mrs. O'Glynn gaping with shreds of meat spilling over her lips, Moira took off her apron and went inside the church hall.

"I've not seen you before," Brian said. "I've been in town but two weeks and wasted them both." He was leading Kathleen onto the worn path leading in the woods by the lake.

"I don't go out much," she said.

"And why not?" His eyes twinkled. "Don't you like having fun, girl?"

She looked down. "I don't know."

"Ah, it's a strange one you are," Brian said, placing his hand easily about her waist. "Now, most girls, they'd be a-chittering and a-chattering. . . ."

"I don't know about girls," she said evenly. "And I don't know about men. But I don't care for talk."

She stood there, dappled with the shadows of leaves on her face, looking directly at him. There was no coyness in her, no fanciful sparring. For a moment, Brian felt a thin chill of discomfort. This girl was like none he'd ever known before. She was cut crystal, pristine and perfect.

But then, he thought, he didn't even know her name. She might be the whore of Kerry for all he knew, but she was willing and it was a fine night for a woman's sweetness. He kissed her then and she made a sound like a whimper. When she pulled away to look at him, her eyes were feverish and there were beads of sweat on her white forehead.

"Here," she said, pulling him to the ground. He unbuttoned her dress carefully, pulling the fabric over her shoulders to expose her breasts. They were cream and pink, fuller than he'd imagined. He passed his hands across them and the nipples stood up erect. Kathleen bent her head backward, exposing her long swan's neck. He touched it with his lips, and he could feel the hunger in her as she pulled him close and kicked her legs free from her dress.

She felt possessed by him. Her back arched, her fingers strained to strip the shirt from his chest. She pressed her face to his naked skin, taking in the scent of him, tasting his salt-dampened body with her tongue. In a fever she enveloped him, wanting him so hard that her belly ached from the wanting. And when he took her, roughly, the way she wanted it, she cried out from the pain and exhilaration of it, for never, never had she felt so alive. And then later, she wept. Because she knew she would never feel as alive again.

"Well, you're a wild one, missy," Brian said gently, stroking her that night in the wood. He pulled the straw-colored hair from her face where it had stuck with the wetness of her tears. "And a strange one, I'll say. Didn't you want it then?"

Kathleen sobbed and held the young man in her arms and knew she would never be able to explain her agony to him. It was she who had been virgin, but Brian was the innocent and would always be.

She could not have explained that to him, even if he had cared to listen.

# CHAPTER ELEVEN

It began to rain on the road leading past Moon Lake. Gusts of cold mist from the water swirled around Kathleen. She was wearing a thin cloak over her fairy gown and she clutched it around herself as she walked toward her home.

She spat to wash some of the taste of vomit from her mouth. She had been throwing up often lately and it had begun to worry her, so much that she had made an appointment with a doctor in Killarney.

Brian was such a child, she thought. It was all well and good for him to mock Seamus Dougherty, but Seamus was something Brian could never be—a man who did things, who realized that after all the talk and the slogans were done, there still had to be someone who acted. Who did. That was Seamus. And that was Kathleen, too, she thought with pride.

She remembered a night a year before when she had walked alone along this road. After they had become lovers, Brian had gotten her a job as harpist and poetry reader at Bounfort Castle, where he was in charge of the nightly shows. Most nights after the show, they would go into town, where Brian would drink too much at Grady's Pub, and then they would go to his rooms to make love—if he didn't fall asleep first, which was happening with greater and greater frequency.

A year before, Brian had mucked up the show, just as he had done tonight, with his stupid Irish propaganda. Kathleen had chastised him for it afterward and they had quarreled. Brian had stomped off in anger. It was his way, she realized, to talk like a big man until someone questioned what he'd said. Then he always ran away to the solace of a pint and the other drunkards who hid their cowardice behind their dreams for Ireland.

For Ireland! In the howling night wind, she had laughed at the stupidity of it. Who but Brian O'Flaherty would leave his woman on a dark road at night because of patriotism? But she had loved Brian then, that long year past. She had loved him enough to accept Ireland as a rival she could not best.

Ireland had never loomed large in Kathleen's thoughts back then. She viewed nationalism with the same suspicion that she viewed religion, particularly when it concerned a country as dismal as her own. For her, Ireland was at best a moderately inoffensive place to live, except for the glut of priests and nuns and other illiterates. The only thing that prompted her to stay at all was that she couldn't think of anywhere better to go.

But Brian, though a blowhard, obviously loved Ireland with his heart and soul, loved the country with an obsession that most men reserved for power or money. He loved it like a soldier, which was why, she supposed, he had joined Sinn Fein in the first place.

Sinn Fein. "Ourselves alone." It was a battle cry of

freedom for Brian, as it had been a battle cry for the Irish since the time of Brian Boru. No matter that the Republic had been severed from Britain since 1921. In Brian's mind, as well as for the thousands of nameless others who pledged their secret allegiance to the Irish Republican Army, the English still occupied six counties of Irish soil, and he wanted it back. For Ireland.

*For ourselves alone.*

She had realized then that it was hard for an atheist to understand a patriot, and she had turned and walked back into Ardath and gone up to Brian's small rooms above the butcher shop.

The apartment was empty. She expected as much, and it made her faintly envious that Brian—that men in general, apparently—could effectively balm their wounds with drink and a pretense of merriment. How easy it must be to be a man, she thought, pushing some dirty clothes off the faded chair next to Brian's bed. She sat down heavily, pulling her cloak around her. Men lived in the pleasure or pain of the moment, unfettered by biological cycles or the moralistic guilt endemic to women. A pint of whiskey could not make her forget the fever she had for Brian. Curling up into a ball on the chair, she had fallen asleep.

Brian, not adequately sozzled despite his best efforts at Grady's, saw her as soon as he entered the room. She looked so small, and his heart and eyes overflowed with saloon sentimentality for her. He closed the door softly and kept the room dark.

"Why've you come, darling girl?" he asked gently, stroking her hair. His anger was gone. His nose ran.

She shivered with the sudden cold of waking in wet clothing. "I want to understand the thing you love."

He held her close to him. "You're what I love, Kathleen."

"And Ireland."

"Aye. And Ireland, too."

They went to the next meeting of the Provisional Sinn Fein in Cork. Although it was legal—the only legal branch of the IRA—the gathering had the look of secrecy about it.

It was held in a dingy hall in an undistinguished quarter of the city, almost in the shadow of Garda headquarters, and Kathleen had the impression that the people there collected together as much for the atmosphere of illegitimacy as anything else. They were a seedy bunch, rather proud of their reverse elitist status. They hung around in groups divided by age. The young, still sporting the long hair and disheveled clothing of another era, smoked cigarettes and spoke in whispers, their hands stuffed into their pockets, their expressions those of indifference and contempt. There were fat girls with pimples and hatchet-faced women taping handwritten slogans to the wall:

A UNITED IRELAND MEANS A FAIR
CHANCE FOR ALL

* * *

IMPERIALIST OPPRESSION MUST BE
STOPPED

* * *

RESISTANCE TO TYRANNY IS THE
DUTY OF MAN

Receding into the corners were the pockets of older revolutionaries, lean men and sharp-tongued women who brushed against one another with the dark familiarity of rats who knew their cage.

Brian lowered his voice as he stooped to enter the low doorway.

"There'll not be a big crowd tonight," he said. "There's no election on."

Kathleen nodded nervously.

A young man in glasses came up to them and put his hand on Brian's shoulder, but he was looking at Kathleen.

"She's all right," Brian said.

The man in glasses shrugged. "Seamus Dougherty isn't the usual kind of speaker," he said, as if he were trying to convince Brian to take the newcomer away.

"I don't know him," Brian said.

"He's an important man. He's just passing through on his way back from New York. We were lucky he agreed to stop in."

"I still don't know what the problem is," Brian said.

The young man waved his hands genially in front of him. "No problem. He just might be a little strong for the uninitiated." He walked away.

"He doesn't want me in your club," Kathleen said.

"Ireland's not a club," Brian said and led her to the rows of folding chairs.

Twenty minutes later, the young man with the glasses introduced the speaker. In his remarks, he said that Seamus Dougherty had helped organize the World Federation of Democratic Youth and he was on the board of the World Peace Council and a half-dozen other organizations. He called him "a freedom fighter who knows that no man is free until all men are free."

Kathleen had never heard of any of the organizations the young man mentioned. Then a small, pock-marked man stepped forward from a chair in the front where he had been sitting quietly, unnoticed.

The contrast between his arrogant manner and the clothes he wore—a cheap blue suit and rubber-soled suede shoes—was almost laughable as he walked toward the front of the room in silence, but Kathleen's amusement faded when the man took his position facing them. Seamus Dougherty had the bearing of a prince. Even before he uttered a word, he took command of the room. His eyes scanned the faces below him as if the people were units of artillery and he were measuring them for suitability.

Kathleen noticed Brian straighten up in his chair as he passed under the silent scrutiny of Dougherty's gaze.

"I am not here to shout slogans about Irish freedom," he said. His words were crisp and measured, and he made no effort to raise his voice above conversational level. To a person, Kathleen noticed, the audience sat forward. There was not another sound in the room.

"You have heard enough of those slogans in saloons and street rallies, and I have heard them until the bile has risen in my throat. For sixty-five years, we have been lamenting the British rule of Ulster and it has come to naught. Some think that if we talk enough and sing freedom songs we will win. But all the songs and speeches change nothing.

"The Catholics—which is to say the real Irish—of Belfast are still oppressed to a standing below cattle, unable to work or to find homes or to live without fear. Tyranny by foreigners is still the way of life in the six counties of the North. There is no more need for talk.''

Dougherty paused and looked once again around the room. Brian shifted uneasily in his chair. He squeezed Kathleen's hand, and she felt he was in some way apologizing for Dougherty's lack of razzle-dazzle. Poor thing, he had hoped for a better show, she thought.

"The fact is, a merger of those six northern counties with the southern Republic would make no difference at all in the condition of the poor and helpless.''

A few heads turned up. Brian's was not one of them. He had already lost interest. He *liked* to hear slogans, Kathleen realized sadly. Rhetoric and bombast were all he could appreciate.

Dougherty continued. "For what difference will it make if our people are oppressed by the Quisling regime in the so-called Republic of Ireland or by the colonial regime in the northern war zone? The Republic is as corrupt as the British territory of Ulster, only more cleverly concealed. You call Ireland, southern Ireland, a free land ruled by a democratic system of free people. I am here to tell you that you are the dupes of a biased and criminal pro-British press. Because what you have here is not freedom. Ireland, as it stands, is no more than a fascist state designed for privileged capitalist sycophants.''

There was a murmur through the room. Some of the older people shook their heads in disagreement. One old man spat on the floor. Dougherty nodded, almost imperceptibly, and from the rear of the room, a burly man stepped forward quickly and removed the man from his chair.

"Communist trash," the old man rasped as the burly man grabbed his arm and propelled him toward the door.

Dougherty went on as if nothing had happened. "We—and by 'we,' I mean the true fighters for freedom in this country and in the world—we do not want a confederation of the South with the North. Nor do we want an independent Ulster. *We want a general dismantling of the existing establishments in the Irish Republic and in Ulster both.*" He pointed out each carefully chosen word with the tip of his index finger.

There was scattered applause. Brian swung his foot, his eyes directed inward, as if listening to some silent music to pass the time.

"Let me make that clear," Dougherty went on. "If we evict the British but all else remains the same, what have we gained? The poor, if they are allowed to work at all, will work for the rich. When profits rise, the rich get richer. When profits drop, the poor get fired and go hungry. It is the worker who will always suffer oppression by the rich and never find himself a penny's worth ahead for his toil."

"For a solution, we must look beyond the boundaries of Ireland and see ourselves, not as Irishmen divided against one another, but as members of a global community."

More applause. Kathleen squinted. What was this man saying? That the "Irish problem" was no longer Irish?

He waited for the applause to die, then asked for questions. He did not smile or in any way appear to seek the approval of his audience. Kathleen felt some-

141

thing stir inside her for this man with the soft voice and the backbone of steel.

There were no questions. Something like panic swept through Kathleen. Dougherty's whispered authority had half intoxicated her. While he spoke, she had felt as if he were whipping her with a velvet cord. Beside his cold precision, Brian seemed like a lump of butter.

Dougherty nodded and began to step away. Before she fully knew what she was doing, Kathleen was on her feet.

"A question," she said, surprised at the clarity and strength of her own voice.

Dougherty looked up. Superciliously at first, she thought. Then his whole demeanor seemed to change as his eyes narrowed and his lips half smiled at her. She felt as if he had plucked an invisible pin from the air and skewered her to the wall with it.

"Yes?" he said, and his voice was laced with honey.

"What solution do you propose?" she asked. Very quietly this time, her voice betraying her.

Someone laughed softly. Beside her, a young woman blew a strand of hair away from her face. Kathleen felt herself stiffen. She clenched her hands into fists and steeled herself for a rebuke, but there was none.

Gone was the momentary seduction in Dougherty's eyes. His gaze shifted away from her as he addressed the room again.

"The only way to insure the well-being of all our people is to nationalize our industries, both in the North and in the South," Dougherty said. "To control the means of production and distribution and to take over the agricultural output of this nation under state-run cooperatives. For this to occur, we must look beyond the boundaries of a narrow national interest and focus on an international goal—the common struggle against colonial and imperialist domination. Any other questions?''

He did not look at her. Cheeks flaming, Kathleen sat down, and Dougherty walked toward a side door.

''What'd you ask that for?'' Brian chided her as the door closed behind Dougherty and the crowd got to its feet.

''I . . . I wanted to know,'' she said. ''That's why I came.''

''Well, this wasn't a very good example of what usually goes on, I'm afraid,'' Brian said. ''Pretty dull stuff.''

The thug who had thrown out the old man tapped her shoulder. ''Mr. Dougherty wants to see you,'' he said, leaning close to her ear.

''Us?'' Brian said, surprised.

The man looked at him without expression. ''Mr. Dougherty's outside, by his car.''

A gray Volvo was parked outside, its driver door open. Dougherty sat in the back seat. He seemed to melt into the back of the upholstery. As Brian and Kathleen approached, the rear window lowered. Dougherty made no move to crane his neck, but sat where he was, expecting them to come to him.

''Your man says you want to see us,'' Brian said through the open window.

Dougherty did not even waste a glance on Brian. ''I'll be at the Essex Hotel tonight. I'd like to talk to you.'' He seemed to be speaking to the back of the front seat.

''I'm afraid we have a long trip,'' Kathleen began.

"Come directly then. Try to make it." Dougherty nodded to the burly man who climbed into the driver's seat. Dougherty rolled up his window and the car drove off.

"What do you make of that?" Brian said, laughing.

The young man in glasses spoke up from behind them. "It's an honor."

"To toady to that simpering pantywaist?" Brian boomed.

The man in glasses shook an index finger in Brian's face. "Seamus Dougherty risked his life to come here. There's a price on his head, you know."

"For making speeches that put people to sleep?"

"Think what you want, O'Flaherty. If he wants something, you can believe it's to a good purpose. You can also believe that he'll get it, one way or the other."

"Well, what's he want with me?"

The young man looked down. "Maybe nothing." He turned to leave but before he did, his eyes met Kathleen's. There was something like laughter in them.

The Essex Hotel wasn't far out of their way. In the lobby, the driver of Dougherty's car was waiting for them.

"He'll see the girl," he said, snapping shut the magazine he was reading and getting to his feet. "Alone."

Brian reddened. "Well, if that ain't . . ."

"That's what Mr. Dougherty said." The roughneck squared his shoulders. He was a few inches taller than Brian and much wider.

"I don't want trouble," Brian said.

"That's why I'm here."

Kathleen looked at Brian and squeezed his hand. "I'll be all right," she said.

"Seven-oh-one," the bodyguard said, still facing Brian, and Kathleen walked to the elevator.

Seamus Dougherty opened the door himself. His blue jacket was draped over a chair. He stood in his shirtsleeves, a leather shoulder holster strapped over his chest.

He motioned her in without speaking. Her eyes fixed on the pistol beneath his armpit, she entered, walking sideways to slide between Dougherty and the door-frame.

The hint of a smile crossed his lips.

"You needn't be afraid of me," he said. His voice was soft, but it still carried the sharp edge of authority. Kathleen suspected that the man was incapable of real gentleness. For some reason, the lack of tenderness in him excited her. She tried to dismiss the thought and cast her eyes down.

Dougherty touched her chin and raised it. "Are you alone?"

She felt herself blazing. "No. My . . . friend is downstairs."

"Pity," he said, releasing his touch. "Do you sleep with him?"

She hesitated.

"Of course you do," he said. "No matter. I suppose the two of you go in for flag-waving buffoonery together."

"Now, just a moment, Mr. Dougherty. . . ."

"I've seen him before, you know. I never forget a face."

"He hasn't seen you," Kathleen said.

"I make it a rule not to be noticed. I haven't seen you before, though."

"I've not had much of an interest," she said.

"In what?"

"In flag-waving buffoonery, as you call it."

"Ah." He raised his eyebrows. "Do you read?"

"Of course," she snapped.

"Not *can* you read. *Do* you read?"

"And I said, of course."

"So much the better. What's your name?"

"Kathleen," she said.

Dougherty moved close to her, slowly. He picked up a strand of her blond hair and caressed it between his fingers. "You're a lovely girl, Kathleen." He examined her face. "Fine features and no vanity. How do you fit in in Ardath?"

She looked up, startled. "How do you know where I'm from?"

"I have a great interest in Ardath," he said. "And I asked." He began to unbutton her blouse.

She tried to stop him, but he forced her hands away. The blouse opened and her breasts spilled out onto his open palms. She watched him, thinking she ought to cry out or run, but she knew her objections would be a sham. Her knees weakened and she felt hot moisture between her legs. Almost involuntarily, her hands caressed the leather holster over his shoulder. The man had power, a power from inside him, and it melted her.

His eyes met hers. "Excite me, Kathleen," he said, pushing her down to her knees. She pulled back with revulsion at first, but Dougherty permitted nothing of her will into their intimacy. At last she accepted him, and to her shame, she enjoyed being forced to please a man.

This was entirely different from her lovemaking with Brian, she thought. Brian was a puppy, lusty, lovable, manipulable. But Seamus Dougherty was another kind of creature entirely, something that stalked, that swooped. He was a bird of prey; she was meat for him. He wanted her to be degraded, and in a perverse way, she needed the same thing from him.

"More," he whispered. She heard a click above her ear. She looked up, momentarily distracted, then gasped. He was pressing the revolver into her temple.

"You'll like it," he promised, grabbing hold of the hair on the back of her head and pulling her forward.

She gagged, flailed her arms, felt herself urinate in panic.

"Take it, Kathleen, because you want this. I saw it in your eyes from the first. You want to whore for me, don't you? You want to do as I say, because you are a child. A child, Kathleen, and I understand you like a father. Take what I give you."

And she opened wider and let him ram himself into her and yes, it was exactly what she wanted, something faceless and irreconcilably wrong and Brian, waiting innocently for her in the lobby downstairs, would never know but she would, yes, she would always know what she really was and when he was finished she sat back on her haunches, feeling dizzy with the terrible shame of it.

Dougherty put the gun away. He knelt beside her and buttoned her blouse. "I'll see you again," he said quietly.

She covered her face. He forced her hands away.

"I said I'll see you again." He stood up, pulled some leaflets and two books from the top of a desk in the room, and handed them to her. "Tell your friend we've been discussing politics. You might even care to read them."

She looked at the titles. One of the books was Carlos Marighella's *Mini-Manual* of urban guerrilla warfare. The other was a cheaply bound volume called simply *The IRA*. Its author was Seamus Dougherty.

"He won't believe me," she said.

"He will. Tell him I have a use for both of you. Now, if you don't mind, Kathleen," he said, nodding toward the door.

"You've used me."

He burst out laughing. "I'd say it's rather late in the day for Victorian pretenses, my dear." He took a comb from his pocket and ran it through her hair. "Come back to me when I send for you," he whispered.

She left, clutching the books to her chest as if they were covering the shame on her. And she knew she would come again.

Whenever he called.

# CHAPTER TWELVE

The morning after Kathleen met Seamus Dougherty, she and Brian were awakened by a pounding on the door of O'Flaherty's rooms. A man was there with a message that Brian must come to see Dougherty immediately.

"To hell with him," Brian said.

"He wants to see you," the messenger said coldly, as if talking to a particularly stupid house pet.

"Bloody well could have seen me last night," Brian blustered. He jerked a thumb over his shoulder toward Kathleen, who was burrowed into the covers of the bed. "The bastard spent enough time talking to her."

The nameless man shifted his weight just enough for his jacket to fall open and for Brian to catch a glimpse of the automatic inside his coat. "Wouldn't know anything about that," he said stiffly. "My orders is to get you to Killarney now. I've a car outside."

"Now? That's a lot of cheek. Suppose I've got something to do?"

"Cancel it," the man said.

Brian stared at the man for long seconds, and Kathleen knew he was deliberating whether or not to punch him. Finally Brian said, with a sigh, "Wait out there till I get dressed." He closed the door on the man and dressed quickly.

"I wonder what Lord Pantywaist wants," he said to Kathleen, who only shrugged.

A few minutes later, after dropping a desultory kiss on her cheek, he left. He had been gone only about sixty seconds when the front door was pushed open. Kathleen was sitting on the edge of the bed, naked. With a gasp of surprise, she pulled the covers around her. Seamus Dougherty's messenger was there, looking at her with no more interest than if she had been a year-old newspaper.

"Is there a telephone here?"

"Yes."

"What's the number?"

She recited it to him and the man said, "Stay close. Seamus will call you."

Brian O'Flaherty tried to engage the messenger in conversation as they took the hour-long drive north to Killarney, but the driver answered mostly with grunts and monosyllables.

"This Dougherty's a pretty big wheel, isn't he?" Brian tried.

"They don't get much bigger," the man said, allowing a small smile.

"That's what they tell me, but all I thought was that he was the head of some youth group or something."

The driver looked Brian over, then turned back to the wheel. Apparently he deemed Brian harmless, because after a few moments, he spoke.

"Seamus used to head up the INLA. You know them?"

"Sure," Brian said. "The Irish National Liberation Army. I've heard of them."

"Well, that was Seamus. The INLA changed the IRA from a lot of talk into action. The only way to win the struggle, mate."

"We'll win it, too," Brian said, his voice thickening with saloon fervor.

"Aye, with men like Seamus Dougherty, we will. He's been in it from the beginning. His father was at the Stensen Institute in 1969, he was. We got our first big shipment of guns then."

"Who from?"

"Everywhere. The world. The world knows we're right. We're all in this together."

Brian stretched his legs out before him in the car. Somehow he felt pleased at being included among the fraternity of freedom fighters. "Seems if all the world's lending us a hand, it shouldn't be much of a problem to roust the Prods out of Ireland."

The man looked at him again, with something like disdain in his eyes, then simply nodded agreement.


In Killarney, the driver, who never did give his name, took Brian directly to a large apartment building monitored by a huge doorman. The messenger nodded once to the doorman, and they were admitted inside without a word.

There was another guard seated outside Dougherty's apartment. He searched Brian methodically, then said, "Wait here," as he went inside.

Brian ran his fingers through his hair and tried to squeeze the fatigue out of his eyes. "What's he want with me?" he asked the driver.

"Told you, lad, I don't know." Brian's worried expression must have touched him, because he added, "It's all right, though. He said you'd be working with us."

Brian's spirits lifted. As the guard motioned him in, he lifted two fingers to his brow in salute. The driver half smiled, shook his head, and walked away.

"I'm sorry to inconvenience you," Dougherty said from a chair in the corner of the spacious living room. "But sometimes we have to work on short notice."

The blinds were drawn and the room was dark except for one small lamp near the entrance. Dougherty was bathed in shadow, and if he hadn't spoken, Brian might not have noticed that the place was occupied at all, so easily did Seamus melt into invisibility.

"Come here," Dougherty said. He switched on a table lamp next to him without looking up. There were papers on his lap. The shadows cast by the dim light accentuated the pockmarks on his face and the dark rings beneath his eyes. Brian moved closer, diffidently.

"I've been researching your background, Mr. O'Flaherty," he said, thumbing through the papers on his lap. "There isn't much. You don't officially belong to any organizations related to us."

Brian frowned, baffled. His brain felt muddy from lack of sleep, and his mouth was dry. He didn't know why this small, ugly man could elicit something like fear in him, but he desperately wanted a drink.

"I . . . I'm not a joiner," he said, feeling stupid immediately afterward.

"That's good," Dougherty said abstractedly.

"It is?"

Dougherty finally looked up. "For our purposes, Mr. O'Flaherty. I'm not sure you realize the extent to which Ireland is at war."

Brian started to speak, then thought better of it and simply nodded.

"We must live constantly with the atrocities of our enemies. Not only England and the armed troops of Britain but the terrorist organizations of the North as well. The Ulster Defense Association has committed itself to destroying the IRA. And the IRA, as you know, is the only hope for our country."

"The UDA is a pack of filthy Protestants," Brian snapped.

"The UDA has killed seven of us in the past three months. And those months are not extraordinary. The press is quick to blame the IRA while it overlooks the murderous evil of the Ulster Defense Association."

Brian felt his legs aching from the tension that Dougherty generated. "How can I help?" he asked finally.

Dougherty stood up. He walked around Brian as if he were a plaster column. Then he took a key from his trouser pocket and opened a drawer in a rosewood desk. From it he extracted a long envelope, which he handed to Brian.

The envelope was unsealed. Inside was a block of money, all old used bills.

"I'm going to ask you to do something without asking me questions," Dougherty said.

"I'm on your side," Brian said. "You just name it."

"I want you to join the UDA," Dougherty said softly. "There's a thousand pounds in the envelope. I want you to go north to Belfast and join up and spread the money around. Tell them you've struck it rich and you want to help them fight the evil IRA. You're a good speaker, Brian. I've heard you. Convince them."

Brian fingered the money bewilderedly. "But . . . but why?"

"You're one of us, aren't you?"

"That I am, Captain. I always have been a Republican and that can be vouched for, even though I haven't joined a lot of clubs and such. Ireland's as dear to me as life itself."

A thin smile poked at Dougherty's mouth. "Then suffice it to say that one doesn't have to understand everything one is asked to do in order to serve the cause." The smile vanished, and Dougherty the leader again took command. "Take the money to the UDA. We've got a contact for you who'll get you in. Make a good case for the donation. Tell them you and your friends are tired of the violence to your country and the world. That's a reasonable facsimile of the British press line, I'd say. Say you want to eradicate the IRA with any means available. Then stay around for a few days. Sign any petitions that are circulating, get your name around. Ask to get on their mailing list. Later, we'll send you back. We want them to trust you."

"I've got it. You want me to be a spy," Brian said. He looked down at the money in his hand. His head was spinning. "Well, Seamus, I'm your man," he said. "But it all is a little sudden." He paused. "You wouldn't have a touch of something on the premises, would you?" he asked meekly.

"I don't suggest you drink much until your project is completed. It might loosen your tongue. You're not an alcoholic, are you?"

"I'm not," Brian snapped belligerently.

"Then do as I say. You'll be watched, incidentally. Don't let it rattle you. It's just too big a project to leave at loose ends."

Brian's fists clenched. "Are you saying that I'm to spy on the UDA or whatever it is and all the while you'll have someone spying on me as well?"

"That is approximately correct."

"Then tell me why. Why me, a Kerryman from the far south, who's not laid eyes on you before yesterday? And why did you take my girl and keep her so long without a word to me about it?"

"I've told you," Seamus said patiently, "that I'm not in a position to explain everything to you yet. But I can ease your mind on a few things. One. You are exactly the man we want and need. Your history has been well documented and there's no accident involved. Two. I interviewed your friend, Miss Pierce, to test her loyalties in this matter. Since it's unlikely that you'd be able to keep much from her for long, I wanted to determine whether or not she's the sort to run to the police if she finds you're working with us."

Brian's fists opened. "She isn't," he said.

Dougherty remembered the creature scrabbling on her knees in front of him. "No, I don't believe she is," he said, half covering his face with his hand. "Not anymore." He rose. "That's all I can tell you for now. There'll be more later if you accept. Do you?"

Brian nodded. "I do."

Dougherty pulled a piece of paper from his pocket.

"Here's the name and address of your contact. He's agreed to put you up during your stay up north. He will take you to the UDA and see that you're looked after. They've accepted him as one of their own. When your business is finished, he will help you get back to Ardath. Under no circumstances will you seek me out or mention my name. Is that understood?"

Brian nodded.

"Good." Dougherty knocked on the door once. It opened, and the guard took Brian outside.

"Exactly the man we wanted," Dougherty said aloud. Then he sat down again in the chair at the far end of the room and wrote a long message in a code decipherable to only one man. He placed it in an envelope, sealed it, scrawled the address with his left hand and handed it to the guard outside the room.

"Place it in a postal box a little way from here," he said.

Beneath the guard's thumb, only three words of the address showed: "Ardath. County Kerry."

# CHAPTER THIRTEEN

She did not want to miss a telephone call, so while Brian was gone, Kathleen stayed in the room and began to read the books Dougherty had given her. While she read, the remembrance of Seamus Dougherty's flesh upon her filled her with shame and longing. The shame was for herself, but the longing was for the man who could make her dance at his will, who could watch her grovel and accept it as his due. His power, even his indifference, was something she needed, an aphrodisiac potent beyond words.

When the telephone rang, it was late afternoon and she had finished both books. Her heart dropped when she realized that the voice on the line was not Seamus Dougherty's.

"Miss Pierce?"

"Yes."

"I'm calling for a friend of yours. Seamus. You understand?"

"Yes," she said, her heart beginning to race.

"He wants to let you know that Brian won't be back tonight."

"Is . . . is that all?"

"That's the message," the impassive voice said.

"What about the castle? The music show that Brian does?"

"Do it yourself, our friend said."

*Do it yourself.* He was mocking her. She felt herself starting to shake and bit her lip to stop the trembling.

"Miss Pierce?"

"I understand" was all she could say.

"He said he would be in touch with you," the man's voice said just before the telephone went dead.

She had never done a solo show at Bounfort Castle before, but she was afraid to disobey. At nine o'clock, when she took the stage, framing an apology for Brian's absence, she was struck dumb for a moment when she saw Seamus Dougherty sitting at one of the spots along the large communal banquet table.

She went through her performance in a daze. Apparently, though, she hadn't embarrassed herself, because she received a warm round of applause when the show was over.

After all the other diners had left, she was alone in the dark banquet room with Dougherty.

"I was surprised to see you," she said.

"I know that," he answered.

"Where is Brian?"

"Do you really care?" Dougherty asked.

Kathleen shrugged. "Just wondering."

"He's doing some business for me. He'll be away for a few days."

He said nothing more, and Kathleen had the feeling that he would be content to sit there alone with her. Did he want to make love to her in that room for some strange reason? Even as the thought occurred to her, he said, "I want you to show me around the castle."

"Certainly," she said, brightening. "Are castles an interest of yours?"

"Yes. A recent interest."

She led him through the banquet hall to a stone corridor. "There isn't much to see, I'm afraid. This is only a portion of the original castle. Most of it has fallen apart over the years, and only this section remains."

She took his hand to lead him through the dark. At first he seemed to recoil from her touch, but then he let her close her fingers around his.

"Down here on this floor, there's only this banquet hall and the small warming kitchen. All the food is actually cooked at one of the restaurants in town and sent up here. We only have to warm it in a microwave oven. Brian and I wait in the kitchen to come onstage, and we serve all the food, too."

"I see," he said. "Nothing else on this floor?"

"Only the bathrooms for people eating dinner," she said.

"All right. His tone was cold and clinical, and Kathleen would not have been surprised if he had started taking notes.

She led him through the tiny food-warming kitchen, where there was a circular flight of stone steps. The stairway curled upward to the left as similar stairways always did in castles. They were planned that way to prevent right-handed attackers from being able to use their swords easily as they tried to fight their way up the steps. Meanwhile, defenders would have the free use of their right arms to hack at the invaders.

There was only one large room upstairs. It was unfurnished except for a wooden table and some hard wooden chairs.

"What's this used for?" he asked.

"Nothing. Sometimes if there's a religious event here, priests use this area for dressing or for whatever folderol they do to get ready for mass," she said.

He let go of her hand and walked over to touch the walls. They were solid stone, a foot thick, and Dougherty nodded and walked to the large French doors at the end of the room. Outside was the balcony, looking out over a large rolling field, still green in the bright moonlight.

"This is where the Virgin Mary appeared?" he said.

"If you believe in all that."

"It's not what I believe that's important," Dougherty said.

He opened the French doors and stepped out onto the balcony, leaned over the stone railing and looked as far to the left, then to the right, as he could see.

"Are you looking for something special?" she asked.

"I've seen what I want to see," he said. "Are there any guards here?"

"Guards? What for?"

"To protect against vandals, say."

"No. There's just one other woman who works here at night besides Brian and me. She takes tickets and fills in but she's no guard, and whoever is the last one to leave just locks up. No guards."

"Excellent," he said softly, still leaning over the rail, looking out across the field.

"I beg your pardon?"

"I said, thank you for the tour. Shall we go?"

"Where?"

"Is there anything wrong with Brian's place?" he said.

"Brian's . . ." She caught his eyes, mocking, insolent. "I guess that's all right," she said.

Dougherty's lips curved in the semblance of a smile. "I thought you'd feel that way."


They drove in Dougherty's car to West Street. It was late and dark and the street was empty. He parked around the corner from the entrance to Brian's apartment, then followed her quietly up the steps alongside the butcher shop. When they stepped inside the apartment, she threw her arms around him and kissed him.

He pushed her away. "That's not necessary," he said. His words stung her with humiliation, but then he smiled—almost gently, she thought—and took her hand. "Don't pretend you love me," he said. "That's for children." He forced her to look at him, and she saw there was no malice in his face.

"I don't even know you," Kathleen said, "but I want to love you. I want you to love me. Anything else seems somehow evil."

"That's a beginning. It's not evil. It's just not— what the poets write about." He lifted her skirt and ran his hand along her thigh. His fingernails scraped against her skin. She winced and felt her nipples harden. "It's what's wrong with most of us. We cover a festering sore with rose petals and declare the patient cured," he said. "Then when he dies, we call it the will of God."

"That's what you said in your book." She moved away from him.

"So the country girl really does read."

"Don't patronize me," she said.

"That's better. I never wanted a servant."

"Is a whore something different?" Kathleen asked acidly.

Dougherty smiled. "Quite different." He laughed at her sigh of exasperation. "I'd like to know what you've learned from the books."

"That you're nothing but a Communist," she hissed, her eyes narrowed.

"And?"

She didn't know what to say. Dougherty reclined across Brian's bed, his head resting on his hands.

"You admit it?" she said.

"Of course. You call it communism, I call it socialism, but it's the only way to eliminate the differences between rich and poor, Catholic and Protestant, Irish and English. Any fool who's given the matter any thought knows that the only way to neutralize tyranny is to eradicate the system that produces it."

"That's not the line you give out most of the time. Brian, the other fanatics you attract . . . even the Americans who send the money to buy your precious guns, for God's sake. They all think it's for Ireland, land of poets and scholars, dear Ireland, the blessed mother of us all."

"Your cynicism doesn't become you, my dear."

"And your cheap tricks don't become you. You're as Irish as Joseph Stalin."

"Bitch," he said with the same relaxed equanimity. "You're wrong. Communism is a global idea. When it comes to pass on a global level, Ireland will benefit. The world will benefit.''

"You talk like a textbook," she said.

"I'm a teacher," he said. "Naturally, we're not about to introduce communism as the solution to the Irish question. Not publicly yet. It's not fundamentally Irish. It will take time to get people used to the idea, but they will eventually.''

She shrugged. "It doesn't matter to me," she said.

"I think it does." He pulled her onto the bed beside him and stroked her hair as if she were a sleek cat. "Your indifference is an attractive veil, but it's not the truth. Why, look at you in bed.''

She flushed. He undressed her slowly, squeezing and pinching and licking her until she moaned.

"Your passion is almost obsessive. I saw it the first time I looked at you," he said.

"It's for you.''

He laughed and hit her hard across the buttocks. "That's false. If it weren't me, it would be someone— or something—else. Take your friend, Brian. The sex with me is better, isn't it, knowing that we're here in his bed and he knows nothing about it?''

"So what? You can buy Brian for a song. He's all puffed up with the spirit of Irish revolution," she said.

"I haven't done Brian any harm. We need the Brians of Ireland, the flag wavers, the shouters. They think the affliction of our country is no more than a paper cut, a little patriotic balm and it's healed. Why frighten them with the fact that radical surgery is needed?''

"I'm not interested in your ideas," she said.

"No. I know what you're interested in," he said.

163

Then he stretched her out on the bed like an idol of flesh and opened her legs and tasted her, burying his face inside her wetness until she cried out with pleasure.

"This time for you," he said.

"Does that make you my whore then?" she asked.

"Certainly not. I was never enough of a Catholic to despise pleasure."

She sat up and straightened her hair with her palms. "I used to be," she said softly. "There was a time when I wanted to find God."

"What happened?"

She smiled. "I gave up the search."


That night was the beginning of what Kathleen wanted to regard as their affair, although she knew the relationship between them could not qualify for even that cautious a term. There was no warmth or sharing between them. Seamus was cold. When he spoke to her, he lectured, and more often than not he did not speak to her at all, except to summon her for physical service.

He left in the morning without a word.

Brian returned to Ardath. She slept with him, but their lovemaking was mechanical, ritualized. He didn't mention what he had done during his time away. He didn't ask about her. He seemed preoccupied with his own thoughts, and Kathleen had no interest in what those thoughts might be. Little by little, the bond that was once between them frayed and thinned until it broke, and neither of them tried to knot it together again.

164

Then three months later, Seamus Dougherty summoned Kathleen to meet him in a hotel in Killarney. Like Brian, he offered no explanation for where he had been, and once again, she asked for none.

It was odd, she thought. Not long ago, she would have felt branded with sin for keeping two lovers at the same time. But there was no sin now, she realized. There was no emotion at all, only the empty pleasure of bodies meeting. And she had herself become one of the nuns in her childhood fantasies: faceless and carnal, hollow inside, gyrating for two men who, in the dark, were interchangeable now.

Throughout the year, Dougherty sent for her sporadically. Sometimes it was twice in a week, after she had finished work at the castle; sometimes several months would pass without a word from him. Brian never questioned where she went; he, too, had become indifferent.

One night, after nine weeks of absence, Seamus Dougherty sent a car to bring Kathleen to Killarney.

She sat on the bed in his hotel room, wordlessly, and began to take off her clothes. She unfastened the top two buttons of her blouse, and Seamus reached over to close them again.

"Not today," he said. He outlined an assignment for her. She accepted it, stolidly, as she had accepted his body, and when he was sure she understood, he called in one of his men and told him to take her back home.

He had not even said he was glad to see her, and she had long since stopped expecting him to.

That had been three weeks ago. Dutifully she had followed Seamus's instructions, and now she was going to see him. Even though she knew Seamus could never love her the way Brian once had, she still ached for him sometimes with a pain she had never felt for Brian. Perhaps, she thought, it was because Brian had loved her and Seamus had never cared. Maybe the fact that she had never been woman enough to conquer Seamus made her want him all the more.

She had stopped seeing Brian, apart from the work in the castle, weeks ago. His Irish Soldier Boy nonsense was grating on her nerves, and after this night's performance in the castle, haranguing the crowd, they would both be lucky if they didn't lose their jobs there. Brian was a fool and it vaguely embarrassed Kathleen to be seen with him.

Her mouth still tasted of vomit. When she got home, she slipped into her house for a drink of water. She could hear her mother's even breathing in one of the bedrooms. Kathleen left the house quietly, started her car and drove to Killarney, where she knew Seamus was waiting in a different hotel, yet another one. Seamus could never stay in the same hotel for long because of the danger to him. He was a man with a price on his head, and she knew there was no prospect of ever making a home with him. And yet she still wanted him, any part of him he would give her.

For a change, he looked happy to see her when she finally got past the ever-present guard who was in one of the outer rooms of the suite.

"You've done well," he said.

She flushed with pride. "I've written to all the newspapers," she said. "And I'll keep doing it." She looked at him hesitantly. "I just wish I knew why you want me to write anti-Catholic letters."

166

He stared at his hands for a moment. "You deserve to know that, I suppose," he said.

"You know you can trust me, Seamus."

"I hope so. Something major is going to happen in Ardath."

"Nothing happens in Ardath," she said with a smile.

"Nothing so far. But something will."

She blinked. "Something . . . violent?"

He nodded. "Probably. Violence is the only way to galvanize a fat, stupid civilian population into active revolution."

"Revolution?" she said, trying to hide a smile. "You think the townspeople of Ardath are going to revolt?"

He sighed. "I guess I don't have anything to share with you."

Kathleen tried to collect her thoughts. "Just a moment, Seamus. Are you telling me that whatever's going to happen in Ardath is so big that it's going to provoke a revolution?"

"Most assuredly," he said.

"What is it?"

"I can't tell you that yet," Seamus said.

"When will I find out?"

"Maybe only when it happens. Kathleen, there is a man in your village. He is a special man to our movement and he may need your help at some point."

"A terrorist? In Ardath?"

"No questions," he snapped. "Are you willing or not?"

She felt a worm of fear thread its way up her spine. "I am," she said hoarsely.

"If you are needed, the man will inform you. He is

called Lazarus. That is how he'll identify himself to you."

"Lazarus," she repeated, her thoughts suddenly back on the convent grounds at St. Anne's School. "If a man walk in the night, he stumbleth because there is no light in him," she remembered.

"You would have made a fine nun," Dougherty said. He touched her arm and led her to the bed.

# CHAPTER FOURTEEN

The door to Wells's room was open, and Cormac found him reading the London *Times*. The room was immaculately clean, as was everything around Wells.

"Ah," he said when he saw Cormac and rose immediately to wash the newsprint ink from his hands.

"This is turning into a waste of time," the Irishman said, tossing his hat on the sofa. "I've talked to everybody in town. Not a clue among the lot. And I'm damned sure nobody in these parts is masterminding a plot to kill the Pope. If you ask me, you're barking up the wrong tree."

"You say that every morning, Michael," Wells said.

"And every morning it's true. I don't see you uncovering any caches of explosives. All I see you doing is reading the newspaper." Cormac helped himself to a leftover sausage from the room's small, old-fashioned refrigerator.

Wells smiled. "Slow but sure, my friend. I told you that one can learn much from the press. Here. Look at this." He folded the newspaper into a square and handed it to Cormac.

The first entry in the Letters to the Editor column had been circled in black marker:

Sir: Instead of always agitating for Catholic control of Northern Ireland, maybe people should start thinking about reuniting all of Ireland under Protestant control. Let's face it, the Catholics have made a perfect mush of our beloved country. As a Briton living in Ireland and a student of history, I can tell you one thing: The only mistake Cromwell made was that he let too many Catholics escape alive. In the future, let's hope that mistake isn't repeated.

Sincerely,
Maire Ruadh.

Cormac looked up and Wells said, "Does that cheese smell a little ripe to you, Michael?"

"That's how much you know about Ireland," Cormac said, tossing the paper back onto Wells's lap in disdain. "Catholic or Protestant, it doesn't matter. Letters, speeches, songs, we've got all the words God ever created and mouths big enough to hold all of them. But it never means they're getting any prompting from our brains." He pointed at the newspaper. "That's just a pointless bit of chaff from some frustrated housewife who married a Catholic and now he spends all his time drinking and she's not getting enough."

"Sounds logical. Which housewife in Ardath fits the description?"

"Ardath?" Cormac said.

Wells nodded. "The letter was postmarked from

here. I've sent for the original. Interesting name on the letter, wouldn't you say?"

Cormac looked at the paper again. "Maire Ruadh. It means 'Red Mary,' " he said. "No significance at all."

"No."

"None at all, except to back up what I say about a frustrated wife," said Cormac. "Maire Ruadh was a legendary Irishwoman. She married a Protestant, and when he made a snotty comment about her ex-husband, she tossed him out of their castle window. A bitch. Just like this letter writer."

"Perhaps," Wells said mildly. "You say you've turned up nothing in your travels?"

"Nothing. I've talked to everybody from the parish priest to the lowest drunks in town. No one has seen a thing, no one knows a thing, there's nobody new in town except you and me and the usual gaggle of tourists passing through and that's all there is to report from the battlefront. I think we should both go home and forget this town."

"That isn't in the cards," Wells said.

"I know. I talked to my boss today, Superintendent Merrion, and he said I'm stuck here until I clean up this case."

"Did you tell him anything about the Pope?"

"No," Cormac said.

"Why not? What about loyalty, old school ties? He's your superior."

"He's also a pain in the ass," Cormac said. "He's been bad enough not knowing what's planned for Ardath. Do you know what he'd be like if he found out the Pope is coming and that maybe somebody's trying

171

to kill him? He didn't ask, so I didn't tell him. Besides, I'm not so sure that anybody's planning to kill anybody at all," Cormac said.

"Too many fingers pointing in that direction for us to ignore it, though, Michael," said Wells.

"I don't see any fingers, pointing or otherwise," Cormac responded.

"They're all over. Let's take it in order. The explosion at the pier."

"All right," Cormac said. "Somebody was doing something with explosives there and they blew up."

"Maybe. And maybe only some of the explosives blew up and maybe there is more and maybe it is stashed somewhere here in Ardath waiting for the Pope to arrive," Wells said. "That's one. Now some explosives blow up and then we find a body without hands or a head. Seems reasonable that the man was killed in the explosion, correct?"

"Indubitably," Cormac said, pouring himself a Scotch from the small bar in the room. "Only it would be nice if we knew who the man was."

"That would help," Wells admitted, "but I don't think it's the most important thing we need. The most important thing is Winston Barnett. We found one of his hands, but what happened to him? Was he killed here in Ardath? Was he killed elsewhere and shipped here? Is he even dead? Was just his hand sent here?"

Cormac sat down. "Suppose Barnett is here, hiding out, the dirty one-handed Protestant thug. Suppose you find it out. Will you go after him with the same zeal you reserve for Catholics who offend you?"

"I'll go after anybody who tries to solve a problem with a bomb," Wells said. "But suppose Barnett is dead and someone shipped him here or his hand here. Then somebody dropped it on the shore of the lake, hoping it would be found and that the identification of that dead body would be made as Barnett. Does that sound reasonable?''

"It does," Cormac agreed.

"Then the question is who? Who did it?"

"I was hoping you'd have answers, not questions," Cormac said. "I ask myself questions all day."

"I'm worried about this one, Michael," said Wells. "I know you've been doing the scut work, going around asking questions of people you'd rather not be talking to. But I've been working from the outside. I've been tracking down every contact I have anywhere in this country, north or south. There just isn't a word of anything big being planned."

"You don't expect that anybody would be bragging about planning to kill the Pope, do you?" Cormac asked.

Wells shook his head. "Not bragging. But there's always a leak. Someone always says something. But not this time, and that's what scares me."

"Maybe it means that nothing is planned." Cormac felt required to point out.

"If it weren't for the explosives and Winston Barnett's hand, I'd be inclined to agree with you. No. What I'm afraid of is that this isn't a big mass operation. That what we're dealing with here is one terrorist. One person who's going to pull the trigger on the Pope. A professional, maybe. Maybe two professionals at most."

"Pull the trigger or push the button. It might be a bomb, not a bullet," Cormac said.

"Exactly."

"Then it'd be a Protestant. The IRA wouldn't have any reason to kill the Pope," Cormac said.

"Time will tell who the terrorist is working for," Wells said.

"If there even is a terrorist. You've got terrorists on the brain," Cormac said. "Especially IRA terrorists."

"I guess I do," Wells said. "Sorry."

He stood up and stuck his hands in his pockets, and Cormac asked, "What was it? Family?"

Wells looked at him, surprised, and waited a long time before answering. "My brother. He was killed in Nicaragua about seven years ago. The war was on then. Some bloody bastard cut off his hands with a machete before he died."

Cormac winced. "I'm sorry. A terrorist?"

"Yes."

"But that wasn't the IRA," Cormac said.

"I don't know that," Wells said.

For the first time since meeting the Englishman, Cormac had the feeling he was dealing with a paranoid. "Come on, Daniel. Be reasonable. Nicaragua. . ."

"Even Nicaragua, Michael," said Wells. "There was no shortage of IRA-trained terrorists in Nicaragua."

"And your brother?"

"A missionary," Wells said. "Killed by an assassin named Lazarus."

"What happened to Lazarus?"

"I found him and I killed him," Wells said.

"I'm glad of that," Cormac said.

"So am I."

Cormac opened the refrigerator again and said, "Nobody can accuse you of wasting food."

"Is that an invitation to lunch?" Wells asked.

"Could you stand to eat with an Irishman? A Catholic, at that?"

"Only if he's buying," Wells said with a smile.


They settled in at Grady's, where the Cork-Limerick football match was in progress on the television. Grady's dog, an ancient, loose-lipped hound with absurdly short, bowed legs, brushed against Cormac's trousers until he was bribed away with a crust of bread.

"On the way over, you said this Lazarus was trained in Jordan, but you think he was an Irishman," Cormac said. "Why Jordan if he was an Irishman?"

"Don't you understand, you Irish ostrich? They're connected. The IRA, the PLO, the Red Brigades and Baader-Meinhof gang, Qadaffi and his trained camels. They're funded through the same sources, trained in the same camps, committed to the same goal. As for your IRA, it's not England they hate, Cormac. It's democracy. The old Irish hatred for the English is nothing but a way for these terrorists to get hold of your country. . . . "

"Jumping Jaysus," Cormac said, starting up from his chair with a scrape of wood against Grady's tile flooring. Wells turned around. Pressed into the window behind him was a lumpen face, surrounded by a dirty red kerchief, the huge squashed nose trailing long hairs.

"Miss O'Shea, I presume," Wells said, pushing his

lunch plate away. Hattie was scratching at the glass with her fingernails.

"I think she wants to see us," Cormac said dispiritedly.

"You," Wells said, bowing his head and extending his arm gallantly toward the door. "I'll leave all the Irish women to you."

Cormac stood up with a grumble and ambled outside.

"Hattie . . . Hattie, I'm here." He reached for her hand, still scrabbling at the windowpane. Her head moved slowly to face him. Her watery eyes blinked in bewilderment. "You be the policeman, don't you now?" she rasped. " 'Twas young Morty O'Sullivan told me, so 'twas."

Cormac was surprised at the old hag's lucidity. "That's right," he said softly.

"I can't talk to Morty no more. In league with the devil, he be. All the while acting like he don't believe me." She cupped her hand around her mouth, her face contorted. When she spoke it was in a loud stage whisper. "But that's just for the others to see. He do believe, you know, but the devil's got him all wrapped up."

"Believe what, Hattie?" Cormac asked politely.

"The ghosts. I seen 'em, rising out of the graveyard. Tortured souls." She made the ancient sign of the evil eye with two fingers. "Their arms was stiff, they was, and they was screaming in anguish."

Cormac cleared his throat. He looked past Hattie, hoping to see someone on the street who could extricate him from this conversation. There was no one.

"What were these ghosts saying?" he asked.

176

"You couldn't understand them," Hattie hushed. "You see, the devil cuts out their tongues, he does, so the dead can't tell us what's waiting for the rest of us. But I seen 'em, sure as I be standing here: I be in the woods, picking the foxglove, and they come. They come, Morty."

"I'm not Morty, Hattie."

"You stop 'em, Morty, afore they steal the souls of us all."

"Oughtn't you be talking with Father Ambrose if it's about souls?"

Hattie looked shocked. "The priest? Why, 'twas in his very own graveyard, wasn't it now?"

"St. Benedict's is the only cemetery in town, Hattie," Cormac explained.

"Well, the corpses is alive there, that's all I know."

"I see." From the corner of his eye, Cormac saw Morty O'Sullivan turning the bend into the square. As unobtrusively as possible, he signaled the policeman to rescue him. Through the dirty window of Grady's, he could see Wells sipping his gin and tonic and laughing at him.

Hattie was beginning to wail.

"Oh, and I can hear that terrible lamentation still, and him with his arms all stiff, blood dripping out of the stumps that used to be the poor soul's hands."

"What?" Cormac said.

"Now, are you bothering this gentleman, Hattie?" Morty O'Sullivan said, with a smile. As ever, his uniform was creased razor-sharp, as clean as a nun's bank statement.

"Wait, Morty," Cormac said, but Hattie had already turned her attention to the young policeman.

177

"Cuirim do gheasa troma draiochta ort, aniar chois amhna. . . . "

"Come along, Hattie," Morty said.

Cormac took her arm and shook it. "Hattie. Hattie. Listen."

"May the devil damn you to the stone of dirges, to the well of ashes seven miles below hell," she said, looking dazed.

Cormac shrugged, and Morty gave him an apologetic look and led the old crone down the street.

Cormac watched her go for a few paces, then looked at Wells through the window of the pub. The Irishman tipped his hat hurriedly and took off after the old woman.

"I can take her home," he told Morty.

"But you . . ."

"Never mind. I want to talk to her."

Morty gave him a blank look as Hattie chanted under her breath. "If you say so," the garda said, releasing her arm.

Cormac walked with her but could not get another word out of Hattie until she was well inside the small junk-ridden yard in front of her tiny cottage, deep in the woods behind St. Benedict's Church and cemetery.

Inside the yard, she walked straight and eagerly to a massive pile of smooth stones and knelt before them, raising her arms high into the air while she shouted in Gaelic:

"I bind you by grave injunction of magic, back from the river, back to the river, may you fall in a nettle patch, may savage dogs eat your liver, may . . ."

"Hattie!" Cormac spoke sharply.

She looked up at him, apparently surprised that she had company. "Who be you?" she asked.

Cormac took a deep breath. "My name's Cormac. I'm a policeman. You knew me when I was a boy."

She sniffed. "Don't hold with policemen," she said in English and slipped back into Gaelic to continue her incantation: "One foot on a mountain, one foot in a grave . . ."

"The ghosts," Cormac interjected.

She stared at him suspiciously, and he held on to her eyes with his own, speaking softly and insistently: "His arms were outstretched. Blood was dripping from them where his hands used to be."

"Aye," she whispered with dim recognition. "Coming from the grave, they was. I seen it myself."

"How many were there?"

She thought. "Well, there was the one, tormented soul he was too. And then the one carrying him."

"Two? Two men?"

"Not men! Ghosts, a legion of them, rising like the vapors out of a poisoned lake, they were, coming out of the ground."

"Anyone else?" Cormac pressed.

She looked at him strangely. "You're not Morty," she said.

"No, ma'am. I'm Detective Sergeant Michael Cormac of the Gardai. . . . "

"You're the new priest, ain't you?"

"No, Hattie, I . . ."

"These are for you," she said, ignoring him. She picked up two of the smooth rocks from her shrine and hefted them in her gnarled hands. "I know what you're planning, priest."

179

Cormac's ears pricked up. "What am I planning?" he said quickly.

Hattie smiled slyly. "You think I be an old fool, but I know. You're talking of putting me away, sending me to some prison for the old people."

"Hattie, I told you who I am." He made a motion to touch her but she pulled back, and before Cormac could gather his wits about him, she flung both stones at his head, then dived into the pile in front of her for more ammunition.

"Wait," Cormac shouted, bounding on top of her. One of the stones had missed, but the other had grazed his forehead, and already he could feel the spot throbbing.

"Guim diochair ar an tigh!"

"For Christ's sake, woman, will you come to your senses?"

"Mr. Cormac," said a gentle voice from behind him. He looked up and released Hattie, who had broken into a fit of coughing. Standing behind him was Father Ambrose, looking stunned and depressed behind his glasses.

"Now, Father, it's not been what you're thinking," he said lamely.

The priest knelt beside him and dabbed at the cut on Cormac's forehead with an immaculate handkerchief he pulled from his long black cassock. His hands were stained a dark woody color.

"There's no need to explain," he said. "Most of us in Ardath have fallen prey to Hattie's eagle aim some time or other."

"Devil," she hissed, pawing another rock with ferocity.

"Now, put that down," Father Ambrose said sternly.

"Take me away, you will, will you?" Hattie's mouth twisted ludicrously. "I'll show you. I'm cursing you now, priest, and it's the true curse that'll see you cut by thistles and die roaring. Fifteen days fasting, 'twas."

"Just put down the stone, Hattie."

"You'll not be dragging me away," she said.

Ambrose reached out his hand and took hers. She spat on his, then laughed merrily at the accuracy of her aim. Father Ambrose's jaw worked and his Adam's apple bobbed up and down as he wiped his hand on the grass. Cormac felt sorry for him because he was sure the priest shared at that moment Cormac's urge to throttle the old hag.

"No one is going to take you anywhere if you don't want to go," Father Ambrose said to her gently. "I just thought you might like to see the home in County Clare. The church sponsors it and it's very nice. You'd have friends there."

"I'll have none of you, you with spirits from hell coming right out of your own churchyard."

"I beg your pardon?" He looked to Cormac for elucidation.

The policeman shrugged. "Says she saw someone near the church, Father. Hands were cut off."

The priest turned pale and looked about to faint. Hattie cackled at his frailty. "Blood just a-drippin', so 'twas," she said, savoring his discomfort. "I'm coming for you, he says. Him and his arms all red, and carrying his hands on a string round his neck."

"What?" Cormac looked sharply at her. Hattie

181

clamped her jaws shut in satisfaction. The priest steadied himself on his hands.

"The last part's new to me," Cormac said. "But she almost sounded as if she was making sense with the other stuff."

The priest said, breathlessly, "Mr. Cormac, I'm afraid Hattie is getting to the age where her imagination runs away with her." He looked over compassionately to Hattie. She was staring off into space, her fingers caressing the round stones of her altar.

Father Ambrose looked down as if he were ashamed of himself. "Some of it's my fault, I guess. When I took over after Father Gervaise died, well, Hattie was working in the church then. But I had to let her go. She was doing terrible things in the church, dark masses and defiling the vestments, and I had to let her go. She's been getting worse ever since. And now she's out of control."

Cormac felt the coagulating gash on his temple. "I know," he said dryly.

"And there's Billy O'Glynn, too. First she broke his arm and then she threw the boy into Moon Lake. I'm afraid we just can't handle her anymore. That's why I'm trying to get her into the church home in County Clare."

"Do you think she has any lucid moments?" Cormac asked.

"I . . . I couldn't say," the priest said charitably.

"Damn your rotten soul," Hattie said absentmindedly.

"There, there." The priest walked toward her, put his arm about her shoulders and helped her inside the house. He came back out alone.

"How's she manage here then, by herself?" Cormac asked him.

"The ladies of the congregation take turns cleaning and buying her groceries. Even with that, I hear ghastly stories about what they find inside her cottage."

"Such as?" Cormac said.

"Leaves, rocks, mounds of dirt, that sort of thing. Dead small animals, I'm afraid. She never remembers where any of them come from. I wish she'd go to the home—they have doctors and nurses there and she'd be looked after—but ever since I mentioned it, she refuses to talk to me. My fault for letting her go."

Cormac put his big hand on the frail man's shoulder. "You did what you thought best, Father. That's all any of us can do."

Father Ambrose looked at him and said, "That seems a nasty cut."

Cormac grunted. "What I deserve," he muttered. Together they walked from Hattie's yard, but as they stepped onto the path, Hattie peeked from the doorway, her gnarled hands clutching the doorframe, and she called after him.

"Go to the graveyard at night. When the spirits rise. Go."

Then the door slammed, and he heard the ring of the bolt from inside.

# BOOK THREE

## CHAPTER FIFTEEN

After punching his lights out the other night, what was Cormac, that so-called big deal Cork cop, doing sitting in Grady's Pub with that smarmy Englishman?

Several sheets to the wind, Brian O'Flaherty pondered that question for a while as he sat in a crowd at the end of the long bar, nursing a pint and pretending to watch the television while keeping a sharp eye on the two men.

They seemed to be getting along all right, not what you would expect from two men who had met in a fistfight. Cormac called the Brit "Daniel" and the Englishman called the other man "Michael" and Brian didn't like it. He didn't like their being together. Come to think of it, both of them had been at the castle for the show last night. They hadn't been seated together but that didn't mean they hadn't arrived together, Brian thought shrewdly.

He ordered another Guinness and watched carefully as the day bartender took the price from the large collection of dull silver Irish coins on the bar in front of him. Brian always watched bartenders when they were near his money because bartenders would cheat you every chance they got. Especially if you were the kind of man who occasionally stood the bar for a round of drinks, because then they got the idea that money didn't matter to you and you wouldn't mind if they stole some. That was one of the things Brian O'Flaherty knew. And another thing he knew was that he didn't like that Irish cop getting friendly with the tall, thin Brit. He looked like a faggot with his neat little mustache. Maybe he was. Maybe they were both faggots. Disgusting, Brian thought.

Then Mad Hattie showed up at the window and Cormac went out and talked to her. Then Morty O'Sullivan came along and he talked to the two of them and then they all walked off and the Englishman was left sitting alone at the table.

Brian didn't like him. Even if he wasn't a faggot, he was too damned neat, for one thing. And he didn't belong in Grady's. He just sat there in the corner of the room, sipping his drink, not minding the football match like the other people in the place. No. That wasn't good enough for him. Instead, Daniel . . . what was a Brit—and probably a Prod, too—doing with an Irish name like Daniel anyway? Instead, he was there, looking out the window at West Street, just watching people pass by. He sat there like a slave trader looking for merchandise, and Brian O'Flaherty didn't like it. He didn't like any of it. He didn't like the Brit sitting in *their* bar and not talking to them and sipping his dainty little drink and looking down his long English beak at them, and he finally took a big slug of his Guinness and decided to tell him so.

He approached the table on slightly wobbly legs. He was surprised at that. He could feel that he was a little unsteady, but he didn't think he had drunk that much. Just a few pints, and that shouldn't be enough to bother even a child, for Jesus' sake. It must be that he was tired. He'd been up much of the night hoping that Kathleen would come back after their argument, and she hadn't. If you didn't get enough sleep, sometimes even a few drinks the next day could make you a little weary.

He stood over Wells at the table. The Englishman ignored him, still looking out into the street. Brian cleared his throat and Wells turned toward him, a faint smile on the corners of his mouth.

"What are you doing here?" O'Flaherty demanded.

"Looking out in the street and enjoying myself. Until now," Wells said.

"You're a smart one, aren't you?" O'Flaherty said. "What's your name?"

"Wells," the Englishman said, turning back toward the window.

"Well, Mr. Longnose Wells, we don't like your kind around here. Suppose you stick that Brit beak of yours someplace else?"

"Brian," the bartender called sharply from behind the bar. "Why don't you leave our guest alone?"

"He's not bothering me," Wells said. "So long as he stays downwind."

"Our guest? Our guest?" Brian snapped. "I don't see any guest. I just see another God-Save-Her-Royal-Underwear faggot, that's what I see. I don't see any guest."

"That's too bad," Wells said softly, looking up at Brian again. "I had always been given to understand that the hospitality of you Irish was legendary."

Brian mocked him, twisting his lips in a mincing

189

manner. ". . . always been given to understand, always been given to understand."

He was going to hit him. Brian had decided. He was going to hit him right square in his English face.

"Shouldn't you be saving your pontificating for your performance at the castle?" Wells said.

"I saw you there," Brian said. "I was talking to you, you know. All that I said, that was for you."

"Somehow I gathered that, Mr. O'Flaherty," Wells said. He was smiling, and Brian was going to hit him now. He didn't like that Englishman knowing his name and using it. He was going to smack the smile right off his big-beaked British face.

"What are you doing in town?" Brian asked.

"I'm on a mission for the Queen," Wells said.

"Oh? And what is that mission?"

"I'm scouring the provinces trying to find the stupidest Irishman in the world. It's been a long search but I want you to know you're one of the finalists."

That was it. He was going to hit him and right now. He swung his big fist at the Brit. Drive him right back off his chair and slam him against the wall.

Except that somehow he missed and the Brit wasn't there and the force of Brian's own blow twisted his body around a little and then he felt a wrenching pressure as his arm was jammed up behind his own back.

The Brit's voice was soft in his ears. "I could break this off just as easily, you blowhard. Now why don't you find yourself a nice street corner somewhere to sing rebel songs?"

Brian felt himself being pushed away. He hit the wall face first. His nose hurt. His arm had been released, though, and he shook his head to clear the cobwebs.

190

When he turned, he saw the Englishman at the bar, paying the bartender for the drinks.

"Sorry about this," he heard the Englishman say.

The bartender shrugged. "The sorrow is mine," he said.

They were both against him. Everybody was, Brian realized. Even Kathleen. He growled deep in his throat and ran across the room, his hand raised over his head. He would hit that sneak Englishman in the skull with the side of his fist.

Wells turned just as Brian reached him, and without a word, without even a hint in his eyes that he was going to do it, he buried a fist deep into Brian's stomach. The big young Irishman sank to his knees. The Englishman wasn't smiling now. He reached down and grabbed the neck of Brian's rugby shirt and snapped his head upward.

"If you ever bother me again, I'll break your arms," he said softly. Then he let go of Brian's shirt, and the Irishman rocked back on his heels.

"This ain't over," Brian yelled after him. "It ain't over yet."

Wells was walking out the door, but he stopped and looked back at the young man.

"It's over," he said coldly.

But it wasn't going to be over that easily, Brian vowed to himself as he left the bar. He drank a cup of coffee and then got on the bus that left from the Park Hotel for the hour-long ride to Killarney.


"What are you doing here?" Seamus Dougherty snapped as he came into the hotel sitting room where

191

Brian was waiting. The young man was nervous now. His hands were in his lap and he was sitting on the front edge of the overstuffed chair as if waiting to be scolded.

"There was something I had to tell you," Brian said.

"Besides that you've had too much to drink?" Seamus asked coldly.

Brian rubbed his red road-map eyes. "Aaaah, I had only a couple of pints. I just didn't get enough sleep. I should be sleeping now but I had to come here to tell you this."

"All right, tell me," Seamus said, keeping his voice level, trying to disguise the disgust he felt for the young drunk.

"There's an Englishman in town," Brian said.

"Yes?"

"He's hanging around with a cop from Cork. The cop used to live in Ardath. His name is Michael Cormac."

"Yes, I know. Tell me about the Englishman."

"Well, they're always hanging around together," Brian said.

"Maybe they're nancy boys," Seamus said.

"I thought that too, but I don't think so. I saw them when they met the other night. They had a fight in a bar. But then last night they was both at the castle for dinner and today they was in Grady's talking like old school chums. Something's going on there."

"Why do you think I'd be interested?" Seamus said.

The bluster had vanished from Brian. "Well, I didn't know," he stammered. "I mean, I know you've been around here for a while and I thought that maybe you was doing something here and maybe you'd like to know what's going on in Ardath. It probably being important to you, and all.''

Seamus ignored the little probe for information. "What did you do when you saw them?" he asked.

"Why, I let that Brit know what I thought of him," Brian said, holding a fist up to his chest.

Seamus was standing at his hotel room window, looking out over the streets of Killarney, rolling and hilly before his eyes. "And I'm sure you did a fine job, too," he said without turning.

"Aye, I did that. I told him what I thought about Brits in general and him in particular and told him that the good folks of Ardath had no room for the likes of Daniel Wells and we would be appreciating it if . . ."

Seamus had wheeled about from the window. His eyes burned into the younger man's, and Brian's words dried up. He glanced away.

"What did you say his name was?" Seamus demanded, his voice as dry as sun-parched leather.

"Daniel Wells."

"And you told him off?" Seamus said.

"I did."

"Tell me, what do you think of this Wells?"

"He's a Brit."

"I gathered that," Seamus said. "Do you think he's a policeman? Or a tourist? What?"

"He's hanging out with that cop. I don't know what he is, but I don't like him. But . . ." Nervous now. "I thought you'd want to know he was in town, whoever he is. If that was wrong . . ."

"You did the right thing," Seamus said, almost sweetly. "I'm proud of you." The slight man saw the

193

big young Irishman visibly puff up under his praise. He glanced at his watch. "Now stay here just a minute. I have to be making a phone call."

Seamus strode off into an adjoining bedroom and closed the door tightly behind him. O'Flaherty walked softly to the closed door, making a show of wandering aimlessly, lighting a cigarette, and tried to eavesdrop through the thick wooden door of the old luxury hotel, but he could hear only partial sentences and words.

". . . our old friend . . . I don't know . . . be careful . . . let me know. . . ."

There was silence, and Brian quickly retreated back to the easy chair and settled back into its soft cushions. When he didn't see an ashtray, he flicked the ashes into the cuff of his trousers.

A few moments laters, Seamus reentered the room and said, "Yes, Brian, you did very well."

"Would you like me to go after this Brit?" he asked. "I mean, he could meet up with an accident real easily."

Seamus shook his head vigorously. "Oh, no. What I want you to do is much more difficult," he said.

"You name it, Captain," Brian said. "You know I'm with you. I went to Belfast for you, remember?"

"I remember. I want you to try to keep an eye on this Wells. See if he goes anywhere. Who he talks to, that kind of thing."

"Is he an important man? An enemy of the cause?"

"He might be," Seamus said. "So I need him watched, and you're my man in Ardath."

"I'll report back to you?"

"No, don't do that. It might be too dangerous. I'll contact you."

"All right, Seamus. As you say." Brian didn't know what to do with his cigarette. The ash was long now and he didn't want to knock it on the floor. "Do you have an ashtray, Seamus?"

"No. Use the toilet." He pointed to the bathroom door and Brian flushed the cigarette away.

"I'll be leaving now," he said when he came back into the sitting room.

Seamus nodded. "You've been doing good work, Brian. I'll be in touch."

"This is what I like," Brian said. "I like to do things. I don't just want to go to meetings."

"Don't worry, Brian. You'll have things to do. Big things," Seamus said.

At the door to the suite, Brian turned.

"Seamus?"

"Yes."

"About Kathleen . . . I mean . . ." His voice trailed off.

"Speak up, lad. What about her?"

"Well, you've been sporting with her."

"Did she tell you that?"

Brian nodded glumly.

Seamus shook his head, came forward, and clapped a small, bony hand on the big youth's shoulder.

"Don't be believing it," Seamus said. "Kathleen is just a promising good student and going to be a good member of our group. I see her because I love her mind. She swallows everything up. Aye, I think maybe she's got a crush on me, but it's not like that at all, Brian."

"She said it was," Brian said. "We don't hardly sleep together no more."

Seamus chuckled. "Women," he said with a smile. "You know how they are. Don't you worry, Brian. I wouldn't lay a finger on your woman."

"Thank you, Seamus. I appreciate that."

"Now be off with you and keep an eye on that Wells fellow."

He closed the door carefully after Brian.

Daniel Taylor Wells.

The Englishman's presence raised the difficulty of their plan by a whole notch. It wasn't just that Wells was one of the craftiest and most vicious of the SAS officers hunting down the IRA. That would be bad enough, because members of the SAS—the elite Special Air Services of the British military—were cruel and resourceful. Any time one of them was around was a dangerous time. But the fact that Wells was in Ardath meant even more: it meant that the Irish government in Dublin had been worried enough to ask the British for help. That meant that everyone was nervous and if Dougherty wasn't careful, the Pope's visit might be canceled.

He was glad that only two men, he and one other, knew of their plans. It made leaks that much more difficult.

He walked to the window and looked out over Killarney. How easy it would be to have Wells killed—but that would spoil everything. Surely the Pope's visit would be called off if such a thing happened.

"Damn it," he spoke aloud in the empty room. If that keg of explosives had not blown up on the pier, none of these complications would have arisen.

Not for an instant did he consider canceling the operation. The opportunity was too good. The chance to finally remove the British from Ireland forever did not arise every day.

He would have to put a lid on things in Ardath, to make it look as if all the problems had been solved. The last thing he needed was an army of trigger-happy police looking for an assassin.

As he stood at the window, he suddenly realized how he was going to do it.

He looked down at the street and saw Brian O'Flaherty, smoking another cigarette, walk from the hotel, across the street and toward a bus stop on the corner.

Seamus smiled. Brian had said that he wanted to do something big for the movement. Well, he was going to get his chance. He would do the biggest thing of all.

He would die.

Michael Cormac waited till nightfall, drank a pint of stout with Doctor O'Connor's grandfather, decided Hattie O'Shea was crazy as a bedbug, then went home to bed.

But Hattie's words kept echoing in his mind. *Bloody stumps that used to be his hands.* . . . How would she know? Had she really seen something this time or was this just another delusion of her twisted mind?

A half hour later, he crawled out from under the covers, and cursing himself, he dressed in dark clothes and headed toward St. Benedict's.

He parked his car some distance away and walked. The night was nearly starless, and black shadows of clouds obscured the pale sliver of moon. He found his way to the cemetery behind the dark church and Father Ambrose's darkened workshop and climbed, groaning and puffing, over the fence separating the graveyard from the woods beyond.

There was nothing out of order here. No blood on the walkways, no signs of a recent struggle. Even the graves themselves hadn't been disturbed, and in the glare of his flashlight, none looked as if it had been recently dug.

Cormac felt like a fool for listening to Mad Hattie, who would be considered insane by anyone's standards. He might be as bad as she was. He remembered for a moment that there was a valley in County Kerry called Glan na Galt, the glen of the lunatics, where if you drank from the lunatics' well, you might be cured. Maybe he should go there and bring Hattie with him. Handless ghosts, indeed.

Hoping to all the saints that no one had seen him crawling around the cemetery at night, he struggled over the iron fence again and brushed himself off. He was heading for his car when he heard a sound that made the hair on the back of his neck stand on end.

It was a moan, perhaps, or a feeble call for help; Cormac couldn't be sure. There was a soughing in the trees and the sounds of the night animals, but he was sure the noise had come from the woods. Pulling his pistol from its shoulder holster, he made his way slowly and carefully toward what he thought was the source of the sound in the trees alongside the graveyard.

He heard something breaking, to the right and ahead. He stopped dead still and listened.

It came again, eerie and faint, something that sounded like a voice calling "darling."

Darling?

There was no mistaking now that someone besides

him was in the woods. There were definite footsteps now, the rustling of overturned leaves. Cormac moved swiftly. From the corner of his eye, he could see a figure in the shadows. Planting his feet, he raised the gun to shoulder level and froze. He aimed the flashlight at the trees and flicked it on.

"Hands up," he shouted. "Police."

There was a wild scuffling behind a tree.

"Get out here where I can see you," Cormac called.

"Don't shoot, don't shoot," a faint voice answered.

Cormac's body was on total alert. Suddenly the light seemed brighter, the sounds louder. "Move out. *Now,* damn you."

Two white hands appeared, shaking as if they were mechanized. Then a face, pale and drawn and impossibly old.

"Old Lanigan?" Cormac said.

"Aye, and I'll thank you not to be killing me neither," the old man said with dignity.

Cormac thrust the .38 back into its holster. "Christ Almighty," he muttered, then shouted at the old man: "What the hell are you doing in these woods this time of night?"

"None of your damned business, Michael Cormac. Why, if your da was here . . ."

Cormac grabbed the man's arm. "You're going to have to come to the Garda station, then."

"Hold on there, lad," Old Lanigan wheezed. " 'Twas looking for me cat, I was, and nothing more. Darlin' run off, oh, it must be three months now. Lost her in this very wood, so I did."

"Darling?"

"Her name. And a darlin' she was, too. Makes me

misty just to think of her cold and alone, or worse, what with them nasty boys around town and Mrs. O'Glynn's Billy the worst of the lot.''

"All right, all right," Cormac said. "Just get on home."

"You ain't seen a fat calico, have you?"

Cormac's eyes bulged. "No."

"Well, then, be on my way, then." Old Lanigan tipped two fingers to his bald head. Cormac nodded in return. When the old man was out of sight, he exhaled noisily.

A cat. If Superintendent Merrion got wind of this, Cormac would be demoted to clerk.

He kicked at the ground. Last winter's dead leaves and dirt sprayed high up into the air.

Cormac stopped. Something was wrong here.

He focused the beam of his flashlight on the area at his feet. The ground was covered with leaves and branches, but it was too soft. Propping the flashlight on a rock, he got on his hands and knees and began clearing away the top growth.

It came away easily. Too easily. Someone had deliberately set the ground cover in place, piece by piece. Beneath it was loose, damp earth, tamped into a mound.

He scrabbled at the dirt with his hands, scooping up armfuls of soil. It was fresh, done no more than a week ago, he guessed.

"Darlin'. . . ."

Cormac picked up the flashlight and aimed it toward the road, where the voice was coming from.

"I told you to get out of here, Lanigan," he roared.

He never heard a response. As he was shouting, he

200

heard a sharp crack and felt the blow come from behind. An instant of pain and then blackness. He fell
forward into the loose dirt and never noticed that his
face was pressed against the crumpled knees of a dead
man.

# CHAPTER SIXTEEN

It was dawn when he came to. At first, there was only the searing, throbbing sensation of unwanted light piercing his eyelids; then there was the scent of grass and earth and rotting leaves. His shoulder hurt. It took Cormac a while to organize his body into turning on its back. And all the while there was a droning above him, along with some sense of urgency.

He opened his eyes. Morty O'Sullivan was standing above him, his head impossibly far away, his mouth moving and the droning sounds coming out of it. Cormac held up his hand for silence and Morty interpreted it as a signal for help. He bent over and pulled Cormac to his feet.

"No, no, no, no, no," Cormac mumbled, but he was already upright, his head turning in mile-wide circles.

"Come on," Morty said. "I'll get you to Doc O'Connor."

"Not yet," Cormac managed. He tried to place where he was. In the near distance, past the first trees of the wood, he could see the church graveyard and beyond it, the rear of St. Benedict's Church. The droning sound was coming from that direction, he realized.

He ran his hand over his hair. Leaves crackled in his ears and then tumbled to the ground. On the back of his head was a huge lump, the hair over it matted with dried blood.

"You got a nasty cut, Mike," Morty said, gripping the older man's shoulder just as Cormac's knees began to buckle. "Who did it?"

"Don't know."

Morty kept speaking but Cormac could not understand the words clearly. He forced himself to turn around. There were the woods, yes, he remembered, and Old Lanigan had scared the shit out of him looking for his cat, and then . . . the ground . . . He pushed Morty aside and went on his hands and knees, feeling the sides of the gaping hole not five feet away. The earth had been removed with a shovel.

"Did you see . . . anybody?" he asked groggily, trying desperately to concentrate.

"I just got here, Mike." Then, making the sign of the cross, he said, "Hattie O'Shea's dead."

"What happened?"

"Natural causes, Doc O'Connor says. Mrs. O'Glynn found her this morning when she went to clean. I was just coming over to get Father Ambrose. I saw Old Lanigan before and he was talking about you last night, how you scared the bejesus out of him, so when I saw your car parked down the road, I thought I'd better check. Good thing, I'd say. I bet this has something to do with the business of the explosion." His eyebrows furrowed.

* * *

Cormac fingered the dirt from the hole. A grave, from the size of it. Whoever had hit him must have known he was getting too close.

"I'll be leaving," Cormac said.

"You'd better not drive," Morty said. "I'll take you after I tell Father Ambrose about Hattie." He clasped Cormac's arm and led him toward the workshop behind the church where the droning sound grew into a loud electrical grating.

"Father's working on his cross again," Morty said, smiling.

The cross had been assembled. Father Ambrose was standing over it, polishing it with an electrical buffer. He looked up from his work and smiled when he saw the two men. Then, seeing Cormac's condition, he turned off the buffer and set it aside quickly.

"What happened?" he asked, his voice hushed with alarm.

"He was attacked, that's what," Morty said.

"Stop it, Morty," Cormac said, steadying himself against a workbench. He saw a keg of nails and sat on the wooden lid. "An accident," he said.

"Not bloody likely," Morty said.

Father Ambrose looked at the wound, turning slightly pale. "I'd better get you some iodine."

"A drink of water would be fine," Cormac said. "Anything but your coffee, Father."

Father Ambrose smiled and said to Morty, "Get some water up at the rectory, please."

When he left, Cormac said, "The cross is beautiful."

"Thank you." He hesitated. "Can you tell me what . . . what . . .?" He gestured helplessly.

204

"I was in the woods below the graveyard. Somebody slugged me."

"Back there?" Ambrose's eyes looked puzzled. "Why? What for?"

"I don't know. When I came to, there was a big hole dug next to me. Did you see anybody last night, Father?"

"I'm sorry, Sergeant, not a soul. Do you think this is somehow connected with the explosion?"

"I don't really know," Cormac said honestly. "Maybe kids bopped me." He looked up as Morty returned and handed him a glass of water.

"What were you doing back there?" Ambrose asked. Cormac thought that the priest was smarter than Morty. That was the question Morty should have asked him but hadn't. Maybe being a village garda was just the right job for the young man.

"It was a silly idea, I guess," Cormac said, "but I was thinking of what Hattie told us, about the body without hands, and I . . ."

Morty spun away from him toward Father Ambrose.

"Love of God, I almost forgot. Father, it's Hattie. She died in her sleep last night. I come to tell you so you can give her the rites."

The priest looked stricken. "But I just saw her yesterday." He looked at Cormac. "We both did. She seemed fine."

"She was old, Father. These things happen," Morty said.

"I . . . I'd better go at once." He looked at the two men. "Please excuse me. I'll have to clean up." He gestured with his varnish-stained hands and moved to leave. But he hesitated in the doorway as Morty said, "Michael, they're after you."

"Who's after him?" Father Ambrose said.

"It's got to be the damned Protestants," Morty said, then crossed himself for the priest's benefit. "Who else would be fooling around with explosives down here? And who else would be hitting him?"

"I don't think so, Morty," said Cormac softly.

"Damn it, man, read the papers. The papers are full of their ravings."

Cormac looked up. "What ravings? What are you talking about?"

"A whole string of letters in all the papers. Attacking Catholics, trying to cause trouble. Damn Red Mary Prod bitch."

"Red Mary?" Cormac visualized the item circled in black in the paper Wells gave him to read.

"Somebody with that name is writing letters all over. They caused such a stir that the *Examiner* reprinted the last one and wrote a story about it. It came from down around here but nobody knows who it is. Michael, I tell you they want to kill us all."

Cormac noticed Father Ambrose shaking his head in sad disagreement, then leaving for the rectory to clean up.

"Morty, I think you're getting hysterical," he said.

"I don't like anybody hitting you on the head," Morty said, and Cormac suddenly understood he was watching a full-blown case of hero worship. He put his hand out on the young garda's shoulder.

"Don't worry, Morty," he said. "We'll find out who did it."

"Damn right we will," Morty snapped, then sighed. "Come on. I'll take you to Doc O'Connor."

"It's all right. I feel better."

Cormac drove immediately to the Park Hotel. Wells was eating in the dining room, the ever-present newspaper in front of him. Cormac snatched it out of his hands. "Why didn't you tell me the Red Mary letters were in every paper in the goddamned world?"

"What happened to your head?"

"The hell with my head. Why didn't you tell me about the letters?"

"You could have read them for yourself," Wells said evenly. "Will you sit down and calm yourself? What happened to your head? Don't bleed on the toast. It's the only edible food I've found in this country."

"Mad Hattie. When we saw her yesterday, she was talking about seeing corpses without hands walking around near the graveyard. So I went there last night to see for myself and somebody rang my bell. When I woke up I was lying next to an open grave."

"You're lucky you weren't in it," Wells said.

"It wasn't a real grave. It was a big hole in the ground, but it wasn't there when I got slugged," Cormac said. "Somebody dug it afterwards. I think something was buried there and I got in the way and they knocked me out and then dug up what they had buried."

"Maybe the explosives. Did you see anything?"

"No. Just a hole. Nothing in it that would tell us anything. I talked to Father Ambrose and he didn't see anybody last night, so that was no help."

"You got this from Mad Hattie. I think maybe it's time we tried to talk to her seriously," Wells said.

"Too late. She's dead," Cormac said.

Wells put down his toast. "How?"

"Heart attack, it looks like."

"How very convenient," Wells said. "She talks to you and then turns up dead."

"Maybe," Cormac said, but he did not sound convinced. He reached his fingers to his scalp and felt sticky blood matting his hair.

"I'm going to the washroom for a few minutes," he said

"Are you all right?"

"Yes," he said peevishly. "I just don't want to bleed on your damned toast."

Cormac washed his wound with paper towels in the men's room and when he came back found Wells again perusing the newspaper.

"More letters?" Cormac asked as he sat back down.

"Not today," Wells said. "But they've been running in the press for the last few weeks. England and Ireland."

"All from Maire Ruadh? Red Mary?"

Wells shook his head. "Only some of them. Some of them are 'Protestant and Proud,' and 'Cromwellian' and a gaggle of names, all of them phonies."

He reached into the inside pocket of his jacket and brought out an inch-high stack of mail. "Here. See for yourself."

Wells sipped at his coffee as Cormac looked through the letters. They were all anti-Catholic, anti-Irish, anti-priest, and anti-Pope letters. Something else was obvious.

"Same writer," he said, looking up at Wells.

"Right. All on one typewriter. You can see the light

M. It's the same on all of them. An old American Underwood manual machine. I had my lab boys in London check it out."

"I didn't know the SAS had labs."

"Scotland Yard, Michael," Wells corrected gently.

"Whatever. So somebody down here is writing these letters."

"Don't get it wrong," Wells said. "It's not as if it's a flood of mail. It's just been a slow trickle for the last three weeks or so."

"At least it's not a Catholic writing. That would send you off into your usual anti-IRA frenzy," Cormac said.

"We don't know that. As I said, it's just a trickle of mail. As if someone were, I don't know, just trying to get something on record without making too much of a fuss about it."

Cormac shook his head. It hurt to move it. "You're priceless, you are. You've already got it figured out that some Catholic is writing these letters to throw some blame or something on the Protestants, don't you?"

"I can't deny that such a thought crossed my mind," Wells said. "After all, everybody knows we Protestants are upright and upstanding and would never get involved in a hate-mail campaign."

"Tell the Pope not to come," Cormac said quietly.

"I've tried that," Wells said. "He's coming."

"When?"

"Next Tuesday."

"I haven't heard a word about it," Cormac said.

"That's one small victory for us. They're going to announce it this weekend. And the Pope is just going to come in by helicopter, conduct a mass or whatever it is you people do, make his speech and then helicopter right out again."

Cormac shook his head again and it hurt again. "Not good enough. They're still risking his life."

"You and I apparently are the only two people in the world who believe that," Wells said. "The truth is, Dublin has some kind of hint that the Pope is going to give an antiterrorist speech, and they want him to give it to try to undercut the support for the IRA. So they've got an answer for everything." He mimicked a bureaucratic voice. "Maybe the pier blew up because some explosives were being moved in and there was an accident. But all the explosives blew up. The dead body was the poor fool carrying the explosives. No loss there. So that takes care of the explosives and the exploder. The hand we found that belonged to Winston Barnett, well, nobody can answer that one away, but what the dickens, how much problem can he be walking around without a hand? I'll tell you, Michael, they've got their heads in the sand on this one."

"What about security?" Cormac asked.

"That's not going to be our problem," Wells said. "They're going to send in army and police teams from Dublin. They'll take it over; they'll do everything that's got to be done at the castle or whatever. We don't have to worry about it."

"Good. Then we can keep looking for whatever's out there."

"Seems like," Wells said. "Like a cup of tea?"

"Christ," Cormac muttered. "Tea's not going to solve anything. You're the worst special agent I've ever known."

"How many have you known?"

"None," Cormac said.

"Then I'm the best," Wells said proudly.

"A cold day in hell," Cormac grumbled.

"You said you spoke with a Father Ambrose?"

"That's right," Cormac said.

"What's his full name?"

"Ambrose . . . er, Ambrose Anthony, I think it is. Good God, is he another one of your suspects? Don't you ever stop?"

"No, he's not a suspect, you defensive Irish lunatic. Just an old acquaintance," Wells said.

"This is it for you, you know. You're out of all your fancy British Army clubs now. For sure," Cormac said.

"How's that?"

"You've got two Irish friends. Father Ambrose and me."

"Who said you were my friend?" Wells said, but he was smiling as he said it.

# CHAPTER SEVENTEEN

He had to see Bonning. There was no getting around it. Cormac had put off the visit and tried to avoid it, and he knew why: he did not want to see Moira Pierce again. The pain of seeing her the last time, even for only a few minutes, was more pain than he wanted.

But he was a policeman, and time on his case was running out. It had to be done, memories or no memories.

With his hat pushed back on his head to cover the dried wound, Cormac knocked on the door of the Pierce mansion. Kathleen answered the door and stared at him, blinking, without recognition. She was pretty, Cormac thought, only there was no life in her, no fire. Next to Moira, she was a shiny piece of coal: beautiful, but hard and lifeless. Moira was the same piece of coal, but burning, ablaze with life and warmth and vitality.

"My name is Cormac," he told the young woman. "I'd like to see Mr. Bonning, please."

"He's sick. My mother's with him. You can talk to her when she comes down."

He nodded and looked around.

"Nice house," he said conversationally.

"Yes," she said. "It used to be ours before we became peasants." She turned then and led him into a sitting room filled with Victoriana.

She made no offer of tea or a drink but simply walked away and left him alone there.

This had been Moira's home, he thought, uncomfortable in his skin. This was where she lived with Pierce, fed him his meals, touched him, allowed him to violate her night after night. . .

He snapped himself to attention. The wound on his head began to throb again. He took of his hat and tried to hold his head still, not allowing so much as an eye to wander. He focused on the wall directly opposite him. It was almost literally covered with framed designs of plants, stretching from a foot below the ceiling nearly to the floor, leaving space only for an oak bookcase in the middle.

From where he sat, Cormac couldn't read the titles of the books, but he guessed from their size and drabness that they were reference works. They extended straight across the case, row after row, the line broken at only one point. Cormac squinted at the delicate thing on the shelf, then felt his heart skip when he recognized it.

It was a small porcelain piece, a basket of violets. He got up and went over to it. Its handle had been glued in several places. He remembered putting it together, fumbling with his big ham hands, desperately hoping he had all the pieces. It had belonged to Moira's mother, a Belleek piece she had won in a raffle. It was the only fine thing she had ever owned, and the old lady had wailed after Cormac had crashed into the bureau that held it and the thing lay in a thousand

213

pieces on the floor. He had stayed up all night with a pair of tweezers putting it back together again.

He wanted to touch it, decided not to. But why on earth, he wondered, had Moira given that piece to Mr. Bonning? He felt a rush of jealousy. Having spent so much time with the annoying little china basket, he felt some inexplicable claim to it. And she had given it away, or left it behind when she moved, perhaps, like the balls of dust in the corners of the rooms.

"Michael, you're bleeding."

He turned abruptly at the sudden sound; he hadn't heard her come in. The movement hurt.

"Sit down," Moira commanded. "Whatever you're here for, we've got to take care of your head first."

She was back in a moment with cotton and water and alcohol and iodine and bandages. Cormac submitted to her meekly. He'd had too little experience with ministering females not to be afraid of them. She snipped and dabbed and pasted. When she was through, a wad of gauze was affixed to the back of his head.

"What happened to you?" she asked.

"I slipped and fell."

"You should be more careful."

He did not respond. He wanted to ask about the porcelain violets. Why did you give them away? Was your betrayal complete then? After a moment, he said, "I'd like to talk to Mr. Bonning for a few minutes."

"He's really not well, Michael."

"It's a police matter."

"Surely you don't think he was involved with that business on the pier." She smelled of soap and new bread.

"People in town do," he said.

She reddened. "Then you must believe I'm a whore and a traitor. They say that, too."

"We're not talking about you."

She made a move to touch him, hesitated, then withdrew her hand. The moment had been lost. "He's a fine man."

Like Pierce? he wondered. Fine and rich and about to die. Maybe this one will leave his money to his mistress too.

"I won't be long with him," he said stiffly.

Her hands fell limply to her sides. "Give me a moment to prepare him for a visitor," she whispered.

He watched her go, moving so comfortably through the old mansion. It had been a quirk of fate that she had lost ownership of it, he thought, but not that she had acquired it in the first place. Moira belonged with fine things, although she had never striven for them—never, except for the one desperate strike she had made when she married Lyle Pierce. And why not? She had chosen between a life of drab poverty, the same life she had always known, unchanging, with a house full of screaming, underfed children and hands bleeding and aged from work, compared with the world Pierce had to offer.

In the Pierce mansion, she had known dancing and laughter and wit. At least she had expected to; from what he'd heard in Ardath, it hadn't been a good marriage. But the choice she made was the right one, the practical one. If Cormac hadn't needed her so much, he'd have made it for her. As her friend, he knew it was right that she leave him.

And they had been friends, first and foremost. He

215

could never have conceived of becoming lovers with a woman as beautiful as Moira if he hadn't known her all his life. It had always been Mike and Moira, skinning their knees as they crawled over Cromwell's Bridge. Mike and Moira, two shadows slithering through the gates into Mr. Leahy's pasture where the ancient standing stones bore their strange messages in a code language the teachers called Ogham.

Mike and Moira would go to the stones at twilight, when they thought the ancient gods were most likely to be watching, to dance and chant in a manner they felt suitable for prehistoric heroes. On Moira's insistence, he had once stolen a sheet from the Pierce family's clothesline while the maids were busy inside. Moira's rationale was the the Pierces could afford, better than anyone else in town, to make a sacrifice to the Ogham stones. They tore the sheet in half and draped the halves around themselves toga-style. And there, among the cow pies and chewing gum wrappers, they transported themselves to a time before the Gaels, before the Celts, when a magical tribe populated Ireland and taught it to sing.

It became a ritual for them, the excursions to the stone circles. When they first discovered them, they went every day, but as the years passed, they formalized their indulgence to meetings on the first day of every month. Sometimes they dressed in the old stolen sheet halves, carefully wrapped in oilcloth and hidden in the space beneath the large sacrificial stone in the center of the circle. In the winter months, they stayed wrapped up in their coats, huddled together on the freezing stone, blowing breath onto their hands, reading poetry banned by the church and pretending to

216

understand why anything so dull could be considered offensive, even by Father Gervaise.

There, on the sacrificial stone of the ancients, they pricked their fingers and allowed their blood to mingle. There, they told each other secrets, formally, one a month. The secrets were the climax of their meetings and had to be things that had not been revealed to anyone else.

Moira's secrets were always better than Cormac's. She told him how babies were made. She showed him a picture, borrowed from a cousin in Wexford, of a Japanese warrior, completely clothed and with crossed eyes, copulating with a geisha. She told him about how she had seen Mad Hattie try to drown herself in her well after her first baby died. Later, after all of Hattie O'Shea's children were dead, Moira told Cormac about the ritual of the curse that she had seen Hattie perform. Hattie had piled the smooth stones high and gone to them, gaunt and straight, and spoken the Gaelic words of the curse for three hours.

Cormac and Moira had tried the curse themselves after that, on Mrs. McDougle, Moira's arithmetic teacher, substituting their own brand of prehistoric chanting and a smattering of English for the Gaelic.

The curse backfired. At their next rendezvous at the standing stones, Moira walked with great dignity and sadness to their spot on the sacrificial stone and took Cormac's hand. Her eyes were filled with tears.

"I'm dying," she announced.

Cormac heard the air whoosh out of his lungs. "What's wrong?"

Her voice cracked. "I'm bleeding. It won't stop."

"Where?" He turned her forcibly toward him. "Where?"

"Down there," she said. "Between my legs, in the place of sin."

"Jesus," Cormac said, crossing himself. "Have you gone to the doc?"

She shook her head.

"Why not?"

"I wouldn't have been able to tell you first," she said.

He held her and they wept together, hugging each other close until after the sun had disappeared, and a few scattered flakes of dry snow blew around them. When they got up, Moira left a red stain of blood behind her on the rock.

Cormac touched it. "Can you walk?" he asked.

"I can."

"We'll go to your house, then. I'll tell your mother. Then I'll get Doc O'Connor."

"No. If you tell, she'll stop me from seeing you. I'll say I fell."

Cormac thought. "She won't believe you. Will she make you leave the house?"

Moira shrugged eloquently.

"I'll come by the back gate at midnight. Have your things ready."

"Where will we go?" she asked.

"We'll find a place. I can work. And I'll see that a doctor looks at you if I have to beat one senseless."

He kissed her for the first time then, and that soft, sweet dying kiss was so beautiful that they both sobbed afterward, hanging on to each other as if to tear them apart one would have to rip their very flesh.

"Midnight," he said brokenly.

At eleven he was at the gate, and he waited.

She appeared a half hour later.

"I'm not sick," she whispered, her eyes frightened. "It's normal. Women do that. Every month."

"Moira . . ." She was trying to spare him.

"It's true. I swear it. My mother told me."

"Every month?"

"That's the long and short of it," she said.

"God," Cormac said, thrusting his hands into his pockets. Women were the strangest creatures on earth.

"But you know what's weirdest about it all," Moira said. "It's called the curse."

"But you're not cursed. Not if it's normal," Cormac said.

"All women are. That's what my mother said. We've got to bear the children and clean the floor and mend the clothes and cook the meals. There's no rest for us. And all because we were born women."

Cormac didn't know what to say. "Seems a shame," he finally blurted.

"You wouldn't understand." She stared at him for a moment, her eyebrows pinched together, her gaze accusing him.

"What have I done?" he asked bewilderedly.

"We're different, that's all. You get to be a man."

She turned and ran back into the house, leaving Cormac out in the snow.

She didn't come to the stone circle in March. Or April or the rest of the year or the next. When Cormac saw her at school or around town, she was distant to him, saying she was busy. And she was. When he walked by her house, she was always sweeping or hang-

219

ing laundry or caring for the younger children in her family.

He began to watch the other girls in his class. One by one, they dropped out, not to marry, but to tend the farms, to care for old unmarried relatives, to replace a lost father or mother. They were drones, bred to work. Physical maturity was the end of childhood for them. When they did marry—late, usually, and often they did not marry at all—they launched themselves into childbearing, a baby a year, to carry on the endless work that brought no comfort, no profit. And those children, too, would play for a few years, and then work, and then bear more children.

Cormac got his first job at fourteen, packing groceries for Mr. O'Sullivan at the market. Morty was born shortly after he started. He was the O'Sullivans' seventh child. Mrs. O'Sullivan was not yet forty years old, yet on the occasions when she came into the store, with toddlers hanging on her skirts like ribbons on a maypole, she looked like a beaten old crone, fat and sour and gray, her hands as red and cracked as a fisherman's.

Cormac, too, had little time for play anymore, but his lot was not the constant work of his sisters. His father, a handyman and carpenter of sorts, would take him to Grady's on evenings when he was not working and slip some Harp into his cider. The young Cormac would listen while the old men sang and swapped stories about the Black-and-Tans and shouted slogans about the coming freedom of Ireland, all while they were in their cups.

They never got beyond the slogan stage. In those days, the IRA was no more than a memory of long-ago patriots who had wrested the land with their own hands from the bloody jaws of the British. These men, the heroes, honored themselves, for want of a wider audience, in the pubs at night, drinking themselves stuporous and longing for the days of their youth, when the enemy was tangible, armed and known. Now, they struggled against time itself, against their own frailty and helplessness. They had done their job well and most of Ireland was free, in a self-governing republic, but it had meant nothing. Ireland had not changed. It was still poor and contentious and sad. The Republic had gained independence only from England's money. In the North, where the British still prevailed, there were factories and jobs; in the South, hopelessness and hunger.

It didn't seem fair. And so they shouted their slogans at the North. The British were still at fault. A new army would one day rise up to cut the cancer of oppression away from the suffering body of Eire.

Michael Cormac listened to them and listened to the younger men pick up the same old slogans and listened to the boys his age as they began to take up the chant, but he could not join them. His spirit was not part of theirs; his spirit was with Moira. She, not Ireland, was the only friend, the only cause he wanted, but she had shut herself off from him.

He ached for her. The parts of him that she had filled with her secrets and quick laughter had been voided and left unfulfilled. He grieved for her every day, and at night he would touch himself and burn with the imagined touch of Moira.

When he was fifteen, on the last day of June, he went to her house. Moira was bringing peat into the house from the shed. Her apron was covered with peat residue, stained brown. When she saw him, she looked quickly at her hands and hid them behind her back.

"Yes?" she asked, lifting up her chin. There was an old woman's furrow between her eyes, a pain behind the defiant greeting.

"Moira, I'm not good with words," Cormac said.

She looked away. "I've no time for them anyway."

"Why haven't you come?" he asked.

"Because it's useless. The dreams are useless, all the fancy ideas we had. . . ." She wiped a lock of hair off her forehead. Her fingers left a dark smear. "They were games for children we were playing. There's no time for them anymore."

"I love you, Moira. I've been waiting to tell you. Every month, I've sat up there in the snow and the rain begging you in my heart to come. I need you so much."

She lifted her face to him and her eyes filled with tears. She opened her mouth to speak, then closed it and walked back to the shed. When she came out, she was carrying an armload of peat bricks. She wouldn't look at him.

The following day was the first of the month. After school, after work at O'Sullivan's, he trudged up the hill and through the woods to Mr. Leahy's pasture. The farmer had built a house on the far side of his holdings since the time Moira and Cormac first started going to the standing stones, so his presence was no longer an obstacle after suppertime.

He waited on the sacrificial stone, cross-legged. He waited, hardly moving, until long after there was any possibility that Moira would come. But still he waited.

And near ten o'clock, when the sky was finally surrendering to darkness, she came.

There were no words between them. She ran to him and he held her, touched her, kissed her with an urgency he had never felt before, not even in the shameful dreams at night, not ever in his wildest imaginings. And she came loose before him: her hair, unbound and gleaming like new copper, her clothes stripped away effortlessly, as if they were useless encumbrances. He hurt at the sight of her, so beautiful, her breasts as big as a woman's, her belly all cream and impossibly tender, a newborn thing. She came to him willingly and he raised her onto the sacrificial stone, the altar to their childhood and their love, and she allowed him to love her with all his hot clumsiness, and she loved him in return. It was all he had ever wanted. It made up for everything, the years without her, the pain of her absence, the nagging necessity of adulthood and responsibility. She obliterated them all.

"He'll see you now, Michael."

Cormac looked up, startled. Moira was standing in front of him, a woman past forty, her hands as red and rough as Mrs. O'Sullivan's had been. And yet Cormac could feel only the same desperate need he had when he'd waited inside the stone circle for her, biding his time, hoping the ancient gods would send her to him. And they had.

She didn't need to ask him what he was going through; she knew. She understood, the way she had always understood him. She smiled, and he wanted to collapse in her arms, erase the empty years between them.

But there had been too many years. And she knew that, too.

"Will you show me his room?" he said stiffly.

She nodded. They walked out of the sitting room, away from the porcelain violets, and up the curving stairwell into the darkness of the upper floor. With each step, they left behind, unspoken, the rag ends of their past and their dusty dreams settled behind them like ashes.

# CHAPTER EIGHTEEN

The odor of sickness and medication permeated the room.

Bonning was a wasted hulk of a man, lying in a huge Victorian walnut bed. From his features, Cormac could see that he had once been a handsome man, and for some reason that angered him. Had Moira lain with him in this bed, too, as she had lain with Lyle Pierce?

"I regret that I can't get up to greet you," the old man said. His voice was still deep and resonant. Cormac had heard that he had been a lawyer. That might account for Bonning's accent-free English.

"That's all right. I'll try to keep this brief."

"On the contrary. Stay as long as you like. I don't get many callers."

Moira asked them if they wanted some tea, then left.

"Mrs. Pierce tells me I'm a suspect in the pier bombing," Bonning said, forcing a thin smile.

"We haven't got any suspects yet," Cormac said.

"I suppose then that the only foreigner in Ardath is a natural start."

"You've been here some time, haven't you?" Cormac asked.

"Almost eleven years. The wink of an eye in an Irish village."

"You're a citizen?"

"Naturalized. My parents were from London. They moved to Dublin in 1916, when I was five years old. There was a lot of turmoil in Ireland then, after the Easter troubles, and a desperate need for physicians."

"Your father was a doctor?"

Bonning nodded. "Harley Street and all that, very comfortable and not at all some Republican rabble-rouser, but he couldn't stand by while waves of typhus were destroying Ireland. He's always loved the country, and my parents spent a lot of time here. I became an Irish national just before I took the bar examinations."

"Were you active in politics?" Cormac said, and instantly regretted the use of past tense, as if Bonning were dead and they were talking about a history that had already been concluded.

But the old man seemed not to notice. He said, with a twinkle, "Oh, I've defended a few old Fenians in my day."

"You sided with the Irish?" Cormac said.

The old man scowled. "I sided with the law, Sergeant Cormac. I still do. Without law, we might as well move back into the caves and wrap ourselves in animal skins. I defended men and women who had been mistreated under the law. Not people who don't believe in the law." He was breathing heavily, his eyes fixed on some invisible point on the blanket. Then he looked up, and his eyes flashed.

226

"My wife was killed by terrorists, you know. She was shopping in Harrod's in London in 1973 . . . it was Christmas week . . . and the IRA launched a mass murder." He brought his hand to his mouth slowly and held his lip before he could go on.

"They bombed everything—stores, streets, the stock exchange. My wife was just one of thousands of victims, dead, injured. The police had them laid out in rows, like damaged goods at a distress sale. Children, babies still with their pacifiers, their limbs gone, old women obscenely violated by the most impersonal kind of killer . . ." He covered his face. His hands shook. "I had to pick her out."

"I'm sorry," Cormac said. The words seemed so inadequate. He had said the same words to Wells about his missionary brother. "It was a terrible tragedy. . . ."

"It was a crime!" Bonning slapped his hand on the bed and sobbed openly. "Not a tragedy, a crime. Not politics but murder. And it's not for Ireland anymore. These aren't old Sinn Fein fighters, rising up out of famine and despair against an oppressor nation. These are killers, baby burners who've desecrated the name of Ireland as an excuse for wholesale slaughter. I guess I always hoped that Ireland would escape somehow, but we couldn't. The killers are here, they're everywhere."

He closed his eyes, took a long, noisy breath and rested back on his pillow. "I just came back from Nicaragua," he said softly. "I'll never go back. The streets are covered with blood. It's too familiar a sight for me."

He laughed then, a dry, mirthless chuckle. "What

have we come to that violent death is an everyday occurrence?''

Perspiration glistened on his forehead, and Cormac could hear his raspy, shallow breathing. He knew he was wasting his time.

''I'm sorry for your misfortunes, Mr. Bonning, and I'm sorry I bothered you.''

''For the record, young man, I don't know anything about the bombing of the pier or the body that was found. Nothing.''

''Thank you, sir. I'll be going now.''

''Leukemia,'' the old man said weakly. ''Makes me tired sometimes. I shouldn't even have seen you, but I did it for Moira. She's a very special woman.''

Cormac only nodded; he could find no appropriate words with which to respond.

''I imagine she's forgotten telling me about you,'' Bonning said.

''About me? When?'' Cormac said.

''Long ago.'' The old man swallowed with difficulty and reached for a glass of water by the bed. Cormac helped him drink. ''She's so lovely and such a good woman. I couldn't understand why she hadn't remarried after her husband's death. She was in such dire circumstances, after all, with a gambling husband who lost everything.'' The old man squirmed, and Cormac helped make him more comfortable against his backrest of pillows. He let the man talk. The memories Bonning was recalling seemed to alleviate some of the old man's pain.

''When I purchased this relic, I offered her anything she wanted from this house, but she refused all but a few pieces of furniture, and not the best pieces, at that.

228

She told me that this part of her life had been cursed. I thought she meant her widowhood, but when I tried to console her, she told me she'd loved a man.'' The old man laughed outright. ''But it wasn't her husband!''

The old man's laughter set him to coughing. ''Can you imagine that, saying something so bold to practically a total stranger? I liked her right away.''

Cormac flushed. ''Moira's always been an honest one.''

''She said it was someone named Michael who had gone off to America. Frankly, I thought you rather a cad for not taking her with you, but then I did a little snooping around town—that was before my illness—and found out the circumstances. Then, a few years ago, we heard this Michael had come back to Ireland. Moira was dropping things around the place for weeks. But Michael never came back to Ardath for her. Until now,'' he said with a wink.

''I'm here on police business, Mr. Bonning.''

''Ah, yes,'' the old man said tiredly. ''We live on our pride as long as we believe life is inextinguishable. It's not until we see the end before us that we realize what a foolish thing pride is when it stands in the way of what we really want.''

''I'd better be going.'' Cormac said.

He thanked the old man and walked quietly toward the door. His hand was on the knob when he turned back for one last question: ''Why did she give you the porcelain violets?'' He felt like an idiot asking, and as soon as the words were out of his mouth, he regretted them.

''Porcelain . . . oh, yes, the broken basket.''

"It doesn't matter," Cormac said.

Bonning wheezed out another tired laugh. "You're so alike. That's what she said too. She got rid of everything in here, you know. All the doodads and bric-a-brac Irish women are so fond of. The church wagon came to cart it all away for the poor, and I saw her standing there, watching it all go, holding the little cracked basket of violets. I asked her if it was something special, and she told me that it didn't matter anymore. She dropped it in the trash, and I retrieved it myself. I thought she'd thank me for it later, but she never has. She just pretends it's not there. Prideful woman."

"I suppose so," Cormac said, embarrassed

"Michael?" the old man said.

"Yes?"

"Don't wait too long." Bonning's voice seemed to gray visibly. Then he sank back into his pillows.


Kathleen Pierce saw him out. She was just plain sullen, Cormac thought, with suspicions in her eyes where dreams ought to be in one so young. Cormac thanked her and left, but as he was walking from the house, he saw that the side door to the garage was open, and something inside it caught his eye.

It was a large garage, big enough for three cars. Only one vehicle was parked in it now, a ten-year-old Mercedes in perfect condition. But Cormac wasn't interested in the car. From his perspective near the gates, he had seen something shiny beneath the car's bumper. It had been no more than a chance reflection of light, but he had caught it. And now, on his hands and knees, he saw exactly what it was: an old Underwood typewriter.

He searched his pockets for his notebook and tore out a sheet of paper. Then he dragged the typewriter out. There was no dust on the keys. He inserted the paper, typed "Maire Ruadh" on it, then the alphabet. He got as far as T when he heard footsteps. He tore the sheet from the machine and pushed the typewriter back under the car.

"What are you doing in here?" Moira asked sharply.

He felt suddenly ridiculous, squatting down on the cement floor. "Nothing, really. Just looking. A fine automobile."

"What do you expect to find here?" She was angry, but the question was genuine.

"I don't know. Something's going on in Ardath that's beyond me."

He knew it was wrong to tell her. So much had happened since their days of sharing secrets. Moira might even be part of the horror he was investigating. But Moira, Moira, he thought, how good it feels to talk to you again.

"Not Mr. Bonning, certainly."

Cormac didn't answer.

"He's dying, you know."

He turned and walked away quickly. He was almost running as he passed through the gate to his car. Still the scent of Moira filled him with hopeless dreams.


When she saw the trail of dust left by his car as it moved away from the mansion, along the lake road,

Moira looked beneath the car and was surprised to find a typewriter there.

She dragged it out. It was Mr. Bonning's and had been in his study the last time she had seen it. It had been in the study for years, collecting dust beneath a pile of papers on ferns and mushrooms that the old man had intended to organize into a book before his illness. She realized she had not seen the typewriter in the study for the last two weeks, but had not until this moment known it was missing from its usual place.

She pulled a piece of paper from her apron pocket. It had been crumpled into a ball, left behind accidentally in a corner of Kathleen's room.

To the Editor:

Isn't it about time that we true Irishmen put an end to the Irish Republican Army and the ignorant parochial views they represent? The truth is the British presence in the North is the most civilizing thing that ever happened to Ireland and if the IRA Catholics don't like it, they should all be blown up with their own bombs. Ditto for the head mackerel-snapper in Rome too.

> Signed, A Thinking Irishman
> (Therefore a Protestant)

Moira had read the note in total confusion, a feeling that was intensified when she looked around Kathleen's room at the IRA posters calling for armed warfare against the British. Her daughter's bookshelves were filled with IRA propaganda and violence tracts, all purchased over the past year. If those reflected Kathleen's views, why was she writing an anti-Catholic, pro-British letter to the newspaper?

When Kathleen had returned home, Moira had waved the note in front of her.

"What's this mean?" she demanded.

The girl was cold as ice, her eyes narrowing, her chin rising. "How dare you snoop in my trash." She held out her hand for the discarded page.

Moira slapped the hand away. "What are you involved in?"

"Nothing to do with cleaning or farming, Mother. It wouldn't interest you."

Moira slapped her face this time, hard. The young woman didn't flinch.

"That's always your way, isn't it?" Kathleen said. "First you beat me and then send me to pray among the nuns, asking God for forgiveness, so that your paltry soul can be relieved of a little guilt. Well, it's not going to work. He's not going to forgive me, because He doesn't exist. And He's not going to forgive you either."

"You're talking like a lunatic," Moira said.

"Am I? Don't you think I know why you've always hated me?"

"I haven't. . . ."

"You had to marry my father because you were already pregnant. Excuse me—Mr. Pierce. He wasn't my father. I don't look anything like him. Who was it, really? The butcher? A traveling tinker?"

"Stop it! Stop it this minute!"

"Am I a gypsy's daughter, Mother? Or just the spawn of a drunken evening with some stranger in an alley?"

233

Moira cried out, the sound choking in her throat.

"What has that paper got to do with me?" Kathleen said, gesturing to the fluttering piece of paper Moira held. "I'll tell you. It's my life. It's something for me to live for besides your embarrassed silences because of your hate for me."

"That's not true. I've always loved you."

"You hated my father. You drove him away."

"I didn't."

"You couldn't stand being an inferior in your own house. That's why you left all our things behind. You made me live like a pauper just to rid yourself of him."

"You've got it all twisted, Kathleen."

"Why don't you take that paper to the police? Turn me in. Maybe you'd be rid of me for good."

"Is it that bad?" Moira asked in a whisper.

"How bad would you like it to be?"

Kathleen laughed. Moira ran out of the place, blindly, running away from her own home, the small cottage near the gates.

From the cottage behind her, she could hear her daughter laughing.


"Excuse me, do you know where I could find Father Ambrose?"

The slight man looked up from his workbench. Daniel Wells could see the Roman collar, half hidden by the plaid shirt.

"I'm Father Ambrose," he said, rubbing his hands on a stained rag. "What can I do for you?"

"I think we had a mutual friend. My name is Daniel Wells."

"And who would our friend be?" Father Ambrose asked.

"The Reverend Robert Wells. A Methodist missionary. You were together in Nicaragua?"

Father Ambrose's eyes widened. "Daniel Wells? Of course. You're Major Wells."

"Retired now," Wells said. "You remember we talked on the telephone. You were in the hospital."

"I certainly do. God. Was it eight years ago that poor Robert . . ."

"Died," Wells finished. Father Ambrose flushed.

"Come in, Major," he said. "Have some coffee." He was still rubbing his hands on the stained cloth.

"None for me, thanks." Wells sniffed. "Is there an awful smell in here?"

"I'm using special varnishes on the cross. They smell like spoiled pork," the priest said. "I'm sorry I can't offer you a chair."

"No need," Wells said, waving vaguely. "The cross is beautiful." He nodded at the highly varnished wood that was taking form on a workbench built across a pair of sawhorses.

"For the church," Ambrose said. "It's become a long-term project, I'm afraid." He paused. "You know, I was too much in shock. I don't think I ever had a chance to tell you what a tragedy Robert's death was to me."

Wells said quietly, "My brother was a good man."

"He was. Just thinking about it still makes my blood boil. How that maniac broke into our little mission and killed those children . . . and poor Robert."

"He was a maniac then," Wells said bitterly. "Today he's a hero of the Nicaraguan revolution. The

Great Lazarus, killed in action against the fascists. They have a plaque raised to him in the capital building.''

"He's dead?" Ambrose said.

'Yes.''

"A hero?" Ambrose's voice shook. "A terrorist butcher of babies. A killer of defenseless clergymen. I often think . . . I don't know how I managed to escape.''

"You were lucky, I suppose," Wells said.

"Lazarus hit me and knocked me unconscious. When I came to, the building was burning. It was filled with smoke and I couldn't see anything. I yelled but I got no answer, so I figured everyone else had escaped or left. It was only later that they found the bodies. You have to believe, Major, how crushed I was. If I had known, I never would have left them behind.''

"I'm sure of that, Father," Wells said.

"You know, Robert often talked about you. His little brother was his favorite.''

"Thank you. That's comforting to hear," Wells said.

"I left Nicaragua right after that. I just couldn't take any more violence. First Belfast, then Central America. I suppose I should have been able to handle the strain, but . . ." His lips tightened. "You said Lazarus is dead. How?''

"After I talked to you, I took leave from the army and went to Nicaragua. I was working with the military there to find him. We got a tip that he was hiding out in a shack in the mountains. I went in and blew it up.''

"And he died?''

"Yes. We found his body in the rubble, or pieces of it anyway. He was blown apart."

"God forgive me," Ambrose said, crossing himself, "but it was no more than the animal deserved."

They were interrupted by a knock on the garage door. When Father Ambrose opened it, a man stood there, holding a package wrapped in red paper.

"Package for you, Father. Just arrived at the post office. Thought I'd deliver it myself."

"Thank you, Liam," Father Ambrose said. He started to take the package from the man's hands.

"Didn't know what it was. But the package said to be careful. Electronic equipment, so I thought it might be real important."

He seemed unwilling to let go of the package.

"It is," Father Ambrose said. "It's my new radio that I've been waiting for."

"Oh." The man seemed disappointed. "I'll be giving it to you then."

"Thank you," the priest said. When the man turned and left, Ambrose closed the door behind him and put the red package on a shelf in the corner of the garage. "Ardath is a nice place, but it has the nosiest mailman in the entire world." He turned back to Wells. "So what brings you to town, Major?"

"I'm just an ordinary civilian now," Wells said. "I was going on holiday when a friend asked me to give him some help looking into the bombing at the pier."

"Sergeant Cormac?"

Wells nodded. "And when Michael told me you were in town, I thought I'd stop by to say hello and to thank you for your kindness in talking to me back when . . . in Nicaragua."

237

"Any Christian would have done the same," the priest said. "I thought you might have trouble getting the news from someone who spoke only Spanish. I just thought it was the right thing. Have you found out who destroyed our old pier?"

Wells shook his head. "Not a clue," he said. "I've stopped looking. I'll be leaving in a few days."

"And Sergeant Cormac?"

"Him, too," Wells said. "I think he'll be happy to get back to Cork."

Father Ambrose said, "I guess there's not much to see in Ardath when you've been living in the city."

The two men talked for another half hour as Father Ambrose told Wells of his missionary brother's last days alive.

"He loved working for the Lord," the priest said.

"I know he did. He'd planned on being a missionary since we were boys," Wells said. He stood up. "Thanks again, Father. I'll be off now. Just one thing, if I may."

"Anything."

"I'd appreciate it if you'd not tell anyone that I was a military man. I'm just another Brit on holiday, and I'd like to keep it that way."

Ambrose smiled. "Just what Sergeant Cormac said. Don't worry, Daniel. I'll not say anything."

# CHAPTER NINETEEN

*Calm down,* Moira told herself. *Sit.*

But she couldn't force herself into one spot, so she cleaned her already immaculate kitchen, set the kettle to boiling and fixed herself a cup of strong tea. When it was all organized, when the exterior trappings of her world were in order, she sat down on one of the wooden kitchen chairs and took the scrap of paper from her pocket. Slowly she opened it, dreading the contents she already knew.

*The head mackerel-snapper in Rome too.*

What was Kathleen thinking? What?

*Blown up with their own bombs.*

What?

Politics were an alien thing to Moira. She couldn't understand her daughter's interest. And what the letter said: Kathleen sounded like a Protestant!

She hunched her shoulders together and rocked, squeezing her eyes shut, trying to wince away the shame of her own ignorance. But the truth was there. Kathleen had spoken it. Moira didn't know anything outside her own small existence, her pots and pans and washing, her little hurts. And she *had* been an inferior with her own family. Lyle Pierce had despised her. He knew she had nothing to offer him but peasant comforts. Perhaps if she'd loved him . . .

No. She'd behaved as if she loved him, but she couldn't do more than that. By the time she'd married Pierce, she'd had no heart left to give. Michael Cormac had taken it all.

And Kathleen knew about Michael. Not the name, certainly, but she knew that Lyle Pierce wasn't her father. The girl had always had an adroit mind, but she had never brought it up before, never questioned her mother. Instead, she waited for the time when her knowledge would hurt Moira most.

It had been a clever way of avoiding talking about the heresy she had written.

*Easy, easy.* She rocked, her hands covering her face.

Kathleen knew.

Moira had never told anyone, had never confessed it to Father Gervaise, had never told Cormac. Indeed, she'd even kept the knowledge from herself as best she could, telling herself it was only her imagination that Kathleen had Michael's chin, Michael's nose. But it had eaten away at her. Kathleen was her unabsolved sin. Her penance for not loving Michael the way she should, but for casting him away instead.

She had been a coward. She hadn't told Michael at the beginning. She was working in the Pierce mansion, cleaning. It had been her job since the end of her school days. It had been humble work, but Pierce paid well. Too well, she thought, until she began to hear the stories about the goings-on in the household.

Lyle Pierce was a manufacturer from Limerick, still a bachelor after forty-eight years, a self-made man from the city slums who had accumulated more wealth than most people in Ardath could ever dream of. He was a stocky man with a barrel chest and short bowed legs, but he never lacked for women. His parties, which he called soirees, were the scandal of the village, and no respectable townspeople would allow their daughters to attend them. The censure didn't bother Pierce in the slightest. His women came from Cork, from Limerick, from Killarney, from neighboring taverns. Loud dance music—not Irish music either, Brigid O'Glynn would whisper excitedly, but American rock and roll—would shriek from the house at all hours of the night, carrying as far on a strong breeze as the parish hall.

Father Gervaise, according to Mrs. O'Glynn, had even gone to see Pierce himself to ask him to curtail the music on Wednesday nights when the Rosary Society was meeting in the hall. Pierce had told the priest outright that he was not a churchly man and didn't care a hang whether he bothered the Rosary Society or not.

Moira's father had been against her working there, but she reasoned with him. Her mother already had the cancer deep inside her and was wasting away. Soon she would have to enter a hospital, and Doc O'Connor hadn't even been paid yet.

"Da, listen to me. Money's money and I'm the only one of the children old enough to work."

"True enough," her father said, "but your good name'll go bad in that house."

"Maybe my name, Da," Moira said, "but not my soul."

Eventually, reluctantly, he had agreed.

Michael Cormac, too, had reservations. "You can't

241

work there," he said, astonished that she would even consider the thought. "Nobody's ever lasted more than three months in that hellhole. Why, Old Lanigan's wife left after two days."

"I'll manage, Michael. My ma's not well. I need the work."

"I've got work," he said stubbornly.

"And where will we live then if you pay for my ma? We've no home of our own yet. You said yourself it'll be two years before we can think of marrying."

He had no answer for her and she had left it at that. She went to work and said nothing when one bleary-eyed woman or another would stumble down the staircase, long after Lyle Pierce had left for his factory, wearing the same disheveled clothes she had worn the evening before. She never talked about the bottles of gin and bourbon she cleared away each morning. She didn't mention the stack of ladies' garments left behind, which she washed and placed neatly in a drawer in one of the guest rooms.

She even kept quiet about Pierce himself, who often touched her when it was not necessary, brushing against her breast or her leg. She never acknowledged him, and he never pursued her beyond those few surreptitious touches.

And so she was utterly surprised when he asked her to marry him. It happened shortly after his breakup with a woman named Carla.

Pierce had been seeing a lot of Carla in the past few months, and when she visited the mansion she left mementoes of herself everywhere: a golden slipper, a negligee trimmed with white fur. One day, a portrait of an attractive blonde woman with stylishly painted eyebrows appeared on the piano in a silver frame. The real article appeared one morning, sitting at the breakfast table when Moira let herself in for the day.

"You must be Moira," the woman said with a British accent that wasn't quite real, and showed her teeth in a smile that wasn't quite warm. "I've made a list of things for you to do. Actually, it's a calendar for the week. On Monday, you'll do the washing. On Tuesday . . . well, you can read it for yourself. You know how to read, don't you?"

Moira said that she did and tried to keep from giggling at the way Carla said "ek-tually."

"Fine. I'm sure Mr. Pierce will appreciate everything being just so."

Little by little, Carla's clothes began to appear in the closet. They were beautiful things, pearl-studded and shimmering, taffetas and satins and fine wools. There were minidresses, still terribly daring for Ardath, and small boots in impossibly bright colors that came up only to the ankle. When Pierce and Carla were both out, Moira would hold the clothes up to herself in front of the full-length mirror and wonder how it would feel to own such finery, to live in a magnificent house, to sip champagne from cut crystal and dine on partridge.

Then, during a frantic afternoon that Carla spent shouting at delivery men, eight trunks and what seemed like a hundred boxes came, and Moira realized that Carla was moving in. Without marriage.

Everybody in Ardath pressed Moira about the details, but she only told them that Mr. Pierce's business was his own. She wasn't delighted about working for Carla and her little lists, but it didn't really matter. She had almost served out her two-year sentence. Soon she would marry Michael Cormac and become mistress of a bed-and-breakfast house. Michael had just been appointed to the garda, so his future was secure.

But whatever bliss Carla found with Lyle Pierce was short-lived. Within a month, the atmosphere in the house began to tense. Carla would sleep until late in the day, emerging woozy and snarling with black mascara smeared under her eyes. Sometimes, Mr. Pierce would surprise Moira by coming in early in the morning, changing clothes quickly and rushing back out in a fresh business suit. On one occasion, she found three decanters of liquor smashed to pieces by the living room fireplace.

But the moment of truth came sometime around the middle of August, when she let herself in at seven in the morning and the two of them were already screaming at each other in the master bedroom. Already or still, Moira couldn't tell which. The argument was so bad that Moira toyed with the idea of leaving, but then Pierce might think she was unreliable, she reasoned. As unobtrusively as she could, she set about working, but it was impossible not to hear them, even in a house as large as the Pierce mansion was.

"Damn chippie, spreading your legs for anybody what buys you a drink," Lyle Pierce screamed.

Carla's shriek matched it in volume. "Well, why shouldn't I? You do. Every night. Fuck, I don't even see you half the fuckin' time, it's so busy you are pumping strange."

Moira raised her eyebrows while she polished the silver. She'd had an idea Carla wasn't any British aristocrat. Her mouth proved it.

"You don't talk to me like that in my house, God damn it," Pierce shouted.

"You fucking bastard, I'll say . . ."

There was a scream—rather studied, Moira thought—and a crash. She must have hit the knick-knack shelves. Then Carla came thundering down the stairs, weaving, arms flailing, eyes wide and bloodshot. "Call the police," she shrilled. Moira picked up Carla's coat from the divan, where it had been thrown the night before, and Carla snatched it, thumping away in her high-heeled marabou slippers.

A moment later, a car engine revved up in the driveway. Twenty minutes after that, Mr. Pierce sauntered downstairs, looking dapper as ever, threw down two glasses of straight gin and left for the office.

It was two weeks later that he sat down with Moira.

"Now, you're a good girl and you've already been taking care of me for years," he began.

"Yes, sir?"

"Well, it's high time I settled down. I've sown all my wild oats, so to speak." He tried to laugh and cleared his throat. "You're very beautiful, Moira."

"Thank you, sir," she said, confused.

"And I can give you a very comfortable life."

She sat stock-still, not daring to move, willing herself not to so much as blink.

"Now, you must understand that I dislike discord," he said.

She nodded.

"And that I'm too old to change my ways. That is, I have certain . . . friendships I may want to maintain. You wouldn't insist upon taking all my time, would you?"

"I'd like to know what you're talking about, Mr. Pierce."

He scowled. "Damn it, I'm talking about an arrangement."

She was silent.

"Well?"

"I see," she said.

"You see what?"

"An arrangement. That's what you might call an affair, isn't it?"

"Well . . ." He stretched out the word to an absurd length, contorting his face around it. "There are financial considerations."

She stood up. "I'm a maid, Mr. Pierce, not a whore. The pay is less but the work is easier." She picked up her handbag and walked out.

The next day, a dozen roses appeared at her family's house.

The day after that, Pierce himself appeared. Her father, despite his low regard for the man's moral character, was obviously awed by the presence of so rich a man in his house. He offered him a drink, which Pierce declined. He stayed only a short while, talking of small things, but when he took his leave, he left behind an envelope addressed to Moira's father. In it was five hundred pounds.

Her father showed it to Moira. He held it trembling in his hands as if it were a talisman of black magic. "What did you do for this?"

"It's what he hopes I'll do, Da. But I've quit him." She snatched the money. "I'll take this back tomorrow."

Her father's eyes followed the envelope. "A lot of

money, that," he said softly, lifting a nearly empty bottle of whiskey to his lips. "What's he want for it?"

"You can guess. He called it an arrangement."

"Aye. A fancy woman." He turned toward the bedroom. In the hushed stillness, his wife's breathing sounded like a bellows.

Moira took his hand. "Don't worry, Da. We'll manage."

Her father threw back the dregs of the bottle. "It's a gift, isn't it?" he said, too casually. He met Moira's eyes for a moment, then failed.

"You know that when a man gives money to a woman, it's never a gift," Moira said.

He pulled back the corners of his mouth tightly. "All right," he said, barely audible.


She was at Pierce's door in the morning. It was raining in a spray of mist, a soft Irish morning when only the tops of the hills were visible, the valleys blanketed in white fog. Moira dressed in a plain blouse and skirt, her head covered by a shawl like an old woman on her way to church. When Pierce answered the bell, she extended the envelope to him.

"You don't have to stand out in the rain, girl," Pierce said, opening the door to her.

"There's no need for a visit. Just take your money and I'll be on my way."

Pierce's features set hard. "You don't have to treat me like a bloody criminal."

She let the envelope drop to the floor inside the door and turned away. He grabbed her arm roughly. "Don't you turn your back on me," he said between clenched teeth. When she tried to push him away, he yanked her inside. With a cry, she fell to the floor.

Facing her, he closed the door with a soft click behind him. "Don't you throw money at me like I was a beggar," he growled. She skittered backward, still on the floor, but he caught up with her before she could get up. "You're the beggar, not me. Understand? No farmer girl looks down her nose at me."

She saw him coming, the bowed legs in their expensive trousers standing over her, the menacing head high above. Then the hand swooping down, tearing off her blouse, buttons flying, fabric ripping, a ragged fingernail gashing through the skin of her breast, a streak of blood.

She cried out. The hand came down again, backward across her face. Then he was on her, the nightmare beginning. He smashed her head against the carpet in rhythm.

"Nobody . . . spits . . . on . . . my . . . money," he chanted over and over as he forced open her legs.

"Nobody . . ."

She vomited.

"Nobody . . ."

"Nobody . . ."

When it was over and Pierce toppled from her onto his side, she scrambled up, frantically pulling the sides of her blouse together, small noises issuing involuntarily from her throat.

"Oh, God, I'm sorry," the man said, rising uncertainly to his knees. His trousers were still open. He closed them hurriedly, his face contorted in shame and disgust.

"Get away from me!" she screamed. She picked up

248

a small crystal lamp behind her. It had been on, shedding a dim light in the gloomy room. Now, as Moira grabbed it, the plug pulled from the socket and it went suddenly dark in her hands, leaving them in shadows.

"Please, Moira, I didn't mean it," he pleaded. He was still on his knees, his back bent in miserable supplication. "I've never done anything like this before. I'm sorry. Sweet Jesus, I'm sorry."

Like a stalked animal, she moved cautiously toward the door, the lamp in one hand, her shawl in the other.

"I'll make it up to you, Moira. I swear I will. I swear it." Lyle Pierce hung his head and whimpered.

When she reached the door, she tossed the lamp onto a chair and ran out. Inadvertently, she kicked the white envelope with Pierce's money inside it out onto the portico.

It was raining harder now. Pierce came outside. The rain pelted him. Moira's running figure receded into the white fog. At his feet, he saw the envelope, soaked, the outline of new bank notes showing through.

# CHAPTER TWENTY

Mercifully, her father was in the fields when she got home, and Moira ran into the bedroom she shared with three sisters, took off her torn clothes and stowed them under her pillow. She would mend them later, but for now, she couldn't bear to look at them.

She got dressed again, dried her hair and looked in on her mother. The woman's skin was gray. Once portly, wheezing with ruddy flesh, the person in the bed was little more than a skeleton lying in deep folds of excess skin.

"Are the children in school?" The voice was a croak.

"They are, Mama. They're fine."

"And you?" The woman ran her tongue over parched gray lips. "How are you doing, darling? I don't get half a chance to see you anymore. Can't seem to stay awake much." She smiled, but the pain in her pulled her mouth crooked.

Moira stood stock-still, waiting for the urge to run into her mother's arms to pass. She couldn't cry now. Her mother already felt more pain than anyone could stand; she didn't deserve Moira's as well.

"I'm fine too, Mama," she said quietly, gently stroking her mother's face.

She saw Michael Cormac that night. Her father barely acknowledged him as he bent over his glass of whiskey near the radio.

He's a good man, Moira thought of her father, staying home night after night to keep vigil over his dying wife and a houseful of children. The children were normally Moira's job, but the older girls were nearly as competent at managing things as she was. There was little for her father to do during all the lonely nights he spent listening to the woman in the bedroom struggling to exist, except to drink himself into a painless euphoria.

He had been drinking a lot. Since they had gotten the news that his wife's illness was terminal, Moira had watched him depend more and more on the bottle of whiskey that always stood near the radio.

"I'm going to buy him a case of Paddy's," Cormac said as they walked through the rain down West Street toward the small fifty-seat movie house. "God knows, that poor devil can use it, and it'd be better on the stomach than that cheap whiskey he's pouring into himself now."

"He'd like that," Moira said, grateful that there was no line for the film. She didn't want to talk, didn't need the strain of having to act as if everything were normal. She wanted to sit in the dark, silent and alone.

The movie was a silly American comedy with Doris Day. She barely saw or heard it and squinted in annoyance when the lights came on.

"Feel like sipping a pint at Grady's?" Cormac offered.

"Thank you, Michael, but I think I'd better go home."

"You don't look well, Moira."

For a moment, she thought of telling him, blurting out the whole hideous story.

But the thought of reliving it, even in words, was just too humiliating, and she said lamely, "I'm fine, Michael."

*Christ, I am not fine!* she wanted to scream. *I have been fouled and cheated and shamed.*

"Just a touch of cold," she explained.


All the lights in their house were on.

The children were all awake, waiting up excitedly. Her father sat in his chair, the whiskey bottle nearly empty, his eyes glassy and bright. He smiled, red-nosed and twinkling, when he saw her. She hadn't seen him smile in over a year.

"What is it?" she demanded. "Why are the babies up?"

"It was your Mr. Pierce," he said, pointing a bent finger vaguely in the direction of the door.

"What did he want?"

The children giggled and her father's eyebrows shot up. His glazed eyes tried to focus. " 'Tis a miraculous thing, Moira. He won't take back the money. He came to bring it back. But that's not the half of it. . . ."

"We'll not keep it," she said, hearing the shrill come into her voice. She extended her hand. "Give it to me."

"But, child . . ."

"We'll not keep his bloody money, I said."

His eyes met hers. He drained his glass, stood up slowly, then threw it against the wall, shattering it. The children scurried in all directions.

"We will keep it, by Christ," he said hoarsely.

Moira sat down, her hand covering her eyes.

"And he's not talking about any 'arrangement,' girl. He's an honorable man, so he is. It's your hand he's wanting, Moira. Your hand in marriage."

The words struck her like a hammer blow. She reeled back in her chair, not daring to speak.

"It's true. Marry him and he's promised two hundred quid a month for us here plus your mother's expenses."

Moira watched her father's face, animated, hopeful. He had already sold her out.

"Don't you see, darlin'?" He clasped her hands. "Your mum can be treated in a proper hospital. We can buy some equipment for the farm. Maybe even another horse for the plowing. The girls will have a dowry when it's their time to marry. The boys will have a start in life better than I did."

Through the wavy vision of her tears, Moira looked toward her mother's bedroom.

"Aye, and if the Lord chooses to take her away from us, we can buy a fine tombstone and a coffin of black teak. . . ."

Moira ran from the house. Her heart was threatening to burst inside her. The rain slapped her like angry hands. She ran to Moon Lake and screamed, screamed for the life she knew she had lost, and at last wept the tears she had held back for too long. They were the consolation of defeat and all the truth she would ever be permitted to feel.

The next morning, she went into the village and waited outside the garda station for Cormac to emerge.

When he did, handsome as a soldier in his uniform, her heart ached. Her feet wanted to run. She would not marry Pierce. It was her life, after all, and she would not live it with a rapist. If she could not be bought for five hundred pounds, why was it that it was all right to capitulate when the price went higher? Her life was with Michael Cormac. It always had been.

But her feet didn't move and her heart stopped thumping. It was necessary and she knew it. Her mother, dying in terrible pain, her poor father, sleeping each night beside the diseased half-corpse, helpless, the horror inside him numbed only by the whiskey; the children, destined to be servants the way Moira herself had been. This was the only chance any of them would ever have.

It was God's will.

Moira stilled her hands and raised her face for Cormac to see.

"Darlin'," he called, striding over to her. He gave her a big kiss on the sunny street. Passersby smiled. It was only Mike and Moira, inhabiting their own universe again.

"Michael . . ." She faltered. The words were too ugly to say.

His brightness vanished. "Go on, now. What's wrong?"

*What's wrong?* She wanted to throw her head back and laugh. Well, it's this way. As a woman, my life belongs to everyone but myself. But then, we already knew that. Therefore, we'll just have to make a small adjustment in our plans. . . .

"I'm going to marry Lyle Pierce."

He stared at her, blankly at first, then with the small uncomprehending smile of disbelief. "What?"

She tried to speak but nothing came out. Her mouth felt soiled. She hung her head, feeling an ache spread between her shoulders.

"Why?" he asked in a whisper.

"Isn't it obvious?"

He touched her shoulder, began to grip it hard. She felt the anger in his hands. Then, as if he were physically tearing himself away from her, he shoved her away.

She staggered backward a few steps. There was nothing but pain on Michael's face. She couldn't bear to see it. She focused her eyes on the ground, on his shiny shoes. The shoes faced her momentarily, looking as if they were about to leap into space from compressed tension, then spun around, leaving whirls in the dust where he had stood. They clacked away smartly, deliberately.

She was sure she would not see him again.


One of the children was sent to inform Lyle Pierce that Moira accepted his proposal of marriage. The following night, he paid a visit at suppertime. The children were all scrubbed and turned out in their Sunday best, and even Moira's mother, weeping for her daughter's good fortune, was dressed and seated in a proper chair.

Moira remained in the kitchen for most of the evening, cooking, serving, washing up. In the sitting room, unconcerned with her, Pierce announced his plans for the wedding. A fine wedding it was to be, the grandest Ardath had ever seen.

When he was gone, her mother's shiny, pain-filled eyes were smiling as Moira and her father carried her into the bedroom. "I'm so happy for you," she said, stroking her daughter's face.

"For all of us," her father said, giving Moira a wink in tribute to a job well done.

Moira kissed her mother's forehead. "For all of us," she repeated.

The wedding was scheduled for the second of October. On the first of the month, Moira went to the standing stones where she had spent so many girlhood evenings with Cormac.

It was a lonely place without Michael. But then, she supposed, Michael didn't belong with her tonight.

She had no illusions about Lyle Pierce. He was marrying her for penance, buying his way out of guilt. Perhaps he thought it was time to have children. If he loved her, at least, there might be some chance. She could learn to live with a man she didn't love, if he loved her. But Lyle Pierce felt no more for her than he had when she worked as his housemaid. A certain lust, soon satisfied, an unthinking appreciation for the orderliness of his home; the unobtrusive companionship of a woman. But there would be nothing more. He still saw Carla. Little secret was made of that, and already the village women were whispering and clucking in sympathy when they saw Moira. And, she was sure, there were others besides Carla. Pierce gambled, too, and was away from the mansion for long stretches of time.

At least, she thought, she wouldn't have to see him every day. It was as small a consolation as her tears.

She sat on the big center stone, brushing away shards of broken glass. In the years since she had first become a woman there, guided by Michael's awkward, loving hands into maturity, the standing stones had become a meeting place for young boys, village toughs who brought their whiskey there and spent the evenings pretending they were men.

But that was in summer. It was becoming chill now, the twilight descending earlier. The broken glass was dust-covered, already becoming part of the earth that would bury and forget everything but the ancient stones themselves.

She held a piece of glass in her hands.

*Buried.*

There was a way out. A moment of pain, and then escape. She felt the sharp edge: it drew blood. Was the neck the best place? The wrists? The spot below the heart? Where had the ancients bled their sacrifices as they lay on this rock? Had they screamed with the pain? Had they thrashed about in violent outrage that their lives would be ended to appease some dim, unseeing god?

Or had they, too, wanted to die?

"Hail Mary, full of grace, the Lord is with thee," she whispered. Sweet Jesus, I know it's a sin to take your own life. I know the punishment is eternal damnation to the fires of hell. But isn't this eternal damnation, too?

"Blessed art Thou among women. . . ."

The glass dropped out of her hand. She jolted to her feet. There was someone in the woods nearby.

The boys, drunk on their whiskey and ready to prove themselves men? Another rape? Oh, Jesus, Jesus.

"Holy Mary, Mother of God, pray for us sinners . . . us sinners. . . ."

It was Michael.

He stopped short when he saw her, then began to turn away.

"Please stay."

He didn't move. "I didn't expect you here."

"Yes, you did," she said and ran to him.

He opened his arms to her, a reflex; she belonged in them, they knew every crook and fold of her. And she filled them comfortably, easily.

"Don't hate me, Michael," she sobbed.

His voice was choked. "Moira. . ." There was no more to say.

She kissed him and for a moment the chaos of her life was gone. He was balm for her, sweet medicine, and as long as she could hold him to her, she would be safe, she would be loved, there would be no damnation, no penance, no hell.

They loved each other again, familiar now, hungry, desperate for the pleasure of each other's secrets, knowing it was the last time, sweet and bitter and needful. Soft and silent. Forever.

There was no forever anymore.

"I'll always love you," he said, and the words so

hurt her that she could only gather up her things and run away like a thief, leaving Michael on the sacrificial stone.

Where he belonged.

Michael left Ardath the next day, the day of Moira's wedding. She remembered the celebration as a noisy blur, full of annoyance and confusion. Only later, when she lay in her marriage bed with Pierce, did she feel the terrible loneliness for the first time.

It would never leave her after that, although the birth of Kathleen nine months later helped alleviate it for a while. She was an impossibly beautiful baby, amusing and bright. And she was Michael's. Moira was sure of it from the first moment she had studied the baby's face and watched her movements. It was a secret, the last one, and the best. Kathleen was a part of Michael that no one could take away from her.

Moira's parents died, first her mother, then eight months later, her father. Moira's siblings were scattered among relatives to whom Pierce gave lavish gifts to take the responsibility of rearing them. Kathleen was all Moira had left.

But something was wrong.

It had never occurred to Moira, even as a possibility, but it had happened somehow: Kathleen preferred Pierce to herself. The little girl loved him with a delirious joy. As soon as she could talk, she was babbling away with him, bringing him leaves from the garden, giggling at the faces he made. When he left on one of his trips, Kathleen would sulk and refuse food. Her

259

father was the center of her life; Moira, an attendant standing on the periphery of her consciousness.

As Kathleen grew older, the preference became even more clear. Father was a man of substance. Mother had been his housemaid.

Penance. Moira couldn't remember when she had first realized it, but gradually she accepted the idea as fact. Kathleen was her punishment for desecrating the sacrament of marriage. The man she loved would never know his child, and the child would have no love for either of them. It was God's will.

Penance . . .

She rocked. The piece of paper from Kathleen's room was on the table, its wrinkles smoothed out by Moira's hands. Her tea was in front of her, cold and untouched.

She understood. Penance could not be avoided. It had to be paid.

She stood up, walked to the gas stove in the cottage, held the paper to the burner, turned on the flame.

Then she walked outside to the garage. Kathleen was gone now, but the typewriter was still under Mr. Bonning's car. She dragged it out and carried it to the edge of Moon Lake, where the cliffs met deep water, and dropped the machine into the lake.


On her way back to the cottage, she saw the afternoon newspaper on Mr. Bonning's doorstep. Unthinking, she picked it up and took it inside for him.

Halfway up the stairs to his room, she read the headline:

**RUMOUR POPE TO VISIT ARDATH**

*Ditto for the head mackerel-snapper in Rome too.*

"Oh, Jesus," she gasped.

She left the paper there, on the stairs, and ran outside. She needed air. She needed to think. It couldn't be true. She was seeing problems where there were none. There must be something she didn't understand. Kathleen wouldn't, couldn't . . .

Penance.

Pray for us sinners.

Feeling sick, she ran back into the cottage.


On a hill overlooking the Pierce mansion, Daniel Taylor Wells stood up, folded his small binoculars, replaced them in his jacket pocket and walked toward his automobile.

# CHAPTER TWENTY-ONE

Moira dried her eyes quickly on her apron when she heard the knock. It took a few deep breaths to calm herself.

Nothing, she told herself. A salesman or a child asking for money, perhaps a tinker or a gypsy. Nothing she couldn't handle.

But the man in the doorway was no gypsy. He was tall, light-haired, good looking and impeccably dressed.

"Sorry to bother you, ma'am," he said cheerfully, edging a little closer to her. Moira pressed the door slightly more to the closed position. "My name is Wells. I'm touring Ireland in rather an unplanned manner and I'm looking for a place to stay."

"I've seen you in town," Moira said.

"Ah, then perhaps you know I've been staying at the Park Hotel." He shook his head. "Terrible place. I've had nothing but problems since I moved in. It simply won't do." He brightened. "So as I was passing by here, I noticed this beautiful old place and wondered if you'd have a room to let in it."

Moira looked toward the mansion. "That is a private home," she said.

The stranger named Wells straightened up in surprise. "Is it? I thought it was a hotel."

"I'm afraid not," Moira said, starting to close the door.

"My error. Sorry, ma'am," Wells said. He left, but a minute later, Moira heard knocking on her door. It was Wells again.

"Pardon me. My car's overheated and I can't turn on the engine for a few minutes. Could I trouble you for a glass of water while I'm waiting?"

She looked him over carefully, finally decided he was harmless enough, and stepped back to let him enter.

"Lovely place," he said, examining the walls, his hands clasped behind his back.

"I'll get you your water."

When she came back with it, he was standing in front of an old picture of Kathleen. "Is this your daughter? Or you as a child?"

"My daughter," Moira said. The photograph had been taken on Kathleen's fifth birthday. She was a confection of lace and smiles. She had belonged to Moira then. "It's an old picture," she said. "She's twenty-two now."

"That's hard to believe," Wells said, looking straight at her with unashamed admiration. Moira felt her throat constrict. It had been so long since she'd been around a man, she hardly knew how to behave. She pictured for a moment how she must look, her hair bedraggled and her nose red, then felt foolish for the vanity. She hadn't been anything more than the Widow Pierce for more than ten years, the aging matron who took care of Mr. Bonning. Even Cormac hadn't responded to her in any way other than as an old acquaintance whose passage through time he found vaguely unsettling.

Wells took the water. "May I sit down?"

"I . . . I'm sorry. Please do."

"I hope I'm not disturbing you."

She shook her head, silent.

He seemed to grope around for a topic, then said, "I say, we seem to be in for a little excitement around here."

She looked at him as if suddenly surprised to see him. "I'm sorry. What did you say?"

"The Pope may visit Ardath. I read it in the press. Quite an event for a town this . . ."

Moira bolted out of her chair into the kitchen.

Through the open doorway, Wells called out, "I beg your pardon. Did I say something wrong?"

"No, not at all," she said, busying herself with the kettle. "Actually, Mister . . ."

"Wells," he said, smiling. "Daniel Taylor Wells."

"Yes. Well, to tell the truth, Mr. Wells, I was in the middle of some things when you came. I hope you understand."

He set down his glass. "Of course. I'm sorry. It was very rude to foist myself on you."

"Not at all. But if you don't mind . . ."

"Please. It was I who imposed," he said.

"You were really welcome," she said, then burst out laughing. So did he. "Politeness can be an endless ritual, can't it?" he said.

She laughed until she cried. And when she cried, she sobbed, uncontrollably, gasping and hanging onto the refrigerator as if it were a block of floating wood on an otherwise empty ocean. She cried until Wells held her by

264

both arms and shook her into sanity. She stopped, he held her, and she did not object.

"Whatever it is, it can't be that bad," he said.

She didn't answer him. But she did not let go, either. Whoever this man was, whatever he wanted, he had given her a moment of peace. He had stopped the crack in the dam before it burst into fragments.

"Maybe you'd like to tell me about it?" he said.

She shook her head. "There's nothing to tell. Just the sentimental memories of an aging woman."

"Now *that* I know is fiction," Wells said.

"It's quite true," she said, pulling back, wiping her hands across her face, ashamed of herself. What had gotten into her that she would bare her soul to a perfect stranger?

"Perhaps we could argue about it over dinner?" Wells said.

"I don't think so."

"What harm? I'm really quite civilized," he said.

She shook her head again. "No, really, Mr. Wells."

"Daniel. Or Dan. That's more Irish. And you're Moira."

She sniffed, startled. "How did you know that?"

"I saw you in town also, and I asked," he said, his eyes smiling. "Please see me later," he said, touching her chin. "I won't pry into your troubles. Really. I'd just like some company."

"Well, I'll be over at Grady's tonight," she said. "They're having music. Perhaps I'll see you there."

"No, 'perhaps' about it," he said.

The door to the small cottage opened and Kathleen rushed in. "What in bloody hell have you . . ." she began, then froze at the sight of the Englishman.

265

Wells acknowledged her with a nod. "So this is the little girl in the photograph."

Moira bunched her apron in her hands. "Kathleen, this is Mr. Wells."

"Get out of here," the girl ordered him.

"Kathleen," Moira said breathlessly.

"We don't need any pig Brit Protestant cop in our house or our town."

Moira fluttered closer to Wells. "I'm very sorry. I don't know what's the matter, but perhaps . . ."

"I'm on my way," Wells said cheerfully. He bowed to Moira, then to Kathleen. Kathleen gave him a look of disgust and left the room.

Sitting inside his car, he faced the cottage studying it.

"Interesting," he said aloud. "Interesting."


Moira waited for the door to close securely before she spoke. "How dare you talk to a guest of mine that way?" she hissed.

"He's an English cop, Mother. How well do you know him?"

"I'm asking the questions here. How do you know he's a policeman?"

Kathleen sighed. "He is. So ask yourself what a man like that wants with you."

The hurt burned through Moira like a poker in her flesh. "I'm more worried about what he might want with *you,*" she said.

"Bloody Christ, he's the gestapo. The Queen's secret army against us."

"How do you know?" Moira screamed.

There was silence. In the tension, in the crackling understanding between them, in the daughter's hatred, which was palpable, no words were necessary. The fewer spoken, the better.

"What'd you do with the typewriter?" Kathleen asked evenly.

"I threw it in the lake." Moira sank heavily into a chair, her hands buried in her hair as if she were trying to keep her skull from exploding. "Michael Cormac was typing something on it in the garage. He's a detective, Kathleen. He knows . . ."

"You showed him my letter," Kathleen accused savagely.

Moira spoke softly, her eyes closed, trying to get through the nightmare. "I burned the letter. But he found the typewriter. It's Mr. Bonning's, Kathleen. What was it doing in the garage?"

"I couldn't very well use it in Mr. Bonning's study, could I?" she snapped.

Moira's hands balled into fists and pounded down on her knees. "Damn it, I don't like the tone of your letter. Did you know about the Pope?"

"No!"

"Your letter talked about him. Why all that hatred for Catholics? You're Catholic, too."

"The letter didn't have anything to do with the Pope." Kathleen paced in angry circles, wringing her hands.

"Then what *did* you mean?"

"Christ, I don't know. I was told . . ." She caught herself.

"Who told you?" Moira said softly.

Kathleen went into her room to the closet where her costume for work hung. Moira followed her. "Who told you what to write?"

267

Kathleen draped the dress hurriedly across her arm. "Don't talk to the Englishman," she said, brushing past her mother.

"Who told you?" Moira shouted.

Kathleen slammed the front door behind her.


The two men sat on a bench in a park at the edge of the lake. When Cormac heard what Wells said, he took the bronze medal from his inside pocket and rubbed it nervously with his thumbs.

"The Pierce woman is involved in this," Wells said.

"Moira?"

"The whole family, I think. Moira threw the typewriter into the lake. Your guess was right, by the way. It matches. All that hate mail was typed on it. I've sent the sample to the laboratory, but there isn't really any doubt."

"You said the whole family," Cormac said.

"I'm just guessing. But I met the daughter, what's her name, Kathleen? A nasty thing. And her boyfriend, that singer, O'Flaherty. Ever since I had an argument with him yesterday, he's been trailing me around. He was loitering outside the hotel this morning. I lost him to go up and take a look at the Bonning house. Then when I got back to town, he was after me again. I lost him to get here."

"I didn't know you two had an argument," Cormac said.

"Nothing to speak of," Wells said offhandedly.

"You saw Moira dump the machine?"

"She tossed it off that promontory that overlooks the lake."

"I know the spot," Cormac said.

"Good. I want you to try to recover the machine tonight."

"They'll see me."

Wells shook his head and smiled as he saw Cormac fingering the medal. "No, Moira is going to Grady's. I told her I might meet her there." He noticed Cormac's eyebrows raise when he said that. "And Kathleen should be working at the castle, so if Bonning's really bedridden, there won't be anybody around. And if he isn't, that's good to know too. Put that medal away. It makes me nervous."

"All right," Cormac said with a sigh and returned the medal to his pocket. "One thing though. Why do we need the typewriter?"

"Truth is," Wells said, "that nobody has broken any law by writing letters to a newspaper, and we don't have any way to connect them to the explosives. But if we have the typewriter, at the very least, we can haul them all in for questioning."

"Say, next Tuesday?" Cormac said.

"Right. The day the Pope arrives. They can be in for questioning and they can watch the ceremony on television if they like. I don't think I'll want them around loose when the Vatican delegation is here. Just a precaution."

Cormac looked reluctant but nodded. "Did you and Kathleen have words?" he asked.

"Nothing, aside from her calling me a pig Brit Protestant cop. I think that was the exact phraseology."

"It sounds about right to me," Cormac said.

"But how'd she know?" Wells asked.

"There's something else I don't understand," Cormac said.

"We can add it to our long list of things. What is it?"

"She attacks you as a Protestant Brit pig rat bastard."

"Don't get carried away," Wells said. "She wasn't *that* exuberant."

"Anyway, if she hates you for being a Prod so much, why would she be writing those attacks on Catholics in the newspapers?"

"I don't know," Wells said. "Maybe she's not writing them. There's the old man. Bonning's a Protestant and hates the IRA enough to stir up some smoke against Catholics. He's not too sick to write letters. Or maybe Red Mary is Kathleen's mother."

"Not if this has anything to do with terrorism," Cormac said. "Moira Pierce is no terrorist."

"You sound very sure," Wells said. His eyebrows lifted.

"I used to know her," Cormac said, embarrassed.

"People change," Wells said.


Moon Lake smelled of kelp. At night, the moonlight reflected the buds of seaweed bobbing out of the water's surface. Cormac rowed the small boat carefully to the area below the promontory. In the boat was a three-pronged grappling hook attached to a length of thick rope.

There was a sound above him, near the house. A car. Its headlights reflected on the water, far out into the lake. Cormac pulled in his oars and floated silently, listening. The car's engine died. A car door opened and closed with a click.

He maneuvered the boat as close to the mud wall of the lake as he could. He could feel, rather than hear, whoever was above him on the promontory. Whoever it was was coming closer.

Then a powerful flashlight shone directly on him.

"Mike?" It was Morty O'Sullivan's voice.

"For God's sake, get that thing out of my eyes," Cormac growled.

"What the blazes are you doing here?" Morty asked, scrambling down the soft cliff edge to the water. "I got a report about some lights here. Guess that was you."

Cormac cleared his throat. "I've got to retrieve a typewriter," he said.

"Can't it wait till morning?"

Cormac knew he was trapped. "I don't want to involve more people on this than I have to," he said.

Morty took a step closer to the boat. "That's why you didn't tell me?"

"Right."

The young policeman smiled. "Well, since I know now, I might as well help."

Cormac broke with relief. "Come on in."

They dredged the area for more than an hour, coming up with nothing but seaweed. "Damn kelp is thicker than soup," Morty said, untangling the grappling hook for the hundredth time. "My hands are cut to ribbons from this rope."

Cormac's hands were blistered and bleeding too. "Serves us right for not wearing gloves," he said, tossing the line overboard again.

"Serves *you* right, you mean," Morty said. "You planned this subterfuge. I'm just a helpful volunteer. Hold on, I feel something." He jerked gently on the rope.

"Trust it to be in the deepest part of the blinking lake," Cormac muttered.

271

Morty leaned over the boat, straining, his arm submerged to the elbow. "I feel it . . . something . . . it's caught, Mike. I've got it."

"Bring her up. You need help?"

"No," Morty said between clenched teeth. "You stay there so we don't tip over. You city fellows are all alike."

He grunted as he pulled on the rope, curling it behind him in wet coils, the boat tossing wildly with each movement. "Here it comes," he shouted.

Out of the water arose a mass of kelp balled up in the grappling hook, plus something else that caught the moonlight. Cormac shone Morty's powerful flashlight on it. It was the typewriter, leaking from every corner. "Easy," Cormac said. "Easy . . ."

"Jesus." There was the scrape of a shoe, a crazy pitch of the boat, and a blur of movement as Morty, the line still in his hands, went overboard.

"Christ Almighty," Cormac mumbled, crouching to the stern end of the rowboat. Morty's head bobbed up a few feet away, covered with strings of seaweed.

"Lost it," he sputtered. "I tried to hang on, but my feet are all tangled in this stuff."

Cormac extended his hand to him and pulled him aboard. "It's all gone then," he said.

Morty looked at his bleeding hands. "I'm sorry, Mike."

Cormac stared at the water. "I suppose there's no use going back for another hook."

"I tried to hang on, Mike."

"Well, you didn't try very bloody hard, did you?" Cormac snapped.

Morty looked up, startled.

"Do you think this stunt is going to get you some pussy from the Pierce girl?"

"What?"

"I wasn't born yesterday, Morty. There've been other cops straddling two sides of the law for a woman."

Morty looked past Cormac to the Pierce mansion on the cliff. "Kathleen? Is she . . ." He let the words die in his mouth.

"Go on. Pick up your oar and row," Cormac said. "There's no point staying here now."

Morty rowed, his jaw working silently as they approached shore.

"I've got a thing to say," he blurted finally.

"Forget it."

"I won't, Mike." The young man's eyes were bright with anger. "You've good as accused me of dropping that machine back into the lake on purpose."

Cormac stuck out his chin, daring a rebuttal.

"Well, it ain't so. Whatever you think Kathleen's got to do with anything, I believe you're wrong. But even so, I wouldn't cover up for her or anybody. I'm a policeman, Mike Cormac, and damned proud of it."

They pulled up to shore and Morty stepped out and sloshed to dry land. "And I'm a damned good policeman, too." His voice cracked. "Good as you, almost."

He got into his patrol car and drove away. Cormac watched him go, the metal disk in his pocket digging fiercely into his palm.

Why had he accused Morty? Just to relieve his frustration at losing the typewriter? To lash out at the young man for his clumsiness? Or was the truth that he hadn't felt anger at all when the typewriter slipped forever into the darkness, that he'd experienced nothing but relief be-

273

cause there was no longer any evidence against Moira Pierce?

So which of them was using his badge to cover up a suspect?

Cormac got into his car. He wanted a drink and a long night alone. Wells was taking care of Moira. That was just as well, he thought. Wells would have a clearer perspective.

"Damned Brit Prod bastard," he said aloud, slapping the car into gear.

Wells was on his way to an early supper at one of the local restaurants when he saw Kathleen Pierce's beat-up old car speeding up Killian Street toward the road to Killarney. He hesitated for a moment. She was supposed to be entertaining tonight at the castle. Why then was she going in the opposite direction?

He ran back into the parking lot of the Park Hotel, got into his car and set out on the road to Killarney himself. After only a few minutes of high-speed driving, he had closed enough of the gap so that Kathleen's car was visible ahead of him. He slowed down to follow her. Moira Pierce would have to be postponed until another night. Too bad.

He hadn't come. Moira was a little sad because, in truth, she had looked forward to spending the evening with the tall, apparently gentle Daniel Wells. And she had wanted to apologize to him for Kathleen's nasty outburst; and perhaps it would just have been pleasant to spend an evening in male company for the first time in she had forgotten how many years. She might even have found out just who Wells was and what he was doing in Ardath. Was he really a policeman? Was Kathleen in any trouble? Was the newspaper correct, and was the Pope really going to visit Ardath to mark the thousandth anniversary of the Shrine of Eternal Peace? Did Kathleen's vicious anti-Catholic letter have something to do with that?

She wanted to know these things, but Wells did not come to Grady's, so she sat in a table in a corner by herself, smiling politely and making a small amount of polite conversation with those who came up to greet her.

The Pope's impending visit seemed to be the most important thing on everyone's mind, and Old Lanigan was saying that "if His Holiness does come, we should all go up and invite him down here to hoist one with us." And Doc O'Connor's grandfather rejoining: "Aaaah, it's not with the likes of you he'll be drinking, you old windbag," and Grady having to separate the two of them before the fight started, it being too early for the evening ruckuses.

She would wait another half hour, she thought, and then she would walk home. Alone. As she always did.


Cormac lay on his bed in the rented room and tried to think about the case but couldn't. All he could visualize was Moira being wooed by Wells, the Briton using her to try to dig information out of her. The more he thought of it, the angrier he became, and he finally got up from the bed and put on his jacket and walked down the street to Grady's Pub. His shoes, wet from the boat, squished as he walked.

* * *

275

"May I sit with you, Moira?" Cormac asked.

She nodded silently. She had seen him as soon as he had entered Grady's and looked around, imperiously, as in the old days when he was young and filled with life and self-confidence and himself. Then he spied her and walked across the room. Behind him, people whispered. The older ones, she knew, were recalling the romance that had once been theirs.

"I thought you'd be with Wells," Cormac said.

"He told you that, did he? she said. There was a snap in her voice. "Did you two have a good time comparing notes about me?" One question answered, she thought. Cormac and Wells knew each other; Wells *was* a policeman.

"It wasn't like that," Cormac said. "I asked him where he'd be tonight is all."

"Cops sharing information," she said coldly.

"He told me that your daughter called him a policeman," Cormac said. "How did she know?"

"Who knows? People talk."

"They certainly would talk about you, sitting here, spending the evening with an Englishman," Cormac said.

Moira turned away to watch the dancers on the floor. Michael had once been a wonderful dancer, surprisingly light on his feet for a man so big. She thought, *If he asks me to dance, I'll say yes.*

But when Cormac spoke, it was not to ask for a dance.

"Let's go," he said. His face was flushed; he did not look at her.

"All right," she said thickly.

They were silent for much of the walk down Killian

Street toward the lake, following the road as it turned left and headed for the Pierce estate.

She heard the squishy sound of his shoes and said, "It sounds like you were trying to walk on water."

"I was out in a boat," he said simply and was silent again.

Finally, Cormac said, "Why were you planning to see Wells tonight?"

"I was lonely."

He was silent again.

"Have you ever been lonely these years, Michael?"

As they walked past the heavy iron gates of the estate, Cormac said, "You could say that."

The cottage was empty. Moira opened the door and stepped inside. "Will you come in?"

He looked at her for a moment. It could never be the same, he told himself. Too much has happened, too much has been lost. . . .

"I will."

Moira had always known how to give comfort. She knew instinctively what Cormac needed. Not love now, but a drink; not passion, but a dry pair of socks. For Cormac, it felt like pampering of the most sybaritic sort. She built a fire and he cozied up to it like an old dog. She filled his belly with soup and bread. She asked little of him, even speech.

It felt as it had twenty years ago; it felt as if he had never left.

"The answer is yes," he blurted.

"What was the question?"

He popped a chocolate into his mouth. "The question was am I lonely. Was I lonely. Whatever. The answer is yes."

"Where did you go?"

"America," he said, turning toward the fire. "A town in Louisiana called Baylor City. The cesspool of the western world."

Moira laughed. Unconsciously she brushed her fingers through her thick red hair, still unstreaked by gray.

"Do you want to know about it?" he asked quietly, not watching her.

"Of course."

"I've never told anyone," he said.

"You can tell me if you like. I've kept your secrets before," Moira said.

"It's not a secret; just a shame. I was an ass." He looked at her for the first time. "Moira, I got married."

Her face seemed to wither. Her hand retracted and balled into a fist, which she covered with the other hand. "Are you . . . still . . .?"

"No. It didn't work." A mirthless puff of laughter came out of him. "She was a prostitute. I don't suppose they make the best wives."

"Michael," she said uncomfortably, but he didn't hear her. His face was bitter and set, and the reflection of flames dancing across it made him look old.

"I worked for a detective agency there. Not as a detective—I wasn't a citizen—but they used thugs from time to time for the dirty work. That was me, one of the thugs. Anyway, to make a long story short, I was assigned to go into a bar and make off with the girl who was working there as a dancer. Naked dancer, you know. Rough crowd. The girl's father hired the agency. It was set up so that the father, the detective who located her, they were waiting outside. All I had to do was go in and get her."

He sipped at his whiskey, beginning to unwind. It had been so long since he had spoken of his life to anyone but a priest in the confessional.

"Well, I did, swooped her right off the bar where she was doing her routine and before I could get her out the door, I got the first bottle on the back of my head. I don't know how many there were after that or how many fists were punched in my face, but I woke up a few days later in a hospital. My pelvis was broken, so someone must have kicked me. My pelvis, my nose, two ribs . . .

"Anyway, the point is that the girl didn't want to stay with her father. Frankly, I met him once and I could see her point. A gross old duck. She ended up right back in the same place."

Moira refilled his glass. "So you married her?"

He laughed. "That was about it. I got to know her, wound up beating up her pimp, then finally she moved in with me." He threw down the drink in one gulp. "Only thing was, she couldn't stay away from the men. She said if we were married, things would be different. So I married her. But nothing changed."

"What was her name?"

"Ellen."

"Are you still married to her?"

"No. She divorced me. She told the judge I was of low character."

Moira tried to suppress a giggle, but couldn't. Cormac scowled at her first, then joined her, and they laughed until tears ran down their cheeks.

"Moira," he said, holding her shoulders. Then he pressed her to him and buried his face in her fragrant hair. "Oh, Moira, why did you leave me?"

"You left," she whispered. "I didn't." When Cormac

wept like a child, she cradled him in her arms. "Come to bed with me," she said.

He tensed.

"I love you, Michael. Whatever's happened, whatever's been broken or lost, I still love you. I always have."

He stood up and took her hand. "Sweet Christ, I've missed you," he said.

They went into the small bedroom together, comfortable as when they were children, sharing their secrets by the standing stones, and closed the door.

# CHAPTER TWENTY-TWO

Killarney is a dark city at night. Kathleen drove through the crooked old streets, swallowing to keep the nausea down.

She had heard it only happened in the mornings. That was a laugh. The sickness was unending. It kept her awake at night, bathed in sweat. It followed her like an accusation.

Well, she thought bitterly, like mother, like daughter. Maybe the line of women in her family was destined to be knocked up by men who wanted nothing to do with them.

She was grateful for a parking spot near another hotel where Seamus Dougherty had taken a room. He had told her that he had been lingering so long in Killarney because of her, but Kathleen knew that wasn't the reason. He rarely had time for her at all.

As she gathered up her raincoat and locked the car doors, she tried to convince herself that he really cared for her but that he just had trouble showing it. Love was alien to him. Love for her, love for anyone. Seamus was limited, in the same way those oddities who could not perceive pain were limited. He could not show love. That was the lack in him. For all his fine ideas of mankind, he had no more soul than a lizard. But he loved her yet. She knew. He had to.

He sounded groggy on the telephone when she called, but he gave her his room number, and she rode up in the creaking elevator.

He had been asleep. He wore an old dress shirt, yellowing with age and wrinkled across the back, and a shabby pair of trousers. The gun—an automatic, he'd told her—lay on the nightstand beside the bed.

"What is it?" He spoke softly but made no pretense about being glad to see her. Every contact was a risk for him. He had made that clear.

"The Englishman. Wells. He was in my house today, with my mother."

"What did he want?"

"I don't know. My mother threw out the typewriter I was using for the letters. He might have been snooping about that. I told him to get out, the dirty Brit."

A stream of air hissed from Dougherty's lips.

"What's the matter with you?" Kathleen demanded, bristling. "I got rid of him, didn't I?"

"That's great, Kathleen. Just great." A closet door had been left open. Dougherty slammed it with a bang that made Kathleen jump. "The matter?" he asked, incredulous. "What's the *matter?* Wells knows we're on to him, he knows you're involved, he's going after you through your frigging mother, for the love of God. Don't you find anything the matter with that? Don't you or that dumb boyfriend of yours have any brains at all?" His voice rose to a frightening crescendo. "Why did you leave the typewriter where someone could find it?" he shouted.

Kathleen fought down a wave of nausea. "It was in the garage under Bonning's car."

"Well, that's an unobtrusive spot," he said, his features twisted into ugliness. "No one would ever get suspicious over a typewriter under an automobile."

"Stop it." She steadied herself on the back of a chair.

"Are you sick?"

She nodded, then sat down. "I'm pregnant," she mumbled.

"Christ!" He lit a cigarette, the flame illuminating his yellow-stained fingers. "You . . ." He cut himself off, waving her away in disgust.

She watched him staring out the window into the dark courtyard and knew he was looking at nothing. He had turned away just because he didn't want to see her.

"You despise me, don't you?" she said in a small voice.

He took a deep drag of smoke, then walked to her and put his hands on her head as if baptizing her. "Of course not. I just don't want things to go wrong."

"What things?" she shrilled. "You've never told me what's going on. Why did you have me write those letters as if I were a Prod? What do you want me to attack the Pope for? What's going on?"

Dougherty hunkered in front of her and took her hands. "Kathleen," he said softly. "There are some tasks that are unpleasant to perform. Sometimes we have to do things that few will understand or condone but which have to be done all the same if civilization is to be saved."

"Please, Seamus," she said, almost in tears. "I don't want any more speeches. I'm not your beloved masses.

I'm the woman who's carrying your child. Surely you don't think I'd compromise you now. Just tell me the truth, no rhetoric, for once. Just the truth. What is going to happen in Ardath?''

Dougherty scanned the corners of the ceiling, deliberating. Finally he spoke. ''There's going to be an assassination.''

''Oh, my God.'' She shrank away from him, folding her hands close to her chest. ''The Pope.''

''It has to be done.''

''Why? What's he ever done to hurt anyone?''

Dougherty rose, annoyed at the need to explain. ''That's just the point. The Pope is the symbol of goodness. He's a rallying point for all of southern Ireland, for most of the world. He's one thing that everyone agrees is good. Whoever is blamed for killing him will provoke the enmity of a billion people. It can change the course of the struggle.''

''You're insane. Why would you want the whole world against you?''

''I said, whoever is *blamed* for killing him. The IRA won't be.'' He touched her hair, stroked it. ''Unless you talk.'' His fingers wound slowly around the blond strands.

''I won't,'' she said. ''Don't hurt me, Seamus. I'm sick. Let me up.'' His hand formed a fist. ''Let me up.''

He released her suddenly and she ran to the bathroom. Dougherty stood without moving, listening to the retching sounds from behind the closed door.

A baby. Women always complicated matters. But the plan was too important for that to be a factor. The cause was what counted, regardless of personal sacrifice. The baby would never have a chance to be born. But it could come in handy to keep Kathleen in line.

"Can I help with anything?" he asked when she came out, careful to keep the impatience out of his voice. She would leave soon enough. A scene and he would be saddled with her all night.

"No, thank you." She managed a weak smile. "Women have been having kids for centuries. They all say it's worth it in the end."

"Yes. I suppose so."

She flung her arms around him. "Oh, it will be wonderful, won't it?"

"What? Oh, yes. Wonderful. When this is all done, it'll be wonderful."

"And whatever you have to do, I'll stay with you, Seamus. I'll never talk. I love you."

"That's good," he said vaguely, patting her back.

"When will it happen?" she asked.

"Next week. He's coming on Tuesday." He straightened up briskly. "Kathleen. Remember once I told you about Lazarus?"

She smiled. "Then you *do* trust me?"

"Of course I do. I think it's time for you to meet him."

"All right," she said, her eyes filled with love. "How do I meet the man of mystery?"

"Go to confession tomorrow."

"Confession?"

"At St. Benedict's. He'll contact you in the crowd there."

She nodded uncertainly. "All right."

"He'll tell you what's expected of you."

"Whatever it is, I'll do it," she said.

"I know." He kissed her cheek. "I think you ought to go get some rest."

"I'll stay here," she said.

"I'd rather you didn't. There's too much risk now."

"But when will I see you?"

"I'll contact you when it's safe. In the next day or two. You take care of yourself."

"Of course I will." There was a trace of fear in her voice. She placed her hands on her belly. "This will be a wonderful baby," she said.

"Yes, it will. Our baby." He kissed her again, on the forehead, and ushered her out. "Be careful going home," he called out softly. "And say nothing to anyone."

In the darkness of the corridor, his voice sounded as mechanical and flat as a recording.

He was relieved that she was gone. Dougherty went back inside his room, lit a cigarette and turned off the lights. The red glow from the cigarette was the only color in the room. A small spot of light in the darkness, Dougherty thought. Like himself. Like Lazarus.

Why couldn't the rest of them understand? For people like Kathleen, a bloody scrap of unformed tissue was more glorious than a whole new order for the world. How did their minds become so small? Both she and that stupid O'Flaherty. It was time for both of them to make their ultimate contribution to the cause of freedom.

As Dougherty stood by his hotel room window, Daniel Taylor Wells dropped a coin into the candy machine at the top of the stairway down the hall. From the corner of his eye, he saw Kathleen Pierce stride past the stairway into the open elevator. At the far end of the hallway, out of sight from where he now stood, two men waited idly in front of the room from which Kathleen had come.

With Kathleen gone, Wells threw the chocolate bar from the machine into the already overflowing metal mesh wastebasket beside him. He took some wet paper towels from the washroom downstairs, which he had laid on top of the candy machine, tore them into strips and scattered them over the top of the debris. Then he set fire to the wastebasket. Once it had burst fully into smoky flame, he kicked it into the corridor.

"Friggin' Christ," he heard one of the bodyguards yell. Footsteps stomped in a run toward the flames. A door creaked open and a woman's voice yelled, "My God, it's a fire."

"Fire, fire," Wells shouted. "Fire. Fire."

Other voices joined in.

"It's caught the rug."

"Somebody call the fire department."

"Fire, fire," Wells shouted again. "The whole floor's gone up."

Wells made way for the stampeding hotel guests. As they stormed into the stairwell, he slipped into the corridor, unnoticed in the shadows of the fire.

The two bodyguards were flailing their jackets at the flames and cursing as people fled past them. One of them stopped momentarily to look at the door at the end of the hallway opened and a small thin man peered out.

"It's all right, Captain," the guard said. "Just a kid's prank."

The small man disappeared back into the room. His face had been visible only for a moment, but the moment had been long enough for Wells.

The Englishman calmly walked down the stairs and out into the street.

The confessional line was long, more than an hour's wait. Kathleen stood, looking around frequently for the sight of a stranger, but there were no faces that were not familiar to her: Mrs. O'Glynn, and her son Billy, his cast blackened with dirt; Old Lanigan, Doc O'Connor's grandfather, Molly Logan.

It occurred to her that she should have worn something more distinctive. She had always dressed as drably as a mouse. Perhaps Lazarus had come and gone without noticing her.

"Nervous as a cat you are," said a voice behind her. She whirled around to see Brian O'Flaherty. "Must have some powerful sins to confess."

She turned away, but he caught her shoulder and pulled her back. His face was strained. He snapped, "You missed work last night."

"Sorry, I was busy."

"With Seamus?"

"Since you know, why tell you?" she said.

"Why the bloody blazes not?" he hissed, loudly enough so that people in the line turned and shifted in their spots to stare. "Maybe you'd like to try both of us at the same time."

She swallowed hard. "We're going to be married," she said quietly.

288

Brian looked at her, at first in shock. Then a broad smile creased his face.

"Are you now?" he said. "That's a rich one. Him marrying his whore." He laughed loudly. People turned again.

Morty O'Sullivan stepped from the back of the line and put a big hand on Brian's shoulder. "This is a church. Be quiet or get out," he said quietly, but in a voice hard as ice.

Brian sputtered for a moment, seemed to be sizing up Morty, then stomped away.

"Are you all right?" Morty asked.

"Fine," Kathleen said.

Old Lanigan came out of the confessional booth and, shaking, Kathleen ran in. She closed the old-fashioned mahogany door behind her and slid onto the hard wooden bench in relief.

"You may begin," Father Ambrose's voice said from behind the screened barrier.

Kathleen blinked. She had been viewing the confessional as a place of refuge, forgetting its real purpose. Lazarus had not come for her. She didn't know what to say.

"Bless me, Father, for I have sinned," she began. In her mind, she began to enumerate the small sins she had committed that she could disclose. Not Seamus, naturally. Not the baby. Not the plan to kill the . . .

She looked around the small booth uneasily. If there was a God, did He know her thoughts? Here, in this holy place, she had acknowledged a plan to murder the Prince of the Son of Heaven. What would God's punishment be?

*The baby.*

She cried out involuntarily.

"What is your name?" the priest whispered.

"What?"

He repeated the question. "K . . . Kathleen Pierce," she said, confused. No priest had ever asked her name in the confessional before.

"And the man known as Seamus Dougherty is close to you?"

She sat back, bewildered. "What? I don't have to answer that," she said. "What's going on here anyway?"

There was a long silence before Father Ambrose spoke again.

"I am Lazarus," he said.

# BOOK FOUR

# CHAPTER TWENTY-THREE

The funeral procession marched the short distance from the church to the gaping fresh grave in the cemetery. The women keened loudly, all of them dressed in the faded black of mourning garments well used.

The men wore shiny old suits and their everyday caps. Father Ambrose walked ahead, praying and sprinkling holy water on the ground.

Hattie O'Shea had had no wake; there had been no volunteers to keep her body. The townspeople attended her funeral as decent Catholics, but not one of the parishioners wanted the taint of a woman who had died a pagan—hating the church and cursing its priest in heathen ritual—on them or their homes.

As Father Ambrose droned through the final prayers, images of the old woman flashed in his mind: Hattie watching him, Hattie knowing.

Hattie had always known about him, he realized, at least to some extent. She could have given him away at any time. But like Cassandra and her prophecies, no one had listened to her.

Not yet. But they would have. Cormac was already

beginning to listen. Wells surely would have. The woman had had to die.

Like so many others.

He remembered how she'd looked that last time, dressed in a long white flannel nightgown, illuminated by the light of a flickering oil lamp.

"Hattie, Hattie, let me in."

There had been the scuffle of hard shoes across the floor, then the sound of the inside bolt sliding open.

"Devil priest," she hissed. "Waking me up in the dead of night."

Father Ambrose slid through the narrow opening and closed the door behind him.

"You're thinking to catch me unawares," Hattie said, "but I'll not be going."

"Going where, Hattie?" he asked softly.

"That home of yours. A devil's prison, so it is, but you'll not be taking me." She smiled lewdly. "For I've talked with the spirits of the dead and they'll see you dead and burned afore I go."

"Don't talk that way." A note of sternness was in his voice. "You were a Christian woman once."

"Aye, and Father Gervaise knew it. But when you killed him, I needed to use the old ways to fight you. The old ways has the magic still in them."

"I didn't kill Father Gervaise," he said gently.

"You did. I've talked with his spirit."

"You were talking to yourself, Hattie."

" 'Twas foxglove you used. Fairy fingers. Makes the heart to wilden. I know magic, the old ways."

"Yes, I know." He took her hand. "And the old medicines are good. . . ."

She snatched her hand away. "He knew you was

294

going to try, you know. He asked me about some of the medicines.''

''That's absurd.''

''Oh, he didn't mention your name. But who else would be trying to poison the father? Now, when I was taking care of the poor dear . . .'' Her eyes glazed over for a moment. When they cleared, she narrowed them stonily. ''You got rid of me so's you could do it in secret, the shameful dirty thing in you.'' She spat in his face. Father Ambrose shook with anger but said nothing. He wiped off the foulness with his handkerchief and spoke very quietly.

''We had to discharge you because you weren't well enough to work. You were frying cigarette butts in the kitchen. You had your cursed . . . your stones over the rectory. You were setting up pagan altars in the church.''

Her face twisted into a contorted smile. She stuck her tongue out and wiggled it lewdly. ''He seen what you done. At night.'' Then she cackled wildly until Father Ambrose turned away from her.

''I talked to the lad, Billy O'Glynn, today,'' he said, facing the wall. ''He bears you no ill will.''

''Billy O'Glynn, Billy O'Glynn,'' she chanted, rocking.

''He's afraid of you. Half the town is, really. You broke his arm.''

''Billy O'Glynn, fell in, fell in.''

''He admitted that he and some other boys were playing with matches on the pier the day of the explosion. He said you saw them.''

''Billy O'Glynn, a sin, a sin . . .''

''What did you see?'' He strode over to her and

clasped her wrist. She squealed and tried to bat the hand away. He shook her. "What did you see?"

"You're hurting me."

He gripped her tighter.

"Billy O'Glynn," she sobbed. "O'Glynn, O'Glynn . . ."

"What did you see?"

"They was burning a cat."

"What?" Father Ambrose said.

"Had it on a spit, with a fire underneath. And it alive, poor thing. I chased them away. They spilled their matches. I freed the cat. So weak it could hardly move it was. Billy O'Glynn, a sin, a sin."

She shook her head rhythmically as she rocked from side to side, tears flowing down her face. The priest released her with disgust.

"Billy O'Glynn, O'Glynn, O'Glynn," she whispered.

He rubbed his eyes. "What were you talking to that policeman about?" he said wearily.

"Morty's my friend. They're not all devils like you."

"Not Morty. The other one. Cormac."

"Morty's not . . ."

"Christ, will you listen?" His voice barked out, and Hattie snapped to attention. "Cormac," he repeated. "The other policeman. You told him to go to the cemetery."

Her mouth opened in a comic exaggeration of sudden understanding. "The poor tormented soul from the grave. Had no hands, so he hadn't. No hands at all. Only bloody stumps. And a rag in his mouth. But even then, I could hear him weeping, waving those stumps like they was flags." Her eyes shifted from the floor to the priest, and they opened wide. "Why, 'twas you the one with him," she said, awestruck. "Not in the cassock you wear, but you all the same. The devil sent you to torment the man's soul, didn't he?" Her gaze moved inward. "The priest from hell, the dead will tell," she chanted, rocking. "The dead will tell, will tell, will tell."

"Go back to bed," Father Ambrose said hoarsely.

"The dead will tell, the dead will tell. Cut off his hands and open your pants." She cackled uproariously.

She was still laughing when Father Ambrose walked over to the narrow bed and picked up Hattie's pillow. She knew too much; perhaps no one believed her now, but sooner or later, the wrong word would go to the wrong ear. He could not risk it.

"The dead will tell, the priest from hell . . ."

And as he placed the pillow over her face, the laughter stopped and the muted screaming began and the old woman's arms and legs pumped like pistons.

"Ave Maria, gratia plena," he said.

*The dead will tell, the dead will tell.*

"Dominus tecum, benedicta tu in mulieribus, et benedictus fructus ventri tui Jesu. . . ."

*Cut off his hands and open your pants.*

"Sancta Maria, ora pro nobis peccatoribus, nunc et in ora mortis nostrae."

*Billy O'Glynn, a sin, a sin, a sin, a sin . . .*

"Amen."

He released her and Mad Hattie fell in a heap in his arms. Her lips were blue. Her eyes were staring.

Father Ambrose carried her over to the bed and laid

her in it, pulling the covers across her chest. Then he closed her eyes and made the sign of the cross over her.

He drove in a cold sweat into Killarney, his whole body itching as if he were covered with vermin. The route was automatic for him. It required no thought. Over the winding, unlit road into the city. Through the maze of brick-covered streets in the commercial section of town, deserted, abandoned-looking. Across the narrow bridge to the district whose name he had never learned, where people walked at night. At first they were women, aimlessly strolling in their cheap, short skirts and made-up faces, harlots who advertised their availability through sullen eyes and painted lips. Then, farther on, where the streets were darker, the people walking were men, not women. Boys, their slender hips swaying, their pants stretched tight across their genitals.

*Cut off his hands and open your pants.*

He parked the car, a clean little yellow Ford Escort, below one of the few remaining streetlamps and got out. He had already walked a few steps before he realized what he had forgotten. He went back, unfastened the clerical collar, and tossed it onto the front seat.

He felt as if he had not breathed for years.

The foot journey he followed also by rote. He passed a bar, a dingy wooden structure leaking American music and the laughter of young men. Outside stood a husky youth in a plastic jacket with a face like Adonis, staring at some point in the distance and smoking. The priest passed him by and turned the corner. It led to a courtyard and a maze of old buildings, some with faded signs advertising curios and shoe repairs, others residences, with straight wooden chairs on the balconies and washed rugs hanging over the railings.

At first glance, the courtyard seemed deserted, but one by one, the figures appeared in the darkness, standing, shadow against shadow, moving sinuously as cats through the alleyways of their turf.

There was an occasional laugh, a buzz of chatter, a billow of white cigarette smoke, but mostly the population of this shadow world merely came and went, without notice, formless, nameless sensations rather than personalities, figures rather than bodies.

Father Ambrose leaned against a crumbling brick wall, feeling the sweat trickle down his face onto his neck. Without the collar, he could feel his own secretions oozing along the skin. Unprotected from his own corruption, he had the sensation that filth was being poured on him like molasses.

"I seen you before."

The voice was soft and dark like the shadows it came from, and the priest welcomed its familiarity. Hearing the sound of it was like finding a friend in a hostile country, although he did not even know the boy's name.

He was young, possibly twenty, but more than likely younger. He was small, with the delicate bones of a girl, but muscularly developed in the shoulders, as if he had had to punch his way through his effeminacy. There was something Mediterranean about the face with its smooth olive skin and enormous dark eyes that still pretended to a cagey sort of innocence, despite what they'd seen. The lashes, Father Ambrose noticed with

299

a certain disgust, had been painted; there were smudges beneath each eye.

In how many rumpled beds had he lain naked today, the priest wondered. How many times had he knelt on the cobblestones while men like himself spent their secret, unnameable lusts into him?

"I haven't got much time," he said, shifting his eyes away from the boy.

"So?" The glistening shoulders moved in a dismissive gesture. "What do you want?"

"Face the wall."

The boy turned around—almost delicately—and Father Ambrose, not a priest now but another anonymous shadow, placed his hands on the boy's waist. The skin was smooth there, over well-muscled flesh. The priest blinked to drive the sweat from his eyes and searched—for what?—with his hands.

The boy said nothing. He rested easily, his palms pressing against the wall, his arms stiff. He allowed the older man to unfasten his jeans, then rolled with slow, experienced movements while they slid down his legs.

The priest leaned against him, the two of them moving together as if in ritual. And so it was, Ambrose thought. The old corrupting the young, death penetrating life and winning, always winning because the shame of the corruption made purity an impossibility.

The boy's flanks were firm and downed with soft hair. He accommodated his customer with an almost sweet easefulness.

How kind he is, Father Ambrose thought. How unlike the other. . . .

* * *

The other. He had escaped from prison, the red-haired boy, and Father Ambrose had found him hiding in the choir loft in St. Benedict's, still reeking of fear from his flight, his clothes torn from God knew how many miles of winter woods, his hands purple with the cold, his limbs weak from hunger.

He was nineteen years old, convicted of several robberies, and rather simple. He had never learned to read, he said. His hair was cut badly and his teeth rotting to the point where they stank. But Father Ambrose had taken him into the rectory and fed him.

He had cooked the meal himself, since Hattie O'Shea had taken one of her increasingly frequent evenings off. Father Gervaise had been in bed for several days with the flu.

Ambrose had watched the boy eat, ravenously, gluttonously, pieces of bread and egg flying from his mouth in an orgy of eating; the boy was suspicious at first but too starved to care, staring, guarding his plate with his arm, then smiling, belching, laughing, talking about his crimes and the prison he'd escaped from, which was most of what he knew in life.

Father Ambrose had let him wash up in the kitchen sink so as not to disturb the ill older priest, then had given him a bathrobe and led him to his own bedroom, cautioning him not to make a sound. The boy had fallen asleep instantly, and in sleep, the priest found the sweetness in his face. His hair was red and straight and farm-tufted; he had freckles all over his back. Ambrose watched him from a chair for hours, before lighting on the bed—oh, ever so gently—and then just to look at him more closely, perhaps to feel the creamy freckled skin.

301

But the boy had awakened and on awakening shouted gross names at him and struck him until Ambrose had to strike back, smashing his face until he felt the nose break under his knuckles and blood spurt out of it like a fountain and Ambrose was kneeling over him, his fist slamming down again and again until well after the boy was unconscious.

And that was when Father Gervaise walked in.

Father Ambrose made his apologies to the old priest, explaining that he had taken in a man in distress, only to be attacked in his bed. He had called the Gardai immediately, but Father Gervaise, in thirty years of being pastor of St. Benedict's, had become a suspicious man. He said nothing, however, not even after the prison officials came and the boy screamed that the priest was trying to bugger him. But Father Gervaise watched; he watched very closely, and finally Ambrose knew that he had to take care of him.

He had used digitalis, the essence of the plant known to the common folk of Ireland as "fairy fingers." It had been liquid, in a syringe, injected carefully. But Hattie had recognized the effects. She was a medicine woman and she had known murder where she saw it.

First Ambrose, elevated to pastor upon Father Gervaise's death, had let her go and tried to have her committed. But she had refused to go to the home, and now she was talking too much and so Ambrose had killed her with a pillow, something soft and white to blot up the stain of what the old woman had known.

Father Gervaise had writhed and prayed and lost consciousness when the injected drug started his heart pounding until it broke down. When his pulse stopped, Ambrose called for Doc O'Connor.

It was finished.


"Am I hurting you?" he whispered into the dark boy's ear.

"I'm used to it."

What a sad thing, Ambrose thought, that pain is less because it occurs frequently. And sadder yet that that knowledge could not stop him from further hurting the boy. He galloped him, shivering with loathing, until he felt himself dying in a spray of lust.

*The priest from hell, the dead will tell.*

And then it was over, the night still. Nothing of any importance had happened. He handed the boy ten pounds and left without even looking at his face.

The bar near his automobile was still open, its tinny music blatantly sexual. Father Ambrose tried to block his ears from the sound. The handsome youth in front had gone; either he had found a mate for the evening or had walked home with empty pockets or a fix of drugs. He didn't matter either. These were people of convenience, visions called at will. They weren't real; real people would not permit them equal status. It was only right. If they were full-fledged human beings with names and wants and sorrows, there could be no morality for the righteous.

He opened the door to his car and gagged at once from the stench. Someone—the youth by the bar, perhaps, or someone just like him—had defecated on the front seat, then smeared the entire car with it. The roof, dashboard, even the steering wheel had been hastily covered. But care had been taken with the collar. It had been defiled deliberately, every inch.

Father Ambrose wiped off what he could with some rags from the trunk. Then he wrapped the collar in the used rags and tossed it into a trash bin.

*The dead will tell, the dead from hell.*


"Pater noster," he began as Hattie O'Shea was laid to rest. The summer air stung him with grief. Another death, another murder, another score for Lazarus and the men and the cause who owned him.

"Pater noster . . ." But he could not finish.

He had forgotten the words.

# CHAPTER TWENTY-FOUR

Cormac and Wells met for breakfast in a small hotel restaurant fifteen miles from Ardath on the long string of roads that made up the scenic Ring of Kerry.

The hotel was a low one-story structure, and despite the advent of the summer season, it seemed to have more cats in residence than guests. The entire staff seemed to be one woman who was reservations clerk, maid, cook, waitress and bartender.

They each ordered eggs, and they came runny and wet with toast as hard as roof tile and sausage so vile that Wells fed his to the cats that lingered about their table. The fourth cat accepted the offering.

"So what kind of day did you have?" Wells asked Cormac.

"Lousy day and lousy night. We had the typewriter but it slipped away and we lost it."

"We?"

"Morty O'Sullivan. The garda. Somebody saw my light and called him. When he came down, I asked him to help. That was a mistake."

"Well, it's no great loss," Wells said. "We'll go back and get it later."

"And then I looked for you at Grady's last night, but you didn't show."

"I was busy. Was the woman there?"

"Yes," Cormac said.

Wells smiled and then tried to nibble on a piece of toast. "I hope she didn't miss me too much."

"No," Cormac said. "She didn't. Why didn't you come?"

"I was following her daughter. She went to Seamus Dougherty's hotel room." He saw the blank look on Cormac's face. "You don't know who he is?"

"No. Should I?"

"Dougherty is one of the top half-dozen terrorists in the North. He's wanted by us, by Northern Ireland, and he's an outlaw here, too."

"How'd you know it was him?"

"After she left, I set fire to the hotel and got him out of the room. I recognized him."

"Many people die in the fire?" Cormac asked.

"Just a small fire. No casualties. What do you think I am?"

"An Englishman," Cormac said. "Did you arrest this Dougherty?"

"No. He's got bodyguards. The ID was what I was after."

"He's IRA, I suppose," Cormac said wearily.

Wells nodded and gave him a look like a fox sitting atop a henhouse. "He was registered as James Devlin. The clerk said that. Now what, I ask, is an IRA terrorist doing down here? And what is Kathleen Pierce doing with him?" He made a face as he sipped his coffee. "Assume for a moment that you're right and that Moira Pierce didn't write those letters. That most likely leaves

Kathleen. Now why would she write pro-British letters, then attack me for being a Brit? And why would she hang out with an Irish Communist?''

Cormac rolled his eyes to the ceiling. ''God, not another Communist. You see them under every bed.''

''Just trust me on this one, Michael. Seamus Dougherty is a terrorist and a Communist. I know the difference between Communists and gently left-leaning softwits. My country is full of the latter, remember?''

''All right,'' Cormac said grudgingly. ''What are they doing together?''

''I don't know,'' Wells said.

''Anything new on the Pope?'' Cormac asked.

''I told you. I sent in my report to Dublin and recommended that they cancel the trip. They won't. I'm sure they're expecting the Pope to rip the IRA apart in a speech. So they won't cancel. But at least they're keeping it down to a stopover. First of all, the security teams are moving in now. They'll have the town flooded by tomorrow. That's when they're going to announce the visit. The Pope will arrive at Shannon Airport Tuesday morning. I guess when the teams move in and take over we'll be off the job.''

''I'm already off the job,'' Cormac said. ''I talked to Superintendent Merrion this morning. He told me to come back to work Monday. He finally got word from Dublin about the Pope's visit.''

''Was he upset?'' Wells asked.

''The earpiece on my telephone melted. He accused me of being a double-dealer for not telling him about the Pope.''

''What did you say?''

''I told him all I had was a rumor and the word of a

British gentleman. I didn't think it was worth bothering him with either of those things, insubstantial as they are," Cormac said, pouring himself more coffee.

"I'll ignore the insults. You're going back Monday then?"

"No," Cormac said.

Wells looked up from his own coffee. "No?"

"No. I told Merrion I'm taking a couple of days vacation. I figure I've spent enough time here, I might as well see His Holiness."

Wells smiled. "Don't give me that guff," he said. "You just don't like this thing finished without being all wrapped up. I know the feeling."

"I don't know," Cormac said. "Maybe in my old age, I'm getting as suspicious as you are. I don't like things left hanging in the air. Tell me, are all the SAS guys as suspicious as you?"

"Scotland Yard," Wells said. "No. But you're right. I'm willing to buy somebody bringing in some explosives. Hell, maybe he was going to remove some tree stumps from his yard. And it blows up and he dies and we get his mutilated body back and can't identify it. That's all right. But I can't buy that severed hand of some Protestant terrorist being found here. Not without a reason for its being here. I've checked in Belfast. Word was that the dead man, Winston Barnett, had a price on his head from the IRA. Nobody was surprised that he hadn't been seen around lately. They figure the IRA captured and killed him."

"They would figure that," Cormac said. "Protestants are as suspicious as SAS people."

"I'd like an explanation for that hand," Wells said. "I'd like to know why someone's writing hate-the-Pope letters when no one knew about the visit. I'd like to know what Seamus Dougherty is doing here. Then I'd be satisfied.''

"Scratch one thing from your list of things to suspect," Cormac said. "Mad Hattie died of natural causes. Looks like her heart just stopped.''

"That's official?" Wells asked.

"Medium official. I talked to Doc O'Connor. He didn't do a real autopsy on her but he said there wasn't any sign of foul play. He figured the heart.''

"That doesn't mean a thing," Wells said. "It could be suffocation, carbon monoxide, a lot of things. Without an autopsy, nothing.''

"Well, forget the autopsy," Cormac said. "She was buried today. Is that O'Flaherty kid still following you?''

"I haven't seen him today. I slipped him last night, and he didn't follow me into Killarney. Haven't seen him since then. Maybe he's found a new game to play.''

"Saloon Irishmen always do," Cormac said. He was idly turning his medal on the table next to his coffee cup. Wells picked it up. "May I?" he asked. Without waiting for an answer, he looked at the inscription. "Valour," he read aloud as Cormac fidgeted uncomfortably. He handed the medal back. "I didn't know I was working with a hero.''

"It's a joke, really," Cormac said, quickly pocketing the medal. "I jumped into Moon Lake after Morty O'Sullivan when he was a kid. My da gave it to me. Just a cheap thing, not a real medal.'' He got up and looked for something to do with his hands.

"You seem to be a real enough hero to Morty," Wells said.

The Irishman flushed and cleared his throat. "Never **was** much for brains, that one. Will you be leaving soon?"

Wells allowed him to change the subject. "No sooner than you," he said. "Our work's not done here."

Cormac smiled. "Then it looks like the Pope's going to have two unwanted cops hanging around."

Wells was silent for a moment as if he were listening to something deep within himself. "Whoever kills the Pope will start a panic that might never stop," he said quietly. "It's what they'd want."

"*They?* Are you back on the IRA?"

Wells met his eyes levelly. "*They.* Anyone who uses a gun or a bomb to make a political point. Catholic, Protestant, PLO . . . it doesn't matter what labels they use. Terrorists are vermin, Michael. They're a disease that's covering the world. They've gotten their way so far because laws can't deal with them."

"Laws were meant for human beings," Cormac said. "Those bastards don't qualify."

"And one of them's right here in Ardath," Wells said.

"Just one?"

"I think so. In assassination, one man is the most effective weapon."

"Then we've only got to find one man," Cormac said lightly. But his fingers strayed to the worn medal in his pocket, and he held it as if it were Ireland itself.

## CHAPTER TWENTY-FIVE

He didn't remember how it had happened, his transformation from a man of God to an assassin. Sometime, in the twilight between hope and despair, between justice and murder, Ambrose Anthony's footsteps had gone off in a direction he had neither planned nor wanted. They led him to parts of the world he hadn't known existed and to a part of himself he had never wanted to know.

Sometime. But when?

Was it as early as his days in the seminary? he wondered. Had his core been soft and blackened, even then?

No. During the early years, he had been clean. He had a vocation. Even the director of the seminary told him as much, granting him special dispensation to research a theological theory during his senior year. At twenty-three, he published a book on the nature of heresy, under the imprimatur of the Vatican. He had been the youngest recipient of that honor in 150 years. By the time he was twenty-five, it was whispered that there would soon be a place for him in Rome.

How proud his mother was. The Genius of the

Church, they called him in the neighborhood in Northern Ireland, his brothers who were out of work, the neighbors who wore their mourning black so often that many of them adopted it as everyday wear. Whenever he returned to visit that pitiless and strife-ravaged place, he suffered with the barefoot children and homeless old men until he thought he could not bear the suffering any longer; and then he would secretly, guiltily retreat back to his teaching position in Dublin, back to the clean order of the church and the placid company of clerics.

Maybe that was when it started, he thought. Back in the days when he first saw his old neighborhood as a man. The squalor repelled him. The illiteracy, in a land known for a thousand years for its scholarship. The alcoholism, always the refuge of the defeated. The chaos of not knowing which of one's friends or family would be dead tomorrow, mutilated by the violence of unseen enemies who were indistinguishable from one's own kind. He prayed for the strength to go back before each visit. And when he ran away from it, as he always did, he prayed again for forgiveness, kneeling in the quiet beauty of the sanctuary, and knowing that penance was easier for him than experiencing the ugly reality of Ireland.

His book was called *The Heretical Believer*. It explored the apostasy of the faithful who believed in God but who lashed out against the Church. His own kind of heresy was different. While he believed mightily in the church and all its tenets, he could not walk down the streets of Derry without tasting the bile rising in his throat. All creations were God's, he reasoned, yet *this* creation, this place, was a horror out of the Inferno.

Why had God chosen to punish his mother, his family, here?

But God was infallible. The fault must lie in his own perception, he told himself, not in the divine plan of the Lord. He knew he had to force himself to see, hear, touch the thing he loathed, or he would never lose his fear of it, and his questions and resentment would crack his soul apart.

He left the seminary where he had been teaching and moved back to a parish in the Catholic Bogside section of Derry. His mother, even though he was back home, grieved for him as if he had died. The hopes for a place in the Vatican were gone; there would be no more lofty books bound in red leather.

The church he was assigned to, St. Mark's, was a dirty place with neither music nor stained glass. A chipped statue of the Virgin Mary in a corner was its only real adornment. At mass, when the offering plate was passed around, the parishioners dug into their pockets for a few coins that none could really spare. The young priest watched the faces of these men and women and their somber children too old for their years, and his bitterness did not cease. It grew.

*What had they done?* He pleaded with God to answer him. Why had these people, living quietly on their own land for countless generations, been made to suffer so long?

He got an answer on January 30, 1972, at a place called Free Derry Corner on a day known as Bloody Sunday.

He heard the crowds gathering in Rossville Street Square while he was preparing for mass. It was an age of demonstrations. The Americans had been protesting

313

their Asian war for years. And while the Church did not condone the assembly, Ambrose personally saw no harm in Catholics banding together for once to protest the Protestant vigilantes who had made what amounted to a sport of beating and murdering Catholics at random.

But the British Army stood behind the Prods. It always had, turning away from the complaints of the powerless Irish Catholics who, after all, had been their enemies for seven hundred years.

The demonstrators collected and began their speeches. Hecklers, as expected, interrupted them but they went on, standing in the drizzling rain, the sea of black umbrellas quivering at attention. Part of Ambrose wanted to run out and join them. It was the first time he had felt any semblance of joy since moving back to the Bogside.

Then the shouting began and the screaming. The army megaphones, the din of a crowd gone to riot.

Then the fire of rifles.

Ambrose ran outside and the sight made him reel back in disbelief. The British Army was shooting at the mass of demonstrators as if they were fish in a bathtub. A man skidded across the wet pavement, spurting blood from his neck. Across the square, past a sea of running bodies, a woman careened backward, her face exploded into fragments. The horror paralyzed him.

While he stood beneath the canopy of the church, gaping, a woman rushed up to him. She was sobbing. Blood covered her face and chest. She carried something in her arms, something equally bloody. Ambrose watched her running as if the scene were in slow motion; it took him a moment to realize that the blood-soaked bundle she held was a child.

The little girl was seven or eight years old. Her chest had been torn open by a bullet.

"She'll be safe here," the mother repeated again and again as she laid the motionless, glassy-eyed little body on a pew inside the church.

Ambrose looked from the child to the open doorway with its horrifying vision of the street beyond. Between the two points, on the threadbare carpet of the church, was a trail of bright blood.

He performed the rite of extreme unction on the girl, then went out into the street to do the same for the bodies lying there, their wounds washed clean by the rain and running in red rivers through the city.

There were thirteen dead in all, every one a Catholic.

The Irish newspapers called the day Bloody Sunday. The British newspapers attacked the Catholics for provoking the British troops. For Father Ambrose Anthony, Christ's apostle, it was the day he lost his fear.

He understood at last why God had made his people suffer. It was because they did not know how to fight back.

Someone would have to teach them how. At the very least, someone would have to try.

The next day, Father Ambrose drove across the border and bought a huge flag of the Republic of Ireland. He stood it inside the entrance to St. Mark's sanctuary, next to the statue of Mary.

\* \* \*

In the weeks and months that followed, all Northern Ireland exploded into civil war.

Underground meetings sprang up all around Belfast and Derry. The Irish Republican Army, taking its name from the citizen-soldiers who had fought for Ireland's independence during the early part of the century, was becoming known in the poor quarters of the North as the last hope of disenfranchised Catholics. Arrests of anti-British demonstrators became too numerous to keep track of. Several members of Father Ambrose's parish disappeared into the prisons and jails that were being packed full in Northern Ireland.

One of them came back.

His name was Brendan Kearns. Father Ambrose remembered him as a big bear of a man, the sort of giant who would have scared Ambrose off the streets when he was a boy, but when he appeared one night at the rectory, he was drawn and emaciated. He looked comically out of place in his too-large clothes. His hair had grayed. Two teeth were missing. His hands shook.

"They're killing us, Father," Kearns said simply. "Standing for days on end without moving. In one place. They give us just a piece of bread once a day to eat, just enough water to keep from dying. Our lips was always parched and bleeding, and the interrogations never stop. They want us to turn in our own families. The questions just keep coming, day and night, and us standing there like that with our legs aching and our bellies empty. All because we had the bloody luck to be born Irish."

The priest played nervously with his tea. "Why are you here?" he asked.

The young man cracked his knuckles, seeming to

work up his courage. "You see, I was only in for five months," he said, "and this is what they done me." His eyes fell down toward his own gaunt frame. "But there's those in for years, some who'll never get out."

"Yes?" Ambrose said hesitantly.

"We need your help, Father."

"I'll give it if I can."

The young man fumbled with his cup, then set it down, rattling the saucer against the table. He cleared his throat. "Some of them's going to try an escape, Father. If they make it, they'll need a place to change their clothes and stay for twenty-four hours."

Ambrose swallowed with difficulty. "Here?"

The man nodded. "The prison's right on Victoria Road. They could make it here through the alleys before the guards could set up a search. They'd leave the next night. There's a bloke with a van will take them south."

"How many are there?"

"Five."

Ambrose stood up, paced the room, then left. He walked to the sanctuary, where above the altar hung a crucifix. The face of the Christ was impassive in His grief. There was no sign there for Ambrose, no encouragement. This time, for the first time since he could remember, the Church would not make the decision for him. He would have to act alone.

Would He have helped them? he asked himself.

But Jesus in His passion remained mute.

"Don't you see, I have to," he whispered, alone in the sanctuary except for the figure on the cross and the faded, peeling lady in the corner. "These are my people."

Even as he said the words, he knew he had said "my" people, rather than "your" people. And why not? he thought in a flash of unreasonable anger. God had turned his back on the Irish again, and they were dying, again, as they had died during the raids by the Saxons, the conquest by the Normans, during Cromwell's purges, the great famine, the exodus of immigration, the terror of the Black-and-Tans, the partition of their land. God had permitted them to live like chattel in their own land during most of their history.

*No,* Ambrose thought. *I will not let them die again.*

The young man looked up hopefully when the priest reentered the small sitting room of the rectory.

"You may bring them here," Ambrose said quietly.


They arrived, stinking and pallid, in the small hours of the morning. Ambrose ushered the men into the basement, where he had prepared basins of water for washing and trays of food.

Brendan Kearns was with them. While the escapees ate, he took the priest aside. "I want to thank you for what you're doing," he said. "There's not many would have taken us in."

"Why did you choose me?"

"The Republic flag in the church. I knew you was on our side."

"Our?"

"Father, the IRA is bigger than you think, and there's always been men of the cloth with us. Did you ever hear of the Stensen Institute?"

Ambrose nodded. "A Jesuit institution in Florence. Why did you ask?"

318

"In 1969, there was a secret meeting there of freedom fighters from all over Europe. The press never got wind of it, but it was a breakthrough for us. You see, working together, we figure we can do what we could never do alone. And Stensen helped. Our men there raised enough support to arm us for the first time, against the Brits. Lorries full of weapons and ammunition, rolling across Europe. That was for us."

He smiled a big, ingenuous grin. "That's why we been defeated for so long. It's not that we didn't have the stomach for it or the spirit. There just wasn't the guns. Now there is."

"But guns only make it worse," Ambrose said.

Kearns glared at him. "There's nothing worse than slavery, Father," he said bitterly.

"Do you plan a war?"

Kearns chuckled and patted the small priest's shoulder. "No, Father, even three lorry loads of arms ain't enough to go to war on. But we'll use them the best ways we can. You don't have to be rich if you're smart." He tapped his temple.

The doorbell rang. Kearns and the other men froze.

"I'd better see to that," Ambrose said. As he started to move toward the stairs, Kearns took hold of his sleeve. He said nothing but held on to the priest for a long moment, his eyes daring Ambrose to betray them. When he released him, it was with a slight, almost indiscernible shove.

"Excuse the disturbance, Father," the officer at the door said. Behind him were two more policemen, looking carefully behind them at the streets. "Did you happen to see or hear anything in the last hour or two, any commotion?"

"Commotion?" He felt himself sweating. "No, nothing I can recall."

"Well, let us know if you do. There's a dangerous element loose. Five men escaped from the Victoria Road prison and looked as if they were headed this way. They're probably nowhere close, though, because none of your neighbors saw anything either. Still, you ought to make sure your windows and doors are locked. And don't go out till morning if you can help it." He touched his fingers to his cap.

"Officer," Ambrose blurted. "What did they do, those men? You said they were dangerous?"

The policeman pressed his lips together. "One of them killed a police officer. Two others set off a bomb in the Protestant section. Killed and maimed a couple. Another two were convicted of lynching a Presbyterian minister and his family in Sneedon."

Ambrose went white.

"Even hanged the reverend's little daughter," the policeman said. "Not seven years old she was, neither. Hung a sign around her neck that said, 'For the thousands of Catholic babies.'" The officer's face struggled to remain impassive. "It's sick people we're dealing with here," he finished hoarsely.

When Ambrose came back down to the basement, the tension on Brendan Kearns's face broke. "You did it, then?" he asked, smiling.

"Yes." But the priest could not bring himself to look at any of them.

Brendan walked over to him. "What's the matter, Father?"

"What was *your* crime?"

His eyes suddenly met Kearns's, and the merriment

on the young man's face vanished, to be replaced by a subtle mockery. "Why, contempt of court. They got me on nineteen counts."

The other men laughed.

"Served out my full term too, so I did."

"In other words, your lawyer got you off on the original charge against you."

Kearns shrugged. "No evidence. They was looking for a patsy, that's all."

"What was the original charge?"

Kearns started to turn away, but Ambrose grabbed him roughly by the shoulder and whirled the bigger man around to face him.

"I asked you a question."

The young man clenched his hands into fists.

"Brendan," one of the men cautioned.

The big hands opened. "They tried to stick me with murder," Kearns said.

"Of whom?"

"Of an army barracks," he said, and the other men laughed again. The laughter was infectious; Kearns caught it and said to the others, "Went up like a blooming bonfire."

"Boom," one of the men said, and they all laughed again.

Ambrose left the room.

A quarter hour later, Kearns asked to speak with him.

"It ain't what you think," he said. "It wasn't murder. It was Brit soldiers on our land."

"They were people," Ambrose said.

"Yeah. The same people what killed thirteen Irish civilians down the street from this church. Maybe if we'd gotten more of them in that barracks, there wouldn't have been a Bloody Sunday.''

Ambrose winced at the memory of those dead, lying in a river of blood on the empty street. "And the others?'' he asked quietly. "The Protestant minister and his family?''

Kearns made a face. "That so-called reverend wanted to kill us all. Called the Pope an instrument of the devil, brought to earth to get the Catholics to multiply like rabbits so's the *real* human beings would have to support us. And it wasn't just in church, neither, though there was plenty of that. He'd go out stumping just like a politician, that one. And every place he spoke, there'd be some Catholic home in flames afterward.'' He stood up straight. "No, Father. Hanging them wasn't no crime. It was justice and a damn small parcel of it for what they done to us.''

Ambrose hung his head.

"I'd like you to come to our meetings,'' Kearns said after a long silence.

"I don't think so.''

"But you must care.''

"I do care.''

"Well, you can't do anything useful alone, can you, Father?''

"I thought I just had,'' Ambrose said.

Kearns grinned. "That you did,'' he said. "But that was tonight. Tomorrow is another struggle, and the day after that and next year, too. But we can do it. The Provos'll win this land back for us if we help them. All of us.''

"The Provos?''

"The Provisional IRA. That's us. We want action,

not a lot of talk in the government the way the original IRA was doing. Why, the Stormont government here won't listen to our words anyway. Ulster never has listened to the Irish. But the Provos . . .'' He gave Ambrose a look of supreme confidence. ''The Provos'll get them to listen. Don't you doubt it.'' He winked. ''Come next Friday to Tomasina's Pub, the back room. We might not have the place much longer, what with the police swarming around arresting everything that moves, but we're safe for a while there. Seamus Dougherty's in charge. I'm a simple man but Seamus is a genius. He'll be able to explain things to you so you'll understand. Will you come?''

''I'll have to see,'' Ambrose said.

''I'll count on you. Eight o'clock.''


Was that when it started, with the first lie to the policeman at the door?

A lie . . . such a small thing, one of many to follow. Lies on lies, until his whole existence had become a perversion of what he had once believed. And after the lies came the savageries, the killings, the unmentionable things that made lies necessary.

For a while, they had not seemed like lies. Seamus Dougherty had made them seem like sparkling truth. But then, Seamus Dougherty understood the nature of a man's weakness. He knew how to find it and exploit it until the truth inside hurt so much that the lies came as soothing balm. And so you came to believe the lies yourself.

Dougherty never had to believe. He had no soul to lose.

At the meeting in Tomasina's Pub, Seamus Dougherty looked like a small boy among the hardened men he led. In fact he was twenty years old. He looked younger, but he commanded like a veteran. Perhaps it was the respect for his father, a man still at the vanguard of the Irish cause, that moved the rowdy followers to listen to this hairless youth whose voice seemed not to have yet finished changing. But Ambrose felt it was something in the boy himself, a center as cold and certain as an oracle, that riveted their attention.

"First, we want to express our appreciation to Ambrose Anthony, who helped liberate five of our comrades from the torture they were suffering at the hands of the British," he began.

Father Ambrose was surprised to hear his secular name used, as if the somber-faced boy had not noticed the cassock he wore. Still, he accepted the handshakes and salutations of the men.

"I'm going to ask Mr. Anthony for something else, here in front of you. It's about the site for our meetings. We can't continue to come here, because the police are watching. I'd like Father Ambrose to invite us to meet in his church."

Dougherty sat back, his arms folded over his chest, just a hint of amusement in his eyes. He knew Ambrose would accept, because weak men always agree to the demands of the strong. Ambrose understood that, too, and his resentment prickled him.

"Only if I can serve mass to you afterward," he said.

"Done." The boy offered his hand. Reluctantly, Ambrose shook it.

*I've won*, the priest told himself. *So why do I feel I've capitulated?*

"Next," the boy went on, "we have to make plans to fight off the violence the Prods are planning. Ever since the newspapers got hold of the story about the prison break, the puppets of the English have been after our blood. The worst faction seems to be the followers of the so-called Reverend McElroy."

He turned to Ambrose to explain. "One of the men who escaped was accused . . ."

"I know of the charge," the priest said. "*And* the conviction."

Dougherty ignored the last remark. "They're planning a raid on the Catholic sector. You all know the Prods have got both the police and the army in their pockets, so there will probably be casualties. It's up to us to keep them to a minimum."

"By fighting?" Ambrose protested. "Don't you see that will only increase the violence?"

Dougherty had been playing with some notes but he set them down now and addressed himself completely to Father Ambrose.

"For centuries we have listened to your kind while you told us it was holy to turn the other cheek. And so, in our despair and helplessness, stripped of our self-respect as we watched our parents and children die under the yoke of British slavery, we were the holiest people on Earth. But no longer. You asked if we will fight. We will. We will fight back. We will fight until the fighting's done and we will never look back."

As he had spoken, the room had hushed. Now it exploded into cheers.

"Will you join us, Father?" Dougherty asked.

"I will not."

He got up and left. Dougherty followed him with his eyes, tilting back in his chair. "His family lives here, don't they?" he asked a thin-faced man standing nearby.

"Aye. Up toward Iverson's Cross."

Dougherty nodded. In his eyes was already the gleam of victory.

The men flooded into the church the following week. Ambrose received them coldly, taking no part in their conference but attending, instead, to the details of the private mass to come. When Dougherty told them that not only did the police have no leads on the five men who escaped from the Victoria Street prison but that an officer involved in the case had been found dead behind Tomasina's Pub, he felt his stomach turn in revulsion.

He would not permit them inside St. Mark's again, he decided, setting out the chalice and the host. God's home was not to be a spawning ground for violence.

Then the messenger came. He was a young man of sixteen or so, his face soot-blackened and terrified.

"They've come!" he shouted. His voice rang eerily through the empty sanctuary. "The Prods have started. Half the houses around Iverson's Cross are on fire."

The men leaped up, all shouting at once.

Ambrose felt a chill rippling through him. His entire family lived at Iverson's Cross. "Oh Lord," he whispered.

"Get your weapons," Dougherty called to the men

as they ran out. "Bring extras. There'll be those who can use them."

He turned to the priest. There was not a trace of alarm on the boy's face. "Coming, Father?" he asked casually, then strolled out as if he were planning to drop in on old friends.

Ambrose stood rooted. God had not done this; His mercy would not let Him. He looked back at the communion table where he had set out the sacramental meal.

*This is my blood.*

He turned his back and ran out of the church.


Iverson's Cross was engulfed in flames so high that the glow from the fire lightened the night sky all over Derry. An overturned ambulance blocked the roadway leading to the burning houses; around it swarmed a mob of men and boys armed with guns and sticks and rocks. Mounted policemen were already on the scene, their horses skittish in the heat. As Ambrose struggled to shove his way through the crowd, he heard the sharp crack of a rifle nearby. A moment later a policeman, his chest burst open, toppled from his horse.

A dozen or more men collected around the body, cursing and beating it with sticks. The priest crossed himself. As he did, he felt a hand reach over to encircle his throat. His clerical collar was ripped off. A fist thudded with a gut-wrenching pain in his abdomen.

"Fuck the Pope!" someone shouted, but the voice sounded dispersed and distant. He felt himself falling, saw the feet about to trample him, when someone pulled him up.

"You'd better get out of here, Father," a strange voice whispered in his ear.

Ambrose tried to focus on the man's face. He was older, gray-haired and stocky. But before Ambrose could thank him, the man fell face forward, blood oozing from a small spot on the back of his head. Behind him stood a teenage boy carrying a board with a nail stuck through it.

Ambrose screamed. Ignoring the body, he dashed through the mob toward the fire.

*What if he wasn't dead?* a voice nagged him from inside. *What if he dies from trampling, this man who saved your life? Couldn't you have gotten him to safety?*

"I have to get to my family," he mumbled aloud. But even then he knew he was lying. He had run because he was afraid.

The heat from the old tinderbox row houses was horrible, distorting the vision and burning the eyes. The women were already moaning over the burned bodies lying near the stone fences. Some were covered with blankets; some, where the fires had swallowed everything, were naked, their skin charred black.

The fire engines were pulled up close to the main area of the blaze, but the thin streams of water hissing into the inferno seemed to have no effect. Several of the firemen were themselves lying among the dead or struggling for a gasp of air on the fringes of the mob.

The house where Ambrose's family lived was no longer visible behind the flames. Occasionally a timber fell, sparkling incandescently. Ambrose ran from one group of mourners to the next, pulling up a familiar-looking shoulder only to find the wrong face. They were the faces of neighbors and childhood friends grown older, and all of them had the same hollow look of human beings who had experienced the unbelievable.

But none of the faces belonged to his family.

Something took hold of his hand. He shrieked and shoved it away, not realizing until a moment later that it was a woman. In the harsh light of the blaze, he recognized her as a friend of his mother's.

"Where is she?" he screamed. "Where are all of them?"

The woman looked at him with sad eyes and gestured with one hand toward the shadows. "Behind the wall," she said.

But Ambrose had seen the wall and the dead laid out before it. His family had not been among them. He searched again among the bodies.

The old woman was still standing, watching him. At least he understood what she had said.

The back of the wall was covered with compost. It always had been, as long as Ambrose could remember. This was where everyone in the neighborhood brought their leaves and their floor sweepings, their few scraps of garbage; it would all be used communally as fertilizer later. He remembered playing in the compost heap as a child and being terrified by the sight of a severed chicken's head under his shoe. Now he knelt there and made the sign of the cross and wished with every fiber of his being that he had died before witnessing the sight before him.

Six headless, naked bodies lay to his left. On his right, in a bowl formed by an indentation in the leaves, were the heads of his mother and her five other children.

*This is my blood.*

"Yours was the first house they burned," the old woman said from the shadows. The din of the fire was lesser here than in front of the wall; by comparison, it seemed like a ghastly silence.

A sound like the cry of a beast escaped from the priest and he stood up, casting the shadow of a giant. Without looking back at the mockery of his family's murder, he ran into the mob, kicking, punching when he could, his rage aimless and unfocused.

His feet knocked against something. Looking down, he saw it was the board with the nail protruding from its end. Perhaps it was not the same weapon that the youth had used to kill the gray-haired man, but he still felt a deep satisfaction that its owner was no longer wielding it. He stooped to pick it up.

Someone kicked him in the side. "Bloody Papist."

He whirled around on the ground, grasping the board and swinging it with all his strength. It struck his assailant in the leg. The man fell, howling, his blood spreading over his pant leg.

Ambrose rose, the board still in his hands. His mind contained nothing at that moment, not pity or mercy or the teaching of Christ to which he had dedicated his life. Nothing remained except for the image of his mother's mutilated body and the rolling heads of his brothers and sisters, massacred in their sleep.

*This is my blood.*

He lifted the board over his head.

"Don't," the fallen man pleaded, shielding his face with his hands. "Please don't, mister."

He crashed it down. The nail on the end pierced through the man's eye. He struck him again, in the throat, on the top of his head, and as the man pitched

330

forward, into the back of his neck. He continued to bludgeon the dying man in his back as the body convulsed in blood-spurting spasms. He hit him and did not stop, could not stop, until he felt hands yanking his arms behind his back.

"It's okay, Father. I'm a friend," a voice said. It was one of the men from the meeting. "You've got to get out of here before the cops see you."

It struck him like a physical blow.

*Father?*

He dropped the board and allowed himself to be led away. When the hands released him, he was standing near Seamus Dougherty.

The boy smiled. From inside his jacket, he produced a pistol. He slapped it into Ambrose's hand.

"Try this," he said.

Father Ambrose stared at him.

"You've got nothing to lose now."

Ambrose took the gun. Ahead a mounted policeman prepared to fire a rubber bullet at two men fighting with each other. The priest pulled the trigger. The policeman's stomach burst open and sprayed blood over the crowd.

"This is my blood," Father Ambrose Anthony said.

There was no turning back.

# CHAPTER TWENTY-SIX

It was April 1972.

Because of the macabre murder of Father Ambrose's family, he requested and received a sabbatical from his churchly duties.

In May, Seamus Dougherty, with a handful of other IRA Provos, attended a summit meeting in Lebanon of terrorist leaders from around the world. As a result of this meeting, the international terrorist known as Carlos began running arms from Lebanese- and Lybian-owned caches in Switzerland to IRA contacts in Northern Ireland.

The IRA was expanding.

In June, Dougherty persuaded "Ambrose Anthony, civilian," to attend guerrilla training in Libya. At the first camp, in Az Zauiah, he learned weaponry, sabotage, explosives and guerrilla warfare. With him at Az Zauiah were Italians, Germans, Turks, Greeks, French Corsicans and men from Brittany and the Basque Provinces. None of them seemed to find it odd that Europeans would be training in the Middle East under Palestinian instructors in preparation to fight for the causes of their respective homelands.

At the second camp, in Tokra, northeast of Benghazi, Ambrose learned from battle-hardened Cuban teachers the most advanced techniques of sabotage known in the world. He became expert at explosives, timing devices, silent killing, subversion, poisoning and terror.

Training began at dawn and continued until after dark, with only a scant meal of boiled barley. The Cuban instructors were tough men, veterans who had lived through every kind of physical challenge from the revolution against Battista to starvation. They drove the trainees until they dropped, grateful for rest, onto blankets laid on a bare floor in a communal sleeping room.

Barracks living did not come easily to Father Ambrose. He possessed a solitary nature and had indulged it in his years of religious life. Even after three months in the camps and a perennial state of exhaustion, he could not get used to sleeping in a room filled with other men.

Mostly he was afraid. His fears were so all-encompassing that it was difficult for him even to define them. He feared for his life, now and later. He feared for his soul. Was it right to fight and kill, even for Ireland? Would God damn him for not turning the other cheek? Or would He be pleased that His priest, through one man's small efforts, helped to save his people and his ancient race?

And he feared the men. Not just the instructors, whose ferocity was part of the training, but the other trainees at Tokra as well. These men were not the young, idealistic Europeans he had encountered at Az Zauiah. Many of them were convicted criminals—murderers, rapists, thieves—who had joined a revolutionary or underground fighting force more for the immediate violence of battle then for any dream of a better society. Others were fanatics determined to wage war on the world for beliefs too obscure for anyone else to understand. Others still were simply mad. But as the training continued, Ambrose realized that madmen too had their place in revolution. They, the fighters, were the tools of the thinkers. They did not make policy, but they were needed to implement it.

In the end, they were the ones who could claim, in all honesty, that they were only following orders.

Ambrose tossed on his blanket, unable to get comfortable. The desert heat was oppressive, and the stench from the bodies of the three dozen men crammed into the small, airless chamber nauseated him. Those bodies, with their rock-hard muscles, their powerful hands and driving, oozing sexuality . . .

The thought of men—as men, not as fighters—bothered him more as the days at the camp wore on. He caught himself watching, his breath suspended, as a smooth-chested Palestinian climbed a wall, his back alive, his buttocks straining. Once, during the evening meal while a swarthy Turk opposite him ate his gruel and a piece of greasy lamb with his fingers, the priest realized with alarm and shame that he had achieved a full, throbbing erection.

He was a virgin. Ambrose had entered the priesthood pure and had never broken his vow of celibacy since. There had been times, in the seminary, when he had been tempted. Other boys did it. He heard them, giggling beneath the sheets or in the washrooms of the dormitory, and he had ached for release himself.

But the stain of guilt was too great. He had, he believed, been chosen by God for his vocation and must not allow himself to be corrupted. Once, in weakness, he had touched himself, alone in bed while the other boys were asleep. The sensations of pure pleasure flooded him then with a power he had never before conceived. His hand moved automatically, uncontrollably, and in his mind he substituted another penis for his own, growing, hardening, thrusting against his hands, his buttocks, into his mouth. It belonged not to him but to some nameless, faceless stranger who weakened under his will, whose body he defiled at his whim, who obeyed each lewd command. He could not see the man's features until the moment of orgasm, when he threw himself back on his pillow with a stifled groan and the seed spilled out of him. Then he saw his accomplice in a blinding instant of light.

It was the face of Jesus Christ.

Afterward, he rubbed his hands with sandpaper until they bled and never touched himself again.

Now, in the camp at Tokra, the old urges haunted him again. It wasn't normal, he told himself. The thoughts that intruded so insistently on his consciousness were perversions, filth. If they had been of women, he could have been more forgiving of himself, but women had never aroused him. Perhaps it was because he never spent much time around women. He didn't know; all he understood was that the scent of the men in the barracks room with him clawed at his desire like the talons of wild birds.

"You."

He lay still, irrationally afraid of the voice.

"Irishman. You are awake?" The words, while whispered, were heavily accented.

"I am," he said.

A young man slipped silently through the darkness onto the blanket beside him. Ambrose knew him. His name was Raffa and he came from North Yemen. They had eaten together more than once.

"I see you moving from the other side. I too cannot sleep," the young man said, grinning, showing two rows of gleaming teeth beneath his thick beard.

Ambrose felt the heat from Raffa's body. "It's very warm here," he said lamely.

"Warm, but not hot, eh?"

"I don't understand."

Raffa made a don't-bullshit-me face. "My friend, we have been at the camps for three months. A quarter of a year. In Yemen, in three months, I would have taken a woman to bed with me ninety times."

"You must have been a very busy man," Ambrose said.

"You do not do the same?"

Ambrose swallowed. "I'm a Catholic priest," he said, so quietly it was almost inaudible among the snoring sounds of the sleeping men. Raffa looked at him, puzzled. "My religion forbids it."

Raffa uttered a word Ambrose didn't understand and slapped the side of his own face with his open palm. "You have never lain with a woman?" he asked incredulously.

"No."

The Yemeni deliberated in silence for a moment. "Or a man?" he said.

"Of course not," Ambrose answered, feeling his stomach knot. Then: "Have you?"

Raffa shrugged. "There is no shame in using a

336

boy." When the priest did not turn away, he said, "Irishman, in my country there is civil war. The streets are covered with bodies. We are forced to fight our own brothers for a piece of land, a bag of millet for food. My people, my family, are starving. Every day is spent in fear of death."

"In mine, too," Ambrose said.

"And so, with death waiting beneath each footstep, we cannot argue about what is good and what is bad in our insignificant lives. The revolution is good. The reign of the theocrats and the English invaders is bad. Everything else . . . unimportant." He smiled. "You understand?"

"It's not the same," Ambrose said.

"Is the same. I show you." He took the priest's hand. Reflexively, Ambrose jerked it away, but Raffa's grip was strong. He placed it between his legs.

Ambrose moaned softly. He wouldn't stop now, he knew; he couldn't. And as he filled himself with pleasure, he squeezed his eyes closed to shut out the sight of the phantom face, its forehead crowned with thorns and streaming blood, that loomed before him.

When the face disappeared, he felt relieved. And empty.

"Don't go," he whispered as Raffa fastened his trousers.

"I must rest now. Tomorrow I come back."

But he did not return the following night, or the next or the night after that. Ambrose lay awake, feverish, like a girl waiting for her lover, while Raffa slept peacefully on the other side of the room.

On the fourth night, he heard sounds and knew instinctively that they came from Raffa's blanket. Someone else was with him. Ambrose turned away, as silently as possible, and tried to sleep.

He could not. The blood throbbed inside his ears, and he let his hand reach down to touch himself. It was dirty, it was obscene, and it was blessed relief.

But when he had done, he heard soft laughter from the other side of the room and then two whispered voices.

Raffa's voice said, "The priest has found love tonight."

And another man's voice said, "Yes. With himself."

They laughed again. Consumed by shame, Father Ambrose rose from his blanket and ran out of the barracks building. He wandered the camp aimlessly and entered the mess building. A pot of coffee was bubbling atop a heavy cast-iron oil-fired stove in the center of the floor.

Ambrose stood in front of the stove. Despite the warm weather, the heat from the stove felt good on his underwear-clad body. It reminded him of home, when he was young, when he was innocent, before he had become a pervert, he thought bitterly, before he had become an object of mocking ridicule among other men.

He held his hands in front of him. Sin and its instruments. He had been a good and decent priest, and now he was a killer of men, one who doubted all he had been trained to revere and obey. He was worse. He was an animal, scorned by others. His hands had visited that fate on him, and as he looked at them, he remembered verses of childhood innocence: "If thine hand offend thee, cut it off."

He extended his hands and then pressed them down on the blazing red iron lid of the stove. He stifled the scream that rose in his throat with the pain. He could smell the sickly sweet odor of burning flesh before he released his touch on the stove. His hands were burned almost to the bone.

Officials at the camp wanted to send him home, but Ambrose refused.

"I will finish my training," he said. For in the moments of his burning, he had come to realize a great truth about himself. The sin was not in his hands, but in his soul. He was a priest, dedicated to God, but the only time he had felt truly alive in his whole life was the moment he had shot that policeman in the Derry riot. Death was his life and he knew now he would offer himself up to it as wholeheartedly, as unquestioningly, as he had once offered himself to the church.

Ten days later the bandages came off his hands. The skin was a twisted mass of scar tissue; there were no fingerprints left, just smooth, hard pads where fingerprints once had been.

Two days later, during a long run across a mined obstacle field, Raffa came up behind him. "You run well, Irishman," he called out. "Your injury has not slowed you down at all."

Ambrose looked around. They were alone, the other trainees having scattered in different directions across the sand.

"That night you didn't come to my bed," Ambrose said, and Raffa nodded. "Why?"

The Yemeni grinned. "Life is short."

Ambrose stopped and smiled back. "It is for you," he said.

Without a word, he thrust his knee into Raffa's groin. When the bigger man dropped, Ambrose dove down onto his face with both knees. He heard the man's nose break. He rolled the man over and ripped down his trousers He entered him roughly, shoving Raffa's broken nose in the dirt when he protested.

When it was over, Ambrose leaned forward and pushed Raffa's face down into the sand until it covered his ears. When the Yemeni stopped fighting, Ambrose released him, stood up, and then carefully covered the body with sand. He turned away and walked toward the coastline.

His training was complete.

# CHAPTER TWENTY-SEVEN

In 1974, the Irish Republican Army branched again to form the Republican Socialist Party and its military arm, the Irish National Liberation Army, a faction even more radical and violent than the IRA or the Provisional IRA. Among the six men who directed the INLA was Seamus Dougherty.

As for Father Ambrose Anthony, he requested an immediate resumption of his duties and a transfer to missionary work. He had had enough of Ireland.

Within months, the church transferred him to Central America, where he watched over a small parish and tended a field of corn and two dairy cows.

And he killed.

He could not stop the killing. After a while he no longer tried. He had created an intellectual justification for it. The world was filled with evil, with corrupters, with those who subjugated the poor and downtrodden. The ways of government and the ways of the Church were too slow to deal with these injustices. What God needed to triumph on earth was a strong right arm. Father Ambrose offered himself up to the task. He would have liked to do it in Ireland, but Ireland was still too painful for him.

Nicaragua in 1974 was under the cruel yoke of the oppressive Somoza dictatorship, but there were rumblings in the hills of popular revolt and people's uprisings, and in the growing boldness of the Sandinista rebels, the priest found a cloak for his own activities.

Government soldiers were found strangled. Police barracks were blown up, buses were run off cliffs. The killings came quickly, without warning, and none knew whom to blame.

The guards at a government storehouse were killed and the store thrown open to the starving peasants. The peasants took the food, went home and ate, and then slyly denied any knowledge of it to government soldiers. The government kept increasing the rewards it offered for the capture of terrorists, but three of the men posting reward notices were shot in the head.

Among the peasants, a legend grew. There was a Robin Hood abroad in the land. He was the man who could not be killed. He was *Lazaro,* the Spanish name for Lazarus, the man who would rise from the dead again and again.

Lazarus had been born.

Three years later, Father Ambrose saw Seamus Dougherty again.

A motorized convoy of Sandinista rebels was rolling through the small village where the priest lived. Father Ambrose was tending his corn in the small roadside field. He looked up as the cars and trucks passed. Then one of the cars skidded to a halt, and Seamus Dougherty stepped from the back seat.

He walked over to the priest, his eyes squinted,

searching the man's face. For a moment, Ambrose did not recognize him. Then Dougherty grabbed the hoe from the priest's hands and tossed it to the ground. He turned the priest's hands over, inside his, and looked at the scars that covered his fingers and palms.

His eyes met Ambrose's and he smiled.

"So we meet again, priest."

Dougherty looked thinner and older, but the knife-sharp zeal of the fanatic was still in his eyes, shining brighter than ever.

"You look poorly, Seamus," Ambrose said.

"I've been a guest of the British."

"You escaped prison?"

Dougherty nodded.

"And why are you here?"

"Perhaps looking for you," Dougherty said.

"You're wasting your time. I'm through with Ireland."

"Ireland's not through with you, however," Dougherty said. "How do you like being ruled by a dictator?"

"I am ruled by God."

"In Nicaragua, you're ruled by Somoza, and God has precious little to do with it," Dougherty said.

"I am not concerned with Somoza or any government. I came here to heal, Seamus. Unfortunately, my wounds are inflicted by the truth. Once one learns the truth about oneself, it's hard to curl up inside a comfortable lie again."

"Maybe you learned the wrong truth."

"There's only one," Ambrose said.

"Is there?" Dougherty lit a cigarette and automatically cupped it into his palm in the manner of a man accustomed to hiding. "If someone asked you if God existed, you'd say He did. That would be the truth, wouldn't it?"

Ambrose nodded.

"And if the same man asked me, I'd say there is no God."

"But that wouldn't be the truth," Ambrose said.

"It is to me. My answer would pass a lie-detector test, same as yours."

Ambrose leaned back against the small wooden fence. "You're still playing tricks, Seamus."

"I still believe I can make a difference."

"To what? World communism?"

"Call it what you want to. I choose to call it equality."

Ambrose snorted in disgust. "What are you doing here?"

"I've come as a consultant to the Sandinistas. Press relations, I guess you could call it."

"Terrorism sounds more like it," Ambrose said. "I've watched the Sandinistas and they don't look much different to me than the Samozans. You just change the names, but they're all the same. The Sandinistas, the IRA, the PLO, there's no difference. A brotherhood of terrorism."

"We're believers in freedom," Dougherty said. "That's all."

"Talk," Ambrose said, dismissively. "More rhetoric, more lies. The people here are starving and they don't know why. Most of them can't even read their own names. They don't care at all about replacing one dictatorship with another one, and you know and I know that that's what will happen."

Dougherty looked at the preist for long seconds. "I could have you killed right now for saying that, you know."

"Aye, you could. And you'd just be proving me right," Ambrose said.

There was sadness in Dougherty's eyes as he turned away.

"I'm sorry, priest. I misjudged you. I never thought you'd wind up on the sidelines booing both teams."

"I don't like either team," Ambrose said, but Dougherty was already getting back into his car and did not hear him.

Ambrose was baking bread when Dougherty returned three days later.

"If you've come to proselytize me again, you're wasting your time, Seamus," said Ambrose.

"Just a man of peace, aren't you?" Dougherty said.

"I try," Ambrose said. He dusted flour from his dirty cassock.

"And Lazarus? Does he try, too?"

The priest sat down on a bare wooden chair and said nothing. The small room was permeated with the scent of baking bread.

"You had me fooled, priest. I'll admit that. But then I found out about this Lazarus, and the Sandinistas don't know any more about him than the Somozans do. When I heard how he killed and how he never left any fingerprints, then I knew it was you." He smiled. "You and I learned the same killing tricks, Ambrose."

The priest's face was ashen. "Does anyone else know?"

"Of course not," Dougherty said. "This is Central America. But what one person learns, everyone soon knows, and your life wouldn't be worth a copper. And I told you, I've got uses for you."

"Not for me."

"Especially for you," Dougherty said. "You're not one of Ireland's Wild Geese, fighting other men's wars in foreign places. You belong in Ireland."

"I'm fighting no war," Ambrose snapped. "What I've done here, I've done for the people caught between groups like your bloody IRA or their bloody Sandinistas and the inept governments you're trying to destroy. I'm not a terrorist; I'm a priest. I want no part of your stinking manufactured revolutions."

"You can't stop it, Lazarus."

Ambrose stared out the small window in his kitchen. "I know," he finally said, softly.

Dougherty put a hand on his shoulder. "Why did you leave Ireland? We trained you. We need you so."

"Ireland corrupted me," the priest said, still staring fixedly at the still cows worrying one of the few tufts of grass in his dirt yard. "It showed me what I was. And what I was . . . was not compatible with the Church."

"You're a soldier, for all that."

Ambrose rose suddenly, pounding his fist on the table in rage. "I am no soldier. I am a servant of God!" Then, as if all the air and blood and strength had left him, he said, "I am anathema."

He stood like a visionary in the small kitchen, his back twisted with guilt, his eyes glistening with the tears of a man who weeps often and uncontrollably. "I have not been confessed in more than six years. The masses I celebrate are a charade. I cannot confess to the sins I have committed because they are so great that not even God would forgive them. And it as because of

346

Ireland. Ireland! Ireland has meant more to me than God Himself and He is showing me His vengeance.'' His hands trembled. He wiped his face with them and sat down.

"Are you ill?'' Dougherty asked.

The priest's answer came in a whisper. "I have syphilis.''

Dougherty swallowed. "How long?''

"Not long enough. I have many years to suffer before my punishment is complete.''

"Come back to Ireland. You don't want to die here.''

"Lazarus returned from the dead,'' the priest said, smiling crookedly.

"We need you. We need your skills.''

"It's not up to me.''

"Request a post in Ireland. For your health. Say this place is too much for you,'' Dougherty said.

"What do you want with me in Ireland?'' Father Ambrose roared.

Dougherty stared, cautiously watching the man in front of him who could turn so suddenly from humility to violence. "I don't think you're ready to know.''

"What's that supposed to mean?''

"It means that when you're ready to come back, Ireland will take you. And it will find work that needs to be done,'' Dougherty said and left.

It was the last the priest saw of Seamus Dougherty for the next two years.

But the legend of Lazarus grew.

# CHAPTER TWENTY-EIGHT

In the time that followed, bridges were blown up and railroad tracks destroyed, preventing supplies and food from reaching government soldiers around the country. Military personnel were ambushed and often found mutilated. Military bases were robbed of their provisions and the food distributed to the poor.

Many were involved in the rebel cause—the Communist-trained and-sponsored Sandinistas, native volunteers and secret troops from Cuba—but for the poverty-stricken residents of the small villages of the mountains and the coastline, there was no protector but Lazarus, the man with no face and no fingerprints, the soldier who led his own army of one.

The Somozan government redoubled its assault, holding secret tribunals where those accused of siding against the government were tortured and killed, often with their entire families. Villages were razed; disease spread like a wave over the country from bodies left without burial in the humid heat.

Through it all, Lazarus brought stolen medical supplies to the villagers at night, along with food. Those who dared to ride alone into the mountains would find the roads marked with the hanging bodies of soldiers.

In 1977, the Nicaraguan bishops objected openly to the ill treatment of the citizens by the government. Now all members of the religious community, both Protestant and Catholic, banded together against the violations of human rights instituted by the Somozan regime.

Father Ambrose took into his farm a young English missionary named Robert Wells, who had been burned out of his own small home. The Reverend Wells brought with him six young children who had been left homeless and orphaned by the growning war.

Wells was grateful. He and his charges tended the small farm during the day. At night, Father Ambrose and the Protestant clergyman conducted services for the dead in the same house. And while everyone slept, Lazarus slipped out to do his work.

But his work produced no result. The war went on; the killings continued. The Somozans had all the resources: an organized army, weapons, transportation, money. They did not have to listen to the bishops. They did not care about United Nations reports of their brutality and repression. The nationwide strike against the government that had touched off the civil war apparently had not hurt them. They had rejected the offer of the United States to mediate a peace settlement. They did not mind the withdrawal of American aid.

The Somozans needed nothing; they would last forever. And the saddest part, Father Ambrose realized, was that the peasants did not care. They did not care who won; they knew their lives would not change at all.

There was nothing left to do. It was Ireland, happening all over again, one organized group fighting another organized group and the people caught, defenseless, uncaring, in the middle. Ambrose stood by his window, watching the sun rise, realizing that Ireland had followed him across the sea, and he wept.

*Oh, Ireland! Is the endless violence all you have to offer your children?*

His tears stopped. A ray of light stung his eyes. His hands fidgeted. The muscles in his neck tightened.

*Violence.*

Not defense but violence, pure and simple. Enough violence to outrage the people into fighting with no weapons, no food. Violence as a prod to action.

Dougherty had known the power of violence from the beginning. Make the people mad enough, frightened enough, and they'll do anything.

*We want to change the world.*

By scaring it to death.

In July 1978, the mayor of a small village was hanged on a telephone pole beside a road. No rope was used. He was nailed to the pole by his neck.

A woman in a neighboring town who had been the mistress of an army officer was covered with gasoline and sent from her house afire. She died on the street, naked, burned beyond recognition as a human.

An old man who had once served under Somoza was hacked to pieces with a machete as he drove his donkey cart into town before dawn.

The people began to cringe. Who was committing these atrocities, directed not toward the military, but toward the common people?

They knew the answer. Only one man moved so swiftly, so silently, that he was never seen.

But why?

Lazarus had been their friend. He had given them food when they were starving. He had protected their families, their churches. He had risked his life a hundred times to save theirs.

Why?

The violence became more random. A bus going from Managua to León was blow up. All the cattle on a government-sponsored ranch were systematically slaughtered. A schoolhouse full of children was exploded.

The masses for the dead grew in number.

In early August, four churches were burned to the ground. A city street crowded with pedestrians was bombed. A nursing home was set on fire.

No, it could not be Lazarus, the people decided. The government had started the killing. It was the government that was escalating it to the level of pure sadism.

The government.

And the government had to go.

In a small mountain village, a woman and five children were murdered, their bodies decapitated and burned.

Ambrose returned in the early morning hours. Robert Wells was already awake, waiting in the kitchen. "You're covered with blood," the young missionary said in alarm.

Ambrose looked at his hands. They were crusted with brown-red stains. "I was helping a neighbor butcher a pig," he said.

Together the two clergymen listened to the news on the small radio in the basement of Ambrose's home. "They fought back," Ambrose said, closing his exhausted eyes.

"They were manipulated into fighting by that maniac," Robert Wells said.

"We'll remember him as a maniac. But as far as history goes, he'll be no more than just another sputtering, power-hungry little dictator," the weary Ambrose said.

Robert looked at him, confused. "I didn't mean Somoza," he said.

"Who, then?"

The Englishman smiled in disbelief. "Why, Lazarus, naturally. He's the one who's turned this country into a concentration camp."

Ambrose stared at the young man, dumbfounded. "Lazarus? A *maniac?*"

"Well . . ." The young man looked around. He didn't know what was happening.

"Lazarus saved the people of this country from slaughter. Ask them! They understand him. They're fighting back now because of Lazarus. The masses had to be prodded into action. They had to be led to the point where they had no other choice but to use force against their oppressors. Lazarus frightened them into defending themselves. Don't you see? They're finally fighting back!

The missionary smiled mildly. "Excuse me, Father, but there's a difference between truth and propaganda. If it weren't for Lazarus and the other Sandinista terrorists, the government wouldn't have started these massacres in the first place. This is the same Communist setup that's been going on all over the world. It's the philosophy of the terrorist."

"Lazarus is not a terrorist!" Ambrose shouted hoarsely. "He is not a Communist. He has served God!" He began to blubber. "He has served God well . . ."

Wells put his arm around him. "Maybe you ought to get some rest, Ambrose," he said gently. "These past few months have been a terrible strain . . ."

"How would you know?" Ambrose cried out. "You

don't know what it's like to be helpless, to resort to your hands because you have no voice and no vote.''

"Father . . .''

"Sometimes your hands are all you have left," Ambrose rasped, drawing back his arm and slapping Wells with the back of his hand.

Wells threw back his head, stunned by the blow, but he did not strike back. Instead, he looked from one of the priest's outstretched palms to the other. Then, studying them, he held Ambrose's hands in his own.

"You have no fingerprints," he said. "What happened to your hands?''

Ambrose snatched his hands away.

"Lazaro,'' Robert Wells whispered. "When you came in with blood on your hands, it was . . .''

"It was for justice!''

The young minister stared in silence for a long moment, then rose, obviously shaken. "The children and I will be leaving in the morning," he said.

"There's a war on.''

"We'll be fine, Father. We've taken up enough of your time and hospitality.''

"Why are you leaving?'' Ambrose asked bitterly. "Am I so evil that you can't bear to share the same roof with me?''

"The reasons don't matter," Wells said, not looking at the other man.

"They do matter.'' He touched the young man's arm. Beneath the fabric of his shirt was the well-defined flesh of a young man at the peak of his physical life. Ambrose thought of his own flesh, diseased, incurably afflicted with the stigma of his sin.

And still he wanted him.

"I am not a killer," he said, begging the godly young man in front of him to believe. But he knew by Robert Wells's expression that he did not believe.

"You've killed hundreds here."

"For a reason," Ambrose pleaded. "There was cause."

Wells nodded. "Good night, Father. Thank you for your kindness to all of us."

It was so English, Ambrose thought, to dismiss him without so much as raising his voice. With utter contempt in his eyes, the young man took Ambrose's hand from his arm and dropped it as if it were covered with vermin.

"Don't you condescend to me," Ambrose hissed, shoving Wells off balance. He could feel the rage in his hands. "Stinking English aristo."

Robert made a move to step past him, but Ambrose blocked his way. "You think I'm just another Irish peasant to be trampled on by your arrogance and power. And why not? You've trampled over the world in the name of your bloody queen. Well, your power stops here."

"You're insane."

Ambrose smashed him across the face. Wells reeled backward, falling, blood spurting from his nose. He reached for a small stool in a corner of the basement and threw it awkwardly at the priest. Ambrose caught it, tossed it away. He walked toward the younger man like a predator after an easy victim.

"Don't," the Englishman said. "For God's sake, Ambrose . . ."

Ambrose kicked him.

Wells rolled over and dragged himself to his feet. He

knew he couldn't make it to the stairs without passing Ambrose. He looked around frantically for a weapon.

On a shelf were a hammer and clamp used in woodworking. He picked up the hammer and waved it menacingly in front of him.

"Don't make me use this," he warned.

Ambrose laughed. "I won't."

He whirled around, raising his leg to land squarely on the man's chest. He heard the crack of ribs breaking. The hammer fell out of Robert's hand, and Ambrose caught it before it reached the floor, swung it once, and connected with Wells's shoulder.

The young man screamed. The hammer struck again, on Wells's left knee. As he howled with the new pain, Ambrose cracked the hammer into Robert's right knee. The young man melted onto the floor, half unconscious with the pain.

Upstairs, there was a flurry of footsteps heading toward the basement. "Go away," Wells shouted through the pain. "Pedro, get the children away from here."

But the child, a boy of eleven or twelve, paid no attention. Seeing the missionary sprawled and bloody, he ran toward the men, leaping on Ambrose to defend Wells.

With one hand, Ambrose grabbed the boy by his hair and threw him face-first against the stone wall. There was a heavy crack as the skull broke open, then the rapid recoil and snap of the boy's neck. As the child lay open-eyed in a spreading puddle of blood, Wells moaned in utter terror.

Five other faces appeared on the stairs leading from the basement. "Go!" Wells screamed the order. "Run. Now."

They pulled themselves out of their frozen horror and

scrambled up the stairs, but Ambrose was too fast for them. One by one he threw them onto the stone floor.

The smallest, a five-year-old-girl, died from the fall. The others huddled around her, sobbing and clutching each other in fear.

Ambrose reached into a dusty crate. He pulled out a machete, its blade gleaming.

"No!" Wells shrieked. With his good arm, he threw the woodworking clamp at Ambrose. The priest deflected it easily. Then, still looking at Wells, he sliced cleanly through the neck of one of the young girls.

"For each attempt on my life, one of them will die," he said evenly.

Wells's face was a mask of horror. "They're . . . just children," he choked.

Ambrose drew the blade across another throat.

"No," Wells screamed. "You said . . ."

Ambrose dragged a child from a corner and cleaved her skull with the machete.

"Dear Jesus," Robert said, sobbing.

He forced himself to kneel, enduring the pain of his shattered knees. He clasped his hands together in front of him and closed his eyes.

As he prayed, Ambrose killed the one child who remained. And as the prayer ended, he kicked Robert onto his belly. He sat astride the young man's back, machete held high.

"May God forgive you," Wells said.

Ambrose brought the blade down. He severed the left hand first, then the right. Wells lost consciousness.

And Lazarus stood up, his cassock heavy with blood, his eyes surveying the nightmare he had created, and thought:

*I have no place with God now. It is time to return home.*
He found the thought strangely comforting.


He stripped to his underwear, leaving the bloody cassock on the floor. Then he took a can of gasoline from the woodshed and poured it in every room of the small house and the one-room church attached to it.

The fire spread quickly, then mushroomed with a whoosh into a spiral of flame.

Ambrose waited as long as he could, then dragged himself out of the building, ran a few yards away, and dropped facedown in the dirt.

Within minutes, he was found and rescued by villagers. As they put him carefully into the backseat of the lone automobile in the village, he peeked at the church. It was engulfed in flames.

He had suffered only bruises at the hands of the mad assassin, and the doctors at the small hospital twenty miles away pronounced him well enough to leave the next day. But first, Father Ambrose had to tell his story to a colonel of the Nicaraguan Army.

It was Lazarus, the priest recounted tearfully. He had been dressed all in black with a black mask covering his face. He had broken into the mission and for no reason at all he had begun killing people. Ambrose didn't know how he had managed to survive. Lazarus had struck him with a pipe. Perhaps he had left him for dead when he set the mission on fire. Ambrose didn't know because the only thing he remembered was waking up in the hospital.

The colonel nodded sympathetically and ordered a telephone brought to the room. He asked Ambrose for one favor. Would the priest talk to the brother of the dead

Protestant minister and tell him what had happened? The colonel smiled apologetically. "My English," he explained. Ambrose nodded and half an hour later was talking on the telephone, repeating his story to SAS Major Daniel Taylor Wells.

He broke into tears during the retelling, and the British officer tried to comfort him over the telephone.

"Will you be all right, Father?" Daniel Wells asked

"I'm leaving. As soon as I can."

"I'll be coming to Nicaragua," Wells said. "Perhaps we could meet."

"No," Ambrose said. "No. That maniac is still loose and I'm leaving here before he comes back to finish the job."

"I fully understand," Wells said.

"I'm terribly sorry about your brother," Ambrose had said. "He was a good man."

"Thank you. I know he was."

Father Ambrose told the authorities he needed a few days to finish his business in Nicaragua before leaving. Then, wearing borrowed clothes, he went out into the hills behind the small village that had been his home, headquarters and hideout for so many years.

On the second day, he spotted a lone rebel. The man's name was Jose. He was a Cuban, and he was drinking with his hands from a stream when Ambrose came up behind him and pressed the fallen branch of a tree across his throat. It was not a blow; Ambrose held the bar, pressing tightly, against the Cuban but left him room to gasp, "Who are you? What do you want?"

"I am Lazarus," he said, then released the grip so the man could turn.

"You are the priest from the village," Jose said, staring in astonishment. "The other priest? *You* killed him?"

Ambrose nodded.

The Cuban grinned, then broke into a chuckle. "You are a great hero of the revolution. Now what do you want with me?"

"The brother of the dead priest is coming here. He is a dangerous man. I need your help to dispose of him."

"I will get you many men," Jose said.

"Only you," Ambrose responded.

"Helping you will be my privilege as well as my duty," Jose said.

Two days later, Jose contacted Daniel Wells by telephone in the capital city of Managua.

"You are looking for Lazarus?" he asked.

Ambrose stood alongside Jose, his ear pressed to the telephone. He heard Wells answer without hesitation, "Do you know where he is?"

"Yes."

"Will you sell me the information?" Wells asked.

"I give it freely."

"Why?" Wells said.

"I too was nearly slaughtered by Lazaro."

"Where is he?" Wells asked.

"Hiding in the mountains," Jose said. He gave Wells exact directions. "Do not come alone, I warn you. Often there are others with him."

"What others?"

"I do not know them."

"Where are you? I must see you," Wells said.

Father Ambrose disconnected the call.

* * *

He and Jose returned to a shack in the hills, which was the target they had given Major Wells. They had loaded the small building with dynamite.

"We will trap him here," Jose said. "It is a wonderful plan."

"It is a better plan than you think, my friend," Ambrose said. He hit the Cuban on the side of the head with the butt of his pistol; the rebel sprawled motionless on the dirt floor of the hut.

When Jose awoke, a cloth had been tied around his mouth as a gag. He saw with horror that dynamite had been wired around his throat and both his wrists. He looked at Ambrose, confusion and terror in his face. He shook his head as if to ask, Why?

"You will be a martyr for a good cause," Ambrose said. "Through you, Lazarus will die, and none will ever seek him again."


They came just after nightfall. Lazarus doubted if the men with Wells were police. The country was in such disorder now that the few policemen who hadn't already been conscripted into the army had their hands full without catering to the whim of an English visitor seeking personal vengeance. More than one of the men limped. Old army, Lazarus guessed, former soldiers who, for one reason of another, could no longer serve except as mercenaries for men like Wells.

They crept up slowly, careful to make as little noise as possible. Through his night glasses, Lazarus saw Wells give the other men a signal to drop back. He was going into the shack alone.

Ambrose fired a shot into the air, then backed away from the shack.

Wells dispersed the men around the small hut. "Come out," he called. "There are too many of us. Come out and you'll stay alive."

There was no response, of course.

Ambrose fired again, and without waiting for Wells's order, the old soldiers with him fired. There was a fusillade of bullets, and then a massive explosion that blew the shack to splinters. Three of the men, who were too near the structure, vanished, obliterated by the blast. Wells himself was thrown back ten yards, cut and bleeding.

He looked at the burning rubble of the hut and screamed, "Die, you bastard! Die!"

Father Ambrose ran.

Lazarus was dead. It was time to return to Ireland.

# CHAPTER TWENTY-NINE

Father Ambrose stood in the graveyard behind St. Benedict's. It was a cloudy night, misted with rain, starless. The flowers the ladies of the church had provided for Hattie O'Shea's grave had already wilted and washed away.

The priest breathed deeply and looked at his hands. Soft hands now, unused to physical work for more than four years. Shaky, unsteady hands. The disease was beginning to affect them. They had been betraying him lately with spasms. Sometimes he awoke in the middle of the night, clutching at thin air, as if his hands were grabbing at something he couldn't see. Soon, he knew, the seizures would spread. He would be a useless thing, a pinched and screaming man, the living acknowledgment of his sin.

God hated him. Any why not? He had shown God more than once that the hatred was mutual. He had broken the most holy of God's laws.

"But I never wanted to sin," he whispered. "I did it for Ireland."

For Ireland, he had returned from his foreign war. For Ireland, he had returned to the priesthood, despite the suffering it brought him to be confronted by his hypocrisy through every waking hour of his life. For Ireland, he had accepted the post as assistant to an old parish priest in a sleepy southern Kerry village. For Ireland he had killed Father Gervaise and Hattie O'Shea, as he had killed so often before. All for Ireland. And for Seamus Dougherty, who *was* Ireland, more surely than the very soil.

Seamus had known for years about the petition to the Pope to visit Ardath. When Ambrose was sent there to recover from the horror of his suffering in Central America, Dougherty had instituted a massive letter-writing campaign throughout the country, pleading with the Pontiff to come to Ardath. It had been done in secret. Some of Dougherty's aides had written hundreds of letters.

At first, Father Ambrose chose not to pay attention to any connection between Dougherty and the Pope. The idea of assassination was unthinkable.

But with the first leaks of information that the Pope was considering a visit to Ardath, he understood what he had to do.

"You want me to kill him, don't you?" he had asked Dougherty.

"I want you to choose sides," Dougherty said.

"Ireland or God?"

Dougherty shook his head. "Not God. Only Ireland. A free Ireland or an enslaved one. That is the choice."

"The Pope isn't Somoza," Ambrose said.

"But the situation is identical."

"That was an open revolt, a civil war," Ambrose said, without believing the words, knowing that his protest was useless, sure that Seamus Dougherty had the answers, because they were Ambrose Anthony's answers, too.

"Why did it occur?" Dougherty asked. "Why then and not a hundred years from now? What prompted the revolution? What made it work?" He lit a cigarette. "I'll tell you: fear. The people will not rebel against a government, no matter how cruel or oppressive it is, unless something prods them to outrage so great that even their lives become secondary to their fury. In the case of Somoza, his own military excesses were nearly enough to bring out that rage. Lazarus tipped the scales. You know your actions were blamed on the government. They brought the government down."

"I know," Ambrose said.

"But the Brits in Ulster are a lot more subtle than Somoza could have hoped to be. The Brits punish the dissidents but not their families. They push, but not too far. They grant concessions; they compromise. They take pains to avoid causing any kind of massive discontent. . . ."

"But the Pope . . ." Ambrose began.

"Exactly. The murder of the living embodiment of God by the British sympathizers will be enough to unite Catholic Ireland, north and south. Together, we can rid the country of every trace of Britain and her descendants within months."

"But first, someone has to kill the Pope," Ambrose said dully.

"Someone has to serve Ireland."

"I'll be killed and you know it," Ambrose said.

Dougherty took a deep drag on his cigarette. "It

would be a better death than some," he said quietly, looking pointedly at the sick priest.

For Ireland, Ambrose thought, sifting through the wet earth of Hattie's grave. First my heart for Ireland, then my soul. Soon, my life. But first, the life of God's supreme disciple.

"Ireland, forgive your sons for what we do in your name," he whispered as he began to dig.

When he got down as far as Hattie's casket, he went into his carpentry shop in the garage at the back of the rectory and pulled the planks from the coal bin. It was an enormous job, backbreaking, leaving his hands bloody and filled with splinters. At the bottom of the bin was a trapdoor. Beneath it was a special compartment and inside that a plastic bag containing the remains of Winston Barnett's body. The body had begun to rot, and even through the heavy plastic, the stench was nauseating. Groaning under the weight, Ambrose carried the bag to the grave and dumped it inside.

After he finished covering the grave, he crawled into the compartment beneath the coal bin where the heavy metal drum of plastic explosives was hidden. He hoisted it up carefully to the garage floor.

He worked through the night, carefully mixing the entire keg of roofing nails through the mass of the explosive. From the red box the mailman had delivered the day before, he took a small metallic device to which he wired a nine-volt battery. There was another object inside the red box, a small hand-held control. He inserted a tiny flashlight battery into the back of it, then walked across the workshop and aimed it at the metal device. When he pressed the button on the control, he heard a click and saw a small spark as the electric circuit on the device was closed.

Ambrose smiled tightly. Even automatic garage-door openers had additional uses these days. Carefully he removed the flashlight battery from the control unit so that it would not be triggered by accident.

Then, working delicately but quickly, he put the electrical switch system into the hollow built inside his massive Celtic cross, then packed around it with the nail-loaded plastic explosive. When he was done, he put the top section of the cross in place, sealed it with woodworker's cement, and stood back to admire his work.

It was magnificent, an ancient looking, hand-carved Celtic cross, a beautiful cross, a cross that could have lasted a thousand years.

But this cross, as the first cross had been, was to be a weapon, not an ornament.

He could see the Pope standing in front of it, blessing it, preparing himself to speak to the crowd. To speak words that would never be delivered. But there was much to do before that moment.

Exhausted, he picked the splinters out of his hands and washed them, although they would not come quite clean.

# CHAPTER THIRTY

Cormac and Wells stood on the edge of Moon Lake as the scuba diver walked ashore, shaking his head. He removed his rubber mouthpiece and said, "Nothing. There's nothing there to be found."

Cormac grunted and the man said, "It's sorry I am to have to charge you for finding nothing."

"Quite all right," Wells said. He paid the man, who walked away and loaded his gear into the trunk of an old, rusted pickup truck.

"What now?" Cormac asked Wells.

"Two possibilities. One, the diver just missed it. Or two, more likely, someone's lifted the typewriter. That being the case, good citizens like us should report that crime to our local gendarmerie."

As they drove back into Ardath, both of them noticed the sudden number of men in both blue and brown military-style uniforms. The advance guard for the Pope's visit had already arrived.

They were walking up the paved pathway to the Garda station when Morty O'Sullivan came through the door. He flushed when he saw them.

"Hello, Morty," Cormac said. The young man nodded curtly. "You know Dan Wells, don't you?"

"I've seen him around town."

"Dan's in the business, too," Cormac said.

"Oh? Here for the Pope, I suppose."

"An advance scout in a way," Wells said.

"Well, the rest of your troop is here," Morty snapped. "The bleeding army, the bleeding whole Garda staff from Dublin, they've moved inside and taken over. I've just been told to go watch for traffic jams and not get in the way. Hell, I'm going to Grady's. I surely won't be missed here."

"Now, Morty—" Cormac said.

"From month to month, from year to year, they don't know Ardath exists. Then one thing happens like the Pope coming, and like a flash all my work's for nothing. They just push me aside and tell me they'll take care of everything."

"Look at the bright side," Wells said. "They'll be gone in a few days and things'll go back to normal."

"Aye, after they're done littering the parks with soda pop cans and fooling with our women. I don't like strangers coming in doing a job that's rightfully mine." He folded his arms over his chest, apparently unaware of the insult to himself. "What's so bloody funny?" he shouted when Cormac laughed out loud.

"Never mind," Cormac said. "I just wanted to tell you that the typewriter we were looking for, it's gone from Moon Lake. Had a diver down there for three hours."

"Well, if you think I've got anything to do with—"

"I don't, Morty," Cormac said quietly. "I was wrong

that night. I'm no diplomat, only a clumsy-mouthed copper."

Morty looked at him for a moment, his eyes softening. "That'll make two of us, I guess," he answered.

Cormac reached up and ruffled his hair. "Have a pint at Grady's on me," he said.

"Will do. Are you coming?"

"Not yet. We'd better stop in here and make our presence known."

Morty cast a sullen glance at the Garda station as if his old childhood hero had suddenly announced his decision to join the enemy, and walked off down the stone path, the leather heels of his mirror-polished uniform shoes clicking on the stones.

"Volatile young man," Wells said, looking after him.

"It's understandable," Cormac responded. "You don't know the Garda perhaps, but their top brass is the most conceited, officious pack of asses in the world. Probably a lot like your SAS."

"Scotland Yard," Wells corrected and followed the burly Irishman into the small offices that served as Garda headquarters.

There were five men inside in dark blue dress uniforms. Two of them were sitting at typewriters—expensive new IBM's, Cormac noted. Of the three other men, one's uniform was festooned with so much braid that he looked like a Gilbert and Sullivan admiral. He was standing at a desk with the other two men, looking down, pointing at a map.

Cormac recognized the officer immediately as Superintendent Desmond O'Keefe, special assistant to the commissioner. Cormac had seen him several times at

369

Garda headquarters in Dublin's Phoenix Park while stopping there on various errands.

O'Keefe looked up just as the two men stepped to the long complaint counter just inside the door.

"What can I do for you?" he said brusquely.

"I'm Michael Cormac."

For a moment, the name obviously did not register. Then O'Keefe smiled and stepped forward from behind the desk.

"Ah yes, Sergeant Cormac. You're the one who's been here for several weeks and found out absolutely nothing. I thought you had returned to Cork."

"I've decided to take a few days vacation," Cormac said, "and spend it here. This is Daniel Wells. He's been assisting here."

"Yes, of course he has," O'Keefe said, still smiling. "I had the displeasure of reading all his reports."

"Sorry you found them so offensive," Wells said.

"Not offensive, just ineffectual. So far as I can tell, the two of you have been vacationing here and sending back reports warning of impending doom and calamity," O'Keefe said.

"Then you know we think the Pope may well be in danger when he visits here," Wells said.

"Not any longer, my friend. We're going to seal this town tighter than a drumhead." The officer accentuated his confidence with a crisp rap on the countertop and a smile so smug that Cormac felt an almost overwhelming urge to flatten the man's officious little nose. "No one will be in or out but those that belong here. We're fencing off the field in front of the castle where His Holiness will speak. There'll be only one way in and we'll make sure that everyone who comes in is safe. We've got in a con-

370

tingent of twenty soldiers already and more are coming, under my direct command. They're in charge of making sure that Bounfort Castle itself is secure and stays secure." He smiled again, broader, showing big, horsey teeth. "Nothing's going to go wrong, I assure you."

"Then you're not worried, Superintendent, about the explosion and the hand and the body that was found," Cormac said, trying to control his anger.

"Winston Barnett. A Protestant terrorist who was stopped by God before *we* had a chance to stop him." The tone of his voice indicated clearly that the result would have been the same in both cases: a dead Winston Barnett.

"But you've read our reports," Cormac persisted. "You know that the hand didn't belong to the body."

"That's an interesting theory for which, I take it, we have Mr. Wells to thank. But the fact is that it's immaterial." He glanced over his shoulder as if to make sure the men under his command were listening to how he put down these country bumpkins. They were. "Whether it was his hand or not, whether there were two men or one men, it doesn't matter. They were bringing in explosives, they blew up and the man or men are dead. Since that time, nothing has happened in this town to indicate any threat to anybody."

"And the presence of Seamus Dougherty in Killarney?" Wells asked.

"We have scoured that city looking for him. There is no indication, other than your suggestions, that Seamus Dougherty has ever been in Killarney. He is not there now and the confidential word we get is that he is in Belfast and hasn't been out of the North in more than a year. I think that in the excitement of the moment, you thought you saw someone you didn't see. I wouldn't worry about it any more if I were you," O'Keefe said.

Wells shrugged and smiled. "I'm glad you have everything under such good control."

"That's exactly the case. His Holiness will come in here, deliver his speech, and leave, and there will be no incidents. I guarantee it."

"What's he going to speak about?" Cormac asked. "Any idea?"

The horse teeth flashed again. "Well, I've heard a few things, but I'm not at liberty to discuss them with you, Sergeant." He stressed the word "sergeant" slightly, just to remind Cormac that more than a wooden countertop separated them. They were also far apart in rank and influence and power.

"Well, we're both on holiday, but anything we can do for you . . ." Wells began, but the uniformed Irish policeman interrupted him.

"Yes. Well, surely we appreciate it but I don't think we'll be calling on you. Everything is in good order now. Under control or, as you British say, 'going swimmingly.' " He turned away from them, and as if on cue, the two typists began pounding their machines again and the two men at the desk hunched over closer to the topographic map of the area.

Outside, Wells snapped, " 'Going swimmingly.' Are all the Gardai such idiots?"

"Only the top brass," Cormac said. "The rest of us are just poor proletarian plodders."

"No wonder Irish cops drink. I'm of a mind to just walk away and let these imbeciles cook in their own juices," Wells said.

"Why don't you? With luck, the Pope will deliver his

speech *before* he gets killed. That seems to be all they're interested in."

"Don't tempt me," Well said and sighed. "This ass is paving the way for terrorists to get away with murder. Michael, I think we're in this for the duration."

In the small rectory of St. Benedict's, Father Ambrose Anthony was serving tea to three monsignors and a bishop when the telephone rang in the paisley-walled room.

"Forgive me, Excellency," he said to the bishop and answered the phone.

"Do it tonight," Seamus Dougherty said.

"Certainly," Father Ambrose said with a smile, then hung up quickly. He grinned apologetically at the four clergymen. "The village is all atwitter at the news of His Holiness. Someone wanted to know if there would be a special morning mass on Tuesday," he said, then sat down, sipped his tea, and prepared to tell the four high-ranking clergymen about his plan for a wonderful procession to welcome the Pope to Ardath.

Moira's face sparkled as she answered the gentle knock at the cottage door and saw Cormac there.

"Michael," she said, then saw Daniel Wells strolling up the path behind him. Two anxious furrows appeared momentarily on her forehead, then vanished. "And Mister Wells. What a pleasure."

"We're here on business, Moira," Cormac said.

"Well, you can come in for all that," she said.

"We'd like to talk to Kathleen," Cormac said.

"She's not here."

"Is she working tonight?" Cormac asked.

Moira shrugged. "The castle is closed because of the Pope's coming. I think she had a date. She got a phone call and went out."

The two men followed Moira inside but declined when she offered them a drink.

"My, this really is business, isn't it," she said lightly.

Cormac said, "Moira, why did you throw that typewriter into Moon Lake?"

"That? Ahh, it was an old thing and I'd been planning to junk it for some time. I finally got around to it, busted as it was."

"I typed on it," Cormac said.

"You must have a stronger touch than mine, because I had to pound to type even a single letter," the Irishwoman said.

"Your daughter was using it, though, wasn't she?" Wells asked.

Moira was utterly unruffled. "Kathleen? I don't know. I don't think so."

"To write letters to the newspapers," Wells said.

"Oh, you must be mistaken. Kathleen doesn't even read the newspapers, much less take any interest in what's in their editorials."

"Did you see anyone down at the lake?" Cormac asked. "In the last day or so?"

The beautiful red-haired woman shook her head.

"The typewriter's gone," Cormac said. "We looked for it today but it's vanished."

"Probably covered over with mud," she said. "You sure I can't fix you both that drink?"

"Daniel, will you wait for me in the car?" Cormac asked.

The Englishman nodded and walked toward the door. He tipped his hat to Moira as he left.

"Moira, we've got to talk," Cormac said.

"That we do, Michael. Why do you bring that man here when you know he's a copper and means no good?"

"I'm a copper too," Cormac said softly. "He and I are working on the same thing."

"I don't know," Moira said. "After what happened between us . . ." She cast her eyes down. "I just hoped you'd come alone sometime."

"Now's not the time for that," he said sternly. "Moira, do you know what's going on?"

"I'm sure you'll tell me," she said irritably.

"Kathleen's in serious trouble."

"Oh, kids don't get into serious trouble in Ardath."

"For God's sake, why are you pretending not to hear what I'm saying?" he shouted. "Someone's planning to kill the Pope, and Kathleen's involved."

Moira sat down heavily on a chair facing Cormac. She shook her head, her eyes squeezed shut.

"It's true, Moira. Would God it weren't, but it's true. That's why we have to talk to her before she gets in any deeper."

"Not Kathleen. She wouldn't . . ."

"Moira, you know she wrote those letters to the papers, attacking the Pope. Didn't you wonder why?"

The woman sat silently, chewing her lower lip, shaking her head. Her hands smoothed the fabric of her skirt over her knees and then did it again. Finally she looked up and said, "I don't know what's going on, Michael. I don't understand why she wrote those letters. But kill the Pope? She would never . . ."

"She may be in the hands of people who would. She

375

may not even know what is happening, how she's being manipulated. Moira, we want to save her and stop the assassination. Where is she?"

"I don't know," she said hoarsely. "That's the truth, as God is my witness."

"Have you seen her with any strangers recently? Has she made any new friends?"

"Kathleen's a lonely child. She hadn't friends that I know of, save that blowhard, Brian O'Flaherty. I can't believe that he'd be involved in anything like that. Why, he's always shouting the praise of Ireland and the Catholics and one country forever."

"What he shouts and what he does may be two different things," Cormac said.

"You're serious about all this, aren't you?"

"Do you think I would have stayed here in Ardath if I weren't serious? Girl, after all the pain and hurt, I wanted nothing to do with this town or . . . the people in it. I'm serious. Someone's going to try to kill the Pope."

Moira twisted the fabric of her skirt between her fingers. "I don't know where Kathleen is," she said in a soft, small voice.

"You must promise me, Moira. When she comes home, call me. We must speak with her. Don't you ask her about it yourself. Call me first. Do you promise?"

"Michael . . ."

"Do you promise?" Cormac said, his voice loud and commanding.

She stared at him for a moment, then nodded. "I promise."

"It's best that way. I'll do what I can to help Kathleen. You know that." He squeezed her hands in his, then walked to the front door.

"Michael," she said.

The policeman turned.

"Do you hate her?" Moira asked.

"Hate her? No, I don't hate your daughter," he said.

"*Your* daughter," Moira said levelly.


Cormac sat down in the passenger seat heavily.

"Did you find out anything?" Wells asked.

"She doesn't know where the girl is," Cormac said in a dull voice. "She'll call us when she hears from her."

"Are you all right? You look as if you'd seen a ghost."

"I'm fine," Cormac answered irritably. "Fine. Let's go find Brian O'Flaherty. The girl may be with him."

As they drove by the gathering twilight gloom, they saw that the gates to Bounfort Castle were closed and military guards had taken up positions outside them. Through the gates, they saw other uniformed men walking over the grounds surrounding the castle, their silhouettes black and eerie against the rays of the dying sun.

"They're searching the grounds," Cormac said.

"They won't find anything."

"How do you know?"

"I already looked," Wells said. "There's nothing in there. Whatever's going to happen to the Pope isn't something that's in the castle now."

"You already looked?"

"Yes."

"How is it they let you in?" Cormac asked.

"They didn't *have* to let me in."

Cormac grinned. "And here I thought you spent all your time reading newspapers."

"Shows how Irishmen jump to conclusions."

* * *

Brian O'Flaherty was not in his apartment above the butcher shop, and his landlady said she'd seen him go out an hour before. No, she didn't know where he was going and he didn't say and it wasn't like her to be asking questions of people, she being a private kind of person and all, and just why was it Michael Cormac was so interested in Brian O'Flaherty?

"Just wanted to chat with him," Cormac said.

"When he comes back, I'll tell him you were looking for him."

"I'm sure you will."


Kathleen and Brian sat in her parked car, in a copse of trees at a far end of town. In the distance, a silver-colored sliver of Moon Lake, glistening in the bright moonlight, was visible. Around them, crickets chirped, and there was a heavy, violent wind blowing that lowered the smallest branches of the trees to swipe against the roof of her automobile.

"I'd like to know what it's all about," Brian said.

"Seamus will explain it all to you. As soon as the person we're waiting for arrives," Kathleen said.

"And who is this person?"

"Seamus's man in the village. I'll let him tell you about it."

"This all has something to do with the Pope, doesn't it?" O'Flaherty asked.

"I'll let him tell you," she repeated.

Brian sighed and drummed his fingers impatiently on the dashboard.

"Does this mystery man have a name?" he asked. "Or are my twenty questions up?"

"He has a name," Kathleen snapped. She looked at him for a moment as if deciding whether or not to entrust him with the information. "His name's Lazarus," she said finally.

The back door of the car on the passenger side opened, and a figure cloaked in black slid silently into the backseat. He carried a long, black cloth bag, which he placed on the floor of the car.

"Let's go," he told Kathleen. O'Flaherty turned to look at the man, but he had a hat pulled low over his face.

"Yes . . ." Kathleen began.

"Lazarus," the man in the back reminded her.

"Yes, Lazarus," she said obediently.

They had driven all over the town and seen not hide nor hair of Kathleen or Brian O'Flaherty. Wells said, "I want to try Grady's. That's one nice thing about Irish villages. Go to the pub, and sooner or later you'll run into everybody."

"Let's hope so," Cormac said sourly.

Inside Grady's, they saw Morty O'Sullivan sitting alone at a corner of the bar. When he saw them, he waved and drunkenly invited them over.

As they joined him, he said, "Here we sit. Three cows out to pasture while the big brass takes everything over."

"I guess the Pope coming to town makes people nervous," Cormac said mildly.

"Makes others nervous and us useless," Morty said

loudly. "They want me directing traffic. Aaaah, have yourselves a drink."

On the road to Killarney, the man in the backseat took off his hat.

"Father Ambrose," Brian O'Flaherty said, unable to keep the astonishment out of his voice. "What are you doing here?"

He ignored the question. "Has Kathleen explained things to you?"

"She said that you and Seamus would tell me what was going on."

"And we will," the priest said. "Seamus will tell you the plan."

"Plan for what?" Brian said, annoyance creeping into his voice. "Plan for what?"

Lazarus's gaze seemed to enter the young man's eyes like shafts of ice, freezing him. "Our country's time has come, Brian," he said softly. "On Tuesday, the British will be driven out of Ireland forever."

Brian gasped. "Praise be God," he whispered. "I'd have given my life to be a part of this."

The priest looked away. *Now you will,* he thought. From the recess of his memory, he saw the severed heads of children rolling in a shallow pit.

*For Ireland. Again.*

There wasn't a light on the road from Ardath to Killarney as it snaked its dangerous way along the edge of rising hills that scuffed the land between the two communities like growths on the earth's face.

From the backseat, Father Ambrose suddenly groaned. "Stop," he whispered.

"What is it?" Kathleen Pierce said.

"My stomach. Stop the car. Please. Hurry."

She pulled off to the side of the road. There were no shoulders to use to get out of the traffic lane, but there was also no traffic late on a Sunday night. Ambrose opened the rear door and walked hurriedly away from the car.

The two young people heard the sounds of retching, and Brian smiled at Kathleen. "Our priest, the secret Republican, seems to have no stomach for action," he said.

"Seamus says he is a very important man in the movement," Kathleen said huffily.

"I'll believe it when I see it. A wafer-pusher's a wafer-pusher."

They heard him call softly. "Brian. Kathleen. Please come. Help me."

Slowly the two got out of the car and walked down the roadside about ten feet behind the car, where Lazarus was bent over a cluster of bushes.

Brian put an arm around the priest's shoulders comfortingly while Kathleen came up on his other side.

Suddenly Ambrose rose. Kathleen screamed as, in the bright moonlight, she saw Ambrose strike with a wooden club into Brian's head. The young man groaned and fell as if the bones of his body had suddenly vanished.

"Father!"

The sound whooshed out of Kathleen as she dropped down beside Brian, unable to believe what she had seen. She looked at the bloody pulp of Brian's forehead, then at the priest's face. It was a different face from any Father

381

Ambrose had shown her before. Impassive, sightless, its eyes promising death: The face of Lazarus.

She scrambled up to run, feeling vomit rush to her throat, but she was too slow. The forearm she threw over her face cracked with the downswing of the club. She fell over onto her back like an unbalanced top, shrieking, kicking her legs out, the broken arm lying useless across her chest.

"My baby," she whimpered. "In the name of God, don't kill Seamus's child inside me."

The dull eyes of the priest never blinked as he moved in close to her. "God forgive you, girl," he said softly. "The Lord doesn't want Seamus to have a child. There are too many of us already." He brought the club down again. Kathleen's face exploded under the weight. She never felt the second blow or the third.

When he finished, her body twisted in one great convulsion, shivered, and then lay still.

Ambrose stood over her for a moment as a cloud passed from in front of the moon and the bloody bodies of the two young people were bathed in pale white light.

*Only two lives,* he told himself. *Two worthless lives.*

He was sweating. He had felt elation during the killings, he realized, a passion close to lust. It nauseated him.

As the sky darkened again, Ambrose lugged both bodies back to the car and shoved them into the backseat, then got behind the wheel and drove off.

A half mile away, the road angled up sharply, overlooking a sprawling peat bog that had once been a battlefield for warring Irish tribes a millennium past.

He turned the car sharply left and stopped it at the edge of the rocky cliff, looking down the steep drop toward the valley. He turned off the motor, opened the hood, and with a knife from his pocket tore open the plastic gasoline line. From another pocket, he took a small flask of gasoline and splashed it around the front seat of the car.

Placing Kathleen's body behind the steering wheel and the body of Brian O'Flaherty in the front passenger seat, he tossed a match under the hood. The car's gasoline-splashed motor burst into flame. He slammed the hood partially closed, then reached into the car, turned on the lights, turned on the ignition key, and released the hand brake.

He did not worry about leaving fingerprints. He never had.

Then he walked behind the car and gave it a mighty heave with his shoulder. It rolled forward, the front wheels dropping over the edge of the rock. It teetered there for a moment, then fell forward, tumbling end over end down the embankment to the peat bog below. As it fell, the flames whooshed out from under the hood of the vehicle, and when it hit, it erupted into a ball of flame.

Father Ambrose watched the fireball roll over one last time before it settled, crackling, into the black fuzz of the bog.

"Oh, Ireland," he said aloud. It was the only prayer he had left. His words bounded off the rock hills surrounding the peat valley and came back to him, unwanted.

*Ireland . . . Ireland . . . Ireland . . .*


Because there was work for most people the next day, Grady's Pub had cleared out early and only the three policemen were left as customers. For the last fifteen minutes, old man Grady had been clearing his throat. When he glanced at his wristwatch pointedly, Wells said, "I think he's giving us a hint to go home."

"Stuff him and keep the party going," Morty shouted. Cormac chuckled. It was the punch line of an old Irish joke about a woman who, at her husband's wake, tells her best friend that she wants to bury her husband in holy ground but he wanted to be cremated and what should she do?

Wells looked at the two of them with an expression on his face that invited an explanation, but Cormac said, "You wouldn't understand, Brit."

The telephone under the bar rang. Grady answered it in a soft voice, then brought the phone on a long cord down the bar and placed it in front of the young garda.

"It's for you, Morty."

"I'm not here," he growled.

"I already said you was here," Grady said and held the receiver toward Morty's ear.

Morty grabbed the receiver with a show of annoyance. "O'Sullivan," he sighed.

He listened for a few moments, then said, "Did you call the station? They do all the work now." He listened again and said, "I know. I'll get right out there."

He hung up the phone and stood from his seat.

"That was Mr. Potter. There's been an accident out on the Killarney Road."

"Potter?" Grady asked.

"No. He was just driving by and saw it. A car went off the cliff. It's burning. I've got to go out there."

"We'll go with you," Cormac said. "You're too drunk to drive."

"You're drunk, too," Morty said.

"But I'm old. I've had more experience driving drunk."

A half-dozen cars were parked alongside the roadway when Wells and the two Irishmen arrived at the scene. Dirty black smoke trickled upward from the car, and around it stood a half-dozen men. They carried torches and flashlights, and in the crisscrossing of the lights, Cormac saw two forms lying prone on the ground ten feet from the car.

They picked their way carefully down the rocky side of the hill. Lights from the men flashed in their eyes as they walked toward the scene. One of the men came forward and clapped a hand on Morty's shoulder. "You'd best brace yourself, lad," he said, his face grim. "It's real bad."

Morty broke away from the hand and ran toward the lights.

"What happened?" Cormac asked the man who had brought the news.

"They're both dead."

"Anybody we know? Who are they?"

The man sucked a tooth. "It's Kathleen Pierce. Brian O'Flaherty was with her."

Cormac groaned. Wells turned to him.

"What's the matter?" he said.

Cormac shook his head. "Moira's girl," he said. He looked at Wells with the confused eyes of a newly caged animal. "Moira's and . . ." He turned away.

Morty was kneeling next to one of the blanketed forms. Cormac approached and saw a broken, blistered face that might have been Kathleen Pierce's. And might not have been.

Morty looked up, his voice anguished as he spoke. "Has anyone called Doc O'Connor?"

"Aye, Morty. We did that right away, but no doctor will help. We called the priest, too."

Cormac knelt down close to Morty. Softly he said, staring at the body, "Are you sure it's Kathleen?"

"Aye, Michael, it's her," Morty whispered, his eyes transfixed by the charred mass of flesh.

Cormac wanted to speak, to say something to the young man who had loved Kathleen, but his thoughts were too confused. Had she really been his daughter, this girl he'd never known? Where had her childhood gone? Would Moira have told him if he'd stayed? Could they have made a life together, the three of them, if he hadn't left so quickly those many years before?

"Moira," he sighed.

Morty looked up at him sharply. There were tears in his eyes. "They was together," he said brokenly. "Kathleen and Brian."

"I'm sorry, son," Cormac said. The young policeman took his hand and squeezed it hard.

"It's her car all right," one of the bystanders said, walking round the wreckage. "Brian was in the passenger seat, so she must have been driving." The man directed his remarks to Morty. "They was both dead when we got down here. I had a little fire extinguisher in the boot of the car and we used it to put the fire out so we could get them out."

"You did right, Will," Morty said, rising slowly to his feet.

Cormac stood up too. He turned and saw Wells, with a borrowed flashlight, looking inside the still-smoking car.

"They was probably in Killarney drinking. They both

had the night off," Morty said. "And then they missed their way and drove off the cliff."

"Probably," Cormac said.

On the overhead road, two hundred yards away, he saw police lights flash as two police vehicles, coming from the direction of Ardath, turned a corner and raced toward them.

A few minutes later four uniformed men were picking their way down the cliffside toward the accident. One of them was Superintendent O'Keefe, the commissioner's assistant from Dublin.

"Just an accident," Cormac said to him. "Not the kind of thing to get a superintendent out of bed over."

"Until the Pope leaves safely, Sergeant," O'Keefe said stiffly, "everything around here concerns me. Even *just* an accident. Hey, you. Get away from there." He was shouting at Wells, who had pulled a long black object from the back floor of the car. "What have you got there?"

Wells put the object on the ground as Cormac, Morty and O'Keefe stepped forward.

"Oh, it's the Englishman," the superintendent said. "What is that there?"

"It was on the floor," Wells said. "This black mesh it's wrapped in is fireproof."

"Open it up," O'Keefe ordered one of his men. He turned to Cormac. "Who was in the accident?"

"Two young people from the village. They were entertainers at the castle." He would tell O'Keefe nothing more, he decided; none of his suspicions about Kathleen or O'Flaherty. They were dead now and nothing O'Keefe knew or didn't know would change a thing.

"They were probably drunk," O'Keefe said. Even

though Morty had said the same thing a few minutes before, it sounded offensive now when O'Keefe said it.

"And maybe they weren't," Cormac said sullenly to the police official.

"Look at this, Superintendent," one of the policemen called.

They had opened the ties that held the black package together. As the material was rolled back, the policemen saw a rifle, fitted with a telescopic sight. There was also a newspaper inside the bundle. As one of the police officers opened it up, Cormac saw it was that morning's *Irish Times*. A front-page story was circled in red marker. The headline read:

## POPE TO VISIT ETERNAL–PEACE SHRINE ON TUESDAY

Another piece of paper was inside the package. Cormac leaned close as the garda opened it. It was a rough, hand-drawn map of Bounfort Castle and the grounds around it. There were two X's drawn near the trees that surrounded the large assembly field that faced up to the castle's balcony. Cormac knew immediatly what the X's represented: spots where a gunman would have a clear, unimpeded shot at someone on the balcony.

"Just two young people from the village, eh?" O'Keefe said aloud, then looked at Cormac with an expression of disgust. "Maybe these were more than just two people from the village. What were their names?"

"Kathleen Pierce and Brian O'Flaherty," Morty supplied.

"Pierce. Pierce," O'Keefe said. "That was the name of the woman who was writing the letters attacking the Pope, wasn't it?" he said to Cormac. "I've read your reports, Sergeant."

"Then you know she's the one we *think* wrote the letters. But we aren't sure."

"I think now you can probably start being sure," O'Keefe said sarcastically, glancing over his shoulder to see if any of his underlings had heard.

He told his men to chase the bystanders away. He was briskly giving orders about securing the area when Cormac noticed something inside the burned-out car.

There was a screwdriver on the floor, its plastic handle melted and twisted. Two lines had been scratched into the dashboard in the rough shape of an X.

"What does that mean?" Wells said from behind him.

"I don't know. Maybe nothing. Maybe O'Flaherty was trying to write something."

"X?" Wells asked.

"Something."

"You look poorly again, Michael," Wells said. "Why don't you tell me what it is."

Cormac looked at the Englishman for a moment, his eyes glazed. "I'll go tell Moira," he said quietly.

Morty laid a hand on his arm. "Thank you, Michael, but it's my job. I'll do it. If you want to leave, I'll get a ride back with the other men."

As Wells and Cormac walked away from the accident scene, they saw that Father Ambrose had arrived. He was bent over the two dead young people, administering the last rites of the church. In all his life, Cormac had never gotten used to sudden violent death, but when he wearied of being a policeman, he could always tell himself he was glad he had never entertained a notion of being a priest. Priests dealt with death all the time, and he would not be Father Ambrose now for anything.

\* \* \*

They were in Cormac's room, drinking lukewarm tea.

"What do you mean you don't believe it?" Cormac snapped.

"I don't believe it," Wells said calmly. He sipped at the tea, made a face, and put the cup down on the metal-topped antique kitchen table. "It's a setup."

"The newspaper?" Cormac said, and Wells nodded.

"All right. He's going to kill the Pope. Does he really need to circle the story in a newspaper to remind himself? That was put there by someone," Wells said. "And the map. This O'Flaherty lad worked at the castle for how long, three years? Would he really need to draw a map to know where to stand on the grounds to see the balcony?"

Cormac bit his lip thoughtfully. "It was convenient that everything was wrapped in fireproof mesh, I suppose," he said. "Who wraps a rifle in fireproof mesh?"

"That too."

"You think they were killed?" Cormac asked.

"I don't know. Maybe that Irish Colonel Blimp of yours and his sycophants will find out something. But I've got problems with a loudmouthed self-proclaimed patriot like O'Flaherty suddenly turning anti-Catholic."

"The girl, too," Cormac said. "Nothing in her background allows for that."

Wells set his cup down with a clatter on the metal table. "Take me home," he said suddenly. "I can't help but think, Michael, that these two were just pawns."

"Whose?"

Wells didn't speak for a long moment. "There are people to whom murder is commonplace," he said slowly. "I saw one of them in a hotel room in Killarney."

"Seamus Dougherty," Cormac said. "Christ, not the IRA again."

"I think I'm beginning to understand at last," Wells said.

"That Dougherty's the assassin?"

Wells stood up. "Men like Seamus Dougherty are never the assassins. Assassins die too easily. The Doughertys of the world keep themselves in one piece, while they destroy everything around them."

Cormac felt the bitterness rising inside him. "If it's Dougherty, he won't be in one piece for long," he said.

"Careful, Michael. You're making this sound very personal."

Cormac tried to blink away the image of Kathleen Pierce's mangled face. "It is," he said. "It is now."

Two police cars were parking in front of the butcher shop as Cormac and Wells drove through the dark streets of Ardath. Lights were on in the rooms above the shop, where Brian O'Flaherty had lived.

Cormac and Wells pulled to the side, across the street, as the door to the building opened and two figures emerged.

The first man was Superintendent O'Keefe, still as spiffy in his highly pressed uniform as if he had just stepped from a shop window. He saw Cormac and Wells as they stepped from the auto and with a hee-haw smile on his face, stepped across to them.

"It's looking as if you misjudged that O'Flaherty," he said.

"How is that?" Cormac said, hating the grin he knew would come. It came.

"Your missing drum of explosives. We found it in his

391

room. There's also a typewriter there that looks as if it had been on the bottom of a lake for a while. Any guesses as to which typewriter it might be?''

Cormac and Wells were silent as O'Keefe looked from one to the other. Then the superintendent said, ''Oh, another thing. His closet was filled with anti-Catholic propaganda. It looked like little Belfast up there.''

''Where'd you find the explosives?'' Cormac asked.

''In the back of the closet, in a laundry bag, buried under dirty clothes.''

''And the typewriter?''

''Right out in the open on his breakfast table,'' O'Keefe said. He turned as one of his men came downstairs holding the typewriter in his arms.

Feeling dimissed, the two men drove away.

Wells said, ''I still don't believe it.''

''You're not alone,'' Cormac said, lighting a cigarette. ''I was in that apartment earlier tonight. There was no typewriter on the table.''


He dropped Wells off at his hotel, then took the lake road and drove by the Pierce estate.

The gate was open and the lights were on in Moira's small cottage, but Morty O'Sullivan's car was not in sight.

He parked and knocked softly on the door. Like a woman who had been waiting on edge for someone to tell her that everything had been a terrible mistake, she opened the door immediately.

Moira's face was stained with tears. Her hair was electric about her head, as if she had been running her fingers through it for hours.

"Oh, Michael," she said.

"I'm sorry, Moira."

"She's all I have," Moira whimpered.

Cormac held her close. Not permitting herself to cry, she clung to him as if he were a talisman that might change the past by magic.

"Kathleen's gone, Moira," he said gently. "Accept it. The sooner, the better."

She pushed him away, wild-eyed. "That's easy for you, isn't it?" she shrilled. "Accept, accept. I've spent my life accepting misery, Michael, and there's never an end to it. Why?"

She stood with her arms rigid at her sides, her throat strained and corded. "Why did my daughter have to die?"

Cormac felt his shoulders dropping. It was as if the weight of her anguish were bending him in half.

"Our daughter," he whispered.

Moira's face broke. He went to her again and this time she touched him, not as a source of strength for herself, but as another victim sharing her pain. She wept now, for Kathleen in her last agony. For Michael, who had never known his own child. For herself, who would have to accept one more hurt in a life filled with pain.

And Michael Cormac wept, too. But not for any of them. His tears were for the useless mockery of it all, because this green land had been fed since the beginning of its history with red rivers of blood. In Ireland, violence was life, and even death brought no peace. There were always more killings. There always would be.

World without end, Amen.

He wept for Ireland.

# CHAPTER THIRTY-ONE

In less than twenty-four hours, the Pope would arrive, and the sleepy little village of Ardath had become a town in frenzy. Television trucks cluttered up the narrow streets. The sidewalks were jammed with tourists. The local merchants, who normally conducted business as if they didn't care if anyone shopped there, somewhere else or nowhere at all, had moved racks of their wares out on the pavement in front of their stores. "No vacancy" signs suddenly appeared in front of all the bed-and-breakfast inns, the "B-and-B's," that dotted the town's two main streets.

Government officials assigned to press relations and to providing public services for the vast crowd that was expected had also moved into the town and taken over the entire municipal building, which was located only a few steps away from the small Garda station.

Superintendent O'Keefe was still in overall charge of security, and when Cormac and Wells met him that afternoon in his small office in the rear of the building, he looked even more smug than usual. With him was a cadaverous man with eyeglasses and a nervous tic in his left eye, who was introduced as a special assistant to the Taoiseach, Ireland's prime minister. O'Keefe seemed to want to show off, and he was making a special point of lecturing Cormac and Wells on their inadequacies as investigators.

"It checks out," he said. "The keg of explosive matter in O'Flaherty's room was the same as the small sample you found at the exploded pier. And the typewriter was the one used to write the Red Mary letters to the press. Add in the gun and the map and the newspaper with the Pope story circled and that would seem to tie a large knot around all of it. They were two pro-Protestant, pro-Ulster, pro-British agitators who planned an assault on the Pope. We were just lucky that they were killed when they were."

The cadaverous official nodded his agreement.

"We think there's more to it than that," Wells said.

"Such as?" the Dublin man said. His voice was bored and tired, as if he had heard it all before.

"First, how do two Irish kids, Catholics all their lives, with no record of being pro-British, suddenly turn up on the anti-Catholic side? How do two kids with no background of violence suddenly show up planning to murder the Pope? And just because he's Catholic?" Wells stared at O'Keefe, waiting for an answer, but the superintendent only returned a look that expressed the quintessence of contempt and boredom. "I saw O'Flaherty at work," the Englishman went on heatedly. "He sounded like Parnell, talking about Irish freedom from the persecution of the British."

The Dublin official looked at O'Keefe, who smiled and said, "It looks to me, Mr. Wells, as if O'Flaherty pulled the wool over your eyes."

"Why do you say that?"

"We have information that O'Flaherty was a secret member of several militant Protestant groups in Ulster. His performances here as a vigorous Irish Republican were just that, performances. His sympathies were entirely on the other side."

Wells looked at Cormac, who shrugged. The Englishman asked O'Keefe, "You are certain of that?"

"Certain. We had fingerprints from the dead man. They turned up in some secret rosters which just became available to us. He was leading a double life and he gulled you, Wells. You were both taken in."

"What about the sign?" Cormac blurted.

O'Keefe lifted an eyebrow. "I beg your pardon?" he asked as if he had been interrupted by a small annoying child.

"The X on the dashboard of the car. It was scratched into the paint with a screwdriver. I think maybe O'Flaherty did it and was trying to tell us something."

"What utter dross," O'Keefe said dryly. "A scratch on a car! Really, Sergeant, this office is too busy to concern itself with your incessant straw-picking."

"And Kathleen?" Cormac shouted. "Is that straw-picking too? Wells here saw her with Seamus Dougherty. Why?"

"First of all," O'Keefe said in the same bored voice, "we had only a glimpse of that man reported by Mr. Wells, so whether it was Seamus Dougherty or not, we don't really know. But there is no trace of Dougherty anywhere in this area. The grapevine tells us that he is in America raising money."

"That's tremendous," Cormac said. "You just hear that Dougherty's in America and you just hear that O'Flaherty belongs to some Protestant organizations.

You just hear, you just hear. Damn convenient grapevine you just keep hearing things from."

Before O'Keefe could answer, Wells cut in. "What accounts for Winston Barnett's hand?"

"He was carrying explosives from a boat. O'Flaherty got away with it. He didn't and that was that."

"I'd feel a lot more sure that that was that, as you put it," Wells said, "if Barnett's hand had belonged to the dead body that was found."

"Come come," O'Keefe said tiredly. "Barnett obviously had help carrying the explosives. The two men were killed during the explosion on the pier. It happens sometimes."

"It happens sometimes too that people try to kill Popes," Wells said sharply.

The Dublin official turned toward the window. "The Pope is coming," he said emphatically.

"To celebrate the anniversary of a chapel? It seems like an awful risk to take with his life," Wells said. He changed his tone: "Let me explain what we think. The hand that was found belonged to Barnett, a well-known Protestant terrorist. But the body was someone else's. How did the hand just happen to float by onto the beach? Where is Barnett's body? If he was carrying explosives, don't tell me that he just blew to bits and the bits were too small to find. And, yes, it was brief, but I know what Seamus Dougherty looks like. It was Dougherty I saw in Killarney, and Kathleen Pierce met with him. If she was a Protestant troublemaker as you two seem to believe, he was a strange person for her to meet with. Don't you see? There are just too many questions now to go through with a Papal visit."

The Dublin man shrugged, "You can always make

a case," he said, "that there are some loose ends. There are loose ends in everything. The Pope is coming and I will tell you, Mr. Wells, in the privacy of this room, that it is more important than simply celebrating the anniversary of a chapel. We understand that the Pope is going to make a very significant pronouncement about violence and terrorism. As far as Dublin is concerned, it is imperative that he make that speech here in Ardath tomorrow."

Wells started to respond, but Superintendent O'Keefe cut him short. "The Pope's visit will not be canceled and that is the end of it," he said. He took a moment to communicate to Cormac and Wells a disdain that most people reserved for crawling insects. "I have the authority to relieve any personnel connected with this case. *Any.* And I am exercising that authority with you gentlemen right now. Please return to your regular work and convey my regards and appreciation to your respective superiors. And by the way, Mr. Wells, you can tell *your* superiors that the Irish Garda force can get along quite well without English interference."

He busied himself with some papers in front of him, indicating that the interview had been terminated. When the two men remained, stunned by the dismissal, he looked up impatiently and snapped, "Anything else?"

Cormac's right hand balled into a fist. "Why . . ."

"Nothing else, Superintendent," Wells said curtly, taking the Irishman's arm.

Cormac, allowing Wells's discretion to hold sway over his own vaulting anger, stormed outside before he could regret following Wells's more careful judgment.

"Damn the pansy weasel to hell," he seethed. "Dublin knows this case isn't closed. They just want the Pope to make his bleeding speech attacking the IRA. They want it so badly they're willing to risk his life by sending that ass O'Keefe out here to run things."

"Michael," Wells said quietly, "it's over. Pull yourself together. We've just been relieved. There's nothing more we can do."

"Christ, don't you know what's going to happen either?"

The Englishman gave a small mirthless laugh. "Of course I know. Better than you do. I've seen it before."

"Jesus!"

"Goodbye, friend," Wells said. He touched two fingers to his forehead in salute.

"You're leaving?"

"I've been ordered to. O'Keefe holds complete jurisdiction here now. Stop by the hotel tomorrow. We'll drink a toast to him before I go."

"Is that all this means to you?" Cormac shouted hotly. "Another job, another muck-up? What about the killer that's running around loose? What about the Pope's life, for God's sake?"

"Politics," Wells said philosophically. "Don't you see, it's not up to us anymore." He smiled wanly at the Irishman. "I'm afraid we've stumbled into a realm far too lofty for the likes of a couple of gumshoes."

Cormac ran his hand through his thick gray hair. Wells watched him silently for a moment, until Cormac's eyes abruptly met the Englishman's. "Well? What's up your ass now?"

"There's something else you ought to know," Wells said softly. "About the Pierce girl. She was pregnant."

Cormac dropped his hand, the fingers still separated.

"I found out the night I followed her into Killarney. She stopped at a doctor's office. I browbeat the information out of him."

Cormac colored slowly. "And why didn't you tell me then?"

Wells looked at his nails for a long moment. "You don't really need me to answer that, do you, Michael?"

The two men waited in silence until Cormac could find his voice. "Jesus," he said finally. His stubby fingers slapped at his thighs. "I feel so helpless."

"Don't we all," Wells answered, his eyes focused far away. "Don't we all."

He walked away. Cormac stayed where he was, his shoulders bowed.

# CHAPTER THIRTY-TWO

All the lights were blazing in Moira's cottage as Cormac walked through the iron gate onto the Bonning property. On the single-step stoop he stopped, took off his hat, and stood panicking for a minute, deliberating whether or not to go in. There were sounds of conversation inside, women's chatter. He didn't want to embarrass Moira now by his presence, even if he had come only to pay his respects on Kathleen's death.

He put his hat back on, but as he turned to leave, he walked into Mr. Bonning. The old man was so frail and light that he reeled backward at the slight jostling. He would have lost his footing altogether if Cormac hadn't grabbed him in a bear hug and set him upright.

"I'm begging your pardon, sir," Cormac apologized, picking up a bunch of flowers Bonning had dropped on the walkway. "I didn't hear you coming up."

"Quite all right, son," Bonning said, coughing. "Oh, it's you. Sergeant Cormac, isn't it?"

Cormac waited for Bonning's hacking fit to subside. "That's right, sir. I'd say it's a bit chilly for you to be out."

"Nonsense. I'm going to die soon enough as it is. No

401

point spending all my last moments alone in that stinking sickroom. Shall we?"

He nodded toward the door, took Cormac's arm and walked up and knocked. "By the way, even from my infirmary, I've managed to hear some strange rumors about that car accident. . . ." The old man fell silent as the door opened. Mrs. O'Glynn filled the space, looking like the figurehead of a ship, a plate of cake in her hands.

"Well," she said, thrusting her nose in the air with comic intensity. "It's Michael Cormac, so it is, Moira," she shrilled into the room filled with women. "And your neighbor as well. The Protestant."

Moira rose from a chair in the corner where she'd been sitting alone and walked past the tables loaded with food toward the two men. She put on a smile for them, but Cormac could see the strain in her face.

"It was nice of you both to come," she said, barely audible above Mrs. O'Glynn's cries from within.

"We've come to pay our condolences," Mr. Bonning began. "It was such a shock. . . ."

"Moira, darling," Mrs. O'Glynn interrupted excitedly, sucking flecks of butter cream from her fingers. "It's seven o'clock, time for the news. We're sure to be in it, what with all them TV cameras around town. Mind if I turn on the telly?"

"No, of course not," Moira said.

As the ladies gathered around the small television, Moira accepted the old man's flowers with a kiss on his cheek. "Thank you, Mr. Bonning," she said. "I was on my way to see to your comfort when some of the women dropped over. . . ." She smiled wanly.

"Aye, old women are as hard to be rid of as the pox," he said rather loudly. "As to my comfort, I'm afraid all

402

your fine ministrations aren't going to make me a randy young goat again. I'll have to leave that kind of work to young Michael.'' He clapped Cormac on the back and laughed, triggering another coughing fit.

"Come on along with me to the kitchen," Moira said. "It's quieter there and you can sit."

She gave him a glass of water and Bonning took a long draft. "Ah, you know that you're old when water tastes better than whisky," he said ruefully, seating himself on a hard wooden chair.

Cormac stood silently against the wall as Moira arranged the flowers in a vase, grateful to be away from the perfumed crush of gossips in the next room.

"They're lovely," she said, setting the flowers in front of Mr. Bonning. "And I appreciate your thoughtfulness. But really, you shouldn't have come. You'll be all tired out tomorrow."

Bonning sighed and waved her protest away. "I wanted to stop by, Mrs. Pierce. I've got some news."

"Yes?" Moira asked apprehensively.

"Oh, not bad news, really. I don't think you could stand any more of that. You've just got to look at it the right way."

"I don't think I know what you mean," Moira said.

"I mean that some things are just plain bad, like this business with poor Kathleen. Nothing's going to make that any easier for you, dear."

Moira stiffened, and her eyes shone with unshed tears. Mr. Bonning reached out with his old, spotted hand and cradled hers in it. "I know," he said softly. "I've lost someone I loved very much, too. I only hope your daughter didn't die as the victim of some shameless killers, the way my wife did."

403

"What?" she gasped.

Cormac cleared his throat and caught Bonning's eye.

"Well, never you mind about that. I'm just a senile old man, blithering."

"But what did you . . ."

"Let me finish my point before I forget it, Mrs. Pierce."

She nodded, looking to Cormac for some explanation, but his face offered none.

"As I was saying," Bonning went on, "sometimes things are really bad, no two ways about it. But then again, some things are bad only if you see them that way." The old man brightened.

"For example?" Moira said.

"For example, me." He chortled. "I'm going to be leaving tomorrow. The venerable Doctor O'Connor tells me that it's time I checked into a hospital in Killarney. Very posh and all that. He assures me I'll be receiving the best of care, but I'll most likely not be leaving there again. I know that."

A deep furrow creased Moira's forehead.

"Now, there you go, looking at the bad side of things again. You've got to see it differently. Try to take my point of view. I've lived a long and interesting life. I've accomplished most of what I set out to do and a few things I didn't. I've made more money than I could ever spend during all my days on earth. And most important, I was blessed with the finest wife a man could wish for. There's only one thing that's weighing on my mind now."

She smiled. "What's that, Mr. Bonning?"

"You, Mrs. Pierce."

"Me?" She shook her head. "I'll be fine. Truly, I will."

"About this tragedy, yes. The human heart is miraculously regenerative. Even broken, it goes on working. I was thinking of more pedestrian matters. Finances, that sort of thing. I might as well come to the point, Mrs. Pierce. I want to leave you my house after I die."

"What? I couldn't accept that," she stammered. "It would . . ."

"Damn it, I know how prideful you are, woman, but I don't have anyone else to leave it to. I've already given most of my money away to charities, so there's only the house left and enough cash to cover its upkeep. And to bury me. Will you see to my funeral? Nothing fancy, mind you."

"Yes, of course," she said impatiently. "But . . ."

"Then you're taking the blasted monstrosity back and that's that," Bonning bellowed.

"I say," Mrs. O'Glynn called from the doorway, wagging a finger at the old man. "In our religion, we don't go about shouting at the bereaved in their own house, so we don't."

Bonning burst out laughing. Mrs. O'Glynn cast him a vile look; then, hearing the shouts from the sitting room, she bustled over to Moira. "Come have a look, dearie. They're starting the piece on Ardath now."

All of them went in to watch the television, where various areas of the town were being shown as an announcer rhapsodized about the "tiny village of miracles."

"Gor, listen to that one," one of the women shrilled. "You'd think this place was Holy Bethlehem."

"So it is, practically," Mrs. O'Glynn said firmly.

"She means 'cause her Billy was born here," another woman said in a stage whisper. They all laughed and Mrs. O'Glynn sputtered, "Heretics, all of you."

The picture on the television switched to Father Ambrose at work in his carpentry shop, placing the final touches on the huge Celtic cross he had fashioned.

"The good father said that his magnificently wrought cross was originally planned to stand at St. Benedict's, his parish church," the announcer said. "But now, since the Pope will bless the cross during tomorrow's ceremonies, Father Ambrose hopes the cross will stand forever on the castle grounds."

The camera cut to a close-up of Father Ambrose speaking. "I would never have had the effrontery to place my poor work at the ancient chapel of miracles, where Our Holy Mother herself appeared, but the occasion seems to demand it," the priest said humbly. "The Lord works in mysterious ways."

The Pope, the announcer said, was reportedly pleased about the new cross decorating the old holy shrine.

"Ain't he a dear one," one of the woman sighed.

Mrs. O'Glynn snorted. "Not more than five minutes, it was, and not one picture of us, after going about in front of them cameras in Sunday best for two days running. Why, there wasn't even a mention about poor Kathleen and that scoundrel O'Flaherty."

"They don't want no bad news now they're talking about the Pope coming," someone said.

"News is news," Mrs. O'Glynn countered heatedly.

"The telly never talks about car accidents, Brigid."

"Accident my foot," Mrs. O'Glynn snapped. "Peter Tynan was there right after it happened. Says he seen a gun and some kind of map in the car."

"Brigid!"

"Well, it's true. Even that Superintendent O'Keefe didn't try to deny it. And her pregnant, too."

The room fell instantly silent except for the drone of the television. Mrs. O'Glynn's eyes slid guiltily over to Moira.

Moira was ashen, her face a blank. Cormac helped her to a chair and set her down, his neck red, his jaw clenched.

"I'm sorry, Moira," he said, trying to keep calm when every instinct told him to swat Mrs. O'Glynn across her filthy mouth.

He wasn't alone. Eyes blazing, Mr. Bonning walked over to the busybody so menacingly that Mrs. O'Glynn put her hands up in front of her face.

"Get out of here, you heartless bitch," he roared.

There was a series of exclamations among the women, which seemed to give Mrs. O'Glynn her confidence back. She raised her chin in defiance, but Bonning made a sharp gesture with his arm, as if about to strike her, and she shrank away.

"Well, I certainly won't be spoken to in that way," she said as she gathered up her purse and shawl. "Not by no Prod."

"Get out!" Bonning looked around the room threateningly. "The rest of you, too."

There was a rustle of skirts and the clink of dinnerware as the ladies angrily picked up the dishes of food they'd brought and moved quickly through the door.

"It's still the truth, Brit," Mrs. O'Glynn shrieked before waddling out of sight.

Alone in the middle of the messy room, Bonning slapped off the television.

"Is it?" Moira asked numbly. "Is it true?"

"Moira . . ." Cormac began.

"Ah, I've made a mess of it," Bonning said, grimacing with obvious pain. "I'm damn sorry, Mrs. Pierce. It was just that woman. She makes my blood boil.'' He sat down, wiping his face with a handkerchief.

''I'll take you home,'' Cormac offered.

The old man nodded. Moira seemed to focus on him for the first time since Mrs. O'Glynn's shattering announcement, and she rose immediately to help him to the door.

''Forgive me,'' Bonning said, sounding sickly and weak.

Moira smiled. ''I'm glad you threw her out, you old dear. You've always been my champion.''

''Then you'll take the house.''

''Aye, that I will and I thank you for it.'' She kissed him on the forehead, but as soon as Bonning turned away, Cormac saw the smile go out of Moira's eyes.

''Will you be all right till I get back?'' he whispered.

She nodded. ''I'll manage,'' she said, closing the door. ''I always do.''


It had started to rain when Cormac got back to the cottage. Moira had cleaned it all, from the dishes to the floor. There was no trace that anything had happened, that a bereavement gathering had ever existed.

Cormac marveled at her resilience. Women, he thought, must be genetically programmed to endure pain, because they did it so well, and perhaps so often. Moira's daughter, her only daughter, had just died, a pregnant girl who had probably been murdered in a terrorist plan to assassinate one of the major figures in contemporary history, and Moira's response was to clean her house. It wasn't that Moira felt less than he did. He knew from experience that the pain coursing through her mind and heart and soul was white-hot and would never be lessened.

But Moira was like the earth: she could be scorched, raped, robbed; she could be flooded, burned, scarred, parched, abandoned. But she could not be destroyed. Underneath the pain, there was something green and eternal in Moira that nothing could touch.

"I love you, woman," Cormac said.

She took him in her arms, and they stood there in silence for a long time, grieving together without tears or words.

"Was it true?" she asked at last. "About Kathleen?"

"Yes. It was true."

"We would have been grandparents, then." It was no more than a simple statement.

Another few minutes went by. They stayed in each other's arms, immobile, as rain danced on the roof.

"What will you do?" Cormac asked. "Later?"

He felt her tears hot on his neck. "This is later," she said.

# CHAPTER THIRTY-THREE

The Pope walked slowly down the steps of the private Vatican jet aircraft and then, in the gesture known to hundreds of millions of people around the world, he knelt and kissed the ground. He rose and lifted his arms above his head, and the crowd at Shannon Airport roared its approval.

In the background waited an Irish government helicopter, its rotor blades spinning idly.

"Well, that's it," Cormac said. "He'll be here inside two hours."

Wells was packing his worn leather suitcase in his room at the Park Hotel. "Will you be staying on?" he asked Cormac.

"Might as well. I'd like to see us proved wrong."

Wells didn't answer. Cormac, watching the television, said, "He seems like a good man."

"Don't eulogize him yet," Wells said. "He's a tough old fox and he's already survived one killer. He might do it again."

"I suppose," Cormac said absently. He turned suddenly to Wells. "What did the SAS say about your being relieved?"

"Scotland Yard," Wells corrected automatically. "They can't meddle in a Republic of Ireland matter."

"But you were asked to come here," Cormac said.

Wells shrugged. "And then I was asked to leave. I look a perfect fool, but . . ." he hesitated. "But my superiors let Dublin know at the highest levels that the Pope might be in danger here."

"Did Dublin pay attention to that?" Cormac asked.

"I guess not. I'm still leaving, aren't I?" Wells said.

Cormac sighed. "Do you know what really bothers me?"

"Something, perhaps, to do with being regarded as a dolt by two governments. It certainly bothers me."

"No, none of that. I don't care anymore about Dublin or London or any of their political farting. It's the car."

"What car?" Wells asked.

"The one Kathleen and Brian were killed in. That screwdriver was on the floor by Brian's seat. He lived long enough to try to scratch a message into the dashboard. I just wish to hell I knew what it was."

"The detective to the bitter end," Wells said. "Unfortunately, I find myself agreeing with Superintendent O'Keefe on that point. When a car runs off a cliff, it's bound to get marked up. The dashboard was a mess of dents. That scratch was . . ."

"It wasn't a scratch," Cormac said. "It was an X. Two intersecting lines, drawn from top to bottom. The peeled paint was still bunched up at the end of those lines. I think O'Flaherty drew that deliberately, probably during the last seconds before he died. That's how important it was to him." He shook his head. "Damn it, I wish I could figure out what he was trying to tell us.''

"I don't know a lot of assassins whose names begin with X," Wells said.

"Oh, stick it up your ass, Brit."

Wells laughed and walked over to the bar. He lifted two glasses. "Short one?"

"No, I've got to get to church. Special mass." He looked at his watch. "Moira's waiting for me now. How long will you be here?"

"Another hour or so. My plane's not till five o'clock, but with all the traffic around here, I might be wise to leave right after breakfast."

"Will you be going back to London?"

"Londonderry, I think. I've got some leave time coming," Wells said.

Cormac frowned. "Derry? Seems like a mucky place for anyone with an accent like yours to take a holiday."

"I may run into Seamus Dougherty," Wells said.

"You never give up, do you?" Cormac said.

"Never."

"If you run into the bastard," Cormac said softly, "mark up one bullet for me." He extended his hand. "So it's good-bye, then."

Wells took the hand and shook it. "I guess it is. Thanks," he said.

"What for? We didn't exactly set the annals of police work on fire."

"For giving me a chance," Wells said.

Cormac reddened and turned to leave, but he turned back. "Daniel," he said. "You're a fine policeman, whoever you work for, you lying Brit."

"And you too, you wild Irish madman. Perhaps

we'll meet again when the blood has been washed from the sea between us." He smiled. "I think I read that somewhere."

Cormac didn't answer. He squeezed Wells's shoulder and then turned abruptly away, walking down the corridor as fast as he could.

As he left the hotel, Cormac saw Morty O'Sullivan directing traffic at the corner of West and Killian Streets, the town's main intersection. Morty looked drawn and weary as he waved through the unaccustomed flood of cars and pedestrians, and Cormac felt a stab of pity for him.

Morty, too, had worked on the case, and his reward had been even less than Cormac's or Wells's. He had not even received a cheap bronze medal with VALOUR stamped on it for saving the O'Glynn boy. And he had lost the woman he loved in the process.

But Morty kept going. He'd accepted traffic duty and, damn it, Cormac thought, he was doing a good job of it, too. He smiled. Honor, he reflected, didn't require medals. It was something inside a person that made him try, even when the trying seemed useless, that told him to hang on where there wasn't any reason to endure any more. Wells had honor. So did Moira. And in the end, young Morty, who had never been very bright or very brave, had it too.

The tiny sanctuary of St. Benedict's Church was filled to overflowing when Cormac walked in. The first rows were occupied by clergymen of such high rank that most of the parishioners from Ardath had never seen their type of vestments before.

Moira had somehow managed to take up enough space for both of them in one of the crowded pews and slid over when he finally located her.

"It's about time," she whispered. "I've been getting black looks from Brigid O'Glynn for twenty minutes." She gestured with her eyes toward the back of the church, where Mrs. O'Glynn and some of the other women from the debacle of the night before were standing beside Father Ambrose's cross.

"Damned cow," Cormac muttered.

"Mind yourself, now," Moira looked straight ahead but placed her hand over Cormac's the way she used to when they were still the center of each other's worlds. And for a time, listening to the comforting, familiar drone of the service, he could almost forget all that had happened between those days and these. For a while, suspended in time, Moira's touch was once again all he needed to live and the feeling filled with an almost drugged peace.

But when Father Ambrose mounted the pulpit to deliver the homily, something jarred Cormac into reality.

"We meet today under special and wonderful circumstances to commemorate one thousand years of a pledge of peace," the priest said. His hands were trembling, Cormac noticed, and he began to understand why Father Ambrose's presence had given him such a start. It was the man's appearance. Cormac hadn't paid much attention to the small man's health when he had spoken to him in the workshop behind the church, but now, against the pristine white linen of his vestments and the polished gold of the altar, the priest seemed unwholesome and gray. He was losing his hair, and what remained on his head looked oddly colorless.

"A pledge of peace," Father Ambrose repeated. "It is a pledge that our Blessed Lady made to us and for us here in Ardath. It is true today as it has been true for ten centuries. We here have always been spared the horror of war and of bloodshed.

"But, O, this poor island, which has known not a moment's peace in that same thousand years. Today we are here to greet our Holy Father from Rome, and we hope that somehow he will be able to extend the peace that we in Ardath have always known to all our brothers, everywhere in this island, to all those who suffer, who have known in their families the terror of sudden violet death, to those who are oppressed and heavy laden. To all these, we hope that Our Lady of Eternal Peace will bless them too as we have been blessed."

Ambrose spoke softly, with no orator's tricks. When he finished, he bowed his head for a moment, then looked up and said, "I hope you all noticed the cross standing near the entrance to the church. To those of you who are guests, it may not mean much, but to all our faithful parishioners, it will answer the question: What's Father Ambrose been doing for the past year?"

He smiled. It seemed to take a great deal of effort.

"Shortly after mass today," he continued, "a procession of men from our parish and these visiting dignitaries of the Catholic Church in Ireland"—he waved his hand toward the first few rows on the left, where monsignors and bishops sat in regal-robed splendor— "will help bring the cross to Bounfort Castle, where

415

the Holy Father will bless it and where it will stand for all time as a prayer from all of us that the peace of Our Lady, brought to this small village so long ago, may one day come to every village and glen and city of our beloved Ireland.''

He stopped, then spoke again, as if in an afterthought.

''Two nights ago, two young people of our village died in a terrible auto accident.''

Next to him on the hard wooden bench, Cormac felt Moira tense.

''Let us remember them in our prayers today, and let our thoughts go out to all our neighbors who knew them and loved them. They share our lives and we share their sorrow.''

Father Ambrose stepped down from the pulpit and with the altar boys began to prepare for Communion.

Cormac walked dutifully with Moira to the altar rail and knelt alongside her, his sharp policeman's eyes watching the faces of the communicants as Father Ambrose placed wafers into their mouths. When Cormac's turn came, he raised his eyes to the priest as Father Ambrose slipped the Host onto his tongue.

He saw then, for the first time, the glass-smooth fingertips stained brown with varnish. In a movement too fast for anyone to forestall, Cormac grabbed the priest's hand and twisted it. The palm was a road map of scar tissue. The fingertips were polished leather pads, smooth and hard, unlined.

Father Ambrose jerked his hand away violently. The other communicants gasped, and a murmur rose up from among the people waiting for a place in line, but for a moment the eyes of the two men locked in deadly truth.

In that moment, Cormac understood everything: Mad Hattie and Brian and Kathleen and the pier and the enormity of what those scarred hands meant.

Lazarus was not dead.

Father Ambrose shoved the tray of Communion wafers into the hands of one of the visiting priests who was assisting him, then walked quickly through a side door off the altar.

Cormac got up from the altar and walked behind the backs of the kneeling communicants to the side of the church where another door led into the back room.

The room was empty. A crumpled white cassock lay on the floor.

# CHAPTER THIRTY-FOUR

The Garda station was a mass of uniformed police-men, shouting above the din of squawk boxes and the noise of civilians outside, packed shoulder to shoulder behind the wooden police barricades that lined Killian Street, moving as thick and heavy as a molasses wave, trying to get to Bounfort Castle in time to see the Pope.

Cormac was wet with sweat, his hat lost somewhere in the crush of people between the church and Garda headquarters. It had been a ten-minute walk that had taken nearly a half hour.

"Where's O'Keefe?" he bellowed.

"What's the problem, sir?" a young officer asked politely while stepping into the opening between the counter and the desks beyond.

Cormac spotted the police superintendent in the rear of the room, a walkie-talkie pressed to his mouth as he watched a black-and-white television set.

"O'Keefe!" Cormac bulldozed his way past the young officer and moved with the inexorable certainty of a tank toward the superintendent's desk. As he approached, the young officer and another threw themselves on him, although they couldn't bring him down.

At the commotion, Superintendent O'Keefe looked up, saw Cormac, and slammed his radio down onto his desk.

"Super, this gentleman . . ." the young officer began.

O'Keefe waved him away. "Are you looking to be arrested, Cormac?" he barked. His eyes were shiny slits in his haggard face.

"No time," Cormac puffed breathlessly. "The priest . . . Father Ambrose . . . he's the assassin. He goes by the name Lazarus."

O'Keefe stared at him blankly.

"He started in Nicaragua and now he's here," Cormac shouted.

"*Nicaragua?* Have you been drinking, man? I don't give a damn who does what in bloody Nicaragua. We've got a near riot on our hands here, trying to get all these people into the castle grounds."

"Listen to me!" Cormac grabbed the man by the front of his jacket. O'Keefe gave him a withering look, and Cormac released him.

"The priest here is a professional assassin working for the IRA," Cormac said slowly, trying to pull himself together. "He's already killed three people. Send out an alarm on him."

"Which three?" O'Keefe asked.

Cormac took a deep breath, running his hand through his hair. It would be no good, he knew, to irritate O'Keefe now. "Hattie O'Shea, and Brian and Kathleen in the car crash. But that isn't the point. . . ."

"A seventy-year-old woman who died of heart failure and two terrorists carrying a rifle. We've been through all this before."

"They weren't terrorists. They were set up. It's the priest, I tell you. Father Ambrose."

"Look, Cormac," O'Keefe said, making an effort to sound reasonable. "I know you're trying to help. But the fact is you've been relieved of duty and this is the worst possible time for you to be here. Now . . ."

"The Pope's leaving Shannon, Super," the young officer said. "We'd better get started." The television showed an Irish government helicopter slowly rising from the ground at Shannon Airport. The Pope's face was visible through a window.

O'Keefe immediately forgot Cormac. He grabbed his radio from the desk, then shoved past Cormac to go out onto the street.

"What are we going to do?" Cormac yelled at O'Keefe's back. Absently, he brought his medal out from his pocket.

O'Keefe called over his shoulder. "Do whatever you want, Cormac. Just stay out of the way."

For a moment, Cormac stood there, confused, uncertain. On the television, a line of people moved slowly away from St. Benedict's Church. At the forefront of the procession was the huge carved cross. The camera moved in closely on the faces of the clergymen who walked alongside it, as well as the villagers who carried the object. Old Lanigan was there and Doc O'Connor's grandfather. . . .

A spear of panic shot through Cormac. One face was missing. Lazarus's face. He was still at the church, then.

Or already at the castle, waiting for the Pope.

Shoving the medal into his top jacket pocket, Cormac raced outside. All automobile traffic had been stopped, the single lane of Killian Street reserved for emergency vehicles. He worked his way through the throng of onlookers, some of them screaming now because they thought they would not reach the castle in time to see the Papal visit. Down Killian Street, Cormac saw a caravan of police cars headed toward the castle. That would be O'Keefe and his men. Cormac kept as close to the barricades as he could for speed, until he reached the Killian–West Street intersection. There he saw Morty O'Sullivan on the other side of the street.

Morty was a link in a human chain of gardai stretched across the width of West Street to control the flow of pedestrians onto the main thoroughfare. Cormac ducked beneath one of the barricades and ran across the road.

"You ought to know better than to run in the street, Michael," Morty said good-naturedly as Cormac came up to him.

"Where's your car?"

"Behind the Garda station. Why?"

"Give me the keys."

"You can't drive down Killian," the young man said, smiling incredulously.

"Give me the keys, I said."

Morty broke off the link with the policeman to his right and reached into his pocket. He handed Cormac a ring of keys. "The square one," he said.

"Thanks. Now I need your help. You've got to get

to Daniel Wells in the hotel. He should still be there. Tell him the priest is Lazarus.''

''Is what?''

''Lazarus, like in the Bible. There's no time to explain. Tell him I'm going to the rectory and then the castle.''

''But I'm under orders. . . . ''

''Do it for me, Morty. I'm begging you.''

Cormac dashed across the street again, up toward the Garda station, without waiting for an answer. Morty followed him with his eyes.

A few moments after Cormac disappeared from view, Morty saw the roof of his own car emerging over a hill. The car sped past him unimpeded as people in the crowd laughed and cheered it on. Others grumbled. Two officers with radios ran behind the car for a few yards. Ahead, policemen darted into the street to stop it, but Cormac weaved around them expertly and as swiftly as if they were hazards on a driving test.

''Must want to get where he's going bloody bad,'' the officer next to Morty mumbled.

Morty blinked. He looked at the officer, then at the policeman on his other side. Then he broke away from the line and sprinted for the Park Hotel.


Inside his room in the hotel, Wells sat drinking a gin and tonic while he watched the television. His feet were propped on an ottoman, and his suitcases were stationed near the door.

On the screen, the Procession of the Cross, as it was being called by the media, was wending its way down the lake road, almost at Bounfort Castle.

422

The cross was heavy. Even in the long shots, where the sweat on the faces of the bearers couldn't be seen, Wells noticed the men's legs wobbling precariously under their burden. Although Wells had never been a particularly religious man, perhaps because of the morning gin he was touched by the spectacle. It was how Christ Himself had carried the instrument of his death, slung over his back. . . .

Suddenly Wells sat bolt upright. He took a pen from his pocket and drew an X on his newspaper, intersecting lines drawn top to bottom the way Brian's mark had appeared on the dashboard of the burned car.

Cormac had been right.

There had been a message.

The message was a cross.

Wells felt his bowels turn to water. The priest. The priest had been Brian and Kathleen's killer.

And the Pope's assassin.

He bolted out the door and down the hotel steps, then fought against the press of bodies on the street to get through.


Cormac parked Morty's car well away from the church and ran to the rectory, keeping close to the walls as he made his way to the workshop at the rear of the building. He moved quietly, wishing he'd carried a gun to mass. If Ambrose was there, he would be armed, and unless Morty reached Wells in time, Cormac would be alone and defenseless against a professional killer.

Damn the Gardai, he thought. He had no business doing this alone. He looked through the small window in the workshop's side door. No one was inside. He was about to turn back for the car when he heard the soft rustle of footsteps behind him. He spun, maneuvering low, but Ambrose was ready for him.

The priest was dressed without his Roman collar, wearing a plaid shirt and blue jeans. The wrench in his hand was already swinging, and Cormac could do no more to ward off the blow than turn his head so that the wrench skidded off the side of his skull.

For a moment, he felt a searing pain, as if his brain had been singed by a flamethrower, and then came a dimness that melted all sights and sounds into a gray mush.

He was not exactly unconscious. He felt the sensation of being dragged across a concrete floor, but he was powerless to stop it. Ambrose propped him on a wooden chair and tied his hands behind his back. Cormac tried to move, but his body would not respond with more than a feeble swing of one foot when the ropes twisted around his ankles, binding them to the legs of the chair.

He dropped his head and let the grayness envelop him. A thousand visions sprang out of the thick jelly of his consciousness like glints of sunlight on a river: Kathleen and Brian, mangled in the wreckage of the car; Wells; Moira waiting for him twenty years ago at the standing stones; and beyond . . . Morty gasping for breath at the edge of Moon Lake, a medal that read VALOUR, a carved Celtic cross. . . .

Then he heard himself screaming. His eyes flashed open. He saw a thin red line following the razor-sharp blade of a machete being trailed across his legs.

"Where's your English friend, traitor?"

Cormac's head felt like the knocker in a huge vibrating bell. The images his eyes took in were blurred and quivering. Only the pain was sharp. He felt the blood trickling down from the cuts in his legs.

"I asked you a question," Ambrose said. There was none of the meek country priest in the man's gray face now. He looked nervous, as impatient and weary as a professional soldier near the end of a long campaign. When Cormac didn't answer, Ambrose lifted the machete with its thin strip of red on its blade and smacked it sideways into his cheek. The blow knocked Cormac over in his chair. "Talk, you ass!"

"Gone. He's gone," Cormac mumbled, his face rubbing against the grit on the floor.

"When?"

"Ten o'clock. To the airport."

Ambrose righted the chair with a sigh. "You should have gone back to Cork when you had the chance," he said.

Cormac shook his head to clear it. His legs were already growing cold under the spreading stain of his blood, but he could ball his hands into fists behind him. The ropes were loose enough to strain against. With enough time, he could wriggle out of them.

Time. That was what he needed. "How many?" he blurted out. It was weak, but all his foggy brain could come up with.

Ambrose switched on a small television set and checked his watch. "What are you talking about?"

The Procession of the Cross had entered the castle grounds and was slowly working its way up the main steps. The camera panned away for a moment and showed the crowd filling the field, easily fifty thousand

425

strong, and another long line of people strung out along the lake road, trying to get into the field.

*Why isn't he there?* Cormac asked himself, twisting against the ropes. With relief, he felt his hands slip out from under one of the strands. *Why isn't Ambrose at the castle?*

"How many have you killed?" Cormac asked.

Ambrose stared at the picture of the human-borne cross on his television, the machete hanging at his side. A drop of blood trembled at the end of the blade and spattered on the floor.

"I don't remember anymore," he said softly.

"Here, then. How many in Ardath?"

The priest looked over to him in mild surprise, as if he had forgotten Cormac was there, and smiled strangely. His gums were gray too, Cormac noticed.

"Well, first there was old Gervaise," he said as if he were reciting a litany. "The priest had to be removed. And Hattie . . . that was a small one, but she was beginning to rave a little too often; and then of course the Pierce girl and O'Flaherty."

"Setting them up as pro-British terrorists couldn't have been your work," Cormac said. His head was clearing now. "They were involved with someone bigger than you. Was it Dougherty?"

Ambrose raised his eyebrows in appreciation. "So you know about Dougherty? Good work, Sergeant." He paused. "I'll have to give credit where it's due. It's Seamus's idea. He is quite good at long-range planning," he said, with a note of bitterness. He pulled over a small wooden keg and sat on it. Cormac recognized the keg from the first day he had stopped to talk with the priest. It had held roofing nails. Another strand of rope slipped loose.

"What about Winston Barnett?" Cormac asked.

Ambrose shrugged. "Barnett was caught by some of Seamus's men up north, a day or so after the explosion at the pier. The episode had already brought attention to Ardath. That's why you came. So Barnett's body was shipped here to take the blame, but in the meantime you'd already found the body of that clumsy oaf who dropped the explosives. So I had a body here that I didn't know what to do with. That was the awful smell you complained about when you came here first. Barnett's body decomposing under the coal bin. I got the idea of cutting off the hand and putting it on the shore where someone would be sure to find it. Later I buried the body but that old witch saw me doing it and blabbed to you. She was dangerous."

"So naturally you had to kill her," Cormac said.

"Naturally."

"So while I was in the graveyard, you came back to dig up Barnett's body and you slugged me," Cormac said.

"Yes." Father Ambrose suddenly giggled. "And then I brought his body back here again. Poor Barnett. He certainly travelled more dead than he ever did alive. Finally, I planted him under Hattie. Good riddance to both of them."

"A lot of bother," Cormac said. "If I were you, I think I would have just scrubbed the mission after the explosion on the pier."

"Seamus wouldn't hear of that." He laughed again, but his voice sounded desperate. "That was the plan, and Seamus Dougherty's plans aren't scrubbed."

"How are you going to do it?" Cormac asked.

"What? Kill the Pope? That's already taken care of," Ambrose said offhandedly.

There was a roar from the crowd on the television. The Papal helicopter had landed in a cleared section behind the castle. It was instantly ringed with police and army troops.

Cormac looked at the picture, then at Ambrose's face. "How?"

The priest smiled. "Enough questions," he said. He rose and snapped off the picture. "Alas, the time has come for us both to depart this vale of tears." He lifted the machete slowly in his right hand. "You see, you should never have come. Suicide is better as a solitary act."

Cormac blinked, confused. "Suicide? For you?"

"Right again, Sergeant."

Cormac worked furiously at the ropes around his wrists. "You don't have to," he said, trying to keep his voice calm. "You're obviously a man with deep problems, Father, and people will understand. Call the assassination off. You don't have to die. No one does."

"It's not in my hands anymore. You see, I'm not supposed to know this, but a long list of credentials in secret pro-British organizations up north has been acquired in my name. It won't take long for those credentials to make their way to the press." His mouth opened and then snapped shut. "I have to die, don't you see?" he shouted suddenly. "It's part of the plan. If I don't do it myself, someone else will take care of that detail for me. It's inevitable."

He ran his finger along the edge of the blade. "Interesting tool," he said vaguely. "It has served me well."

Cormac knew there was no use trying to reason with the man. But he needed time. There was only one strand left in the ropes behind his back. He knew his wrists were bleeding. He could feel the sticky fluid trickling onto his palms and fingers. He only hoped that it wasn't forming a puddle that would attract the priest's attention. "I suppose you used that thing to cut the hands off Wells's brother," he said, bullying.

"It's quick," Ambrose said.

"Not if you bleed to death."

Ambrose took a deep breath. "I've already done more penance than your humanistic guilt can give me, Sergeant. And there's an eternity of damnation still ahead for me. You see, there is a God, a jealous God. I've been certain of that ever since I placed Ireland before Him in my heart."

"Ireland!" Cormac hissed. "You've never helped Ireland. You've sunk her into the mud and smeared your stink on her, you and those vampires you work for."

"You're wrong," the priest said quietly. "It's Ireland that's the vampire. She needs blood, you see. The dead—my dead—all had to die. Their lives were necessary to feed Ireland."

His eyes locked on Cormac's. "I never killed without reason," he said. "Every one of the deaths was absolutely essential." His hands fluttered. "As were all the deaths before Lazarus ever existed, I suppose. Ireland is a hard mistress."

He stood in front of Cormac and held the machete

in both hands like a baseball bat. "I'll do it cleanly, across the neck."

Cormac spat in his face.

The priest recoiled, so surprised that he backed away and bumped into the workbench on which the television rested.

*One strand.*

Ambrose wiped his cheek with the sleeve of his plaid shirt. "You'll pay for that, Brit lover," he said hoarsely, rising to his feet. "You'd like to know how Robert Wells died? I'm going to show you."

Cormac swallowed, his fingers moving behind him in a frenzy.

*One bloody strand!* Cormac's sweat was running into his eyes. *Jesus, if You've got any heart in You, get this frigging rope off me,* he prayed.

"I'm told there's no sensation at all until the bone breaks," Ambrose said, coming forward. "There's a gush of blood, of course, from the main arteries. It'll be all over the wall. . . ."

Suddenly he fell silent and turned his head in a quick mechanical motion toward the door leading outside.

There was the sound of footsteps and then a voice called, "Michael?"

"Morty . . ." Cormac yelled but stopped as Ambrose swiped a greasy rag from the workbench and stuffed it into Cormac's mouth.

"Wells wasn't at the hotel. I thought maybe I could help. Hey, what's this?" Morty said as he stepped through the doorway and saw the two men.

He reached for his gun, but the machete was already flying. It imbedded itself diagonally from the side of his neck to the center of his chest. Morty looked down at the trembling blade in astonishment and at the wall of blood cascading down his chest. Then his legs buckled and the gun, unused, tumbled out of his hand, and as he fell to the floor his mouth opened and the last of his life bubbled out of it.

Cormac squeezed his eyes shut.

*Oh, Morty, your blood, your wasted blood . . .*

The last strand broke.

Cormac dived forward, his hands clutching at the priest's pant legs. Ambrose fell, and Cormac, dragging the chair still tied to his ankles, managed to scramble on top of the smaller man. He had a grip on the priest's neck. Ambrose's face was darkening, a deep gurgle sounding within his throat, when he wedged a leg between them and kicked fiercely into Cormac's stomach, sending him hurtling backward onto the nail keg.

The chair smashed apart on impact. Cormac got up, splinters of wood still tied to his legs, and lunged at the priest, but Ambrose already had reached Morty's gun. He spun around, both arms rigid behind the trigger, and fired into Cormac's chest.


"Heavenly Father, I do not ask for forgiveness," Ambrose said, kneeling on the cement floor in front of a small crucifix nailed to the wall. The machete had been wiped clean and was resting across his lap.

"I know that my destiny is to burn in the fires of hell for all time to come, and I go to that destiny without absolution but without hesitation or a cry for mercy. I only ask that You look into my heart at the hour of my judgment, for there You will find Ireland.

Ireland is why I lived and Ireland is why I killed and for this blood-drenched island, Father, do I die."

He raised the machete with both hands to his neck.

"Hail Mary," he began, "full of grace . . . ."

Cormac's eyes opened. Unbelievably, he thought, he was still alive. His chest was burning and covered with blood, and there was a stabbing pain in his ribs. But he was alive.

". . . the Lord is with Thee; blessed is the fruit of Thy womb, Jesus. . . ."

Cormac was struck by a jolt of adrenaline when he saw the priest, Lazarus, the killer. The man was kneeling with his back to Cormac, the long blade poised at his own throat. Morty's gun had been tossed on the floor behind him and Morty's body lay sprawled in front of the doorway, his face chalk white, the dapper Garda uniform soaked in a pool of blood.

*I should be dead like Morty,* Cormac thought. *Why not?* But, trembling, he slid his hand across the floor and picked up the gun.

". . . Holy Mary, Mother of God, pray for us . . ." The machete dropped. Cormac stood in front of the crucifix, the gun inches away from the priest's face.

Ambrose looked up, surprised.

"My judgment," he whispered.

Cormac fired. The range was so close that there was no blood. Only a dark hole appeared in the middle of the man's forehead, but the back of his head exploded as he toppled over backward, the astonishment still showing in his eyes.

* * *

Cormac ached. He reached for his chest and felt a hole in the breast pocket of his jacket, but inside the pocket he found the bronze medal. Ambrose's bullet had slammed into the middle and then deflected. The word VALOUR no longer existed, wiped off by the bullet's impact. The metal was still warm, but the medal had saved his life.

Underneath, he knew that ribs were broken. The pain was beginning. The deep cuts on his legs throbbed. For a moment, his body allowed itself to begin falling apart. He wiped his sweat-dripping face with his sleeve and then heard someone coming through the door. He crouched, unaware of the widening slits in his legs and the new gush of blood from them, and held the gun in front of him.

Wells hit the floor and rolled, out of sight, as swiftly as an acrobat before the Irishman could fire.

"Jesus," Cormac shouted, sticking the gun inside his belt. "How'd you get here?"

"O'Flaherty's message was a cross," Wells said, putting his weapon away as he bent over Morty O'Sullivan's body. "I figured it might mean the priest. I was headed for the castle when I saw Morty running in this direction. Bloody shame." He closed Morty's eyes. "Looks as if you had a bit of a row yourself. Are you hit?"

"Broken rib, I think," Cormac said.

"Your legs."

"Never mind about that."

Wells had gone to Ambrose's body and was examining it. He lifted up one of his scarred hands, stared at it, then dropped it. Slowly he looked to Cormac for an answer. "Lazarus?"

The Irishman nodded mutely.

"Bloody bastard." Wells's gaze lingered on the staring eyes of the dead priest. "And I thanked him."

"There isn't time for that now," Cormac said abruptly, switching on the television.

The camera was set back in the crowd, and from a long shot, it showed the balcony and the big Celtic cross standing in the background. Roman Catholic clergymen flanked it on both sides, waiting for the Pope to come onto the balcony.

"He had no intention of going to the castle, he said," Cormac related. "He said the assassination was already taken care of. How? How?"

The Pope was at the center of the screen now, beginning the long climb up the castle steps.

"There's got to be something here that'll tell us," Cormac said, looking about frantically. He glanced at Wells, who was still standing, dazed, looking down at Ambrose's body. Cormac pulled him off viciously. "Help me, god damn it."

Wells stared at him, then blinked. "The nails," he said. "Shrapnel."

Cormac looked over at the spilled keg of roofing nails. A week before it had been full. Now only a few nails were scattered on the floor around it.

"A bomb then," Cormac said. "We know that. But **where?** Something big enough to take a keg of roofing nails and enough explosive to blow them. Where?"

"Cormac." Wells pulled a red cardboard box from a garbage pail.

"What's that?" Cormac asked.

"The other day when it arrived, Ambrose said it was a radio. But this says it's a garage-door-opener. Radio-controlled."

434

"So?"

"This place doesn't have a garage door."

"A radio signal." Cormac understood. "What's the range?"

"Short. A bomb at the castle couldn't be detonated from here."

"The car's outside," Cormac said.

Wells left instantly. Cormac limped behind, conscious of his loss of blood and the ache in his legs and chest.

The pain was making him nauseated. He rubbed his eyes. "Jesus on the cross," he muttered.

The television blared. ". . . handworked for over a year. It is a gift from the townspeople and the priest of Ardath as a symbol of peace."

Cormac lowered his hands as if he'd just been struck by lightning. On the screen was a full-length view of Father Ambrose's Celtic cross.

Outside, he heard the car start.

He limped out to it as fast as he could and got inside; Wells shot away up the lake road.

"It's the cross," Cormac said, feeling cold.

"Oh, my God," Wells said.

"Hurry."

Near the entrance to the castle, Wells skidded to a stop. The road was lined with people on both sides, held back by ropes, and three police vehicles had been parked sideways to seal off traffic along the road.

"As far as we go," Wells said. He jumped from the vehicle, and a uniformed policeman stepped from one of the cars, where he had been sitting listening to the radio.

"Here now," he said, waving his hand at Wells. "You can't leave that car there."

"Are you in touch with the Pope's guard by radio?" Wells asked.

"No."

"Backwoods donkeys," Wells snarled, bolting past the garda and running toward the castle gates.

"It's all right, we're police," Cormac told the startled officer as he lumbered past him after the Briton. He caught up to him at the gate. The heavy iron gates were slightly ajar but two uniformed Irish soldiers blocked the opening with their bodies.

"I'm Colonel Wells of the SAS. Radio upstairs and tell them to remove the Pope. There's a bomb on the balcony."

"Well now," one of the soldiers said with infuriating slowness. "You wouldn't mind showing us some identification, I'm sure."

Suddenly there was a deep, long cheer from the crowd. Thousands of voices were raised calling out the Pope's name.

"He's out there," Wells yelled frantically. He started to push by the guards. One grabbed him by the arm, but Wells spun and dropped the big man with a fist to the jaw.

As Wells ran toward the main entrance to the castle, the other soldier drew his firearm. But then he lowered the gun as Cormac stuck the muzzle of Morty O'Sullivan's pistol into his back.

"We'll have none of that," Cormac said as Wells ran into the castle's main entrance. As the second soldier climbed slowly to his feet, Cormac yanked the radio from his belt. He depressed the talk button and said: "Alert. Alert. This is Sergeant Michael Cormac. Remove the Pope. There's a bomb on the balcony in the cross. Remove the Pope. This is an emergency. The Pope is in danger."

The radio crackled a response. In a harsh whispered voice came, "This is Superintendent O'Keefe. Identify yourself."

"Dammit man, this is Cormac. There's a bomb in that cross. Get the Pope out of there."

"Now listen, Cormac . . ."

"Get the Pope out of there," he roared and shoved the radio back into the soldier's hands. "Just repeat what I said. Maybe you'll find somebody with brains to talk to."

He squeezed through the partly opened gate. The metal brushed his chest, and he almost screamed with the pain. As he ran to the side of the castle, he pulled his billfold from his wallet and hung his gold police badge from his top jacket pocket.

He brushed by a number of uniformed police and then stopped for a moment. The field was packed solidly with people. Had he come here to find Seamus Dougherty? One out of fifty thousand, a hundred thousand? He'd have as much chance of finding one particular blade of grass. And he knew Dougherty only by a photo Wells had shown him.

A woman saw the revolver in Cormac's hand. She looked startled for a moment, as if considering a scream. Cormac slipped the pistol into his jacket pocket. The entire castle was ringed with soldiers who stood behind a rope barricade. The first rows of standees under the balcony were mostly priests and nuns.

Cormac looked upward. The Pope, wearing the mitered hat of his office and his brocaded white robe, stood, his arms raised, looking out over the crowd, which greeted him with wave after thunderous wave of cheers.

They hadn't removed him.

The fools, they hadn't removed him, Cormac thought with a sinking feeling.

The Pope was still there, and behind him, looming against the sky, was the twelve-foot-high Celtic cross. Alongside the cross, just inside the archway that led into the castle's single upstairs room, was Superintendent O'Keefe, polished and shining and stupid. He had ignored Cormac's message.

The Pope was going to die.

Cormac looked around helplessly. Some were looking at him curiously because of the rips and blood on his clothing, but he saw no one to appeal to. He was surrounded by people. There was no way, in this throng, of finding Seamus Dougherty. The terrorist could be anywhere.

No. He couldn't.

He was going to use a garage-door opener to set off the bomb. But it was a small transmitter with only limited strength. To be foolproof, its effective range would have to be very small, particularly with so much background interference from radios.

Cormac moved out of the crowd and back toward the balcony. The front rows of priests and nuns stood, staring upward in rapt attention.

The Pope began to speak. In heavily accented Eng-

438

lish, he said, "We come to a place of peace, to pray for peace in a troubled land," he said.

He waved his hand at the Celtic cross behind him. "We come to bless this cross for peace."

The crowd was murmuring; then it stilled. And then there was a gasp of astonishment, collectively, simultaneously, from thousands of throats.

Cormac looked up at the balcony. He saw Wells push past Superintendent O'Keefe out onto the balcony. The Pope stopped speaking and turned to the intruder. Security people moved from their unobtrusive posts along the sides of the balcony to intercept the Englishman. But Wells ran past the Pope, ignored the guards and threw himself at the tall cross.

His weight and the force of his charge swept the cross back off its easel, and it fell backward through the open archway into the room behind the balcony. When it hit the floor, Wells was atop it.

Then came the sound and the light of death, grand and dark and muffled by the weight of Wells's body. Before the billowing cloud of black smoke began to pour over the balcony, in the split second between the act itself and the evidence of the act, a severed arm tumbled weightlessly across the open archway like a prop in an Italian farce.

The hand of Lazarus had killed again.

Cormac groaned, watching in horror as the Pope was pushed to the floor of the balcony by security guards. The very walls of the ancient castle shuddered, and a deep crack opened along the west battlement. Blocks of stone crashed down on the spectators so crowded together that they could not move out of the way. Piercing screams of the dying punctuated the already deafening noise of a mob in panic, the low din of thousands of feet scrambling for escape, the shrill of police whistles. A television cameraman, his equipment hoisted on his shoulder, fell and was trampled.

On the balcony, Superintendent O'Keefe was standing, talking into his radiophone as he scanned the crowd below with a blank, frightened expression on his face. Then the platform itself began to move, and the Pope was pushed inside, into the dust and smoke of the chapel, as two stone rails broke away from the balcony and fell to the ground. Below, an armed guard had already gathered to escort the Pontiff away as soon as he reached the bottom of the steps.

But Wells, Cormac knew, would not be coming out.

He turned to face the crowd. The rows of priests and nuns in front were moving in an orderly mass, directed by the soldiers.

All but one.

One slight priest was walking east, swiftly, alone, keeping near the walls of the castle, heading toward the woods around Moon Lake. He picked his way gingerly through the settled rubble, ignoring the pleas of the people injured or trampled, ignoring the shouted instructions of the police.

Cormac followed him, pressing his hand to his chest where he could feel the broken rib. In the field between the castle and the woods, he saw the glint of metal on the grass. It was a thin metallic object about the size of a cigarette package, with two switches on its face. It was the radio unit that had set off the bomb.

"Dougherty!" Cormac called. "Seamus Dougherty."

The man broke into a run. Cormac drew Morty's

440

gun, fired, missed. He felt as if his heart would burst as he lumbered into the woods behind Dougherty. He squeezed off another shot. It whined off a rock.

The small man never stopped, never looked back. Cormac loped along doggedly, far behind, his shoes stained with blood pouring from his legs. He saw a movement ahead of him and fired twice; some squirrels chattered as a flock of birds flapped noisily away.

He was running now, his breath coming in painful spears as the woods darkened. It was quiet here. Except for the wail of ambulance sirens in the distance, the commotion at the castle was no more than a background drone to the sounds of birdsong and the rustle of trees and the heavy fall of Cormac's feet on the undergrowth.

Then a shot rang out, to Cormac's right. He hit the ground, nearly screaming from the pain of the bullet burning the side of his stomach, and fired. There was no sound from the place in the woods ahead. He pulled the trigger again. The gun was empty.

Cursing, he dropped it and got to his knees. The spot had come from the east, toward the old Pierce estate. He willed his legs to stop shaking, spat out a mouthful of blood. Bracing both hands against a tree, he inched his way upright.

He didn't know now what he could do with Dougherty if he found him. Without a weapon, he would be helpless. But then, he thought, Wells had been helpless, too. All he'd had to fight with was his life.

And they'd taken it, the faceless killers, the bomb throwers, the baby burners, as they'd taken so many others that the numbers weren't known anymore. No one could stop all the Seamus Doughertys of the world, certainly not one fat, middle-aged man without enough blood left in him to fill a cat's belly. But he would try, once more.

By God, he would try.

He staggered a few feet, but then the second shot came. It thudded into his right shoulder, shattering the bone. Cormac jerked backward and rebounded into a rock. He fell where he stood.


It was a long time before he heard the shouts of the men.

"There's somebody up ahead. Looks like he's hurt, too."

"Go back. Get a stretcher."

Cormac tried to raise his head, but he didn't have the strength.

How many dead? Hattie, Barnett, Kathleen, Brian, Morty, Ambrose, Wells. The innocent who had fallen victim to Lazarus's bomb. And the Shrine of Eternal Peace on which, after ten centuries, the Holy Lady had finally turned her back.

"Ah, Daniel," Cormac whispered. He pressed his face against the earth that smelled of home and the lake, and he closed his eyes.

# EPILOGUE

It was nearly autumn, the endless Irish autumn that still smelled of summer. The dead had been buried, their graves already beginning to sprout thin blades of grass, and Ardath once again slept peacefully in the bosom of Kerry's green hills.

In the gathering twilight, Cormac and Moira stood side by side in Mr. Leahy's meadow, in the low shadows of the standing stones. Moira was thinner, and for the first time, a few strands of gray shone in her copper flame hair. Cormac's shoulder was still bandaged under his jacket, but the other wounds had healed during his stay in the hospital.

"Why are you going back to Cork?" she asked.

Cormac shrugged. "It's where I live."

Moira looked down at her hands. "Well, I've got the house now. It's so big and I've been thinking it's not really that far away from Cork."

"Why, Moira McLaughlin. Are you asking me to marry you?"

"Certainly not!" She blushed furiously.

Cormac put his arm around her waist and pulled her toward him. "You're not? Well?"

She hesitated for a moment, then raised her chin in her old gesture of defiance. "Yes. Yes, I am, Michael Cormac. And why not? You're a lame old fool with no one to look after you."

"Not all of me is lame, girl," he said, tickling her.

"Stop that. Michael, you're the devil himself, I swear. Stop or I'll scream."

"Scream away, wench. I've got you in my clutches now. Hey." He bent to rub a red mark on his ankle where he had just been hit.

A boy stepped out from behind one of the stones. It was Billy O'Glynn. He raised a slingshot and pinged off another stone at Cormac. "Traitor," he said, as the rock hit the dirt in front of the man.

"Whoa, there, Billy O'Glynn. What's the matter with you?"

"Brit lover," the boy called over his shoulder as he ran away.

Moira sat down on the sacrificial center stone and covered her face with her hands. "Will they ever stop?" she asked wearily.

"No," Cormac said. His voice was soft. "It's easier to hate than to think."

"The police keep saying they're getting close to that Dougherty man. They've got his picture on the telly every night, but I'm beginning to wonder if they'll catch him."

"It doesn't matter," Cormac said. "There are hundreds of Seamus Doughertys and more in the making." He cocked his head toward the field where the O'Glynn boy had run. "Like that one. There's still enough stupidity and hatred to recruit an army of terrorists. No matter how often they've been exposed for what they are, more people just line up to join.''

''What do we do, then?'' Moira asked.

Cormac looked over the stones to the blood-red sky and took out his bronze medal. The word VALOUR had been shot away; the slug had left a deep dent in the medal that made it unrecognizable. He fondled it absently. ''We live, Moira, the way we've always done,'' he said. ''We're Irish. We've been starved and hanged and flogged and shot but we're still here. And Ireland's still here because of us. We go on. And some-day the hate and the killing will stop.''

He bent down awkwardly and dug a small hole with a rock. Into it he placed the medal. Moira looked at him, puzzled.

''For valuor,'' Cormac said. ''For Morty O'Sullivan and Daniel Taylor Wells. It belongs in the ground, with them.''

He covered it with earth and crossed himself.

Moira came beside him then, in the place where the two of them had once shared all their secrets, and to-gether they knelt and prayed and said an Ave there for the dead.

And they prayed, too, for those yet unborn, for the generations to come who would one day look on their wild and ancient land and would weep for her suffer-ing, but still would take their strength from her. For after all the words had been spoken, those Irish too would stand for freedom. They too would bury the bro-ken bodies of their dead in Ireland's eternal soil.

They too would endure.

## THE FINEST IN FICTION
## FROM ZEBRA BOOKS!

HEART OF THE COUNTRY                                    (2299, $4.50)
by Greg Matthews
Winner of the 26th annual WESTERN HERITAGE AWARD for
Outstanding Novel of 1986! Critically acclaimed from coast to
coast! A grand and glorious epic saga of the American West that
*NEWSWEEK* Magazine called, "a stunning mesmerizing perfor-
mance," by the bestselling author of THE FURTHER ADVEN-
TURES OF HUCKLEBERRY FINN!
   **"A TRIUMPHANT AND CAPTIVATING NOVEL!"**
        *—KANSAS CITY STAR*

CARIBBEE                                               (2400, $4.50)
by Thomas Hoover
From the author of THE MOGHUL! The flames of revolution
erupt in 17th Century Barbados. A magnificent epic novel of
bold adventure, political intrigue, and passionate romance, in the
blockbuster tradition of James Clavell!
      **"ACTION-PACKED . . . A ROUSING READ"**
          *—PUBLISHERS WEEKLY*

MACAU                                                  (1940, $4.50)
by Daniel Carney
A breathtaking thriller of epic scope and power set against a
background of Oriental squalor and splendor! A sweeping saga
of passion, power, and betrayal in a dark and deadly Far Eastern
breeding ground of racketeers, pimps, thieves and murderers!
              **"A RIP-ROARER"**
            *—LOS ANGELES TIMES*

*Available wherever paperbacks are sold, or order direct from the
Publisher. Send cover price plus 50¢ per copy for mailing and
handling to Zebra Books, Dept. 100 , 475 Park Avenue South,
New York, N.Y. 10016. Residents of New York, New Jersey and
Pennsylvania must include sales tax. DO NOT SEND CASH.*

## ACTION ADVENTURE

**SILENT WARRIORS**                              (1675, $3.95)
by Richard P. Henrick
*The Red Star*, Russia's newest, most technologically advanced submarine, outclasses anything in the U.S. fleet. But when the captain opens his sealed orders 24 hours early, he's staggered to read that he's to spearhead a massive nuclear first strike against the Americans!

**THE PHOENIX ODYSSEY**                     (1789, $3.95)
by Richard P. Henrick
All communications to the USS *Phoenix* suddenly and mysteriously vanish. Even the urgent message from the president cancelling the War Alert is not received. In six short hours the *Phoenix* will unleash its nuclear arsenal against the Russian mainland.

**EAGLE DOWN**                                     (1644, $3.75)
by William Mason
To western eyes, the Russian Bear appears to be in hibernation — but half a world away, a plot is unfolding that will unleash its awesome, deadly power. When the Russian Bear rises up, God help the Eagle.

**DAGGER**                                             (1399, $3.50)
by William Mason
The President needs his help, but the CIA wants him dead. And for Dagger — war hero, survival expert, ladies man and mercenary extraordinaire — it will be a game played for keeps.

*Available wherever paperbacks are sold, or order direct from the Publisher. Send cover price plus 50¢ per copy for mailing and handling to Zebra Books, Dept. 100 , 475 Park Avenue South, New York, N.Y. 10016. Residents of New York, New Jersey and Pennsylvania must include sales tax. DO NOT SEND CASH.*